MAGIC

IMAGINATION

the keys to magic

NICK FARRELL

SKYLIGHT
PRESS

This edition first published in Great Britain in 2013 by Skylight Press,
210 Brooklyn Road, Cheltenham, Glos GL51 8EA

Parts of this book were previously published as *Magical Pathworking* in 2003 by
Llewellyn Publications, Minnesota, USA.

Designed and typeset by Rebsie Fairholm
Cover photo by Nick Farrell
Drawings by Paola Farrell
Golden Dawn Temple Tarot Deck created by the Wendrich Arthouse
Olympic Spirit sigils by *asterionsoccultart.blogspot.com*
Publisher: Daniel Staniforth

www.skylightpress.co.uk

Printed and bound in Great Britain by Lightning Source, Milton Keynes.
Typeset in Adobe Caslon Pro. Titles set in Cal Beneventan Miniscule. Symbols
set in Segno Pro and Adobe Hebrew.

British Library Cataloguing in Publication Data.
A catalogue record for this book is available from the British Library.

ISBN 978-1-908011-72-5

To **Marian Green**, *writer and occultist,*
who has selflessly worked to foster the
Western Mystery Tradition in the United Kingdom

and
Paola Farrell
and the
Magical Order of the Aurora Aurea

Olympic Spirit: Hagith by Paola Farrell

CONTENTS

ACKNOWLEDGEMENTS

This book is the result of countless experiments into pathworking and the imagination. Its success is due to the patience of many who worked with the techniques even though we were initially uncertain of their effects. To these brave people I acknowledge their contribution, particularly Jane and Anna.

Rufus Harrington enabled me to see that some of the life healing techniques in this book could be used in modern conventional therapy and counselling.

Marian Green was the first to get me interested in the workings of the magical imagination and the writers W.E. Butler, Gareth Knight, Dion Fortune and David Goddard, who were all influences.

Thanks also to Peregrin Wildoak and Anita Hoener for giving this new manuscript the once over for me.

Without all these people it is unlikely that this book could ever have been written, or completed. Indeed my life would not have been as interesting as it has been without them.

INTRODUCTION

Refining one's personality is the first thing that a magician needs to tackle in their path, and that was what the first edition of *Magical Pathworking* approached. It was designed to help people use magical techniques in a psychological way to improve themselves and overcome the blocks to their development.

When I wrote the first edition of this book more than a decade ago, I used psychological ideas a lot more than I do now. The book was designed to make public the magical imagination techniques I used in my successful psychological experiments.

As my spiritual path has progressed, the emphasis on the psychological interpretation of imagination techniques has become less of a personal focus as I started to understand its wider use in magical practice.

Concentrating on the psychological use of imagination, as I did in the first edition of *Magical Pathworking*, had its limitations as I came to develop my own theories of imagination, and I felt that the book did not provide a complete picture of what the technique was capable of doing. By taking the technique to another level it was possible to look at the use of imagination in ritual magic and also to merge personal imagination with that of God. This interests me more because it widened the remit of the techniques I had suggested in *Magical Pathworking*.

In this edition I have reworked the previous material and added new chapters which aim to open the techniques for a more magical and spiritual purpose. This includes developments on group work, divination, visiting other inner world dimensions and working towards what I call 'objective pathworking.'

It was the realisation that these techniques could breathe new life into such an established magical system as the Golden Dawn that encouraged me to build the Magical Order of the Aurora Aurea (MOAA).

MOAA is a Golden Dawn group that specialises in using that system in a practical and experimental way. Utilising the magical imagination techniques in this book it was possible to make contact not only with those spiritual forces behind the Golden Dawn, but also beyond, to the roots of creation itself.

If *Magical Pathworking* was about the psychological work that I was experimenting with a decade ago, then *Magical Imagination* reflects the sort of magic I am doing now.

Imagination is our inner vision, our human skill to see different realities. It can take us to the throne of God, it can connect us to the stream of infinity and enable us to see the universe for what it really is. It can help us take up our crown as a co-creator with God and build our own universe. But this same tool can also trap us into our small human lives until we are prisoners imprisoned in matter, forced to look at shadows on the wall which life has convinced us is reality.

As a child I often created worlds and disappeared into them when the pressures of life were too much. Being asthmatic with a complete disinterest in sport, growing up in New Zealand made such imaginary worlds an increasingly attractive escape from the bullies and weird waltzes of early relationships.

Like many of those the writer Colin Wilson would label Outsiders, I was a people watcher and inhaled psychology books to learn more about the way they worked. In my late teens my knowledge grew, and upon entering into my adult life these day-dreams became less important and my psychological knowledge just became another tool for understanding the life around me.

But occult study reactivated my interest in these subjects. Books by Marian Green, Dolores Ashcroft-Nowicki and John and Caitlín Matthews started to convince me that these imaginary worlds of mine were not only real but also had a direct magical purpose. Builders of the Adytum, my first magical school, taught me that these visualisations could actually change my material world.

In those days 'pathworking' was still discussed in the hushed whispers that follow the public disclosure of a technique once closely guarded by the mystery schools. Now, only 15 years later, it is so commonplace that it is almost regarded as a beginner's technique.

Few have tried to work out what is happening with these magical imagination states or even teach how to create them. This has blunted the technique to a point where entering a pathworking is a lazy way of filling half an hour on a workshop or a lodge meeting or circle. I have sat through many pathworkings where it would have been more valuable to me to sit and watch television. This book aims to present what I have learnt about pathworking and show how it can be constructed for the maximum effect.

Pathworkings are only the start of Magical Imagination techniques, indeed its uses are an untapped well waiting to be explored by magicians and witches in the 21st century. This book will show that there is a direct link between psychological states and those environments created in imagination. Neurotic complexes, that do so much to spoil and limit our lives, have the same reality in our imaginations, and therefore it should be possible to correct them using magical imagination techniques.

Instead of waiting for a person to dream to hear the voice of their unconscious, creative imagination would give direct access, enabling not only communication but also a way of repairing faults.

The only way to prove this was with experimentation. Over a number of years a group of magicians and friends of mine worked through various techniques and found that pathworking was a door to our psychological states. Healing these complexes initially seemed so easy that we overkilled the amount of work we tried to correct. We forgot to take into account the tremendous fall-out that follows each experiment. Unpicking a complex in a day that has taken years to develop has a result that is felt over months or years, and at the time we were doing one of these workings a week. Not something I recommend now.

After the dust settled we were completely different people, free from many of the shackles which had bound us. I have subsequently handed the technique on to several counsellors and they have also found it effective.

It was during this period that I joined the Servants of the Light (SOL), which ran a correspondence course employing the concept of using pathworking to create an environment which represents the inner self. This 'Inner Kingdom' was set in an Arthurian mythos with a castle representing the physical body of a person. Written by W.E. Butler and embellished by Dolores Ashcroft-Nowicki, the course aimed to awaken magical energies within a person to enable spiritual development. But what interested me was that it created an Inner Kingdom which had to be maintained for some time (the course lasted five years). During this course my Kingdom not only taught me spiritual things, but gave me a symbolic insight into the way my life was going.

If an Inner Kingdom was built, it would be possible to see the world as my unconscious saw it. What was learnt from that perspective was that I was the ruler of my own Inner Kingdom and if I made a change at that unconscious level it was possible to change my life.

The guts of the SOL course was published by David Goddard in his book *Tower of Alchemy* and before I left the group there was talk of replacing the course with different techniques.

My experimentation with Magical Imagination continued. For the best part of 14 years I have been using the magical system of the Order of the Golden Dawn – a magical order that started at the end of the 19th century – and in its teachings found an explanation for many of the Magical Imagination techniques I used before. It was these techniques that inspired the poet W.B. Yeats and are also included here.

The mystical use of pathworkings as a method of contacting the divine within has become more important. This use is still rarely talked about as it is considered too dangerous for beginners. I remain sceptical about these fears, as a person experimenting with mystical states will see God at their own level of understanding. I have yet to hear of someone being sent into an H.P. Lovecraft style mania from doing a pathworking. I have met people who find Magical Imagination techniques addictive, to the point where they do not wish to exist in the real world. I can also accept that those suffering from dissociative mental illness could face many problems. But these are the sorts of problems that would be true of any magical technique.

There are occultists who might object to the publication of these techniques or the revealing of the secrets of magical imagination. However, it is important that they are available for those people who really want to work them. I am a firm believer that the casting of pearls before swine is preferable to burying them in a locked box where they cannot be found by the profane. I have yet to see a pig with a matching pearl necklace and earrings, but a pig farming mate of mine used to say, 'pigs are funny animals' and you are never sure what they are going to do next.

The book also includes pathworkings and examples of techniques. Although these have been all tested and work in their own right, the aim of this book is to encourage development and experimentation in this new and exciting esoteric field.

This book also looks at how magical imagination works and how its techniques are vital for the development of a working magical system.

Nick Farrell
Rome
November 2012

Chapter One

(T)AGICAL IMAGINATION

(T)AGICAL IMAGINATION is a tool to change your consciousness to rebuild aspects of your life and self to bring about a transformation of your environment. It also contacts the forces of life behind the universe so that you can experience different aspects of reality subjectively.

Everyone builds around them an impression of reality – a unique image of the universe from their own perspective. This universe is built from countless experiences since birth. These are the lessons that we have taught ourselves or accepted as gospel from our parents, teachers, friends and society. Over the years our universe becomes more defined, meaning that we can handle more of what our life throws at us.

Sometimes that world picture is incorrect. What our parents or teachers present to us as fact is sometimes bigoted or just wrong, and being children and not having any evidence to challenge that information, we accept it and paint it into our world view. Sometimes we build in features in our Inner Kingdoms to protect us from hurt. This is particularly true of people that have been victims of abuse, who have elaborate defence mechanisms designed to overcome the intense psychological stress such abuse triggers. The behaviour patterns learnt to avoid the pain in such instances are often applied to the rules of our whole Inner Kingdom. Everything that looks similar to the original situation is incorrectly treated in the same way. A lover, with whom you are extremely close, can suddenly become the manipulative father who terrorised your childhood, just by making the wrong gesture, because in the rules of your Inner Kingdom the people who make that gesture are the bad guys.

Occultism teaches that our mental picture of the universe is such a powerful force for stability that it eventually creates the circumstances that maintain it. In other words, how we see our universe becomes a self-fulfilling prophecy. The person who is rich either in material or spiritual terms is unlikely to be poor, while the poor will be locked in their misery.

But occultism teaches that since such a universe is built by the imagination, that great magical wand of the magician, so it can be changed. Over the millennia countless different techniques were developed that enabled people to master their personal universe using their imagination. This enabled them to change the wiring of their minds to let in things like success, happiness and wellbeing.

Imagination has had a bad press after the scientists of the 19th century looked for purely materialistic theories for what they saw around them. To them, imagination was day-dreaming and unnecessary. Just like a grumpy school teacher who tells off a school boy for staring out the window, science shouted at us to PAY ATTENTION without actually realising what powers imagination had. Science was brilliant at saying what was happening now, but what of the future? Inventions and human developments are 99% the work of dreamers and imaginative people – those same men and women who did not pay attention.

There is a stigma attached to imagination techniques. I recall a scathing book review of David Goddard's *Tower of Alchemy* which deals with a good imagination technique. The reviewer said that the author seemed to believe that if you day-dreamed your problems away all would be all right. This book aims to prove the reviewer wrong. To be fair to the reviewer, it was a mistaken belief I once held.

Many years ago, after some successful Magical Imagination experiments with the British magician Marian Green, I derided my experiences as "just imagination". She pointed out to me, somewhat bluntly, that my problem was that I didn't really know what imagination was. She was right. There was no scientific definition of imagination in my head that would work.

For example, the *Concise Oxford Dictionary* says that imagination is a "mental faculty forming images or concepts of external objects not present to the senses" or "the ability of the mind to be creative or resourceful". However, this does not define the sort of imagination which creates spontaneous imagery in the mind. Ideas are not simply formed out of existing material, whether intellectually or emotionally, they were often created out of new experiences without any conscious input from me. It seemed that thoughts and emotions were simply the kindling to an imaginative flame which was coming from outside my personality.

To prove this, let us perform an experiment. Shut your eyes and imagine a castle. After a few seconds open them and describe that castle out loud. You will have a very full picture of what the castle looks like after a few seconds thinking about it. Where did all that information come from? You could argue that it was based on a memory of a castle you might have seen or read in a book. Have you actually visited that castle? If so, have you visited it from that exact spot? I would argue that what you have done is painted the picture using your imagination and it was based on a simple phrase "imagine a castle". All that detail, which did not come from your memory, came from somewhere else. Later I realised that imagination came from a deeper aspect of me, a part which the psychologist Jung would call my Higher Self.

It is clear that we are dealing with something more important than mere fancy. In fact, one of the greatest magicians in the 19th century, Dr W. Wynn Westcott, who founded the famous magical group the Order of the Golden Dawn, said that Imagination must be distinguished from Fancy, which is "mere roving thoughts, or simply visions". He said that Imagination is "an orderly and intentional mental process and result. Imagination is the creative faculty of the human mind, the plastic energy – the Formative Power."[1]

Westcott added that the power of imagination to create images enabled it to produce external phenomena by its own energy.

> "It is an ancient Hermetic dogma that any idea can be made to manifest externally if only by culture, the art of concentration be obtained. Man by his creative power through will and thought was more divine than the Angels for he can create and they cannot."

ThE MIND AND ThE BRAIN

Like philosophy, those who study the mind fall into two broad camps. There are the rationalists who believe that everything is limited to the world we experience through our senses and there are the idealists who argue that the whole of the world is mental.

Many rationalists have tried to say that the brain is the centre of consciousness. The most recent notable attempt was in *Astonishing Hypothesis: the scientific search for the soul*[2] in which the writer Francis Crick argued that the mind was the sum total of millions of brain cells.

---

1   Order of the Golden Dawn Flying Roll V.
2   Simon and Schuster, 1994 edition.

Most occultists opt for the more philosophically 'idealist' idea that all things are thought and the brain is just an organic radio set that picks up memories and thoughts from outside the body. Medical science may disagree with this particular point but equally it cannot disprove it either. Experiments on patients who were conscious when their brains were operated upon reported having memories, or feeling sensations, when parts of their brains were stimulated. This does not mean that those memories were in the brain, but rather that switches were flicked in the person's brain that connected to the real memory which was outside the physical body. Likewise when people suffer accidents or mental disabilities that prevent them remembering or cause them to see things in unusual ways, it is because this organic radio has been damaged and cannot see outside itself effectively. Saying that all knowledge is in your brain is like saying all the knowledge of the Internet is in your personal computer. It is subjectively true in that the knowledge ends up on your PC, but if you disconnected your computer from the phone line you are unlikely pick up any information.

The ancient Greek philosopher Plato (who inspired many esoteric schools) said in his book the *Phaedo* that the mind was imperishable and immortal and as such had knowledge of the Universe. In fact the whole of the universe was the action of a Universal Mind which was creating using imagination. Your mind is just a reflection or a specialisation of that larger Mind. Once you get it out of your head that your mind is your brain then you can truly start to see how free and immortal you are.

United States comedian Bill Hicks[3] summed up how the Universal Mind worked as part of his act: "We are all one consciousness experiencing itself subjectively. There is no such thing as death, life is only a dream and we are the imagination of ourselves."

There seem to be clear boundaries between us and a realisation of the true nature of this Universe. These are walls that define our individual selves as separate from the rest of humanity and the universe. Unless we are extremely enlightened, or mentally ill, we see ourselves as individuals who have clearly defined boundaries between ourselves and the rest of the world. This is mostly because our consciousness is deliberately limited by the design of creation. We were built to see a very small part of creation and experience it consciously. We are like a meditation on a specific subject being carried out by the Universal Mind.

---

3   Bill Hicks, who died in 1994, was a so-called 'shock comedian' who in my view made accurate observations on political, social and spiritual situations. The fact that he could do that and get a laugh was incredible.

When we were born, a little part of the immortal Mind was placed at the core of our being. It has been called the Ghost in the Machine or the Rider in the Chariot, but it is the real YOU. It experiences matter and the bewildering aspects around it called life and after a while it forgets its divine self and gets on with existing. You may have noticed something similar when you drive a car. After a while our consciousness expands until we are less the person driving and more an entity called 'the car'.

Throughout our short history on this planet humanity has produced people who discover their own divine self and co-operate with the Universal Mind. Firstly they work out how their own mind works and how they use it. Then they balance themselves away from emotional, intellectual and social extremes so they may truly express the will of the Universal Mind in their lives. This leads to fulfilment and access to powers that many consider miracles. This enables them to do more within creation. The interesting thing about aligning yourself with the Universal Mind is that it does not make you super-spiritual or even particularly Godlike. Instead it makes you more intensely *yourself* and you have an interesting life with all the challenges that get thrown at you.

hOW ThE mIND LEARNS

When we are born, the physical body is surrounded on all levels by the Universal Mind. At the centre of this is the spark of divinity from which a personality will develop. This spark forms a link with the developing body, centring itself in one of the energy centres in the heart. Surrounding itself with energy, the spark can pilot the body through life. Initially it has some difficulty in that it cannot use the developing brain, which has not been programmed yet. What the spark does is to quickly train the brain with a set of experiences that enable it to function. Initially a baby's brain will not allow it to have a concept that it is separate from the world which surrounds it. The spark has its work cut out in the initial phases, as the baby rapidly learns things like up, down, light and dark and as it does so it slowly builds a mental framework for what will become its own Inner Kingdom. It is also during this time that early life patterns are established and crucial programming is performed by the Universal Mind to move the soul towards the life purpose that it has mapped out for it. This process takes time and requires the spark to make frequent trips into the Universal Mind to recharge its batteries and process the data it is getting from the brain. This is done during sleep and possibly explains why babies need so much.

One of the downsides of this process is that as the Universal Mind depends on the sensory experience of the newly born brain as its anchor on the material plane, it becomes limited and unable to function at its full potential. It forgets and will spend the rest of its physical plane life re-discovering part of what it already knows.

This process is accentuated during the next phase when the baby accepts that its mother is a separate identity from itself and it has enough of an inner reality to start asserting itself on the physical levels. This usually happens around the age of two (the aptly named terrible twos) when the individuality makes its first declarations and yet still lacks the communication skills to articulate its personal needs, leading to deep frustration. The price for such individuality is a conscious disconnection from the Universal Mind and the reality that the child sees around it. It still feels its presence in sleep or daydreaming, but generally the child's focus is on the world around it. It starts to learn by cause and effect. It learns that if it touches something hot it will hurt, so touching such an object is a bad idea. It is important to realise that the part of the child that is learning is the brain. The Universal Mind already knows what will happen if it touches a hot plate, but it is vital to get the body to realise what will happen. It is not so much learning as remembering what the reality is. It is only by experience that our physical form remembers much of our true reality and our brains gain access to more aspects of the Universal Mind.

Because of the way this process works, humans need experience to develop and grow. Good and bad events flavour our lives, enabling our Inner Kingdoms to grow and become rich. In experiencing more, the Universal Mind at the heart of the personality grows too.

Associations develop like logical trees with each experience mapping onto another one. So that not only touching a hot plate is bad, touching hot objects becomes bad and soon other associations become loaded in with the association 'bad'. An example of this was the famous experiments conducted by Ivan Pavlov, who found that he could condition a dog to slaver on demand by ringing a bell whenever it was presented with food. After a while the dog was so accustomed to associating the bell with food it would slaver if the bell rang.

Unfortunately some of these associations are incorrect. For example, a child might see an adult it respects recoiling in terror from a spider and assume that spiders are as dangerous as the hot plate. Later in life they will be unaware why they are so frightened of spiders.

The association process builds until things that are like the original fear also produce the same response. In one particularly unethical experiment conducted in 1920 by Watson and Rayner they took a baby called Albert and showed him a white rat and then made a loud noise. Like Pavlov's dog, poor Albert started to associate the rat with the loud noise and became frightened every time he saw one. However Albert's mind also associated the white rat with 'white fur', rodents and all small furry things and so was frightened of these too.[4]

But fear is not the only conditioned response. A person can be conditioned to do practically anything if they think it is going to let them avoid suffering from pain that they have experienced in the past. For example, one woman who was shouted at by her live-in boyfriend for not locking the door of the house went through an elaborate ritual of making sure it was locked whenever she left the house. Sometimes it could take some 60 seconds of leaning on the door to make sure. Later this pattern extended to checking the handle of the car door which she performed so rigorously that the handle fell off.

When associative patterns of behaviour become so elaborate, they become what psychologist Jung[5] called complexes. When a person is operating in the grip of a complex, they often find themselves behaving in strange ways, often without knowing why.

For example, a boy is struck by his mother for standing on his bed but she fails to give a reason for hitting him other than saying a single word 'dirty'. To avoid the pain of being hit again the boy never stands on the bed but associates 'bed' with 'dirty'. He becomes involved in a church group and during a sermon the minister, who he respects, refers to sex as being 'dirty' causing the boy to link the word 'sex' with 'dirty' and therefore by association the word 'bed', so it is not surprising that when he has his first sexual experience he has a complex about doing it on a bed. It was only by tracking the association trail backwards that he could see that was how he ended up with this complex.

The mind develops these associations to enable it to provide a rapid reaction to events that unfold in the child's daily life. In fact your Inner

---

4   This is what psychologists call classical conditioning. Psychological tests on children are now considered about as ethical as bear baiting.

5   Carl Gustav Jung was an associate of Freud, the founder of modern psychoanalysis. He broke with Freud after publishing work which emphasized the role of symbolism in the unconscious.

Kingdom is made up of millions of these different complexes which your mind orders and links together with a symbolic language.

SYMBOLS ARE THE KEY

The word 'symbol' comes from the Late Greek word *symbolon*, meaning token or sign. A symbol is something that stands for another object which it resembles in some way. A white dove, for example, is a symbol of peace, because in the biblical story of Noah a dove brought an olive branch, indicating the tempest was over. However symbols are much more than that. In a world which is built by a mind, a symbol is a language that can key you into various thoughts and feelings built up over millennia of human history.

Throughout a study of occultism you will see symbols drawn on paper, on talismans, in magical books. Some of these are common, like a crucifix, others are rarer, such as the elaborate pentacles contained in the medieval spell book the *Key of Solomon*. All are designed to stimulate the mind so that they can contact the deeper, more powerful realms of the unconscious Universal Mind.

A symbol links associations together. For example, in your mind all dogs will be linked with a symbol of a dog. When you see a dog your mind will instantly access those files that are associated with it. Upon opening the file it will see all the associations, good or bad, that you might have about dogs (which are themselves stored under appropriate symbols).

Some symbols are unique to you. These are ones which you have built yourself from your own experiences. Someone who was bitten by a dog in their childhood might associate the dog symbol as a bringer of pain and fear, while another might have happier connections and see them as a symbol of loyalty.

There are two types of symbols. Primary or archetypal symbols are basic and only designed to stress a single idea. Then there are symbols which have other details added, to stress certain points whose meanings may have been obscured in the drawing of a primary symbol. Take for example a drawing of an equal armed cross. This primary symbol says (basically) there are four elements, which when they meet in balance enable a fifth. You could emphasise this by making it a secondary symbol by placing a rose in the centre to represent the spirit. You could then turn it into a tertiary symbol by colouring the arms of the cross red, blue, yellow and black to represent the four elements. The primary symbol is usually the most powerful because it has more potential to lead the mind in wider directions.

One of these symbols is a plain cross and the other is the Golden Dawn's Rose Cross of the Elements. Look at one for a minute and then write down everything that occurs to your mind. The lists that you get will be different because the plain cross is used by Christians and therefore any feelings that symbol will drag out of your unconscious could say a lot about your relationship with that religion. The Rose Cross is perceived as more magical and the list you will get from it will probably be tinged with 'occult' teaching.

But if you look at that teaching you will find that the Rose Cross is explaining information that is already in the plain cross, and if you stared at the crucifix with an open mind you would get the same 'occult' information. The more you look at primary symbols, the more teaching you will receive. This teaching is very often not 'intellectual'. For example, a study group, when given this exercise, all said they received a lot more intellectual information from the Golden Dawn cross; however, they felt that the purity of the plain cross provided them with more spiritual information that said more than plain intellect.

You can see your symbolic language in the seemingly anarchic visions of your dreams. Such dreams only make sense when you look at each composite symbol in the light of your own experience. A dream where the cast of *The Sound of Music* came around to your house to sell you homemade jam would have to be pulled apart symbol by symbol. What does *The Sound of Music* mean to you? It could be a symbol of heroes escaping from Nazi oppression. If you hate the film, they could be a symbol of mindless fantasy with an irritatingly catchy soundtrack. What did the jam represent? If you associate jam with long summer holidays when your mother made it, it could mean that your subconscious mind is advising you to relax. If jam represents calories and sweet things (and you hate *The Sound of Music*) then it could mean that you are having unconscious fantasies about fattening things.

Other symbols called archetypes are common to most of humanity. These are and were 'discovered' by the psychoanalyst Jung[6] who realised that some symbols in his patients' dreams had no personal meaning for the dreamer but still felt important. Some of these symbols were common throughout human history, appearing in myths, religion and creative writing. Jung reasons that these common symbols were drawn from the Universal Mind, which he called the collective unconscious. These are the big symbols that seem to enter a person's mind just by virtue of the fact they are human.

Every religion has an archetypal figure, whether Zeus, Isis, Jesus, Abraham, Moses, Buddha or Allah. Myths and legends vary between cultures, yet they all seem to contain archetypal figures such as the Fool, the Seeker, The Maiden, The Crone, the Mother, the Father and the Hero. This adds weight to Plato's idea of an archetypal world dominated by primal ideas from which all other things proceed.

These very important primal images are vital for our wellbeing. Within our Inner Kingdom they can become distorted and effectively strangled by the complexes built by our life experiences. For example, there was one person I knew whose mother was a prostitute, and when she could not be bothered to sleep with her clients, would send them to her underage daughter's bedroom instead. This twisted the young girl's Mother archetype until, instead of becoming one of nurturing care, it became one of fear and mistrust. The girl's natural father had long since disappeared and so the only impression of the Father archetype came from her mother's pimp, who was the only stable man in her childhood, but he also sexually molested her. The fact that these archetypal figures

---

6   I use the term loosely. Archetypal figures had been a key part of magical tradition for centuries and Jung simply re-defined them. He was then able to go back through the huge amount of occult and alchemical literature and point out the archetypal figures to a round of applause from his students.

were so corrupt meant that all the pleasant things normally associated with parents were totally corrupted and associated with distrust and fear.

One of the key areas controlled by Mother and Father archetypes are relationships, because we tend to see the opposite sex through our initial impressions of our parents. As a result, this young woman's relationships with men and women were based on a mistaken belief that they would always betray her, and this became a self-fulfilling prophecy. We will look a little later at how we can begin to heal these archetypes.

ThE LITTLE UNIVERSE

We have mentioned how we are a little universe, or a microcosm of a larger macrocosm. In the Order of the Golden Dawn this mini-universe was an energy field which reflected everything in the bigger one. This field surrounds the body and is the key to understanding how magic and imagination work.

In modern New Age terms, this energy field is called the aura, but in the Golden Dawn it was dubbed the Sphere of Sensation, which is a much more involved idea. In fact the Sphere of Sensation is a canvas upon which an auric energy system can be painted. Golden Dawn adept John Brodie Innes wrote[7] that the Sphere of Sensation was an egg shaped aura around the body which was made of 'Akasha'. Akasha is an Eastern term meaning 'Ether' or lower forms of 'spirit'. In pre-Einstein physics, ether was the unseen energy that held the universe together. Although you could not see it, it was still a semi-physical force. In the Indian philosophy which influenced the Golden Dawn, Akasha was also the spirit that bound together the four elements. When Brodie Innes said that the Sphere of Sensation was Akasha, he meant that it was made of an unseen spiritual energy. Akasha is the memory of the Mind of God and it contains everything in reflection. One drop of Akasha, he explained, contains a reflection of everything seen, unseen, past and present.

This makes the Sphere of Sensation "the Microcosm and the Universe as the Macrocosm; regarding the former as a reflection in miniature of the latter, as in a grass field full of dewdrops each drop might present a perfect tiny image of trees and mountains, the sky, clouds, the sun and the stars." It is a hologram of the universe that can be cut multiple times and still contain a complete likeness of the original.

7   Flying Roll No. XXV by J.W. Brodie Innes.

The Sphere of Sensation behaves automatically and fairly passively but it is packed with the memories of everything and has links to every point in the universe.

In the ideal person, the Sphere of Sensation would reflect the world of divine ideas and bring these into manifestation. However, humanity has become blinded by the material world. We have become like the prisoners in Plato's cave allegory[8] who are lost in worlds of shadow and only dimly aware of our previous divine existence. Most people's Spheres of Sensation are tuned to looking towards the physical world and reflecting that. The tools of imagination are locked so that they interpret these shadows and just create more illusion.

Some of this is caused by the process of birth. When a person is born, the Sphere of Sensation is orientated by the planetary and zodiacal energies of their natal chart. When a baby is born, the first view of the universe is based on its astrological chart. The rising sign is in the East, the Mid-heaven above and the descendant behind. This is the natural way of things, but it is not the ideal. Our ascendant, which is how we appear, is rarely how our true self, as represented by our sun sign, wants us to be. We have been born facing the wrong way. We start life facing nature rather than our spiritual self. This pathology means our Sphere of Sensation shows us a distorted vision of the Universe. Our lives are based on incorrect perceptions based on clouded understandings of the symbols. We often see symbols but can only see them in a glass darkly. As life continues and fails to fulfil childhood optimism, the small becomes large, and our view becomes narrow and clouded. To make matters worse, people form links with others through shared magnetism. If one person can have a corrupted idea about reality, then a group can build a hell.

As people age, they become more fixed and are unable to see any new Universe which is being born around them. Instead they either keep symbols of their own universe, or just live their lives as they always have done. In such circumstances the Higher Aspects of the personality lose their ability to influence the Sphere of Sensation and the person finally dies.

The Golden Dawn provided its students with a vision of the Sphere of Sensation in its version of Key 21, The Universe. In this tarot card, nature is shown dancing between two poles, while her sphere of sensation moves around her. The sphere of sensation contains the signs of the zodiac and all the angels which hold it together. The Golden

8   Book VII of Plato's *The Republic*

Dawn used the Angels of the Schemhamphoresh, which are shown in the card by the smaller circles. These were reinforced by the Kerubs, or four holy creatures.

The Sphere of Sensation, when viewed psychically, is brightly coloured because the seer looks at the outer shell of it first. As we can see, these are the colours of the Macrocosmic constellations. A skilled seer would be able to pierce this and see into the microcosmic colour range too. Truly gifted psychics would be able to make out prominent symbols in a person's life; they might also be able to make out what the Golden Dawn describes as veins of symbols that make highways through the Sphere of Sensation.

These are collections of symbols that lead by association to craft a person's inner kingdom. Modern psychology calls these complexes. They may be good or bad, but build up a person's spiritual, mental and physical personality.

Most psychics also see chakras or wheels of energy at certain points in the Sphere of Sensation. It is usually easier to see the heart and crown centres, because these are the places of associated with the Higher Mind and the seat of the self in Western Culture. This does not mean that spirit really is in the heart or the crown, simply that the psychic viewing of the Sphere of Sensation puts them in this place.

The Golden Dawn also suggested something radical, which we will go back to a number of times in this book. *By changing, or adding, a symbol in someone's Sphere of Sensation it is possible to change their universe.*

ChANGING OUR UNIVERSE

It is an occult principle that, as the universe is built from thought, it can be changed by thought. Thought can be used to enter to the deepest levels of consciousness and to touch the very hub of the Universal Mind: God itself. As an adept of the Order of the Golden Dawn, Dr Berridge once said you have to accept that your imagination has a reality. "When a person imagines he actually creates a form on the astral, or even some higher plane, and the form is as real and objective to intelligent beings on that place as are earthly surroundings are to us."[9]

The method that occultists have used throughout the ages to bring about what they want is a very powerful technique called visualisation. Put simply, this is to imagine what you want as clearly as possible and to wish for it with the very essence of your being. The latter is an important part of making what you want happen. According to Berridge, to change one's environment using magic, the magician must also ensoul the image in the mind with the Will. Imagination can only create a finite image that will fade over time. On its own, Will, or simply the desire for something, will only create something which is vague and insubstantial. "However when the two are conjoined – when the imagination creates an image and the Will directs and uses that image, marvellous magical effects may be obtained."

By making a powerful image of what is wanted in your mind, and ensouling it with emotion and desire, it is possible to bring about your wishes. This has been a key principle behind the popular visualisation movement of the 1970s. This movement was based around books with titles like *How to get what you want* and *How to Win Friends and Influence People*.

Visualisation techniques expressed on these methods are effective in most cases, and many sales training courses are based upon them.

9   The Order of the Golden Dawn Flying Roll number V, *Imagination*, by Dr Berridge

Essentially, this approach attempts to influence potential customers by visualising them agreeing with the sales person. Another technique involved a sales person visualising their commissions shooting through the roof or a customer leaving the shop with the product in their hands. Other systems artificially enthuse the sales person towards this goal, making them believe in their product so much that the sales process is conducted with the same zeal as a missionary trying to save a person from hell by converting them. Such ideas activate the Will so that the sales person wishes to make the sale with all of their being. If this sincerity is achieved along with the appropriate visualisation then the sale is almost certain. Another sales technique worth mentioning is for the sales person to get the customer to visualise themselves using that product. That way the customer starts the process of visualising it for themselves.

The visualisation movement flounders because, while it can explain success, it has a greater difficultly explaining why it does not always work. There are many things that can prevent a visualisation having a full effect. This is mostly because when the new image is planted within your Inner Kingdom it immediately has to fit within the framework of what is already there. Those things which fall short of the *status quo* are swiftly destroyed. This happens because you are your Inner Kingdom – it is the sum total of your past visualisations. If you do not believe in success, you have effectively crippled yourself from making new visualisations. The new visualisation is like a seed cast on stony ground and dies before its results can manifest.

Another issue is that you might get what you want, but it may not manifest in the way you wanted it. For example, you may have visualised yourself driving an expensive car as a symbol of you winning the lottery. After months of visualisation you receive a job that involves you delivering such cars to wealthy lottery winners.

In the famous one-act play called *The Monkey's Paw*, a middle aged couple are cursed with three wishes. They initially ask that they will have enough money to pay for their new house. Their treasured son is killed in a factory accident and they collect his insurance money. Distraught, the mother wishes for her son to be alive again – and then they realise his mangled rotting flesh has just crawled from the grave, and they wish him dead again. While never so dramatic, occultism is littered with similar stories of people getting things that they did not really want.

A magical school called Builders of the Adytum, of which I was a member, insists on the first page of its visualisation course that people should not turn over the page before answering the question *What do you want?* At the time, despite my desperation to move on with the course, I could not really work out what I wanted. It was some weeks before I finally realised that what I wanted more than anything else at that moment was to turn the page and continue with the course. If you can answer the question 'what do I want', the next one you need to work out is 'why?'

The answer to the 'why' question usually indicates what you lack in your life. The thing you then have to ask yourself is whether acquiring this particular thing fulfils your wish. Visualising the woman or man of your dreams sweeping you off your feet, for example, is probably one of the most pointless things to do, particularly if you have someone in mind, because what you are really lacking is love in your life and what you want is to be more lovable to attract the right person. Generally people looking for a white knight (or lady), or the love of their life, are looking to escape any real surgery to their personality. They want someone to rescue them from their own Inner Kingdom rather than change it so that such a person can enter.

Having answered why, the next thing you need to work out is what you are prepared to do to assist your goal to manifest on the Earth level. There are many that visualise a good job for themselves and then do not open the paper, let alone search or apply for a job. It is an absolute myth that money will magically appear out of nowhere with no effort on your part. Many magicians rarely perform magic to increase their income, not because they think it is unethical, but because the Universal Mind tends to give them more money by making work to do.

Below is a visualisation technique worked successfully by many magicians in the Western Mystery Tradition. I suggest you practice it before you move onto the other exercises in this book. Try it with something small first, such as acquiring a book. The unconscious mind might actually work to prevent you from achieving a bigger goal, because it is tied up with previous behaviour patterns, but most people's unconscious will let small things through, like books, so it is best to experiment with something where you are least likely to have personal blocks against its success.

A few successes will result in the system being adopted by your unconscious mind.

BASIC VISUALISATION

1. Sit in a chair. Make sure your arms and legs are not crossed and relax as deeply as possible.
2. Think of a clear image of what you want. Build it as intensely as possible. Think of the colour of it. If it is a physical thing, work out what it feels like, smells like, tastes or sounds like. Take your time over this stage because the clearer it is, the more likely you are to get it to manifest.
3. Next you have to stimulate your desire for the object. All else has to be put aside at that moment; all you can want is the object.
4. Visualise yourself as clearly as possible getting the object. Visualise a scene with you owning the object and then another with you owning the object in the past as if you already owned it.

If you followed the above technique to get a book you would visualise the cover as clearly as possible. Feel your desire for the book. Then visualise opening it and reading a book plate with 'this book belongs to ...' and your name on it. Then see yourself putting it on your bookshelf. Next think about the book as if it were already on your shelf.

If it was for something less tangible, like a new job, you would visualise yourself doing the job. During job interviews, if I have decided that I want the job, I ask to be shown around the office. This sounds very keen, but enables me to get a clear picture of what it is like to work there for a visualisation session later on. You would empower that visualisation with all the desire you can muster. Next you would imagine yourself hearing on the phone that you had the job and how you feel about it. Shut your eyes and imagine you are already working there.

The last stage is important in visualisation because it anchors the visualisation in the past, meaning that your mind does not get the chance to think of this as something for the future (remember as far as your mind is concerned the future never happens).

HOW IT WORKS

By taking control of the tool of Imagination, you are building a new symbol within your sphere of sensation and this will build itself a new reality. It starts a vibration within your personal sphere of sensation that sets up a resonance in the bigger universe. If you play a note on a violin you can see the sound waves cause ripples on the surface of a glass of water. In this situation the creation of a new image on your sphere of sensation will create a similar one in the macrocosm. This is possible because the Universe is made up of spiritual matter which vibrates at different frequencies. The lowest frequency is matter or the world we see around us, whereas the highest frequency is pure spirit. There are many different pitches that this energy works at but it is essentially an expression of the One Thing working at different levels, in much the same way that electricity works in a light bulb or a television. For simplicity, occultists grade this energy into four different levels or worlds. The first is Divine, the next is Archetypal, the next is the world of Formation and finally there is the Material world.[10]

Occult teaching says that each world is influenced by the one above it and the once below it. For example, an act on the material plane would affect the world of formation and vice versa. So if I wanted to make a change in my material existence I would enter the world of formation and place an image of what I wanted to happen, ensouled with my will, inside my own sphere of sensation. This image would attract to it all the components needed in the world of formation until it had enough structure to manifest in the next world.

The next level up is the world of archetypes, which are what Plato called 'forms'. He believed that everything had an ideal version of itself that enabled us to identify what it was. Take, for example, a bed; each one is almost entirely different from another in colour, shape and size yet we can identify it as a bed. That is because at the archetypal level there was a true bed form, from which all others derived. It would have all the essence of 'beddiness', apart from the fact you could not sleep in it.

The essences at the archetypal level are extremely powerful and affect the material plane by influencing the world of formation. Normally these archetypal figures have a clear run down through the levels to the material plane through the world of formation. This enables us to recognise the things we see and experience. Some archetypes have a rough ride, as they pass through the world of formation and encounter the thinking and experiencing part of the personality which interprets them incorrectly. An example of this would be the woman I described earlier whose mother was a prostitute. In that situation the 'Mother' archetype would flow down the levels to the world of formation, where it would be met with the experience the woman had with her real

---

10 I am of course referring to the four Cabbalistic worlds.

mother. These feelings of mistrust, fear and anger would block much of the positive side of the archetypal figure and only allow the negative sides.

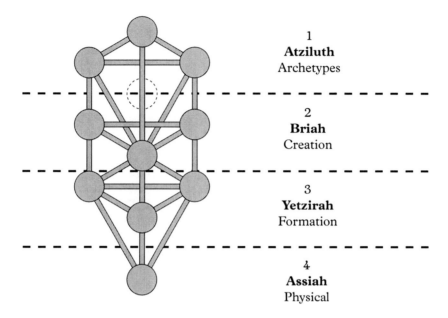

1
Atziluth
Archetypes

2
Briah
Creation

3
Yetzirah
Formation

4
Assiah
Physical

ENTERING THE MIND

Throughout this book you will be given techniques to explore the Inner Kingdom of the mind and the sphere of sensation. But before that we actually have to work out a way to get there. It is one of my pet peeves in magic that there are countless 'experts' in occultism who describe various exciting Inner Kingdoms without visiting them themselves. They will usually give details provided by some other occultist's experience, as if that counts for something. "Of course," they would say, "when Aleister Crowley visited the 32 Aether[11] he saw a being with 14 arms covered with bacon fat, so I am sure that your experience must be wrong." If you ask them about *their* experiences when they visited that level they usually change the subject. Such people are like those experts watching the Travel Channel coverage of foreign holidays and talking as if they had been there.

---

11 This is a reference to the astral cartography of a 16th century magician called John Dee who was given a description of 32 levels of existence between the Earth and Heaven called Aethers. Crowley used the Esoteric Order of the Golden Dawn's method to visit these Inner Kingdoms.

In fantasy novels magicians visit magical kingdoms or other dimensions by waving a wand. At their command a vortex forms and then they step through into the other world just like a transporter in *Star Trek*. In fact there are some similarities between Magical Imagination and that particular fantasy image.

In Western and Eastern magical systems, entering another reality involves some form of meditation which shuts down the body, centring the mind and switching consciousness from one level to another. This is achieved by relaxing as much as possible, regulating breathing until you get as close to possible to sleep (which is another time you enter an Inner Kingdom). Breathing evenly, and as deeply as possible, you keep yourself from nodding off.

But relaxing is no easy thing in this stressful world, and in fact there are countless experts charging business people small fortunes teaching them to relax. Below is a standard technique that really works and which will prepare you for deep meditation.

RELAXATION TECHNIQUE

Sit in a straight backed chair with your hands on your thighs. This is the position depicted in many Egyptian statues and is believed by some occultists to be showing someone performing a meditation.[12] Your back should be straight, your knees at right angles to the floor and your legs uncrossed.

When you are comfortable, regulate your breathing. Breathe in and out as slowly and as deeply as you can. Say you yourself, as I breathe out, all tension is leaving my body and as I breathe in, I shall relax further.

Now think of every part of your body starting with your feet. Say to yourself 'as I breathe out any tenseness in my feet will leave and as I breath in my feet shall relax.' Repeat this until the feet are totally relaxed and continue with the other parts of the body.

There will be some parts of the body that will be more tense than others and will require special

---

12 I don't believe a word of it as it is a common position in Egyptian statues. There is one image I have seen that shows the so-called meditator with his wife with her arm around him, which is not really indicative of a good meditation session. Still, the sitting on a chair is the most comfortable position without being so comfortable you fall asleep!

attention, but the more effort you pay to them, the greater the rewards later in your meditation.

When you have completed your relaxation process (and this can take 15 minutes to half an hour for the first few times) say to yourself "I will now become more deeply relaxed".

Visualise a lift[13] before you. You enter the lift with the floors marked from 10 down to 1. You are on the tenth floor. Press the button marked '1', saying to yourself, "as this lift descends I will become more deeply relaxed". The lift descends and when it arrives you are probably at your most relaxed. Allow the doors to slide open and you will find a plain wooden door before you. This is the entry point to your Inner Kingdom. Over the lintel is a symbol of protection. What that symbol is will be yours and yours alone. For now just note what it looks like, as it will be possible to use it in hours of need.

To leave this doorway to your Inner Kingdom you only need to take the lift back up. Say this to yourself: "As this lift rises I will become more aware of my physical body and surroundings." Step out of the lift and see yourself as part of your own body.

The rest of this book contains powerful exercises. Before you attempt them you should master the above process. After a while you will be able to relax quickly and not need to use the visualisation. Instead you will just have to visualise the doorway.

MEDITATION

Meditation broadly describes the process of entering into an alternative state of consciousness. The two main types of meditation are called active and passive. Passive meditation is when you enter an altered state and images are allowed to enter the consciousness. Active meditation engages the intellect more and tends to be directed. It is the most common magical technique taught in occult schools because it takes control of the thought process. Using a set of intellectually understood symbols, active meditation guides the meditator along a particular thought process towards a realisation or spiritual goal.

Passive Meditation

Earlier I described how we develop association chains when we are growing up by associating one idea with another. Passive meditation

---

13 American people will of course use an 'elevator'.

uses this to find a root cause behind each symbol by mentally travelling down the association chain. If you started with a symbol such a cross you would look at it until another idea entered your head... say an image of a hot cross bun. You would follow that association, perhaps to Diana the goddess of crossroads and magic. By the time you have finished you will have explored a whole network of associations in your mind.

It is a tricky form of meditation because you shoot off at tangents and can get very lost in bizarre associations quickly. Using this technique I once started out with a symbol of pentagram and ended up with a pot of blueberry jam, which contained very limited spiritual information. The trick is to push away associations that you know are going to take you away from your target. For example when using the symbol of a white dove it would be good to follow the association with purity but not a good idea to wander down the guano association.

Earlier I gave an example of passive meditation on two different forms of crosses. Here are two more for you to try.

Passive Meditation I

Start with the lift visualisation, relax your mind as deeply as you can and regulate your breathing. When you get to the wooden door see before you a circle with a dot in the middle. Ask yourself 'what does this mean?' Allow the door to open and then allow images to appear in the door frame.

Initially you will see symbols that relate to intellectual information you have about circles and dots. Then when you have exhausted that stream of information, wait, and after a while new information will arrive. Merge into the symbol so that you become it, and it becomes part of you. How do you feel? Allow more information to rise into your consciousness.

Passive Meditation II

This uses chant of a Divine name to have some form of mystical experience. Relax as before, take a deep breath and chant the divine name IAO[14] (which is pronounced EE AH OH). Breathe in and vibrate it again. Repeat.

In these exercises you will get an effect which is uniquely your own. In some ways passive meditators are like someone who takes acid, in that

---

14 This is an extremely powerful Greek name of God and it is said that vibrating it opens a connection with the divine force behind the universe.

they have no control over what they experience. Sometimes, due to their mood, or the psychic state of their environment, they may experience all manner of horrors. Like many mystics, they may see the throne of God and experience great elation. Unfortunately they can often never repeat the experience because there is no ordered method of approaching it. They are also unable to explain their experience because they lack the language to understand it. Often they will get new information and gain new insights on a subject.

Active Meditation

Active meditation uses symbols to build a road of ideas to a particular spiritual idea or goal. These symbols are designed by people who have gone before them and have obtained results by applying them in various combinations. It has the advantage in that although the problems of association chains remain, the mind can be steered away from heading down meditative blind alleys. The system's weakness is that its practitioners can become obsessed with the intellectual meaning of the symbols or become too reliant on symbols at the expense of spiritual progress so that they are unable to drop them when the time comes. Sometimes a person might be led to a mystical experience in a pathworking but cannot abandon the symbol at the last minute to experience it fully. However if a spiritual realisation happens they have a symbols to describe what they have experienced to others.

Active Meditation I

After your usual relaxation, choose one of the following sentences.

> *The seed of Light*
> *All things are an expression of the One Thing*
> *The Kingdom of God is at Hand*
> *Who am I?*
> *What do I want?*

Mull the sentence over in your mind until you understand it. Take each word and cut it apart with an intellectual knife, work out all its meanings, consult a dictionary if you have to. Remember that each word is a symbol and some of them are loaded with powerful archetypal meaning.

Next, relate each sentence to your life and then to each other word in the sentence. See the sentence as a collection of symbols that are designed to teach you. Ask yourself what are the implications for the universe? How can you tie all this knowledge together?

When you have run out of all the intellectual information related to this sentence, something new will happen and you will suddenly see the sentence, and the world, in a completely different way.

This particular technique is wonderful if you are confused about how to approach a life crisis. Firstly you have to convert your situation into a single sentence question, which is in itself a wonderful problem-focusing exercise. A seed idea is generally always positive, so it is not a good idea to choose the sentence "why am I so useless?" The idea would be to find the seed of the problem and to meditate upon it. For example, someone who has just ended another dud relationship could work out what they really want to know and come up with something like "Why do I have bad relationships?" There are three key words in this sentence which will generate interesting material: these are *I*, *bad* and *relationships*. After meditating on this one for a week, one person realised, much to her horror, that she *chose* bad relationships and that the reason was that she did not believe that she deserved any better. She also discovered that her definition of a relationship was wrong. Her mistake was that she saw the romantic overtures of the relationship's beginning as a sign that there was a relationship, rather than simply a shallow dramatic play for her affections by men with limited imagination to form anything more lasting. True, she had obtained romance, which was what she thought she wanted, at the expense of a relationship which she really did want.

Active Meditation II
Relax as normal and go to the doorway described at the end of the relaxation technique. Open it and you will find yourself in sea of silvery mist.

After a while the mist clears and you find yourself in a cave.

In the centre of the cave is a white stone which fills the cave with light.

As you watch, a stem of a plant grows out of the white stone, buds and becomes a rose.

The rose opens and the cave is filled with its perfume.

In the centre of the rose is a tiny golden child.

Bending over, you look at the child.

It looks at you with eyes of someone who has lived many times.

This is your higher self.

It grows and matures until it becomes a mirror image of you and raises its hand in a blessing.

You bow and depart through the door through which you came.

A Balance is Best

Sometimes I get asked which is the best form of meditation for those on a spiritual path of development. The truth is that both have their advantages and disadvantages. There are those who say that active is better for beginners who have yet to master the subtleties of inner vision, while others accuse it of killing creativity.

Ideally you should use a combination of both active and passive techniques. You should develop a system of symbols, but just pause in an active meditation to see what happens. For example, in Active Meditation II, a passive element where you talk to your Higher Self could be added.

USING IMAGINATION TO IMPROVE YOUR MEMORY

The first time we see the imagination being used in anything like modern pathworking is in memory systems developed to help poets and orators remember their speeches. These were codified during Greece's Golden Age by Simonides of Ceos (556BC – 468BC). Although we are uncertain what Simonides actually invented, a 3rd century BC tablet called the Parian Chronicle credited him with inventing a system of memory aids. This is backed up by Roman writers Cicero, Quintilian, Pliny and Ammianus Marcellinus. We do know that all the Ancient Greeks used a system that is uncannily close to modern pathworking. These can be summed up by a 4th century fragment known as Dialexeis:

> "If you pay attention you will be able to see things better. Repeat again what you hear, for by hearing and saying the same thing, what you have learned is easier to remember. What you hear, place on what you know."

In other words, if you want to remember that Ajax was a soldier in the Trojan Wars, you could imagine him standing next to a statue of Mars in your bathroom, cleaning the bath, with a big map of Greece in the background. You would remember to put all Ajax's soldiers in the bathroom. So if you were going through a speech, you would mentally walk through your house until you got to the bathroom. In your mind's eye you could see a soldier cleaning the bath, remember Ajax[15], see the map of Greece and recall he was on the Greek side of the Trojan war.

Obviously this example is a little clumsy and the Greeks and Romans needed to codify things better to cover the long lists needed to remember their speeches. They already had a list of Gods, who were attributed to the different planets. In memory terms, all they had to do was see a statue of the God and then they would immediately think of the planet. Cronos (Saturn) would be a link to words like death, time, inheritance and blackness, while Zeus (Jupiter) would connect to things like rulership, wealth and purple. The net widened to include the zodiacal attributions. This meant that if they were making a speech about War with the Persians they would use a magical image of a statue of Mars with the various points of their speech being placed around it.

Here is another one developed by an occultist friend of mine, Elliot James, who used a memory system to give a tricky speech to his fellow American Civil war re-enactors in the summer of 2001. He decided that his speech needed a number of quotes from the Articles of War – specifically Article 5, covering political speech by troops – and Article 54, covering behaviour of troops in friendly territory.

He designed three rooms:
1. a hallway for my introductory remarks,
2. a drawing room with French windows,
3. a garden with a terrace.

And then broke down his speech into various visual pictures.
For article five:

> "Any officer or soldier who shall use contemptuous or disrespectful words against the President of the United States, against the Vice-President thereof, against the Congress of the United States, or against the Chief Magistrate or Legislature of any of the United States in which he may be quartered, if a commissioned officer shall be cashiered or otherwise punished as a court-martial shall direct; if a non-commissioned officer or soldier shall suffer such punishment as shall be inflicted upon him by a court-martial."

On the face of it this would be murder to memorise but Elliot pictured himself moving into a room with French windows:

---

15 Although there is an outside chance you might call him Vim, Flash, Jif or some other household cleaner.

In the room was a table with a soldier's cap upon it - link this idea to: "Any officer or soldier who shall use contemptuous or disrespectful words…"

Then he saw a picture of George Washington:
"…against the President of the United States…"

Then a picture of John Adams:
"…against the Vice-President thereof…"

Then a snow-shaker with a model of the Capitol on the desk;
"…against the Congress of the United States…"

Then a picture a feather-boa (trade mark of Jesse Ventura, Governor of Minnesota); "…or against the Chief Magistrate…"

Then a sculpture of a four-horsed chariot (as on the capitol building in St. Paul); "…or Legislature of any of the United States, in which he may be quartered…"

Then picture a sword on the desk with the point towards you; "… if a commissioned officer shall be cashiered or otherwise punished as a court-martial shall direct…"

Then a picture of a row of chairs behind the desk;
"… if a non-commissioned officer or soldier shall suffer such punishment as shall be inflicted upon him by a court-martial."

Having finished that part of the speech, Elliot moved to the French windows, opened them and then moved on to the next part of his speech.

There was a side effect of using this system; people using it started to pick up new information about their subject. This side effect was noted and explained by the philosophers Plato and Aristotle. Both considered obtaining knowledge as simply recovering information (remembering) which had been forgotten when we were born, and fell from our perfected state in the higher realms of existence. So when people were using these memory systems it was no surprise that they 'remembered' something else about the subject at the same time.

It was perfectly reasonable then that memory systems could be used to teach by bringing new information to the conscious mind of the practitioner. This is important when you consider that in contemplating esoteric symbols, information would have been remembered by the person using the system.

In the Middle Ages and 16th century, memory systems were developed further, particularly among Renaissance magicians. One of the great researchers into memory systems, Frances A. Yates, in her book *Art of Memory*,[16] suggests that it is these techniques which may have evolved into the medieval magical system called the 'Ars Notoria'. Under this system, she says, the magician would stare at magical symbols, recite a prayer and gain knowledge of all arts and sciences.

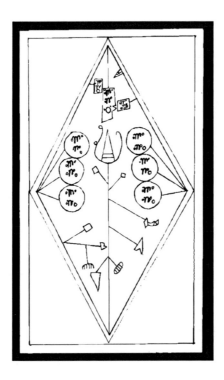

This memory picture comes from the Sixth figure of philosophy. It was designed to help the person understand the nature of the Universe. While staring at the figure they would say the following prayer:

"Gezemothon, Oronathian, Heyatha, Aygyay, Lethasihel, Iaechizliet, Gerohay, Gerhomay, Sanoaesorel, Sanasathel, Gissiomo, Hatel, Segomasay, Azomathon, Helomathon, Gerochor, Hojazay, Samin, Heliel, Sanihelyel, Siloth, Silerech, Garamathal, Gesemathal, Gecoromay, Gecorenay, Samyel, Samihahel, Hesemyhel, Sedolamax, Secothamay, Samya, Rabiathos, Avinosch, Annas, Amen."

16 *Art of Memory*, 1966, Routledge & Kegan Paul, London

Then the following:

"Oh Eternal King, Oh God, the Judge and discerner of all things, knower of good sciences; instruct me this day for thy Holy Name's sake, and by these Holy Sacraments; and purify my understanding, that Thy knowledge may enter my inward parts as dew falling from Heaven and as Oil into my bones, by Thee, Oh God, Saviour of all things, who art the fountain of goodness and origin of piety. Instruct me this day in those holy sciences which I desire. Thou who art One God for ever. Amen."

Then knowledge would slowly filter its way into their conscious mind either by dream, a person instructing them, or simply understanding.

Perhaps closer to these memory glyphs are those pentacles found in the famous magical grimoire the *Key of Solomon*. These were symbols, usually painted on wooden disks, that were held in the hands of a magician when they invoked a spirit. I know a number of magicians who have received insights or 'memories' when staring at these symbols, perhaps because they hold links to the spirits behind them. It is my view that more research needs to be done into the use of such pentacles in this manner before less experienced people start to tinker with them. There are several pentacles attached to each planet, with different spirits attached to each one, and some are easier to deal with than others.

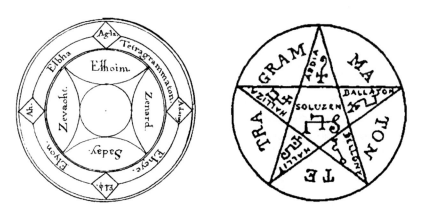

There were more obvious images that were associated with memory which were not only more widely circulated, but also give us a safer method of remembering the things we want and gaining new insights. These memory pictures of the Middle Ages give us archetypal figures for each of the planets that can provide the sort of information you want.

Below you will find seven planetary images that were designed by a 16th century magician Cornelius Agrippa to have the maximum possible impact on your unconscious mind and allow you to understand the planetary forces. Some of the images are familiar, others will strike you as strange. This is because they were in the language of the unconscious and everyone knows that the unconscious mind can produce some strange and disturbing images at times! If you want to remember something, make a story out of the magical image that included what you want to remember. If you want to remember that the password on your computer is 'Badger' you would place a badger on Mercury's[17] lap, perhaps with the word 'password' written on it. If you have a fault with your computer and are trying to find the answer without bothering the helpdesk, you would visualise the magical image and ask it for help.

A word of caution here, just because the magical image gives you an answer does not mean that it is right or that you heard it correctly. Sometimes (particularly when you ask a magical image about your love life), your lower unconscious mind will put the words it wants to hear in the magical image's mouth. For example, when I was a lot younger I had a crush on a woman and hoped that she was interested in me. I approached the magical image of Venus and asked and was told emphatically 'yes'. However, I noticed that the image actually shook her head when she said yes (in other words the image was saying 'no' but my lower self was blotting this out). Confused, I asked again and this time the head nodded and the voice said yes. All that had happened was that my lower self had realised that the image was shaking its head and made sure it could not do this again. So when using magical images it is always important to listen, watch and accept that the first thing you were told was the proper message. Then test what you have heard against logic and reason. It is possible that you have been conned by your lower self so you have to be careful.

WhICh PLANETARY IMAGE DO YOU USE?

Saturn ♄
Fate, time, the past, limits and boundaries, form, structures including houses, old age, ambition, bones, knees, skeleton, shins, ankles and circulation, rheumatism, arthritis, envy, suffering, feet, guilt, toxins,

---

17 Mercury rules computing.

repressed aspects of the self, death, vermin and lice, politicians, scientists, architects, teachers, mines, mountains and wastelands.

Jupiter ♃

Lawmaking, opportunity, growth, progress, evolution, money, banks, rulers, royalty, faith, hope, charity, redemption, freedom, spiritual wisdom and development, hypocrisy, hips, thighs, feet, lawyers, priests, counsellors, actors, open spaces, public places and panoramic views.

Mars ♂

Wars, anger, action, sexual desire, physical energy, guards, courts, justice, courage, protection, transformation, revenge, destruction, surgery, the head, genitals, excretory system, rashes, red spots, migraine, predators, soldiers, surgeons, athletes, furnaces, and metal work.

Venus ♀

Love, eroticism, desire, pleasure, inspiration, joy, partnerships, peace, friendship, creativity, the arts, beauty, evaluation, promiscuity, overindulgence, lewdness, gentle animals, the throat and neck, kidneys, lower neck, diplomacy, artist, fashions, bedrooms and gardens.

Mercury ☿

Communication, movement, messengers, computers, the media, language, trade, theft, magic, skill, learning, intellect, psychology as a science, science, rationality, cunning and mischievous animals like monkeys, digestive system, arms and hands, merchants, clerks, accountants, scholars, universities, examinations, shops, schools, airports and train and bus stations.

The Moon ☽

The unconscious, habits, instinct, sea, rhythm, the astral realm, mysteries, women (particularly their health), mothers, childbirth, psychics, menstruation, mental health, the stomach, breasts, warts, sterility, obsessions, delusions, insanity, cleaners, brewers, midwives, sailors and harbours.

The Sun ☉

Leadership, general health, healing, organization, arrogance, display, drama, fathers, power, individualisation, the heart, the back, the lungs, kings, directors, managers, actors, palaces, and theatres.

OLYMPIC SPIRITS – IMAGINATIVE DOORWAYS TO RELIGION

Buried in the side corridors of magic is an imagination technique which can lead a person to understand the principles of religion through direct experience. The Olympic Spirits make their first appearance in a ritual magic handbook called the *Arbatel of Magic*, which was bundled together with the *Fourth Book of Occult Philosophy* of Cornelius Agrippa in the 16th century.

The *Arbatel* says that the Olympic Spirits have control over the world and can do what they like, provided they do not upset God, who is the guide of all things. This is to remind the reader that really it is God that does everything. Each spirit was assigned a planet and they had control over them.

The names of the Olympic Spirits are Aratron, Bethor, Phaleg, Och, Hagith, Ophiel and Phul. But these are 'titles' and a means to approach them. The *Arbatel* says that each spirit, when approached, will tell you their true name. However, these are unique for every person and will only last for 40 years, perhaps because each force changes over time and after a 40 year cycle it is so different that it can't be called the same thing any more.

RAY	COLOUR	OLYMPIC SPIRIT	PLANET	DAY OF THE WEEK
1	Violet	Phul	Moon	Monday
2	Indigo	Aratron	Saturn	Saturday
3	Blue	Bethor	Jupiter	Thursday
4	Green	Hagith	Venus	Friday
5	Yellow	Och	Sun	Sunday
6	Orange	Ophiel	Mercury	Wednesday
7	Red	Phaleg	Mars	Tuesday

Reading the *Arbatel*, more questions arise than are given answers. But the process of asking provides a picture of these beings which makes them more godlike. Firstly since this is a late medieval document we must understand what is meant by the term 'spirit'. In magic we are taught that in a planetary hierarchy we have God, Archangel, Angel, Intelligence and Spirit. Spirits are the least possible to control and must always be approached through the other three hierarchies. However, it is clear that the Olympics are supposed to be approached directly and will send minions to do their bidding. They are not 'spirits' in that sense, but in the late medieval period everything that was not God or material was considered to be a spirit. For example, we have the 16th century magician John Dee calling Aniel a Spirit and she was an archangel.

It seems that in looking at the names of the spirits, or becoming focused on their planetary nature, we missed the fact that by calling them Olympic, the *Arbatel* was implying they were the seven main Greek gods that dwelt on Mount Olympus. These would be Apollo, Selene, Ares, Hermes, Zeus, Aphrodite and Chronos. These were named by the Romans as Sol, Luna, Mars, Mercury, Jupiter, Venus and Saturn. Notice that we are *not* talking about the planets, but the God that rules the planet, just like the *Arbatel* says.

The *Arbatel* makes a clear division between the Olympic spirits and the divine. In doing so it would be following the line that Christians had taken up to that point, that the Olympic spirits were minor when it came to the spectacular unity which was God.

Thus it is tempting to suggest that the Olympics were just a blind for the pagan gods of the Greeks and Romans. The 'secret names' of the gods and goddesses were accessed through the Christian religion without them having to worry about the accusation that they might be worshipping pagan gods.

But if the inventors of the 'Olympian Spirit' system had coded the pagan deities, it is clear that the names were not that important. They do not say 'Zeus' or 'Ares', they have different, more occult names. It might have been because they feared that they would be persecuted, but during this period of history it was becoming acceptable to look at Pagan symbols if hidden under an appropriate Christian cloak. But it is possible that they were saying something a little more heretical.

Although God is One Thing, it expresses itself in seven different ways as it passes into matter. These are the seven primal ideas of deity. Earlier we mentioned that Plato thought that the world was made from ideas which were born in the Divine Mind. But God itself is also an idea; a reflection of a reality that cannot be really expressed. When the human tries to order this idea, it creates seven different versions.

The Ancient Greeks had a habit of classifying all gods and goddesses using their system. Every time they encountered a new god or goddess they worked out which one was closest to their system. Thus we find the Jews being told that they worshipped Zeus because their God tended to sit on mountains and lob thunderbolts. The Ancient Egyptian Thoth was called Hermes because he represented writing, and the Celts' worship of Alator was associated with Ares. But equally it could be applied to the more obscure Greek gods and goddesses. So for example Athena was a form of Zeus, Dionysus was another expression of either Apollo or Venus. The fact was that all gods and goddesses of religion could be placed under seven broad headings which loosely fitted within the planets.

Monotheistic exoteric religions could also be placed in this seven-fold category. If Judaism fits into Jupiter then Christianity does quite nicely as a Solar cult. But then we start to notice that when a religion fragments, it often becomes a different expression. The puritan Christianity of the 17th century was very much Chronos, while the happy-clappy 'born-again' Christians in many respects act like a Venus cult. Early Pauline Christianity was practically a Venus love cult when it was first established, but when it became an official Roman religion it became similar to worship of Selene with her virginal priests worshipping Mary. Similar 'pagan' fragmentation may be found in the Muslim religion. Note that I am not saying that monotheists are worshipping these gods by name, but are approaching religion through a similar avenue to the worshippers of that pagan god.

In other words, these seven make up all the gods that rule the earth. As the spirits once told the magician John Dee:

> "*Seven rest* in seven: and the *Seven* live by *seven*. The *seven govern* the seven and by *seven*, all *Govern*ment is."

Just as white light is divided by a crystal into seven colours, violet, indigo, blue, green, yellow, orange and red, so is the real religion of unity split into seven aspects.

In the Eastern-influenced system of Alice Bailey they were called Rays, although these are her impression of a tradition that goes back to Ancient Greece. When Zeus takes the bull-form known as Taurus in order to win the heart of Europa, his face "gleams with seven rays of fire." The idea of seven rays appears in the Mysteries of Mithras and Dionysus, the Chaldean Oracles. The Gnostics and others worshipped a God of Seven Rays. While it is not clear what these rays were, they were often seen as an expression of the sun.

But if the seven rays are the seven archetypal gods on which all religion is based, then all our attempts to find God through them are chasing shadows. The Olympic Spirits are fragments of the Divine Unity, as we are, and therefore must be brought together in the mind of the magician as part of the journey home. They also provide us with direct control of planetary power. According to the Hermetic work *Isis to Horus* :

> "Seven wandering stars are there which move in the spheres before Olympus' Gate... To these stars the human race is committed. We have within us Mene, Zeus, Ares, Paphie, Kronos, Helios and Hermes. By this means are we destined to draw from the living Aether of the Kosmos our tears, mirth, anger, our parenthood, our conversation, our sleep and every desire."

Religion is a vital part of the development of any magician, and in the Golden Dawn rituals one of the more important officers is called the Hegemon who carries the mitre-headed sceptre which she says "represents religion which guides life".

So why is our religion not balanced? It is simply because each person is born with one or more rays predominant and so they are naturally drawn to one Olympic spirit over another. If you look at your astrological chart you will see that some planets are weak and others cancel each other out so you are left with one or two predominant rays. As you begin your religious quest you will first be drawn to that Olympic Spirit that is closest to those predominant rays. Society often dictates what religion is available but each of the bigger ones is capable of containing all rays with their 'church'. A Christian who is on the Och ray will be drawn to those churches which emphasise death and resurrection. Those who like lots of psychic experiences, such as speaking in tongues, will probably head to the churches where the Phul ray is predominant.

Everyone is trying to find that Olympic spirit which is predominant in their creation and when they find it they will get an appropriate set of rules and guidelines for living in the universe which was created by the Gods.

With the fall of Christianity within Western society, many people have lost touch with the various Olympic Spirits. As such they have lost their spiritual guidance and are feeling a bit lost. Some managed to find the same spirits behind the masks of other religions but until a new modern religion replaces the Church then people will have to keep looking. It is probably for this reason that the neo-paganism movement has managed to gain so much ground. Worshippers are returning to the Olympic Spirits almost directly and finding that they have something to say.

However, each ray is in itself unbalanced and subject to corruption. Solar religions tend to end up killing people, usually through a Leonine arrogance that they are completely right. Lunar religions end up castrating people either physically or metaphorically. Mercurial religions often play mind games, Saturnian religions are big on guilt and so on. But for most ordinary people the mystical power they provide is what they need to live out their life on earth. As the *Arbatel* says, the Seven spirits decide people's destinies.

That should read "ordinary people". The magician is different. Their destiny is not to worship the Olympic Spirits but to balance them in themselves and then move on to attain a unity with the God who expresses itself through the seven rays. This balancing act is probably what was suggested by the Gnostic idea of Aeons. When you die, you face each of the Olympic Spirits. If you have mastered all of them, you are permitted to go on your journey into the reality of the universe. How do you master them? You take the lessons and spiritual guidance they have to teach you.

Firstly you have to find out which ray and therefore which Olympic Spirit you are attached to. Primarily it should be the predominant planet in your chart. So take for example this nameless person.

Leo: Sun (in the first house)
Scorpio: Moon
Leo: Mercury
Libra: Mars
Virgo: Venus
Gemini: Jupiter
Pisces: Saturn

With the Sun in the first house and in its favoured sign of Leo, it is very strong. Mars in Libra, Pisces in Saturn, Mercury in Leo are not well placed and therefore weak. Jupiter is strong, as is Venus. Therefore the main Olympic spirit will be Och, although the person will also be influenced by Bethor and Hagith.

Another case:

Gemini: Sun
Gemini: Venus
Taurus: Mercury
Leo: Mars (12th house)

Libra: Moon
Leo: Saturn
Taurus: Jupiter

In this chart Mars in Leo would be the strongest but being in the 12th house it is blighted. The expansive Jupiter would not like the conservative Taurus. Saturn would not like the expansive Leo and Mercury is also weak. This leaves the Sun, Venus and the Moon as the strongest, although neither are particularly obvious. Looking at the person's chart, however, we see that the Moon is not blocked by any bad aspects and actually is in a trine and sextile with the Sun. It would mean then that their Olympic Spirit would be the Phul, although Och and Hagith would be also involved.

What does this mean in terms of the religion that both these cases would follow? The first case would look for a religion that followed solar cycles of death and rebirth. The religion would probably have a healing angle and may follow the ideas of re-incarnation. The second person would be attracted to a more mystical and psychic religion, where feminine roles were more important and sexuality was sublimated. But for both of these people, if they followed just their primary Olympic Spirit, they would be badly unbalanced, and fortunately have back-ups in their subsidiary rays. It is probably fair to define the fundamentalist in any religion as one who only sees one Olympic Spirit. If either of these two were occultists, it would be important for them to work with and understand those Olympic Spirits which are blighted in their charts. Their natural tendency will be to manifest Och or Phul, so they must work consciously to involve the others.

SEALS OF THE OLYMPIC SPIRITS

We approach these beings through our imagination and by using their seals or sigils. Earlier we mentioned how images and symbols were used to open the sphere of sensation to different teaching and understanding. We are using a similar imagination technique here.

The seals of the Olympic Spirits are a complete mystery. All but the seal of Ophiel are based on horizontal and vertical lines. Ophiel is more like a lightning flash. Phul appears to have departed slightly from the square boxes of the other sigils and relies on a curved line which might represent a lunar crescent.

It is possible that the symbols are primal and are connected to the same symbols used to denote gods in stone age iconography.

The figure of Och, for example, could be a symbolic shorthand for the sun showing three rays emerging from it, or it could represent the solar stag with its horns. Unfortunately this is unlikely, as one of the most important symbols in cave paintings and carvings is the spiral and these characters are all linear. If it represents the sun with three rays then the symbol has become corrupted as there is an important lateral line to the figure. Likewise the stag is not an animal associated with this figure. The stag is associated with Phaleg and the antler motif can be imagined, but it is a little dubious.

Generally then, it is better to see these symbols as links to the primal power of which we have no intellectual knowledge yet.

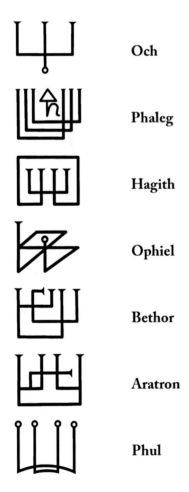

Och

Phaleg

Hagith

Ophiel

Bethor

Aratron

Phul

The colours of the seals are based on the colours of the ray associated with them, which is tied to the colour of the planet.

The *Arbatel* gives fairly simple methods of approaching the spirits. You should get up at sunrise on the day assigned to the Olympic Spirit and say a prayer of request. The Prayer is:

"Omnipotent and eternal God, who has ordained the whole of creation for your praise and glory and for the salvation of man, I beseech you to send your spirit N.N. of the Order of the Sun, who shall inform and teach me those things which I shall ask of him or that he may bring me medicine against the dropsy &c. Nevertheless not my will but Thine be done through Jesus Christ, Thy only Begotten Son, our Lord, Amen"

There is a warning that you should not talk to the spirit for longer than an hour unless he is the Spirit that is linked to you.

"For as much as you came in peace and quietly and have answered my petitions I have given thanks to God in whose name you came. Now may you depart in peace to your abode and return to me again when I call you by your name or your Order or by your office which is granted from the Creator, Amen."

If it were performed literally it would not work. It is as if the writer of the *Arbatel*, having given some detail about the Olympic Spirits, had given up trying to tell any other details. But there are clues even here about what to do.

To call any of the seven lamps, you have to invoke the single light that is behind them.

The writer invokes the Omnipotent and eternal God who *organised* the *whole* of creation. You would have to do the same thing to provide the white light which becomes the seven others.

After invoking the light behind the lamps, you must then invoke the Olympic Spirit while staring at the seal.

This can be done by vibrating the name of the Spirit while looking at the symbol. If you do this for at least ten minutes, you should find yourself going into a light trance. Then, when you shut your eyes, you should be able to see the image of the seal clearly.

Allow images to appear in your mind. This is where it will become hard. You will know you have mastered it when you find yourself close to a temple or some other form of religious hardware. You might find that the temple is generic and there are statues of many different gods and goddesses that manifest its ray or it might only appear as one. There you will find the spirit.

When working with Olympic Spirits you have to treat them as if they were God. Worshipping is possible, but only if it is in your mindset. I am not one to go around telling gods or goddesses how big and impressive they are, so they don't tend to believe me when I do. Respect goes a long way, but so does a feeling of awe before something infinitely bigger than you. One of the interesting things about early so-called pagan religion was that it was very matter of fact. There is little indication of a mystical expression outside the Mystery religions. Everyone knew the gods existed, they also sought to placate them with respect and doing the right rituals. If something went wrong with society or a family then it was important to find out which gods had been insulted and attempt to placate them. But the feeling was that if you were pious the gods and goddesses left you alone and sometimes did you a favour. The Mystery religions were the first to take gods out of that cycle and look for a more intimate relationship.

The Olympic Spirits are like the One Thing on a lower arc. They are fragmented aspects of its Power. However I have yet to see any proof that the One Thing demands worship. There is little in the way of logic that suggests that a being so vast and multi-dimensional gets anything out of being told how wonderful it is. Humans might feel that power and want to express it, but it is not a necessary part of the equation. In fact the rational occultist might not want to do even that. Jewish religion treats the idea of worshipping fragments of God, just as humans, gods and angels with horror. Thus it is more likely that the Olympic Spirits want to be understood and have willing assistants in the destiny of creation.

Once you have a clear image in your mind's eye of the Spirit, you can then ask the personal name by which that ray manifests in your life (it might be a god, archangel, etc). Remember that the Olympic Spirit is the archetype of all gods and goddesses that are part of that ray. They are there to provide you with advice on your life course, but they still *act* like gods and goddesses. Bethor is just as likely to throw a thunderbolt at you as he is going to help you win the lottery. If Bethor manifests to you as a bearded YHVH he will talk in absolutes. However, he only understands things in terms of his own power. As the *Arbatel* keeps saying, only the complete God knows all the answers. However, it is the nature of gods to want worship.

Ask it to deal with your question or problem. If it agrees, it will give you advice or assign a spirit to do the task. You should ask for the name of any servitor and you can work with it directly on the day of the Olympic Spirit who gave him to you. This spirit might be another god. Remember that the Olympic Spirits are the sources of all Gods. Rudd gives us descriptions of only some of the sorts of spirits that are under the main Olympic Spirits. It is fairly clear that rather than being absolute descriptions, they are what Rudd got when he tried it.

These are mostly planetary. For example, the creatures that belong to Phaleg are tall brown, filthy, red with horns like a hart, griffin's claws and make a noise like a roaring bull. You know if you get one because there is always thunder and lightning around your magic circle. However you have to remember that Rudd was a Christian, so seeing the leader of the Wild Hunt (which is fairly clearly what he is describing) might have

Phul

scared the willies off him. The Spirits of Hagith, however, are all beautiful maidens who charm to come and play. These sound like classical Greek nymphs. The impression he had of the spirits that were assigned to him by Mercury were fully armed knights who move like clouds and bring fear to those whom they are around. Before we lapse into Tarot symbolism as a way of explaining this symbol, let's look to see if there is anything Mercurial that would fit this description. Mercury was seen as a protector of travellers on journeys and was often seen as the person who led the dead to Hades.

However the Celtic bear god Artor was thought of as being a form of Mercury, who later evolved into King Arthur. Another spirit who fits the bill is Odin, who was also very militaristic and carries the souls of the dead to the afterlife. Odin was also said to inspire fear.

You can also ask the god a question, or for a spirit who will provide you with something you want. Olympic Spirits are 'gods' and cannot be ordered about. You cannot threaten them or do anything which is a standard tool of grimoire magic. You are getting in touch with one of the prime religious motivators in the universe and the most powerful source of magic. However, they act according to the will of the One Thing's own will and according to its plans. In some cases they will not give you want you want, and in other cases they will let you have it, even if it is not a good idea. Gods are like that.

My own experience, and the experience of other magicians that have invoked the Olympic Spirits, is that they feel much like an intense religious experience. Your invocations have to be emotional and almost mystical in their approach – lots of appropriate candles, chanting and perhaps the odd sing song. In some ways they are the most simple and approachable magical experience you can have. In other ways they are hardest to achieve.

OLYMPIC SPIRIT	GODS	MEANING
Och A King riding a lion, a crowned King, a Queen with a sceptre, a bird, a lion, a cock, a yellow or golden garment, and a sceptre.	Osiris Helios Apollo Dionysos Sol Shamas Ra Anextiomarus Atepomarus Bel Maponus	Birth and death cycles Healing Sacred Kings Rulership Corn gods Summer Men generally
Phaleg A King riding a wolf, a man armed, a woman holding a shield on her thigh, a he-goat, a horse, a stag, a red garment and wool.	Ares Mars Hepaistos Vulcan Ninurta Horos Sekmet Camulos Cernunnos Belatucados	War Mechanical skills Metalwork Justice Power Energy Overcoming evil Active protection Young men
Hagith A King with sceptre riding a camel, a young woman clothed and dressed beautifully, a naked young woman, a she-goat, a camel, a dove, a white or green garment, flowers and the herb Savin.	Venus Aphrodite Ishtar Turan Hathor Bast Sucellus Epona	Love Sex Creativity Grace Music Art Joy Beauty Nature spirits Young women

Ophiel A King riding a bear, a fair young man, a woman holding a staff, a dog, a she-bear, a magpie, clothes of changeable colours, a rod and a little staff.	Mercury Hermes Turms Nabu Thoth Seshat Cisonius	Communication Trade Writing Magic Messengers
Bethor A King with a drawn sword riding a stag, a man wearing a mitre in a long robe, a young woman with a laurel crown adorned with flowers, a bull, a stag, a peacock, an azure garment, a sword, a box tree, and lightning bolts.	Jupiter YHVH Zeus Athene Poseidon Minerva Tinia Marduk Hapi Maat Leucetius	Thunder Storms Justice Wisdom Abundance Rulership Order Sea Gods
Aratron A bearded King riding a dragon, an old man with a beard, an old woman leaning on a staff, a pig, a dragon, an owl, a black robe, a hook or sickle and a juniper tree.	Kronos Saturn Hera Juno Ea Neth Ptah Demeter	Time Death Motherhood Home Building and construction Harvest
Phul A King like Arthur riding on a doe, a little boy, a woman hunter with bow and arrows, a cow, a little doe, a goose, a green garment or silver, an arrow or a creature with many feet.	Artemis Selene Luna Hecate Diana Sin Tivs Khonsu Hades Isis	Underworld Women generally Witchcraft Divination Hunting Childbirth

Obviously the above list is just a start and some of the bigger gods and goddesses could appear under different Olympic Spirits. Isis could appear in several different slots, depending on what she was doing. This is not because the Olympic Spirit was mixed at any point but simply because early religions often swallowed other religions' mythology. Paul's version of Christ can fit under most Olympic spirits.

Chapter Two

MODERN MAGICAL IMAGINATION TECHNIQUES

AGICAL SCHOOLS continued to develop the use of magical images and symbols as methods of training. Most of them, like the mystical secret societies, implanted a set of symbols within the minds of their members during initiation rituals. The advantage of performing a ritual is that it exposes a person to a dramatic presentation of a symbol and the effect that it will have on a person's life. The candidate would study these symbols as part of their training within the school until they could walk the symbolic paths depicted by these rituals.

An example of this is the Freemasonic system where a candidate is presented with a set of symbols and allegories during an initiation ritual. The symbols are those of a worker building Solomon's temple, and by meditation and use of this allegory the candidate is expected to become a better person. The Golden Dawn used a technique where a candidate would be shown a diagram, while at the same time the officer holding it would place that drawing in their sphere of sensation. For many years this technique was lost, and while it was missing, Golden Dawn initiations lacked much of their power. We will be looking at the ritual use of imagination later on.

In the 18th century, magical schools started to develop another mind technique based on the idea of a journey through an inner landscape, or through a myth where the practitioner was the central character. Usually these journeys were carried out in the rarefied setting of a magical ritual, which gave the journey more impact. One Napoleonic period ritual manuscript[18] shows the candidate identified with the myth of a page

---

18 I will not reveal the name of this group because part of this early ritual is still being practised as part of a particularly powerful initiation system.

heading towards King Arthur's court. During the page's journey (which is described by one of the officers in the ritual) he has several adventures and after each one is rewarded with the knowledge and control of the elements of fire, earth, water and air. By the time the ritual sequence of the page is completed, he arrives in Arthur's court where he encounters more adventures and is finally knighted (a symbolic integration of the soul and the body).

In the late 19th century this technique developed into something called 'travelling in the spirit' or 'rising through the planes'. Although this sounds flowery, it is essentially where a person in deep relaxation visualises themselves undergoing various experiences. Perhaps one of the greatest exponents of this was the Order of the Golden Dawn.

GOLDEN DAWN

The Order of the Golden Dawn[19] was pivotal to the way Magical Imagination material was developed for nearly a hundred years. It influenced many magical groups that are using its techniques. For this reason it is worthwhile looking at some of the teachings of the Golden Dawn in regards to Magical Imagination.

The Order's basic technique involves sitting in a chair, relaxing and regulating your breath and then visualising yourself ascending upwards towards God. This was called 'rising through the planes' or 'spirit travel'. It was also possible to enter into a Tarot key, or any other mystical symbol, using this technique.

---

19 There is a tendency to believe that the Order of the Golden Dawn, or the Golden Dawn (in the Order) was called the Hermetic Order of the Golden Dawn. However, this name was first coined by Israel Regardie, and adopted by some of the modern resurrections of the Order he helped to establish in the 1980s. Since then a number of modern Golden Dawn groups have been established, and although the Esoteric Order collapsed at the beginning of the 20th century, it is surprising how many of these modern groups attempt to gain kudos by claiming direct descent from it. If they really were direct descendents they would not call themselves 'Hermetic Order' but would refer to themselves using the original name. (Of course if there is a sudden upswing in the numbers of groups advertising themselves as the Esoteric Order now, you will know why.) After the Esoteric Order collapsed it divided into three different groups: the Alpha et Omega, the Holy Order of the Golden Dawn and the Stella Matutina. Of the three only the Stella Matutina survived, finally shutting its doors in New Zealand in the late 1970s. All these groups used the same rituals; however, although much of the teaching was the same, the emphasis varied from group to group.

According to a Golden Dawn Instruction paper[20] the adept should:

"Proceed to the contemplation of some object, say a Tarot Trump: either placing it before you and gazing at it until you seem to see into it; or by placing it upon your forehead or elsewhere and keeping your eyes closed. In the last case you should have given previous study to the card, as to its symbolism, colouring analogies etc.

In either case you should then deeply sink into the abstract ideal of the card; being in entire indifference to your surroundings. If the mind wanders to anything disconnected with the card no beginner will see anything spiritually. Consider the symbolism of the Tarot Card then all that is implied by its letters, number and situation.

The vision may begin by the concentration passing into a state of reverie or with a distinct sense of change (something allied in the sensation to a faint with a feeling urging you to resist. If you are inspired, fear not, do not resist, let yourself go and then a vision may pass over you)."[21]

The same manuscript gives a detailed example where two senior adepts entered into the Tarot Key the Empress. They found themselves in a pale green landscape with a Gothic Temple.

"Here there appeared a woman of heroic proportions, clothed in green with a jewelled girdle, a crown of stars upon her head, in her hand a sceptre of gold. She smiled and said: 'I am the Mighty Mother Isis, I am she who fights not, but is always victorious. I am that sleeping beauty whom men have sought for all time. Such who fail, find me asleep. When my secret is told it is the secret of the Holy Grail."

This secret turned out to be the heart of nature, the love that runs behind and supports everything.[22]

Later in its life one of the adepts who participated in this pathworking, Florence Farr, developed an organisation within the Golden Dawn called the Sphere group. This was designed to work solely with Magical Imagination techniques with the aim of 'turning evil into good'. Although it featured many different journeys during its work, its central operating method was to get participants to visualise spheres of divine energy around the area, globe, solar system and universe.

---

20 These were called Flying Rolls.
21 Flying Roll Number IV.
22 So no surprises there!

The main inner work of the Golden Dawn used a Christianised version of the Jewish mystical system of the Cabbalah as a roadmap of consciousness. This was based around a diagram called the *tree of life* which showed ten aspects of God connected by 32 paths (see diagram). The meaning of the glyph is complex because it can be read as both a roadmap for the evolution of a human and a description of God itself.

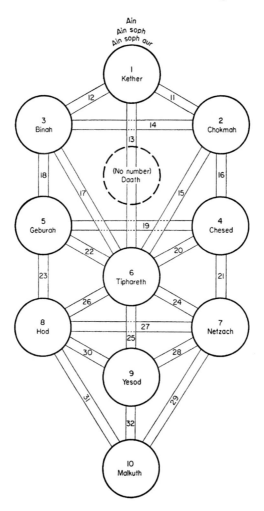

The ten stations have 10 aspects of God; the Crown, Wisdom, Understanding, Mercy, Severity, Beauty, Love, Splendour, Foundation of the Creation and finally the Kingdom. Since Cabbalah, and the Bible, say that humanity is made in God's image, these stations have a correspondence within each of us. The Kingdom is our physical body;

the Foundation is our unconscious mind; Splendour is our intellect; Love is our higher emotions, and Beauty our spiritual self. The other spheres are more abstract aspects of ourselves. Severity is the way we destroy; Mercy is the way we build. Then we have within us the creator god and goddess (Wisdom and Understanding) which are divisions of the One Thing (The Crown).

These stations on the tree of life were linked by 32 paths which were agencies that make up these spheres. The paths were considered important by the Golden Dawn because each one represented a Hebrew letter, a Tarot trump, a planet or zodiacal sign, an Archangel and angel, and certain other symbols. The Golden Dawn believed that by travelling along these paths in your mind's eye you would come to understand the deep meaning of the symbols and unlock the keys to the spheres. The result of this would be mastery of yourself and then mastery of the Universe. Travelling along these paths was called 'pathworking' by later magicians, who used the Golden Dawn techniques.

The method for ascending these paths involves visualising a doorway with the symbol upon it. They would step through the doorway and into an imagined landscape. During the Golden Dawn's elaborate system of initiations they were given passwords and signs that would be fused into their unconscious mind. Any beings they met on the other side would be tested using the Golden Dawn's many grade signs and passwords to make sure that they were not being deceived by a malicious spirit. If the spirit did not reply with the correct password they knew that either the spirit was mischievous or they had not attained the right state of consciousness. For example, once a Golden Dawn initiate encountered a being who gave a password which indicated it was a water entity, when he believed that he had pathworked into a fiery element. Since water was considered 'below' fire in the particular pathworking this adept was attempting, it was clear he still had a way to go to get to the state of mind he needed.

Halfway through the journey a symbol appears that would give an indication that it was time to come back. The journey would always end when the adept stepped out the door back into their own time and space.

We will be looking at the Golden Dawn imagination techniques in more detail later, but below is an example of a Golden Dawn pathworking for you to try. It is along the Path of Tau and leads to the lunar aspects of the Sphere of the Foundation. Since it has been designed for those who are not Golden Dawn initiates, it is impossible to 'test' the visions that you see with the grade signs and passwords (as any self-respecting

Golden Dawn initiate would do). If you would like to try some more Golden Dawn pathworkings, I suggest the book *Self Initiation into the Golden Dawn* by Chic and Tabatha Cicero, and the *Tree of Life* by Israel Regardie. The Tarot key is the Universe and is from the Golden Dawn Tarot Deck designed by Tabatha Cicero. I recommend you see this card in its full colour glory to have the best effect.

JOURNEY TO THE MOON

A Golden Dawn pathworking

After you have relaxed and regulated your breathing, visualise a doorway before you. On the lintel of the door is a Hebrew letter ת. Over the door frame is a violet curtain with a picture of the Tarot key 21 'The Universe'. Take your time to visualise this as clearly as possible, soaking up the symbols until they seem to take on a life of their own.

Step into the curtain and you find yourself in a sea of silver mist.

This slowly clears and you find yourself looking at the mouth of a cave. In your hand is a lantern. Instead of a candle light there is a Hebrew letter י and it glows with a cold blue light.

You enter the cave and find yourself going along a passage that is getting slowly narrower until it becomes an entrance around which are carved the images of a bull, an eagle, a man, and a lion.

You step through the door and into a cavern. In the centre is a hermaphrodite, who holds two wands and is dancing. The hermaphrodite radiates a light which sends shadows into the cave dancing in tune.

Then the hermaphrodite vanishes, but leaves the ghostly outline of the Hebrew letter ת in the air.

You walk along the cavern until you come to a dark underground river. There is a boat here and a boatman looks at you with cold eyes.

"Only the dead may pass over the river Styx," he says with a voice like the grave. "By what token do you seek passage?"

You draw in the air the Hebrew letter ת and he motions for you to get onto his boat.

"He who has hung on the cross of the elements may pass both ways through the gates of Death."

Without another word he rows you across the river to a beach. You get onto a beach, then into the mouth of another cave.

This winds upwards, but the cave is narrow and you have to crawl on your hands and knees. Sometimes you feel that you will become stuck, but somehow, with some scrapes, you end up emerging into another cavern.

You hear the rushing of the ocean in the cave and the air smells of salt. You walk out of the cave and onto a sandy beach. Soft hazy creatures of light move around you and you see that the beach is full of them. They are watching the full moon rising. You hear on a wind their gentle voices almost whispering *'Gabriel'*.

Then, as the moon sends a silvery pathway across the sea, you become aware of a bright light coming towards you. Unlike the other creatures, this light has substance and power. It has the head of a beautiful woman with a face of alabaster and blue hair. She has a slim body, from which blue and white wings beat. In her hands she holds a silver chalice and in her left a wand with two snakes curled about it. Around her feet walks a lion. This is Gabriel.[23]

Her power is overwhelming, almost knocking you off your feet. The wispy creatures[24] move through the air, hoping to touch this being, but she approaches you. What does she say?

After she has spoken, you ask her for a vision of the Divine aspects of the moon, of the foundation of the Universe.

---

23 Although this may seem a strange vision of a lunar archangel it has been built according to a Golden Dawn formula using the Hebrew letters of the angel's name. (See *Making Talismans*, by Nick Farrell). While it may be odd to see a female version of a 'male' angel it is important to realise that angels have no gender and their form is in accordance to the task they are performing, in this case the feminine lunar role.

24 These are Air elementals or Sylphs. The sphere of Foundation is attributed to the element of Air.

"Look into the Moon, Son (or Daughter) of Man and pray that Shaddai El Chai shall appear in his glory."

You look into the moon and wait. Then something happens. What happens is up to you.

When the vision has departed, you find yourself back at the cavern where you saw the dancing figure. You retrace your steps through the cave and back out the door. Turn and you see the tarot card on the door fade into a purple light. You then slowly become aware of this time and this reality.

MODERN DEVELOPMENTS

The Golden Dawn pathworking techniques were almost universally adopted by those magical groups which followed in its footsteps. Perhaps the most significant was the Society of the Inner Light, which was founded by Golden Dawn initiate Violet Firth, who is better known by her pseudonym Dion Fortune. Fortune made a lot of the Golden Dawn's teachings more accessible to her students, allowing them, for example, to take part in a pathworking to the Inner Temple of the Order before a ritual took place. This enabled those taking part in the Order's rituals to work on a physical and an inner level at the same time. Something like a pathworking was performed before a Golden Dawn working, but only by a select few senior adepts in the temple. We will be looking at this in a later chapter.

Fortune was greatly enamoured by the almost spiritualist practice of establishing contacts with inner plane beings whom she met using similar techniques to pathworking. It must be said that the Inner Light still followed the Golden Dawn's formula and as far as I am aware still do. It took one of the Inner Light's favourite students, the writer Gareth Knight, to start seriously tinkering with the Golden Dawn's system of pathworking during the 1960s.

Knight wondered what would happen if you used the standard pathworking technique, but focused on different symbols or legends. This was a time when another former Inner Light student, the writer William Gray, was also experimenting along similar lines.[25] Some of his

---

25 Bill Gray, although an inspired magician who was responsible for a number of interesting developments in the British magical scene, was a self confessed racist who felt compelled to leave after his initiation into the Inner Light when he discovered that some of the officers in the Inner Light were African.

students and associates included Marian Green and R.J. Stewart. This led to an explosion of experiments among the esoteric groups in the UK and mirrored a change in occult groups towards less rigid structures. The techniques developed between these people resulted in a dramatic change of the way in which we do pathworking.

Suddenly a pathworking was an exploration of an inner world. A guide would take a group or individual on a journey to explore that particular region of inner space. Some of the results could be interpreted in psychological terms, but others clearly gained something spiritual and nothing that required much in the way of structure, other than knowledge of symbols on the part of the guide or teacher.

The work in the UK was mirrored by some non-occult research in the United States carried out by the Foundation for Mind Research. During this period the Foundation was looking at the creative process and exploring trance states. The result was the development of systems that occultists would call 'pathworkings' and in some respects was a more scientific re-invention of the wheel. Much of the material was published in 1972 under the title *Mind Games*, co-authored by Dr Robert Masters and Dr Jean Houston. This book had a series of 'pathworkings' which had the same goals and techniques of many occult groups.

Pathworking had now become a key part of the training of occultists in the UK. When W.E. Butler wrote a five year correspondence course for his school, the Servants of the Light, he based it entirely on an inner landscape using the Arthurian myth. Using pathworking techniques, he was able to have his students prepared for Higher Magic by training them in an inner landscape and unconsciously opening the gates for the energies he wished to be activated to make them ready for initiation.[26] We will be looking at a similar concept to Butler's in the next chapter.

By the 1980s, pathworking had become commonplace in the UK, thanks to the writings and workshops of Marian Green and Dolores Ashcroft-Nowicki. Ashcroft-Nowicki's *The Shining Paths* was a modern take on the old Golden Dawn system using Hebrew letters to ascend the Tree of Life. Its structure was far looser by the time she wrote another series of pathworkings on Tarot cards a few years later, *Inner Landscapes*, where journeys were completely fluid and more inspired by the card rather than a structure of pathworking. Pathworking techniques within her school now meant a journey to a particular Inner Plane temple or location and often included a meeting with a spiritual being.

---

26 The kernel of this system was published by a former Servants of the Light supervisor David Goddard in his book *Tower of Alchemy*.

Here is a more modern pathworking to try, which is based on a journey to read the Akashic records. Occultists believe that nothing is forgotten and that every life in its minute detail is recorded forever within the Divine Mind. If it is possible to tap into that Universal Memory, a person could understand all history from the standpoint of someone that was actually there. It works as a sort of telepathy across time. Many branches of occultism have a belief that we have lived many lives before and sometimes it is possible to remember them. This pathworking will help you find images of your past lives to explore. I should point out that this may not actually find you a real past life. It may just give you an image of another time and place and enable you to see the world through another's eyes. Whatever your experience, there will be a reason and logic to it. It might provide you, in symbolic form, an indication where your current life is going. I personally think that 99.9% of 'past life' memories are simply this. Too many claim to be priests and priestesses of various gods; one person was adamant that she guided the fleets of Atlantis to the shores of Britain. But like the magician W.E. Butler, "I have never met someone who has claimed to be an ancient Egyptian dustman."

ThE UNIVERSaL LIBRaRY OF CONSCIOUSNESS

Open your inner eyes. Before you is a revolving door which turns slowly clockwise. On the right hand of the door, on a brass plate, are the words *Universal Library of Consciousness*. Beneath this is written 'Open all hours'.

You enter the revolving door and find yourself in a large corridor which has a heavy desk at the end of it. Above the desk in imposing letters is the word *Enquiries* and beneath the sign is an unimposing man with small round glasses and a wispy, white beard. He is carefully covering a book in plastic so that it will survive the rigours of life on the shelves, and is doing so with such concentration and precision that he hardly notices you approach.

You clear your throat and he looks up, peering over the top of his horn rimmed glasses.

"Yeeers," he says in a tone mirrored by countless librarians throughout the ages. "Can I help you?" The tone suggests such disinterest in your actual reply and an obvious hope that you will go away.

"I would like to have a look at a certain book please," you tell him. "It is an autobiography on my life."

"Is the book finished?"

"Finished?"

"Are you dead yet?" he asks in his imperious tone.

"No."

"Then go the 'Living' reading room, sit down at a counter, type your name and date of birth into the computer and your autobiography will appear in the slot beside you. One volume for each incarnation. You may in the living reading room request any former incarnations. Return the book by placing it back in the slot."

The sentence is delivered as if it had been the same for centuries, with each initial letter emphasised for effect. He directs you to a double door, through which you step and find yourself in a corridor.

On your left is a sign which points towards *Living Reading Room* and on the right *Catalogue of former incarnations, History (Civilisations current), History (Civilisations expired), Mammal Wing, Fish Wing, Lizard Wing, Plant Wing, Insect Wing, Organic Matter Wing.*

"Of course," you think. "Everything from a human to a stone has a memory and this must be recorded in this place."

You walk down the corridor until you come to a double door with a sign above it which says *Living Reading Room*. You open it and find yourself in a huge circular room. At its centre is a massive circular computer bank from which lines of desks emerge like spokes of a wheel. Above the desks is a huge dome, on which is depicted the sun.

Hunched over the reading room desks are countless people of different races and religions, all reading from different books. Their eyes are glazed over as if they are not really here at all, but have been transported to another place and time by the words they are reading. Occasionally someone will blink, shut the book and look thoughtful.

People come here instinctively when they seek to discover something about themselves by evaluating their past. They do not of course need the symbol of the Library to get to the information.

You sit at a desk. In front of you is a computer screen and a keyboard. There is a slot on the right hand side, like a letter box. On the screen in large friendly letters is the phrase "What name do you want to access?" You type your full name. "What date of birth?" You type in the information. "Which place?" You type in the place and hit the enter button.

The screen goes blank except for the word *searching...* then the computer prints out your name, address, date of birth, time of birth and asks you if this is correct. If it isn't, type 'no', and it will search again. (This occasionally happens if you have a common name). When you have the correct name type 'yes'. On the screen there appears a message: "Book of Life found and being delivered." There is a whirring noise of conveyer belts, and after a while a large black book is poked through the hole by unseen machinery.

On the cover is your name, and on the spine is a number and name which is not yours. The name is the secret name of your Higher Self and the number is the amount of times you have incarnated. Deep in the stack room of the library there is a long shelf with a line of books with this name upon them and this book you are holding is the latest volume.

You turn to the back of the book and open it. Words are appearing as you look.

"Slowly I read the words which magically appear before me. This is a strange book, I think. I wonder what is in the front. I shut the boo…"

You shut the book and turn to the front. There is a big picture of your birth, but seen through your eyes. As you look at the picture your eyes begin to glaze over and suddenly you are remembering the whole incident. You can remember the light, the confusion, the pain of the cold air – everything.

You squeeze your eyes shut and you are holding the book in the library again. *Right,* you think. *I am going open this book at random and find a memory in my past, which I need now to understand something that I am going through.*

You open the book at random. There is some text but there is also a picture of a scene. You look at the scene and experience it.

When you have finished you shut your eyes, open them again and you will be back in the library.

Now it is time to find out about your past lives. You note the number and name on the spine of the book and return it into the slot.

On the screen there appears the message "Do you want another search?" You type "yes".

On the screen is the phrase. "What memory do you want to access?" You type the name which appeared on the spine.

A message appears on the screen. "That is a soul name, is that correct?"

You type "Yes" and the computer asks you for a number. This is the number that appeared on the spine. If you want to know about your last life you would type the number minus one. (For example if the number for this incarnation was 34 you would type 33.)

When the book arrives it will tell your name, date of birth, and details of your life and death. Each incident in that life will have an illustration which you can enter by staring at it.

Experiment for a while and learn. Think about this past life which you have experienced. How relevant is it to the life you are living now? What did this person do right that you can learn from and what did they do wrong which you too are experiencing in your life? Carry these lessons in your heart and meditate hard on them. When you have finished, return your book and leave the library the way you came.

ThE PERILS OF PAThWORKING

There is a certain amount of danger in pathworking because it is a form of willed dissociation, and some psyches cannot deal with too much of it. Some people suffer from mental illnesses of which dissociation is a symptom, and therefore there is the danger that they might disappear into the imaginary realms and not return.

Pathworking can be addictive, particularly for those whose lives are not that pleasant. These people can ascend into pathworking as a means of escape from their world rather than an attempt to change it.

In the late 1970s a form of a pathworking called Dungeons and Dragons was developed and it gained huge popularity in the 1980s. These sorts of pathworkings were not conducted in the altered states of esoteric methods. A game would be controlled by a Dungeon Master who would describe what was happening, and players, playing the roles of fantasy heroes, would recount what they would do in response. As the game progressed, the imaginations of the players would be expanded until they started to get as excited as if it were real. The more imaginative the Dungeon Master and his players, the more real it would become. So much so, that if the player 'died' they would have an emotional response far above that which would be expected for a simple game.

As games became more elaborate, some players wanted to remain in the character of the heroes that they played in their games. They looked at their lives and decided that Dungeons and Dragons was better than the real world so they retreated into it, some living just for the game and as much pizza as they could eat in a game session. They became trapped into the framework of the game, and reality had become meaningless; which is a pity because Dungeon and Dragons was otherwise harmless and useful at enhancing imagination.

I am talking about an effect on a small number of people here, but it should be remembered that the same thing is possible with pathworking, which is littered with more powerful symbols. There the addiction is not gained through winning treasure or rescuing a princess, but is based on the spiritual release that the use of such symbols can provide. It is possible to forget that the goal of pathworking is to bring about change, and simply write and perform it for its own sake.

This is why I always suggest that each pathworking should have a goal to bring about change in the material world.

You should not do more than one pathworking a week when you first start. More experienced people can manage one every three days. However good and experienced you are at pathworking, you need three days simply to process what you have experienced.

The exceptions to this are workshops where people have to fit a certain amount of experience into a short space of time. In such workshops as many as five or six pathworkings can be packed into a weekend, leaving teachers and students a little burnt out by the experience. Some teachers limit any negative effect by talking about the results of such pathworkings in some detail to help the person earth the experience. I also recommend that people do not do any pathworking for at least ten days after such an intensive session to give the pathworkings a chance to have an effect.

DIFFERENT TYPES OF PATHWORKING

There are two main forms of pathworking: directed and passive. A passive pathworking is when you are given the barest outline of a scene and leave the person taking part to see what they want to see. Although it is largely uncontrolled, passive pathworking is good for allowing access to a person's unconscious and allows aspects of a person's higher mind to communicate with the lower personality. A passive pathworking would have extremely general instructions such as "visualise the God Anubis speaking to you" but the rest of the pathworking is left to the spontaneous imagination of the person. It is from passive pathworking that a person receives inspiration and new material.

During a directed pathworking everything is controlled to achieve a specific effect on the unconscious mind of the pathworker. Directed pathworkings must be designed with an aim, like an understanding of cosmic love, and be littered with specific symbols to allow that goal to be achieved.

An effective pathworking contains elements of both passive and directed methods. A more controlled pathworking might take a person through a series of symbols to meet a guide. Then a period of passive meditation might take place where the guide gives specific information unique to the person who is taking part in the pathworking. The person is then guided back to this reality as the pathworking becomes more controlled.

There is a third, rarer form of pathworking that is unique to magical groups. This is when a group of people are taken to a place on the astral using directed methods and then, once they have arrived, each group member describes what they see until a collective picture is built up. What is unusual about this method is that after a while everyone sees the collective scene so clearly that it has a tremendous impact.

Below is an example of a transcript of exploring a particular inner realm connected to the element of earth, by three magicians who I will call A, B, and C. After the group leader had taken them through a door by a directed method, they were left in an image of silvery mist. Once this cleared, they collectively built up the scene.

A: It is cold.

C: I am standing on shingle rock.

A: I am getting that too.

B: I can see that the sky is black, but I don't think it is night.

A: Yes it is hard to imagine any stars in that sort of blackness.

C: There is vegetation, it looks like dark cactus.

B: Yes I can see them, they look like the tall Cactus Jacks you see in the desert.

C: I have just tried to touch one and it has split into four. It is hollow and full of something like gas.

The story continued until they met one of the beings of this place – an angel.

C: He spells his name Z A Th[27] B E L

B: So he is a Hebrew angel.

A: He has a cube in his hands. Ask him what he does?

B: He says he is a catalyst and his job is to speed up chemical reactions.

A: So how can we use him?

---

27 This is an English transliteration and the Th is the Hebrew letter Tau.

C: He does not understand – I don't think he is something that can be called upon – he is just a force within nature.

A: In the rock itself yes. What are the cacti then?

C: Zathbel does not see cacti – he sees – I am picking up a word like insubstantial symbol.

A: The cacti are a symbol to us but to Zathbel they have a different meaning?

C: Yes that is it! They are a symbol that the densest matter is really not as solid as it looks.

A: Zathbel is nodding

B: Yes I can see that too. He is saying that once the element of earth is examined closely, it is as insubstantial as air.

The conversation went for many exhausting hours before everyone got tired and decided to return. The result for this group was that they had the name of an angel they could use if they wanted to speed up a magical reaction. What was interesting about this pathworking was that it was to a specific part of the Earth which was identified later as being Serbia. This was several weeks before trouble in the former Yugoslavian republics boiled over into war and ethnic cleansing. Zathbel seemed to be working to make things happen quickly.

PATHWORKING AND ASTRAL PROJECTION

It is easy to confuse pathworking and astral projection. When you astrally project, your body is left behind with just enough of your consciousness to keep your body functioning. Your disembodied consciousness floats within an astral shell through the various levels of creation, which are still shaped by the mind of the astral projector and so they encounter creatures and a landscape but there is a feeling of reality. One important way that it differs is that the colours and feelings are intensified. It is possible for an intelligence to be a colour or a geometric shape. The strangest thing is that whatever you want to happen, or wherever you want to go, you will be there almost instantly.

There are those who believe that when they are doing pathworkings at a deep level and they lose awareness of their physical bodies they are actually astrally projecting. Unfortunately this is only partly true.

A pathworking, however deep, is a vision of the astral with your mind's eye and it is not the same as taking your entire 'self' there for a look. It is a bit like watching a movie in which you might feel that you are part of the scene, but you only have to blink, or hear the person in front of you scrunching a potato crisp packet, to be returned to reality. No-one watching a Western would say that they have astrally projected to Tombstone, however deeply they were absorbed with the movie. If you astrally projected into a movie you would be like the person in Woody Allen's film *The Purple Rose of Cairo* and could interact with the characters and change the plot.

The similarities between pathworking and astral projection mean that the former is training for the latter. The first time I astrally projected I was completely disorientated. However, I suddenly remembered all the pathworkings that I had performed over the years and could control the experience. Pathworking techniques give you all the information you need for a safe astral projection. The only difference is that you do not leave your body.

WRITING YOUR OWN PATHWORKING

On the surface, constructing a pathworking is like writing a short story or novel. In conventional writing you are most likely to have a beginning, a middle and an end; it has characters, a setting, a plot and a theme. Unless a pathworking is simply going to be reading a work of fiction to a bunch of very relaxed listeners, it has to be a little more than that.

At the heart of every pathworking is a magical objective, which might be to understand the nature of the element of fire, or to understand why a person is frightened of spiders or lacks self-confidence. The 'plot' of the pathworking is based around that particular objective. The philosopher Plato wanted to explain the fairly complex concept that our reality was simply a shadow of a deeper truth and he used an allegory, which if it was turned into a pathworking, would look something like this:

PLATO'S CAVE

Imagine you are a prisoner in a cave, chained facing a wall. You are chained about your neck so that you cannot move your head to the right or left. All you can see is a small amount of wall in front of you.

There is a fire behind you and it casts flickering shadows on the wall. You are aware of other prisoners chained in the cave but because you cannot see them, conversation between you soon dries up. All you can focus upon are the shadows on the wall in front of you. Soon they become a means to escape, they take on a life of their own and you are swept away in your imagination with these dancing figures. The occasional cry from the other prisoners indicates to you that they have found the same thing.

Years pass and your mind has taken on the belief that the shadows are all that there is, short of the disorientating moments when food is thrust into your mouth by your jailer. In those shadows your life plays out in a flickering grey show.

Then suddenly one day you are unchained and led out of the cave. As you pass the fire, you see that it made the shadows which had been the focus of your life for so long. Then, as you are led blinking out into the light, you see the world is bright and full of colour, lit by the sun.

You bask in the glory of that which you had forgotten over the years. There was a real light, real colour and real life.

After a while you start to think of the other prisoners in the cave, chained to their shadows without a hope of the light that you now see. You rush back into the cave to tell them what life is like outside.

One by one they tell you to go away. "Our lives are these shadows," they say, "we have much invested in them." Not only do they not believe you about your 'tales' of light and colour, but they do not want to hear the truth.

Allow the scene to fade.

In the above example the entire plot is centred on trying to make the pathworker understand the central theme. Once that happens at this deep level it will have a considerable impact on the pathworker. It will have bypassed the conscious reasoning of the person and allow them to see it in a totally new light.

The other important element of a pathworking is the use of symbols. Scenes within a pathworking should be built around a central archetypal symbol that reacts with the person's unconscious. This adds considerable psychological power to the pathworking and helps to raise it in intensity. In the above example the central symbols were chains and shadows. They sent a symbolic message to the unconscious that the pathworker is bound to a false reality.

Meetings with gods, goddesses, hermits, wise people and animals in a pathworking are all steps along the way towards unlocking particular aspects of the unconscious and building up an emotional and spiritual effect. These symbols do not have to be in the pathworking's centre stage, you could make the pathworker walk alongside a fast flowing river in which salmon are swimming upstream. There need be no explanation of this particular symbol in the pathworking, as the unconscious mind will pick up the symbol and act upon it. It understands that the salmon, which is a symbol of wisdom, is going against the flow of the river, which symbolises the mass mind. Such a symbol would be important if you had designed a pathworking to help someone break free from conventions that were keeping them chained to the shadows.

Knowledge of what these symbols mean takes some experience, which is why pathworkings are rarely written by beginners. If you meditate on symbols, their meanings will become apparent over time. Fairly obvious ones are easy to uncover, such as the archetypal figures of Mother, Father, Wise person, Fool, and Trickster.

The meanings of animals can be found within the shamanic tradition. *The Druid Animal Oracle: Working With the Sacred Animals of the Druid Tradition* by Philip Carr-Gomm could be a good introduction.

The elements of fire, air, water and earth can provide powerful symbols for a pathworking.

Fire: energy, power, destruction, transmutation, illumination, the Sun, the father, conception, wisdom.

Water: compassion, understanding, mutation, the moon, prophecy, the mother, the unconscious, gestation.

Air: communication, healing, intellect, mind, speed, mercury, the son, growth.

Earth: resources, both natural and material, sleep, the planet earth, cold, darkness, the daughter, death.

Having read the list above, you should be able to tell what would happen if you wrote a pathworking with a magical well of prophecy which is activated by plunging a torch into its waters!

WRITING A PATHWORKING

Words are symbolic guides in a pathworking. They should be written with care so that they do not lead you from the atmosphere you are trying to create. In some books on pathworking you might find writers saying that it is important to use clever language and poetry, usually lifted from writers like Blake, Coleridge or Yeats. The logic is that the evocative language used by great writers and poets may inspire the reader to achieve great heights in a pathworking.

I disagree. While it is true that words are symbols and the likes of Yeats knew what they were doing when it came to using them, the use of another's words in a pathworking you are writing is at best lazy (and a little pretentious) and at worst outright dangerous. A poet, like the writer of a pathworking, is trying to use words for a specific purpose. Although the poem might say it is about Joy, the words that the poet is using are actually pointing to a moment in his life. This is fine if you are reading the poet's work but using those same words will lead your pathworkers down the same route. Hijacking the poet's purpose is a bit like using a hammer to knock in screws – it might work but you are more likely to end up with a lopsided set of shelves.

The same applies to lifting whole tracts of sacred and religious verse. Sacred texts are usually written in a different era and a different language and lose much in translation. It is not that the words are wrong, but they will lead your pathworkers to an ancient place which is alien to their modern minds. The religion of Ancient Egypt was never the religious Utopia that many New Agers would like to believe. The various gods and goddesses all have their dark sides. Even the beautiful mistress of magic, Isis, has her black aspects. It is impossible to know what I am going to access if I incorporate what seems to be a beautiful evocation to her from the pyramid texts into a pathworking.

It is possible to use these sorts of texts in pathworking, we just have to adapt them using our own modern minds and symbolism. If I had written a pathworking where the person meets the crocodile god Sobk, I *could* quote the original utterance 317 from the pyramid texts and end up with something like this:

"I have come from out of the waters of the flood. I am Sobk, green of the plume, watchful of face, raised of brow, the raging one who came forth from the shank and tail of the Great One who is in the sunshine.

I have come to the waterways which are in the bank of the flood of the great inundation to the place of contentment, green of fields, which is in the horizon that I may make green the herbage which is on the banks of the horizon, that I may bring greenness to the eye of the Great One who dwells in the field."[28]

---

28 *The Ancient Egyptian Pyramid Texts*, R.O. Faulkner, p.99, Oxford University Press, 1969.

On the face of it this is an evocative piece of writing that would look good in a pathworking. But even the translator R.O. Faulkner has to guess about what parts of it mean, and he *assumed* that since the Great One is described using feminine words, it is probably a reference to one of the great goddesses like Neth. The upshot is that if I use this in its ancient (even translated) form, I may get more than I bargained for. So I have to work out what I really want this god to say, so that it sounds similar but is in keeping with the pathworking's direction. I have to use my symbols and my words to make this happen. Since the theme of the pathworking in this case is the "beauty in nature", I rewrite Utterance 317 until it becomes:

"I am Sobk who comes forth from the sacred waters of the Nile.
Watchful am I,
Still am I.
A raging one who was born from the sky goddess who holds the sun.
I come with the blessings of the Gods on the sacred land.
I stand on the land so that it may be fertile and green.
I bring a beautiful vision of nature to the Great Goddess
As she watches over us."

It is not the same text, but it has been inspired by the original and has some of its flavour. But it is anchored symbols I want and it will not go anywhere I don't want it to.

When writing a pathworking, words should be used sparingly. It is vital that the imagination of the pathworkers is allowed to blossom in the pathworking. It is the rogue elements that you do not put into your script that make the pathworking personal and magical. If you drown the pathworker's imagination in a sea of prose they become lazy and don't have to imagine. This means that they will not have the chance to really use their inner eyes and pick up new and exciting symbols. One of the most frustrating books I ever had to study in school was John Steinbeck's *The Pearl*. This was because everything in it was described in so much detail. It seemed to me that, although I could see things with my imagination, Steinbeck insisted on describing everything to me including lots of information that I did not need to (or want to) see.

Keep your descriptions as brief as possible and sentences short. If a teacup is blue don't call it a frail, egg-shell, turquoise teacup with a dark blue vine leaves upon it. Unless the symbols of the vine leaves are important, the tea cup should remain a 'blue teacup' and nothing else.

The phrase 'you are in a dark forest' will be enough, without describing the meanderings of snake-like vines and sinister trees that look like ancient, bearded men.

There are exceptions to this rule. If you want to make a point in a pathworking, use a suddenly dramatic descriptive word which is packed full of meaningful symbolic words. For example:

"You are in a dark forest.
You have the feeling that you are being watched.
Pressing down the pathway, you come to a clearing.
In the centre is the remains of a burnt out fire.
This place smells of fear and the trees look as if they have been tortured."

The last sentence is designed to give the pathworker a sense of dread. Notice that it does not say 'the trees were twisted and bent like they had been tortured', you have left that to the pathworker's imagination.

The other place where you can go to town with your language is in the speech of the characters your pathworker will meet. This is because the language should give the pathworker a sense of the character of the being who is talking. Normal people do not speak in short sentences, but they don't often use long and colourful words either, and to put such language into their mouths does not make for a plausible conversation. In a Norse pathworking a peasant should say: "It is raining so heavily out there you can hear old Odin's hammer in the hills." And not "This precipitation lashes like a cat-o'-nine-tails against the windows of our fair lodge. Harken doth that not be the hammer of Ancient Odin crashing and rumbling against the grey stone mountains as he furies against the Ice Giants?"

You might want to give your characters an accent or use words that are out-of-date to give a pathworking a historical feel. One of my teachers loved to have his angels use plenty of Old Testament style language with the argument that the unconscious understood and responded to ancient language better. This was, he said, because the unconscious was an old part of the human psyche and understood old language. I beg to differ. The English language may look the same in print as it did 400 years ago but the words were spelt and pronounced very differently from modern English. For example, the word 'nun' was pronounced 'noon'. Shakespeare's English would have sounded like West Country English, only with so thick an accent that it would be very hard to understand. In my view it is better that modern languages are used and that the pathworkers understand it.

A pathworking should not last longer than 20 minutes. This is about the maximum a mind can stand without slipping into sleep or starting to feel uncomfortable. Almost all of what you write that happens after this time will be lost. If what you want to achieve cannot be written in a 20 minute pathworking, then break it up into 20 minute sessions with a pause to discuss things in the middle. After about 30 minutes the mind will be rested enough to go on. However be careful here, although the mind does see the same pathworking as a solitary action, a series of them lasting many hours requires the endurance of marathon runner. One 'all day' pathworking I took part in once left me feeling so spaced out it took me a couple of days to recover.

A pathworking should always end where it began, and it usually starts with a doorway. Convention says that the doorway should look like the historical period into which you are entering. If you are pathworking with an Egyptian theme, you would use a doorway in the style of Ancient Egypt with a winged sun disk on the lintel; a Celtic doorway would be two sacred trees or even a cromlech. The reason for this is that it enables the person to unconsciously re-orientate themselves afterwards and trains the unconscious mind always to return to the place it left. This is particularly useful if a person later develops their astral projection skills.

You should also include phrases at the beginning of the pathworking which give the people a chance to enter an altered state. This would be a period that allows people to relax and regulate their breathing. You should try to make the pathworker as confident and relaxed as possible about what they are about to do. Reassure them that if they feel frightened they only have to say a word and they will return to the doorway through which they entered the pathworking. You should also suggest to them that throughout the process they will always hear the sound of your voice. This is important because if they lose the ability to hear you they will find the trip back harder.

You should also write an ending to the pathworking that enables the person to become fully 'earthed' afterwards. My favourite is a ritual formula that I learnt from one of my teachers which I have adapted over the years. After the pathworkers have returned through the doorway I say:

You are a creature of spirit manifesting in the material world.
Feel the elemental vehicle in which you travel upon the earth.
Feel the heat in your body – this is Fire.
Feel the air in your lungs – this is Air.
Feel the water in your mouth – this is Water
Feel the weight of your bones and flesh – this is Earth.
You are a creature of the four elements and spirits.
Open your eyes, stamp your feet, for you dwell in Earth again.

NARRATING THE PATHWORKING

Narrating is harder than it appears. Pathworking sessions, whether passive or directed, generally have one leader or guide who leads the person or group through a particular sequence or narrative. This person is usually the group leader or teacher because it takes a special knack to do properly. Their role is not just to read a story to a group of pathworkers so much as guiding a group of people through a mystical realm. They need to be able to read the story while at the same time 'seeing' in their mind's eye what is happening. People in a pathworking do stray off from time to time and it is important that if you see this you work out a way to get them back to the group.

Group leaders have to be wide awake on the earth level to look after the people in their vulnerable altered state. If anything happens, the guide has to be able to bring the pathworkers back quickly. If they come back too fast they could be at best disorientated or at worst in a state of shock.

Group leaders should also endeavour to experience the pathworking themselves to ensure that they receive the benefits. This requires a sort of split-level working, where the group leader ascends and descends often. After a workshop or a day's worth of pathworking I am usually very tired because of the effort that this sort of activity takes.

The pathworking should be read slowly with long pauses between each sentence. This allows the pathworkers a chance to see what is being described to them, and any new things that have not been written into the pathworking.

This also takes a bit of a knack to get right, because although a pause may seem a long time for the person reading it, it may seem very fast for the people experiencing the pathworking. This problem is eliminated if the reader is really with the pathworkers taking the journey.

After a pathworking is complete, the group leader should go through it with each person in the group. This process is to help the individual remember their experience. This is important as pathworkings are a little like dreams in that they are forgotten very easily if they are not written down or discussed quickly. This also gives the group of pathworkers the chance to discover similarities between what they saw. One of the strange things about group pathworkings is that people do see the same things, even when these are not written into them. There are often slight variations, sometimes in colour or shape, but often these are differences in the person's inner symbolic language. One person might see red as a colour for excitement, while another might see it as a colour for violence and prefer yellow. If these two saw an Angel of Excitement wearing a tabard, one will see it wearing red, while the other will see it as yellow.

One thing you will notice is that some group members might feel that they have fallen asleep during the pathworking. They typically say they 'lost' the thread of the pathworking at a certain point. This was a cause for concern for me as a group leader and I used to watch these people closely during a pathworking. To my surprise, despite their complaints that they feel asleep, they were usually with the group throughout the pathworking and they always 'woke up' when the pathworking was finished. It was occult teacher Marian Green who came up with the answer to this problem as a result of research with her many students. She believed that, rather than 'losing it', the pathworkers had slipped into a deep level of consciousness. So deep in fact they had lost the use of their short term memory. They were experiencing the pathworking but they could not remember details of it. Her answer was to discuss what happened with them after they thought they had 'lost' consciousness. Sure enough, it was possible for them to piece together what they had missed. Even if they could not remember the pathworking at a certain point, if they wake up with the others then the full effect of the pathworking has gone into their unconscious.

There are exceptions to this, as sometimes people do fall asleep during pathworkings. They tend to snore or don't wake up when the pathworking has finished, sometimes their heads fall forward and they wake up with a start. Such people need to develop better concentration skills and also make sure that they get enough sleep before they perform the pathworking.[29]

---

29 There was one esoteric group who had an elderly member who decided to die during a pathworking and no one realised until they all came back. It was assumed that he was concentrating adequately and did not die in his sleep.

Sometimes there are those who always fall asleep and there might be a medical condition that needs to be explored. One American occult teacher who had a problem with one of her students nodding off all the time carted him off to the doctor for a blood test and found that he was coming down with the early signs of diabetes. When he underwent treatment he was able to stay awake.

UNUSUAL ThINGS WhICh hAPPEN TO A PAThWORKER

There are a number of physical side effects that happen to a person when they are in deep meditation or taking part in a pathworking. None of these conditions are harmful, particularly if you know what is happening.

Paralysis

This is when the person for some reason becomes aware of their body during a pathworking or meditation and focuses on it. However the awareness is only partial and most of the person's consciousness is still taking part in the meditation or pathworking and so it is hard to rouse the highly relaxed body. To the momentary returning consciousness the body feels like it is paralysed and cannot move. This sometimes creates a moment of panic, causing the pathworker to return and fully rouse the body. This sometimes occurs naturally during sleep and is nothing to worry about. In fact in some Eastern systems of magic yogis train for months to achieve a really good state of paralysis.

Pain, Itches and Twitches

This is very common, particularly among inexperienced meditators or pathworkers. Although sometimes it is caused by the person not sitting correctly, it is more often the lower aspects of the personality attempting to assert itself. The lower self feels threatened by the pathworking because it knows that the exercises will bring about change. The lower self is fairly inert and it likes things to stay the same so that it does not have to think too much. What it does is generate pain, or more commonly, itches, that force the person to scratch them, causing them to come out of a deep pathworking. The first few times this happens it is important not to give in to it. It may spoil the pathworking but you should ignore it. Eventually the lower self will give up on that tack if it knows you are determined to ignore it.

The Body Feels Like it has Slumped or Moved

The first time this happened to me was when I was hypnotized and it is a strange sensation. I was convinced that my head had slumped onto my shoulder. I could feel it there, and in the vision that I was trying to follow it felt as if I was watching it with my head cocked to the left. After the session was over I remarked to the hypnotist that the session had been spoilt because my head had moved and I was too relaxed to bring it back up again. He seemed surprised, as my head had not moved at all and I was sitting bolt upright throughout the session. Much later I discovered that this is common amongst people who are in a deep altered state. Their consciousness slips out of the body and becomes free from it. This is part of the early stages of astral projection. If the person is unaware of what is happening, the freed consciousness stays put or slumps. This happens more frequently with people to whom astral projection is easy.

Seeing Things

This happens when a person is not properly earthed after a pathworking. They see shapes, darting images and other people's auras. This is because they are so used to seeing with inner vision that when they return they still use it. This might seem like fun (and in some pathworkings it is a good idea to get people to open their eyes so that they can see their surroundings with inner vision) but usually it is disorientating, and if someone is attempting to drive afterwards, downright dangerous. A good hot drink and something to eat generally sorts that problem out. Sometimes physical activity also can help.

Chapter Three

BUILDING YOUR OWN INNER KINGDOM

THE BEST WAY to learn about Inner Kingdoms is to build one and explore it. This chapter will show you how to do that and give you a taster of a system of meditation which if you wish could be the basis of your meditation patterns for the rest of your life or give you the inspiration to build one that closely responds to your own personality. It uses some of the 'active' techniques we examined in the previous chapter but has a significant passive pathworking element. There is much that you will need to discover and build for yourself, but the aim of this chapter is to create the framework for self discovery. I have included more structured pathworkings within each section of the Inner Kingdom so that you can see how it works, but you will get much more out of it when you start to plan your own. Your Inner Kingdom is a living and breathing creature of your imagination which is more personally powerful than any artwork you might create. In fact many artists would say that their art is only a shadow of their imagination.

Earlier there is described a door to your Inner Kingdom and the question was left open as to what you would see on the other side. Generally that is up to you. The truest picture of your Inner Kingdom is the chaos of your dream state. However, there is some evidence among occult schools that if you accept a standardised glyph of an Inner Kingdom it is possible to slowly shape your unconscious. When maps of these Inner Kingdoms are drawn they often become elaborate symbolic diagrams or mandalas.

The Servants of the Light esoteric school used the Arthurian landscape for its mandala and focused on a castle which it defined as the physical body of the operator. Locked in the basement of the castle were those prisoners or complexes that you did not want to deal with, and at the top was your spiritual self. One exercise involved walking around the medieval village of Camelot with the goal of interacting with the wider part of your unconscious – the part that you shared with other people. Still further away from your castle were parts that belonged to others, many of whom were spiritual beings. It was possible in this exercise to see yourself in relationship to the rest of the spiritual and material universe.

Because all of these places are seen through the glass of your imagination and coloured by personality, some of the visions have to be interpreted symbolically. For example one magician was shocked when she saw the people of Camelot having a bear-baiting contest in the middle of the town square. It would be tempting to see this as an example of the evil that is contained in humanity which tortures animals. Since she was the 'King' of Camelot she was in a position where she could make a change, perhaps issuing an edict banning bear-baiting, and then such cruelty would be outlawed. The effect is that the 'law change' would go some way to limit cruelty to animals.

It is more likely that the bear baiting means something more personal to the person viewing it, and many have walked through that particular Inner Kingdom without seeing it. It was probably a psychological image that she could work out using her own symbolic language and the legend of King Arthur[30] as a reference. In her world view she believed that the world was against her and would tear her to bits if she trusted. The name King Arthur was probably derived from the Celtic god Artor, the 'Bear', and in the SOL mandala the pathworker was King Arthur and so it is possible to interpret the bear-baiting image as the pathworker's belief that people were ready to torture 'her'.

The Arthurian world is a good design because it merges the pagan and Christian worlds, is unreligious but loaded with archetypal symbolism. As a King you are in charge of your Inner Kingdom and responsible for it.

There are other mandalas that can be used, either from a historical epoch or from yours or someone else's imagination. Material from fantasy, historic or science fiction books can provide good landscapes, so if you are a *Lord of the Rings*, *Star Trek*, or C.S. Lewis fan this gives you the opportunity to incorporate the symbols that moved you into your own Inner Kingdom. I know of one person whose Inner Kingdom was centred on an office with him as the chairman of a company. Another built a science fiction *Logan's Run* style dome complete with

30 We will be examining the use of legend in Magical Imagination later in this book.

laser defence systems. Then there was another who was an English Civil War re-enactment buff who built a fortress with musketeers, pikemen, cannons and cavalry.

Below is a fairly simple map of an Inner Kingdom. Not only will it give you some ideas to play with, but it is complete and has been tested to see that the symbols work. It is based on a Celtic mythos, but could have easily be adapted to Medieval, Arthurian, Ancient Rome, Greece, Egyptian or Atlantean worlds. Remember that this world has a reality of its own with a unique time and space, but this makes it no less real than the world outside.

To visit this kingdom I recommend you study the diagram and then record the description or have someone else read it to you. Make sure that each sentence is read slowly and there is a pause after each sentence. This gives you time to imagine what you see. You will only need to do a directed journey once to make sure that you know where everything is and build the basic structure. Thereafter you can visit and rely on your memory of what you saw the first time.

Take note in a diary of everything you notice that is not described.

To enter this kingdom use the relaxation exercise to journey to the door, let it swing open into silver coloured mist. Step into the mist, which slowly clears to reveal the scene I describe...[31]

ThE hALL OF ThE hERO

As the mist clears you are looking at a roaring fire; the smoke is rising upwards towards a hole in the thatched ceiling.

Surrounding the fire are roughly cut tables and chairs.

There is freshly cut straw on the floor.

It is a large chamber. Behind you is a long table with a larger chair in the centre. This is your chair.

You are the chieftain.

On the table is a sword. It is a broad slashing sword with two serpents for a guard. It is your sword. With it you rule your tribe and your territory. On the right of your big chair is the chair for the Bard and on the left is the chair for your partner.[32]

---

31 Before anyone complains about the stilted nature of the writing of this particular pathworking I should point out that it is written to be read in a pathworking. Some sentences are designed for emphasis.

32 The partner can be male or female. It should not be someone who is 'real'.

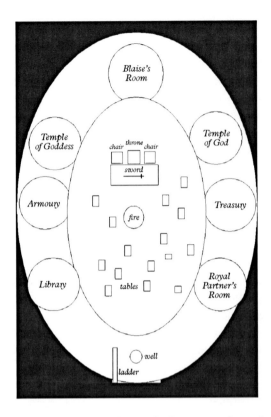

Around the walls are shields, and there are four doors on your right and four on your left. Behind you is another door and there is a large doorway which leads to a courtyard with a well. The courtyard is enclosed by a stockade, which encloses the hall. Beside the well is a step ladder which leads to a tall watchtower.

You are a mighty Celtic chieftain. Your hall is large and has ten chambers.

The first one, closest to the door, on the left as you enter, is a library where scrolls of knowledge are kept.

The door on your right as you enter is where your partner sleeps. It is a room dedicated to love.

The next door on your left is the armoury, which is full of weapons and armour. Traditionally it is where you would try tribespeople when they have broken the law, and arm them for battle against the enemies of the Kingdom.

The next door on your right is the treasury where you keep the laws of the land. You go in there if you want to change an unjust law or to distribute treasure to the tribe, either as a reward or if they are in need.

Slightly behind the throne on the left is the room dedicated to the Mother Goddess.

Slightly behind the throne on the right is a room dedicated to the God.

The door behind the throne is where Bard Blaise sleeps and composes his magic. You are indeed fortunate for your tribe is a host to the greatest magician and bard in the land. Blaise taught the legendary Merlin the Enchanter and it is he who is your guide and he who helps you arrive at the best decisions for your land. However, he sometimes gives you advice which is wrong, not out of malice, but because it is important that you know to stand on your own two feet. So you must weigh his advice carefully. No one goes into his room, for the ground is considered even more holy than the temple of the God and Goddess.

As you walk out of the hall you are in a small courtyard with a well. Some say the well is magical, and many people enter the courtyard to deposit small coins into it for luck. The courtyard is surrounded by a stout stockade and there is a gateway into the village outside (see diagram).

Notice in which room you sleep, as it will say a lot about your orientation. If you sleep in the library you might be more head orientated, in the armoury you could be defensive or aggressive, either the mother or father goddess rooms could indicate a paternalist or materialistic phase in your life. You will also notice that where you sleep will change. Try to think why these changes might be happening. Notice the colours of clothes that people wear. Try to see what these people represent to you. The well outside represents your unconscious. In times of stress its waters will seem troubled, other times you will be able to use it to see into the future. When you are experiencing a period of conflict in your life the armoury door will be open with different types of weapons or armour made ready. These could tell you the best way to deal with the problem. If the sword is there it means that you will have to get close and fight with your adversaries. A spear would mean that you will have to fight but should fend off your opponents and are not too closely involved. A bow means you have to keep your distance and strike from afar. If there are no weapons, or the door to the treasury is open, then you must not fight and must either be kind or forgive. If neither door is open there is no action for you to take at this time.

This part of your Inner Kingdom is to do with your personality and physical body. People who enter the hall are almost universally aspects of your personality. This is particularly true of the warriors who you will find populating your hall. The arrogant warrior who sows discord among the others and insists on making conflict is a part of you, and you must find a method of bringing him into line. This process of externalising your personality traits is a powerful way of finding out about yourself. Your role as a chieftain is to bring peace to your hall and sometimes it is going to mean banging some heads together. At other times it is going to mean some skilful diplomacy.

One example would be if one of the warriors comes to you complaining that another has stolen his horse. On the surface this would seem to be a traditional gripe in a Celtic society and was normally dealt with by a trial by combat. In your role as a Chieftain you have to assess what this symbolically means. After questioning, the warrior who is making the complaint seems to represent how you relate to your partner. The warrior who has 'stolen' the horse, a symbol of power, is your work. In other words you are working too hard and allocating too much power to it and your relationship is suffering. It might be in your interest for the work warrior to keep the horse for now, and the relationship warrior to be compensated.

Always check to see how the warriors respond to your decisions. While you might have the final say, your job must be to make sure that all sides are happy and the tribe, which is your overall personality, is not put out by the decision. For example, if the relationship warrior still remains unhappy it means that the compensation you are proposing is not enough. It is an unconscious warning that your partner is about to get angry about the way they are being treated and your relationship will not survive unless it gets its power back fast.

Sometimes it is impossible to please the whole tribe, even with the most sensible decision, and this is because you are destroying a complex or a pattern of behaviour that is entrenched in your psyche. In most cases if you look closely at what you are changing you will find out what the cause of the problem is and you might have to really work at forcing the warriors to obey your ruling.

Besides receiving a warning from your unconscious that your relationship might be heading towards trouble, this imaginary conflict has shown you the best way to handle it. You can take counsel with Blaise, who represents your spiritual self, over some of the trickier decisions.

Remember: things that change in your hall will gradually change in your own personality.

Feast Days

You can use the Hall of the Hero to hold imaginary feast days to invite your warriors to meet with other beings to learn more about the land. These have to be conducted carefully as you are allowing beings that are not necessarily part of yourself into the centre of your imaginary Kingdom. The best way to do this is to ask Blaise to visit the surrounding lands and invite beings who he thinks the kingdom would benefit from meeting. Blaise will bring warriors, priests, peasants, doctors and so on, one at a time into your hall. You should receive them politely and sit them beside you, listen to what they say and think about it. Always make a ceremony of thanks and farewell and see them leave. Each feast should be a single meditation session and if a stranger outstays their welcome they should be escorted from the building by your warriors and Blaise. Blaise will usually step in and threaten to satirise the wrong-doer in every hall in the land if he does not leave, and this will motivate him into moving.

An Adventure in the Hall of the Hero

Today there will be a feast to celebrate the day when the warriors of the tribe declared you to be their Chief. The fire burns brightly in the centre of the hall, which is filled with the scent of burning wood.

Warriors noisily shout, cheer and dance to a song being played on a Celtic bagpipe. Wine has been flowing for some time and everyone is a little the worse for wear.

Banging your tankard on the table, you call for silence and slowly the room comes to order.

"Warriors of the Kingdom," you say in your best public speaking voice. "Unaccustomed as I am to public speaking..." The room erupts into laughter but you continue.

"Unaccustomed as I am to public speaking... this being the anniversary of my succession to this chair... it is time for me to declare a boon to the first warrior to touch my cup."

As you say this you hurl your cup into the throng of drunken warriors. This is a traditional event and your warriors are ready for it. Usually the strongest and least drunk would win the resulting scramble, and win a prize. Sure enough the warriors leap for the cup, but before they get there a child runs among them and grabs it.

It is a boy of about seven years old. He has a mop of dark brown hair and wears clothes which look like they have been stitched from some ancient material which may once have been cloth. There is stillness in the hall. None of the warriors have the heart to snatch the cup from a small boy, particularly one so poor.

Suddenly one of the older warriors starts to laugh at the situation.

"It seems we have been bested by a boy no taller than my knee, he must be a great warrior indeed, so the boon is his." The laughter and cheers pass around the hall and the boy slowly and thoughtfully walks up to the chair.

"You seem to have lost something," he says carefully and in a measured tone.

"Yes," you say. "And what boon would you like? Clothing, a house, money?"

"If the Chieftain would hear my story maybe he would like to decide," the boy says.

You agree and the hall is hushed to hear the boy's tale.

"I was born in a village close to the edge of the great forest. There the people lived in fear of the faery folk, who out of mischief would steal food and property from houses while the villagers were out in the field. Sometimes they stole children too and the villagers were so afraid of this that they started to leave out food for the faeries, hoping they would leave them in peace. One summer the crops failed, and there was barely enough food for the villagers, let alone leaving out any for the faery folk. So they came and they took a small boy who was the son of a Chief. They treated him well and taught him many things. Soon he started to miss human children and his parents. Initially the Faery would not let him leave but after a while they saw that he was so unhappy that they realised he needed to be among his own kind and escorted him back to his village.

When he arrived he found that time had moved on, and although seven months had passed in the Faery realm, more than 70 years had passed in the outside world and his village had been destroyed. The boy declined the kind faery who offered to take him back and raise him as their own and decided to search for humans in other villages because he wanted to be among his kind.

I walked until I came to this hall, and hoped that here I might find the home I am looking for."

Blaise touches you on the shoulder. "This little boy is something that has been lost to the kingdom. Something which you, as the embodiment of Kingdom, have had taken away from you, perhaps when you were very young."

You lean down to the boy and ask him. "What are you that has been taken away from me?"

The boy tells you.

Think about what he says. And then allocate a family for the boy to live with, and know that your kingdom is stronger now that something which has been lost has been restored.

This pathworking is about elements of ourselves that are taken from us or which we give away to others. These parts of ourselves are prizes, for when we access to them we gain the power that was taken. This is an emotional pathworking when done correctly, and the emotion we feel is the power being restored to us.

The Watchtower

Before you explore the wider aspects of your Inner Kingdom it is important to make a reconnaissance. It is for this reason that your hall has a watchtower. If your village is attacked, the elderly and children would hide in the great hall, protected by its stockade. The watchtower enables the chief, if he is not personally in combat, to see enemy troop dispositions and issue directions to his warriors to on how to repel the invaders. Since Celtic fortifications were often on raised ground, a person standing in a watchtower could often see very far away and have warning of any impending attack.

As part of your pathworking, slowly climb the ladder. Below you is the village of your tribe. Immediately abutting the gate are the stables where your mighty war chariot is stored. We will be examining this later.

The village is surrounded by a stockade and tall earth bank, but the rest of its makeup is up to you. Those things that are closest to you, such as your family and friends, will have huts, or houses closer to your great hall. Your workplace will be represented by a big hut with lots of people going in and out. Unlike your great hall, the people you associate with look like they do in real life, but their role in your village might be a little different. For example your boss at work might be a wailing child being carried by a more powerful secretary.

From your position in the watchtower it is possible to see how these people relate to each other. In your village they may act differently to each other from the way you would expect because they are being seen from your unconscious perspective. In some cases you might be unconsciously frightened of some and they may appear more fearsome in your village. The inner vision includes subtle details that you may have missed; a couple at work might have feelings for each other that you have not seen. A colleague might have been more hurt by one of your actions than you had previously thought, or someone might be secretly sharpening a dagger to stick in your back.

Be careful here, as such perceptions are often loaded by your own preconceptions. If you are worried that your partner is having an affair and in your village you see him or her in the arms of a stranger, do not see that as evidence. All it shows is that you are convinced deeply that something is going on.

Remember what you are seeing is a self-fulfilling prophecy unless you do something to change it and what is manifesting in your village will actually happen to you. If you see something you do not like, it is important that you change it. However, to do that you have to step outside the walls of your Great Hall.

Looking towards the horizon you can see other kingdoms and territory from your watchtower. These are the kingdoms of those closest to you, and if you were to visit them you would start to see them as they really are rather than as they appear in your realm. For example the rat catcher in your realm may be a wonderful king in his own kingdom.

Everyone rules their own Inner Kingdom and guards their borders as jealously as you. If you actually entered one of these kingdoms you would be challenged and repelled by extremely strong forces. Sometimes a bard might appear in your hall who might invite you into another kingdom's hall with the aim of learning something new from you. This is unlikely to be someone you know and is more likely to be the Inner Kingdom of a spiritual guide or teacher. Some magical orders and groups have Inner Kingdoms of their own and it is possible for them to invite you to one of these to receive instruction. It is through these inner states that people can get occult teaching without actually being a member of an esoteric order.

At the boundary of your kingdom and those of others is the Forest of Adventure. This is where you will spend much of your time. Once you have watched from your watchtower it is time to go out of the protection of your great hall and into the outside world.

Greater Albion

As you leave your hall you will strap on the Sword of your Kingdom. You might want to visit the armoury and chose a spear or armour. Just take a note of what has been left out for you to wear because it will flavour your journey. The Treasury door might also be open, which means that you will require money[33] for this journey. Once you are dressed and armed you leave the Hall of the Hero and step into the village.

You might want to explore your village in more detail first, and interact with people at a level that you would have never experienced before. Remember that what you are seeing, like anything in your Inner Kingdom, has to be interpreted symbolically rather than literally.

Firstly check the walls that surround your great hall. Holes in the wall, or part of the stockade that are in a poor state of repair, indicate weaknesses in your aura. It is important to find out what caused these weaknesses. Ask one of the villagers, as they often know, or failing that ask Blaise. Fixing any holes will require help from a wood worker and a group of labourers. You must find these people in your village and ask them to do the work. Some of them will work for money, other times they will ask for payment in kind. What they ask for will give you a clue as to how the problem can be fixed deep within the psyche.

For example, a woman who was sexually and psychically abused by her boyfriend found herself depressed and unable to leave him. Using the village formula she found that part of the wall had been torn down. She asked a child how this happened and was told that she had ordered the wall to be torn down because she wanted a giant to have easy access to the hall. If the wall was there he would have to batter the gate down and so she had decided that it was easier to leave a hole there. It did not take much to realise who the giant was and that her aura was leaking like a sieve because she was not resisting the giant. Anyone who has suffered from what psychologists call a co-dependent relationship will recognise that it is easier to be a victim than it is to stand up to the person.

Obviously there would be no point repairing the wall if the giant was going to just tear it down again.[34]

A macho response would be to suggest that she should try to kill or subdue the giant; however that would be counter-productive. In a co-dependent relationship the roles of victim and aggressor are always swapped, and fighting the giant would simply be perpetuating that

---

33 Remember that money is a symbol of your power, energy and time. You may find yourself having to give money to a being in the outside world. This will indicate that you must be prepared to spend time, energy and effort towards that cause in real life.

34 Just as there is no point going to an alternative healer to have your aura repaired if you are just going to allow someone to damage it again.

process. This is like the person who thinks they can make their alcoholic or abusive partner better by bending to their will. It hardly ever works, and simply perpetuates the cycle. The person will always be a 'giant' however tame they appear to be.

It is far better to banish the giant from your kingdom. It is the right of anyone to banish someone who they find harmful. You gather your warriors together and order the giant to leave your kingdom and never return. You then escort to them to the village gate. They might put up a fight but the sheer numbers of warriors you have will overwhelm them (remember since you are not trying to kill them, there is no need to draw weapons or hurt them). More often they will leave voluntarily.

What will happen then is that there will be pressure for that person to leave, or unconsciously you might find it easier to leave them. In this instance the woman decided to leave her abusive partner and by coincidence he happened to be out of town two days after she made that decision. She rallied her friends and moved out of the house before he got back. She removed everything that connected her with him (including deleting him from her address book on her mobile phone) with the intention of truly banishing him from her life.

Once she had recovered, she set about going to restore the wall and found that the villagers, so relieved that the giant no longer bothered them, had repaired the wall for her without asking.[35]

Once you have repaired the walls of your great hall it is important to pay attention to the walls that surround your village. These represent the ability of your lifestyle to hold its own against the problems of the outside world. These walls should be strong, but not inflexible. This is why I have chosen the symbol of a stockade rather than a stone wall. The purpose of a stockade was that it provided a good level of defence but was flexible enough to be expanded and contracted or even moved. Your lifestyle should be able to hold its shape, but you must never be frightened of changing it. Once again it is important to find out what caused the holes so that they may be filled or replaced.

For a long time I had a section of wall which kept falling down because of bad soil underneath it. By examining the houses around the breach, I worked out that the wall was my job, which was no longer financially or emotionally rewarding. Enemy warriors could sally forth

---

35 What had happened was the woman had concentrated on finding more friends and developing a social life now that the abuser was out of her life. This made her feel much more self-confident and healed her. In other words the villagers (her friends) had made her feel better.

into the breach, thus weakening other areas of my life. Fixing the hole (and changing my job) meant this did not happen.

Remember: Whatever you change in your personal village will result in a change in your immediate environment.

An Adventure in the Village

Every life has moments of conflict, either at work or at home. This pathworking is designed to uncover the root cause of these and attempt to resolve them at a psychological level.

There is a cry from the watchtower. The village is under attack! Horns of alarm sound and warriors rush to strap on their weapons and remove their shields from the walls of their houses. Villagers rush to hide inside and the guards slide the huge gates shut and bolt them.

You quickly run to the watchtowers by the gatehouse and climb to the tower's top, which gives you a panoramic view of the village and the hill that surrounds it. Sure enough, there are several warriors at the bottom of the hill.

They had hoped to sneak in, but they were seen and the alarm was raised. Now they were at the bottom of the hill plotting their next move.

You ask the warrior on guard duty who they are. What does he say?

You then ask if he can work out what they want from your village. What does he say?

Blaise has walked to the gatehouse and is muttering magical words against the bolts of the gate. They glow with power, meaning that it will take more than a physical assault to break them.

You climb down the watchtower and ask Blaise for advice.

He looks at you and says you have three options. Fight the warriors, agree a treaty, or surrender. What else does he suggest?

The Chariot

Now it is time to leave the village and enter the dark forest of adventure. In the stable is your chariot which is drawn by two ponies, one black and the other white. You have a chariot driver who, sometimes with difficulty, will keep these two steeds moving in the direction you want to go.

Note the state of repair of the chariot, the horses and the driver. The car of the chariot is a symbol of your physical body; the horses are your emotions and the charioteer is your sense of reason. If any of these are in bad shape it is worthwhile finding out why.

The Western Mystery Tradition is legendary for its lack of emphasis on the physical body. Unlike Eastern systems, which have their martial arts or yoga, the West tends to go towards extremes. On one hand there are the food-faddists and on the other the chain smoking, heavy drink or drug takers. Either way the poor body gets a rough time of it. It is important to get regular exercise and eat a balanced diet. This seems to create the environment for spiritual progress. In fact my first spiritual breakthrough happened when I started going to the gym and took up karate. Others notice changes when they give up smoking or change their diet.

The emotions are always a difficult thing to control, as they will pull us in directions that we do not want to go. The only way of stopping this is with the intellect. The New Age movement has smeared the intellect in favour of the emotions. Thinkers are often told that they are out of touch with their feelings, which for some reason should be allowed a free rein. It has led to what I consider a psychosis of the modern New Age movement, a sort of tree-hugging mush that never really gets anywhere because it is stuck in a child-like appeasement of emotional satisfaction. But Western magic is all about balance, and as the symbol of the chariot shows, without the drive of the emotions the chariot is not going to move, and without the direction of reason the chariot is going to go nowhere interesting. The charioteer must understand the ponies, and know them well enough to prevent them from going to places they shouldn't.

When this combined symbol of the chariot is ready, it is time to take it into the forest of adventure.

Journeying to the Great Forest

Your village is sited on a hill with several natural wells. This makes it easy to defend, as an enemy cannot drive you out, and gives it a clear view of the land surrounding it. The gateway is flanked by two watchtowers, from which guards oversee and admit those who wish to come to trade. The two gates are made from solid English oak and sealed by two enormous slide bolts. As these swing open, they reveal a causeway and a primitive road. On either side of the causeway is a deep and wide ditch, which is designed to make it hard for attackers to approach your village wall.

Once your charioteer has ridden along the causeway, the road slips quickly downhill and it is a little bumpy. You have to hang on to the sides of your chariot here, as the wheels bounce off the ruts made by countless carts and chariot wheels.

After a while the road levels out and you are on a fairly straight road through cultivated fields. Farmers till their crops and raise sheep, cattle and pigs on this rich farmland to provide food for the village. As you ride by, they wave to you, acknowledging that this part of the world is still under your direct rule.

It is a bright and sunny day. The rhythmic drumming of the ponies' hooves seems oddly energetic in comparison to the stillness of the outside world.

Soon the farmland gives way to less cultivated land. This land is only recently acquired by you and although it has been explored, it has not been fully developed. In this area you are aware that there are magical springs which can provide healing or in whose limpid waters you can see the future. There are small villages here.

This land represent skills that you are starting to obtain, new people who are coming into your life and new wisdom.

As you ride further you come to the periphery of an enormous and dark forest which surrounds your kingdom. This is an ancient forest and in it are contained many wonders and dangers.

When you banish anyone from your kingdom, they usually have to pass through this forest to the outside world. Many stay here as outlaws, causing trouble for outlying farms. Occasionally these outlaws have been known to join marauding armies in the hope that they can have some part in your downfall and resume their previous status in the village.

The forest is magical and changes all who stay too long. Slowly they start to become less human and more like monsters and demons. Many have been here since long before you were ruler; they are great and ancient demons that are a threat to the whole of Britain and not just your little kingdom.

A number of times you have thought about building a huge wall to keep the forest dwellers from your village. But Blaise has warned you against it, telling you stories about several kingdoms that built huge walls to keep evil away from their kingdoms. Behind these walls the evil grew, while people became effete and unable to fight any more and after a while there would be a fire, or an earthquake which would damage the wall and then all manner of evil would force its way into the land, finding a people too weak to resist.

"It is better to watch the forest dwellers," advises Blaise. "Try to understand them and help them to re-integrate into village life. Some you will have to fight and drive deeper into the forest, but always remember they will return until they are either killed or adapted to village life."

Occasionally you will send Blaise out to bring back some of those who are banished, to see if they are ready to return to civilisation. At other times you will go yourself.

The forest contains many wonders. There are hermits who live in caves and huts who will dispense advice and teaching. It is full of magical groves and springs, where talking trees reveal much about Nature, their goddess. There are nature elementals, the Gnomes, the Salamanders, the Undines and Sylphs and the nature spirits like Elves, and Goblins, Trolls and Giants. Some live on their own, while others, particularly the Elves, live in established communities with hierarchies much like humans.

As your kingdom grows into a place of peace, more of these magical beings will choose to allow their part of the forest to become part of your kingdom, and themselves your subjects. This will bring many magical treasures from which you and your kingdom will benefit.

What you experience in the Great Forest will result in changes to your inner and outer world. It will change habits, fears and phobias and neurotic behaviour at a very deep level.

As you face each trial you will face those parts of yourself which you sought to banish from your life. In integrating them you become a more complete and a stronger person. Sometimes you will find imprisoned princesses or princes. These will be parts of yourself that you gave away to other people – perhaps a relationship, or a parent, in order to please them. Often they are protected by the memory or fear of that person and in their Inner Kingdom they often appear as some kind of monster. Its defeat will bring back what you have lost, and often provide you with a clue about fixing the problem. This is the essence behind the shamanic technique of soul retrieval which seeks to make a person whole.

The Tiny Giant

Here is an example of how a psychological change can be brought about in this pathworking. A five foot one woman whose self-confidence was apparently smashed by her ex-partner. She said she had always been intimidated by her partner, who had towered over her, demanding that she conform to a bizarre routine centred on him. Having left him, she now found it impossible to have another relationship as she felt too shy to approach anyone.

When taking part in a pathworking similar to this one, she saw herself locked in a tower guarded by an enormous version of her former partner. She had always been intimidated by his size and physical presence and this had meant frequently bowing to his will under threat of violence. When she had stood up to him, he raped her to confirm his physical prowess. The answer was obvious; if she was bigger than him, he could not fight her. In real life she was only five foot one, but in her Inner Kingdom where magic rendered everything possible she set out in search of a potion to make her giant-sized, and in another glade she found a wizard. This wizard said that if the woman put on a magical ring she would become a giant. The only problem was that once she wore it she could never take it off. The reason he had never attacked the giant was because he was frightened of always being so big, but a warrior maiden like her should have no problems, if she had courage.

She put the ring on and became a giant. She faced the giant who represented her ex-partner, who fled before her. Upon freeing the princess she had a sudden belt of emotional power, as if something had been returned to her. She realised that since her teens she had associated her powerlessness with her height, when power was really a state of mind. An emotional shock was caused by her realising this and suddenly having access to a part of herself that had remained locked up because of her insecurity.

When looking at this case it is possible to see how the woman's imagination drew her to a conclusion that was slightly different from her own idea of the problem. She had always believed that her ex-partner was responsible for creating her insecurity, rather than the relationship being a symptom of the wider problem. It is also interesting how she unconsciously generated the wizard in the imagination who had a 'cure' that fixed her true problem.

This was an example of a passive pathworking of a type I called *psychological magic* which will be examined in detail in the next chapter.

Meeting Other Beings in the Great Forest

Earlier I said that the Great Forest contained non-human beings. These are creatures like fairies, goblins and elves. While it is possible that such forces have made an appearance in your Inner Kingdom, it is more likely that they represent magical potential within you or random parts of yourself that are not under clear control or direction. Just because they might only be part of your psyche that does not mean that you treat them any differently! In fact you should treat them as if they really were those characters in myth. This suspension of disbelief is a vital part of pathworking and in this case enables the magic that these beings represent to actually work.

If your pathworking takes you to an Elven feast, you will politely ask to speak to the Queen. In the case of Thomas the Rhymer, she liked him so much that she gave him the gift of poetry and song. This represents that magical part of the psyche unlocking its latent powers. I know one creative writer who managed to write a novel after a series of successful inner world encounters with an Elven queen. Not only did he dedicate the book to his fairy queen,[36] but also named his baby girl after her.

Care needs to be exercised when dealing with the inner representations of fairies and nature spirits, as they can be quite harmful. Like their counterparts in legend, they can be devious, malicious and want to play with your mind. In some pathworkings they will represent rogue complexes or irrational parts of your character, so it is vital that you are in control when they appear. Information is your best weapon and you should read all you can about fairy legends so you know how people were tricked, and in return tricked the fairy folk. There is much common sense lore tied up in these legends and if you don't see the links when you are reading them, your unconscious mind will present the same principles in an understandable way when you do your pathworkings.

Guides and Hermits

The Great Forest contains beings that represent your higher aspects. These appear as guides and wise ones. When they appear it is at least interesting to understand what they are trying to tell you, as they can often give clues to the resolution of a particular problem or issue.

In some cases there may be a psychic communication with another entity, either a human, or what is known amongst some occult groups as an inner plane teacher. Some care needs to be taken here, as the vast majority of contacts made in a subjective meditation are likely to be aspects of the self. There are far too many people who claim they are in personal communication with a spiritual entity in their meditations. Of

---

36 In this case it was probably a representation of the writer's feminine creative side or Muse.

these, few have a genuine contact and those that do can't contact them in every meditation session. The reason is that to keep such threads of communication pure, a person has to disable the personality sufficiently that the message is unimpeded by the wish-fulfilment of the lower self. This takes an enormous effort which, given the egos of many in the esoteric world, is a little like asking someone to stop breathing for a couple of hours. Much of the drivel that comes from such guides is usually so wishy-washy as to be useless or contained in the mind of the occultist already.[37]

In worst-case scenarios they can be beings which are actually harmful to your development. If good guys exist on the astral plane it is logical enough that there are some inner-plane beings who are not nice. As in all Inner Kingdom conversations, you have to be careful. A good rule of thumb is that no good inner plane being, or higher aspect of yourself, will ever tell you what to do. At best they will only suggest and not really care if you ignore their advice. Like the outer plane worlds, the bad guys work by flattery, bribery and cajolery to convince you that their way is the best. If anyone arrives and tells you that you are to head a New Age religion and that you are really the son of God (or the devil), it is probably a good bet that they are not a good contact or are a megalomaniac aspect of your own persona. The best at being bad guides are those who suggest little things at first and gradually increase their demands while simultaneously inflating the ego.

You should not assume that because a being shows up dressed in the form of a god or a historical personality that they really are (or were) that being. Often the form is simply a symbol for what that guide represents, or is created from the wish fulfilment of the meditator. A head of a magical school to which I once belonged had a contact with an inner plane being who had many forms but the most common was the Egyptian god of the dead, Anubis. A disproportionate number of her students had this god making appearances as their contact in their meditations. Being charitable, it is possible that they associated teaching with this particular human being, and wanted to be plugged into the same source. Being uncharitable, it could be possibly be a wish that they were just as important as the head of the school. This does not mean that the students were not in communication with something, or

---

37 There is nothing more boring than a contact talking for hours about how they are working to achieve peace and healing among all beings when the audience wants something more concrete, or a 'contact' reciting from a book from which the mediator has just read.

even the highest aspects of their selves when addressing the Egyptian god of the dead. It was just that their unconscious minds had built this imaginary vehicle for teaching and their Higher Self or the Inner Plane contact used it as the only symbol going.

Another issue is the problem of asking the guide practical information about your life and accepting it as gospel. No guide will ever offer you advice on such matters, they will only tell you the principles behind the problem. Guides do not tell you to dump your boyfriend or the best brand of toaster to buy, but they will tell you about the nature of relationships and how fire elementals convert bread into toast.

This rule has confused a lot of really good magicians over time. My favourite story is when Dion Fortune asked her contact if her soya bean factory was going to continue to be successful, and was given the sage advice that "the soya bean will look after itself."[38] Some heads of magical orders fail to follow this advice and, having reached a decision about a course of action, will perform a pathworking and approach their contact who will, surprisingly, agree with them. The result is that you get some wacky decisions that are presented as coming from the authority of the contact. There was one school, School A, that told its members not to talk to people at School B, because the contact had warned that 'its teachings are dangerously incompatible'. The contact must have had a short memory because School A was a daughter of School B and all of School A's teachings had come from the allegedly incompatible School B. When the surface was scratched you discovered that the person in charge of School A was a little worried about students joining School B, leaving her with no one to teach. These sorts of petty ego squabbles litter the history of groups and orders within the Western Mystery Tradition and the use of the authority of contacts to provide justification for it does the system no credit.

If the guide figure is not a discarnate super-being they can be in a pathworking to highlight deeper aspects to the issue that you are meditating upon. Hermits or guides are archetypal figures which can, if you permit, bypass aspects of your personality which stand in the way of a clear message to the rest of yourself.

When you are building a pathworking through the forest it is always best to allow yourself a stopover near a sacred well or a hermitage. If such a place is visited, it is possible to talk to one of the sorts of characters that live there. Sometimes they will speak in riddles or in strange, seemingly meaningless phrases. This is because, as was said in the previous chapter,

---

38 I always thought that such a priceless pearl of wisdom should be put on a tee-shirt.

the unconscious mind is blocking the message because it is frightened that you will actually act upon it and it will be forced to change. Like a dream, this message can be pieced together with some thought, or by example when the pathworking progresses.

In a pathworking, a hermit once told me with great pomp and ceremony that "wishing for custard squares out of the refrigerator does not deliver Danish pastries, the cook has to get into the kitchen". When I asked him what he meant he just repeated it. At the time it made no sense, but afterwards I remembered that when I was a child my mother occasionally made really nice custard squares with real chocolate icing and Danish pastries. She only did it once or twice because they were too difficult to make and despite the pleas of my sister and I, we could never get her to make them again. Later when I became good at cooking I never made them, presumably because of my mother's complaint that they were too hard. Custard squares and Danish pastries had become a symbol for something nice that I had waited for in vain. What the Hermit was trying to tell me was that in such matters the only alternative is for me to create my own. Oddly, the issue I was meditating upon was nothing to do with my parents, or cooking in general, it was about latent skills which I had never developed. My lower self therefore had a vested interest in keeping this information secret because I would then spend a lot of time doing more creative work and less time in front of the television.

Sometimes a hermit or similar being will offer to guide you through a particular scenario. When this happens you should be careful not to simply blindly follow the guide but remain aware of what is happening. I can remember one scenario where my guide took me through all sorts of adventures and walking around in circles. When I berated him for it he laughed and asked if I had 'got the message yet'. In my case the question was about my dependence on a particular spiritual teacher and what my higher self was trying to show was that I should never be entirely reliant on another being for wisdom.

In the Inner Kingdom pathworking I have designed for this book, the character of Blaise is a guide and a source of wisdom. If you design your own symbolic Inner Kingdom you might like to replace him with a similar archetypal figure, like Merlin, Thomas Aquinas, Plato, or John Dee. There is no need to have a historical character either; figures like *Star Wars'* Obi-Wan Kenobi or Yoda work well if you are moved by that symbolism. *Star Trek* is full of similar archetypes to draw upon, as is Tolkien's *Lord of the Rings*, or (if you have a really good sense of humour) the Harry Potter series.

Meeting the Wise Woman

This pathworking is designed to give you a link to the feminine energy of the Earth. It provides advice but not in an intellectual way. When people have tried this particular pathworking they have found that the wise woman does not say anything but instead they have a feeling of warmth and of love. Others have found this exercise hard because it deals with the Mother archetype and many have had difficulty with their mothers. The symbolism is associated with the Mother and Venus, but the majority is taken from an Arthurian legend of Owain, with a slightly different result. This pathworking will give you an answer to some of the questions relating to life and death. It also has a strong redemptive element and is very effective at removing pain and hurt. Its use was taught to me by a very clever priestess who loved to stir things up in my life for a while – which is exactly what this pathworking does.

The road opens out into a clearing and there is a narrow track off to the left. A glint of copper in the trees catches your eye and you leave your chariot to investigate.

Walking down the narrow path, you notice that everything has gone quiet. You enter a clearing which is covered with wild wheat. In the centre are a well, a fir tree and an ancient stone. Hanging from a tree branch by three lead chains is a copper bowl.

It is such a strange combination of things that you are left wondering what to do. Suddenly your thoughts are interrupted by the appearance of a tiny, dark man emerging from behind the well.

"Hello," he says. "I would not even think about doing that if I were you."

"Doing what?" you ask confused.

"Lots of people have done it but she has always got them."

"Who? Do what?" You are starting to get a little cross that the man is not telling you much.

"The old Wise Woman. She is summoned by pouring water on the rock. But the danger is that when she comes nothing is ever the same again."

"What does she do?" you ask.

"Some she kills, others she rewards, but no-one comes away unscarred." He pauses. "You are going to do it, aren't you?"

"I thought I might."

"Hell's bells, another sucker," says the man. "Don't say you were not warned." And with that he turns on his heels and runs into the forest.

You take the bronze dish from the chain and fill it with water from the well. You notice that there is the sound of humming all around you and a gentle breeze whistles through the fir tree. The sun goes behind a cloud.

Here goes, you mentally say and pour water on the rock.

Suddenly there is a clap of thunder. Dark storm clouds fill the sky and the wind becomes stronger.

The earth starts to shake and you lose your balance.

Rain pours down from the sky and the wind becomes so strong that it is impossible to stand, even if the earth were not shaking.

Then as suddenly as it all began it stops. First the shaking ends, the clouds part and the sun shines.

There is a fluttering of wings and hundreds of birds fly into the tree and start to sing. It is all so beautiful and you feel relaxed. *Surely nothing can be so bad now*, you think. Then you notice the dark shape enter the glade.

He is a warrior dressed from head to toe in black. On his head, covering his face, is a dark helmet. He has a huge slashing sword of coal-coloured iron in his left hand.

"Who is it that poured water on the Wise Woman's stone?" he asks.

"I did, but I meant no harm," you say.

"Harm or no, the punishment for pouring the sacred water on the stone is death," he says as he advances towards you.

"Can't we talk about this?" you ask, drawing your sword.

"No, the universe is a fairly difficult place to understand at times and dealing death gives me a sense of purpose," says the warrior, swinging his sword at you.

"Well everyone has to have a purpose in life," you say, parrying his blows.

"Glad you see it that way," the black warrior says.

"Not at all," you reply.

The fight becomes a complex ballet of swords. Sparks fly as you each fight your way across the glade. You seem easily matched and each slash he makes you can parry and vice versa.

After some time it gets tiring and the black knight lets down his guard for a moment, giving you a clear over hand blow to his helmet.

The helmet splits.

"Bugger," says the dark warrior and promptly vanishes.

Well that was strange, you think.

Another being enters the glade. She too is covered from head to toe in a black cloak.

"Er, hello," you say, fully aware that the last person wearing black advancing upon you attempted to kill you.

"Hail to thee slayer of the black warrior. Why do you approach the Wise Woman of the forest?"

You think about this. Why would anyone embark on a quest for knowledge?

"I seek to know in order to serve," you reply.

"Serve who?"

"The land and its people, for I am their Chief."

The woman draws back her veil and looks straight at you, into the depths of your soul.

"I am she whom you seek to serve and you are born of my blood," she says. "What would you ask of me?"

You ask her any question and she will reply.

After she has finished she says.

"I am the river which supports and in which you sink,
I am the water that carries you through life towards the endless sea,
I am with you until the sun has left the sky
And the stars are no more
I wash at the waters for you at the ford between the worlds
On the morning of your last battle in life.
And carry your soul to the Isle of Apples
Unclasp your troubles
Release all the pain that I have mixed into your life
No longer clench agony
No longer cage joy's flight
Come to me and let me wash the pain away."

And with that she takes water from the well and pours it over your head. It does not feel like water. It feels like healing and any pain you have felt starts to subside and any tension you may have is released.

She says:

"You may return to my glade whenever you need such healing."

And with that she vanishes.

When this inner world map was tested upon several groups of people there were some interesting results which fall into the category of psychological magic, which we will look at in the next chapter. The first was that, although the design of the hall was the only thing that was really described, there was an unconscious urge for many of the participants to change the layout. Those who know something of Cabbalah will be aware that I have based it on this model, however more than one person wanted to change the rooms around. One in particular thought it was important that the room dedicated to her partner should be placed behind her instead of the room dedicated to the 'God' (which has a connection to the archetype of the father) and her parents should really be in those front rooms where she could see them. Psychologically what she was saying was that she felt the need to 'replace' her father with her partner and place the role models of her parents in full view instead of in the shadows behind her.

Another found her warriors made too much noise and she could not feel comfortable. She also did not feel like she had any control over them and became a little frightened and frustrated. When asked if she had a busy life, she replied that it was too busy, there were too many things going on for her to cope with and she felt out of control.

Another woman who had just left her depressive husband after many years of being focused on him, found that there were few warriors in the hall. This was because all the parts of herself had been focused on a man who was no longer there, and effectively he had taken all her warriors! Her first response was to use the remaining warriors to recruit some more from the village and outlying region. These are indications that the Inner Kingdom was working. All of these things show that the unconscious was using it to tell the participants something about themselves. Everything that happens, every desire you feel in your Inner Kingdom, is a symbolic clue to your true state of being.

The pathworking had also given the opportunity for the pathworkers to actually change those things about themselves they didn't like. The woman who felt that she was not in control of her Inner Kingdom could visualise herself banging her sword on the table and ordering them to be quiet. It is easier to gain control of the beings of your Inner Kingdom than it is those in the material world. But once control has been obtained and you acknowledge yourself as the ruler of your Inner Kingdom, it will start to percolate down the levels until you are equally in control of your material world. The warriorless woman discovered that after she had issued her order, she found herself surrounded by new friends.

Chapter Four

USING IMAGINATION TO CHANGE YOUR PSYCHE

THE PREVIOUS CHAPTERS have shown how pathworking can have psychological effects. The aim of this chapter is to focus specifically on this facility and use it to find and repair weaknesses in the psyche. The techniques we will look at are the result of some seven years experimentation with a variety of different people. During that time we found a fairly simple formula which could be examined as part of an ongoing therapy. Although it was developed by occultists not psychologists, some counsellors in England who were asked to comment on its effectiveness tried it out with some striking success.

Some considered a simpler variant of Neurolinguistic Programming or NLP which uses imagination to identify the way a person has been "programmed" to think, act and feel. But the idea of basing treatment around a single pathworking is unique as far as I am aware. 'Psychological magic'[39] was based on the occult concept of working on the astral level with the images that rise into a person's mind during a passive pathworking. As we have said earlier, occultists knew that these images, which are generated mostly by the lower personality, had a direct effect on the material world in which a person lives, and changing those images enabled a person to change their material world. But in the early nineties a few of us started to reason that if these images were being changed, there must also be a fundamental change in the person's psyche to bring them about. Someone who is 'a loser' can never achieve in occult terms, unless they lose the elements in their psyche that make them destroy their own life. So it is reasonable to assume that if the power of pathworking was brought to bear on the psyche, it would be possible to find out the root causes of neuroses and eliminate them at the source.

---

39 Like most things in the occult world this was affectionately shortened by the group who practiced it into the phrase 'psycho magic'.

The effect was explosive, particularly as the early experiments started to coincide with dramatic changes in all our lives. I personally think this was because those neurotic crutches that had propped us up all our lives were suddenly kicked from underneath us. Married couples suddenly discovered that the reasons they were together were not actually based on love, but a desire to mimic the disasters of the their parents; another found that his hatred of women was based not on competition with his brother, as he always thought, but on a long forgotten form of child sexual abuse; another Pagan found that his early Christian upbringing was still having a dramatic effect on the sort of relationships he was choosing. While this self-discovery was one thing, the magical altered state of the passive pathworking gave the person a chance to change their psychological response to the various parts of their past and build a new future.

Unfortunately this technique did stir things up. It seems that if you removed one neurosis, like a house of cards, much of a person's worldview came crashing down with it. While many would consider such techniques dangerous, the occultist, along with the alchemist, accepts this particular stage as vital to becoming a true 'integrated' person; that is, someone whose personality works in tune with their higher self. The result of the technique is an initial feeling of empowerment, as energy trapped in the neurotic complex is freed. This is followed by a sense of purpose for the future and then sometimes an urge to return to the safety of the past. Some reported a sense of depression, as the road map for your life feels altered and the things that gave you joy are suddenly tasteless shadows. In alchemy, this period is called nigredo, which, according to the great 16th century alchemical text *The Rosary of the Philosophers*,[40] is when the brain turns black. Alchemy describes in horrible terms what this feels like using the imagery of rotting corpses. From this mass of depression rise the buds of something greater which the alchemists called 'whitening', where the blackness is purified.

Fortunately the nigredo period following the session was rarely as bad as was described by the alchemists, because the technique was only focused on one aspect of the psyche rather than the complete personality. Removing a selected neurosis did not usually take down a person's entire world view all at once. However, the follow through process was usually unpleasant.

---

40 *Rosarium Philosophorum* was in *De Alchemia Opuscula complura veterum philosophorum*, Frankfurt, 1550.

From a psychological point of view you are rushing the person through to a realisation, something that usually takes a long time in therapy, where the conscious mind is in control and the therapist has to rely on Freudian slips and other tricks, smattered with the odd dream interpretation, to reveal the state of the unconscious mind. However, by using this technique, the unconscious mind is opened before the analyst and it is up to them to interpret the findings.

As we have seen earlier, each personality is built from the lessons we have learnt from the past. These lessons always start from a single lesson that was taught to us by experience or by teachers, friends or parents or situations. There is an occult law which says the first thing you hear about a subject of which you know nothing will become part of your Inner Kingdom from which you will judge all other information.

But that association becomes much more than that, we actually build a life based around this lesson until it is a complex tree of ideas linked by association. Take a fairly simple example.

When I was a child a Christian teacher told me that they had found chariot wheels in the Red Sea, and this proved that Moses had crossed it, closing it on Pharoah's chariots. It was an important point for me because this little bit of knowledge covered all manner of flaws in fundamental Christian philosophy. The information was given by someone who I deeply respected as a teacher and who was a role model for me at the age of 11. I reasoned that if Pharoah's chariots had been found then Moses had a fixed place in history and there was an obvious element of literal truth in Bible stories. Throughout my teens I carried this 'literal' image of biblical history and its obvious association with the literal theology of fundamental Christianity. All was well until my interest in Ancient History turned towards archaeology in the Biblical period and I discovered that the chariot wheel statement was complete fiction. My universe was shattered. Everything that I had been told by this teacher was now in doubt. I applied research to everything that I had accepted as fact and found it wanting, finally abandoning fundamentalist Christianity entirely in favour of a personal revelation. Some years later I found a friend from that period of my life to whom that brand of Christianity remained important. He asked me why I had 'abandoned my faith' and was told about the teacher and the chariot wheels. He looked at me as if I was stupid. "But they *have* found chariot wheels in the Red Sea," he said. Initially he thought he had read it somewhere, but like me he was able to trail the information to the same teaching session. Unlike me, the information did not break his faith.

We can draw the associations that my mind made from that one incident into a tree.

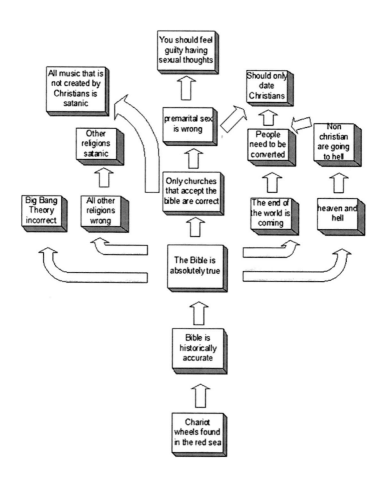

While it would probably be shallow to suggest that my Christian faith was entirely based on that one incident, it propped up many of the fundamentalist Christian ethics that I stood by in my teenage years. Destroy the roots – that first association – and the tree will fall.

What I am describing is a loss of interest in a religion, and many who have lost their faith report something similar. An event happens which undermines the first association they had with that faith. War, for example, can shatter a person's belief if that faith was based on an association of God being all knowing and all loving. If, they would say, God was all knowing and all loving, why has He allowed this to happen?

Faiths based on guilt can be rejected if the person realises that there is nothing wrong with doing things that are considered a sin.

However the same thing applies to any belief pattern or world view. Such a pattern begins with a single seed that grows by association after association until it is a dominant life force. This can be good if it is a positive seed from which a life grows. My parents built much of my life around a seed form which was something like 'always ask questions'.[41] One school of magic, of which I was a member, described initiation as 'planting the seed of light'. In other words, the symbolism of divinity, once planted in the unconscious, would build a new personality based on a divine plan. More often the things we need to remove are the negative associations which we may have made by accident.

Remove the seed and it is possible to destroy most of the associations that sprang from it. This allows new and correct information to replace the corrupted programming.

It is for this reason that the technique uses the symbol of a tree as an accurate depiction of the problem. It cannot be a very nice tree because it is in the position of causing trouble in your life now. In the technique this tree is shown as sucking the joy from your life. Below is an outline of the formula so that it is possible to discuss how it all works. We will look at the full pathworking later in this chapter, but before we give an explanation it is important to provide an outline of the process.

OUTLINE

1. The person is taken on a pathworking to a beautiful garden.
2. They are told it is a garden of their Inner Kingdom. There are pagodas representing each area of their life, work, family, etc.
3. Their eye is drawn to an ugly old tree which seems out of place in their garden. Its twisted roots seem to be sucking the life out of the garden and the pagodas.
4. They approach the tree and try to destroy it but discover they can't.
5. A guide approaches and shows them how to get into the tree.
6. They find themselves inside the tree and are taken down a corridor where rooms open up into the various times when whatever is behind the complex is manifested.
7. On each occasion they are made to confront the behaviour they see and change it to a more appropriate situation with a positive conclusion.

---

41 My mother always said this worked well until I started to question my parents.

8. After at least four of these experiences (more if the guide cannot work out what the common thread is) the person is guided to the roots of the tree.
9. At the roots of the tree there is a dark room where symbols are spontaneously allowed to be generated that illustrate the root of the problem.
10. The root of the problem is resolved using symbols, and as the tree breaks up, the person plants a seed of a new affirmation. This grows into a white rose.
11. The candidate sits in the petals of the rose and rises through the decaying tree to the Garden.
12. The white rose has replaced the old tree and the garden is healed.

Before the pathworking begins, the person is encouraged to relax as much as possible, but is told that they will always be able to describe what they see and feel. They will also never lose the ability to hear your voice. I tend to place the person in a chair in the centre of the room and walk around them clockwise during the pathworking. This seems to help the process by providing energy to the person and also ensures that they do not associate your voice as coming from a particular direction. Direction must be defined by what they see in the pathworking and not by any 'compass' from the earth level.

The person is taken to a beautiful ordered garden and told that it represents their life. The garden is a variant on the 'Inner Kingdom' that we looked at in the last chapter. The different aspects of their life, such as work, are seen as things that would appear in such an ornamental garden: pagodas, pools, bridges, trees, bandstands, summer houses etc. These are shown in a positive aspect to remind the person that, except for this problem here, life would be OK. Although a person might have many complexes that are causing problems for their garden, it is important to tackle them one at a time and not to try to see others.

The complex is depicted as a tree that drains life from the garden. Cutting down the tree is impossible. It is either too big, or if cut down it will spring up again. Trying to do this only represses the complex set. It is still there, its roots deep in the ground, but you are refusing to see it. The person must be shown that this is not an option, that they must recognise and face this complex.

A guide is called, or appears, to assist the person to remove the tree. This guide can be anything in authority that the person accepts and trusts. Some use gods; others use relatives whose wisdom or protective influence they respect. The function of this imaginary guide is to make the person feel comfortable and protected as they deal with the sometimes frightening experiences within the tree. It should be discussed who the guide should be before the pathworking begins.

The guide opens the tree and it becomes like Dr Who's Tardis, bigger on the inside than it is on the outside. Holding a lantern the guide leads the person deep into the complex, which is seen as a corridor carved out of the wood, and the very knots in the wall whisper those voices in your head that describe you as weak.

The technique also recognises that what a person thinks is their problem is likely to be the tip of the iceberg. By the time a complex becomes intrusive or compulsive it is likely to have manifested in countless other situations and experiences. Even though you are unlikely to know the root cause of the problem in the initial stages of the technique, it is important to see some of its outcomes and if possible repair them.

This is achieved by having the person approach down a corridor within the complex. They are told that when the door opens they will see the last time the problem manifested. Initially they are allowed to see the scene as they would a film. Then they are asked how they feel about what happened. Then they are asked to experience it as they did when they were there. They are again asked how they feel and if they could have done anything better. Then they are given the opportunity to change the scene where they act in a stronger, more confident way. It does not matter if it is absurd, it is just important that the outcome is changed to become more positive.

For example, one woman had trouble with her boss, of whom she was terrified. The first door opened and a scene replayed where he was bullying her. When the scene played out she could see that she was frightened and more to the point he could see her fear. She could also see that he was enjoying the fear he put into her. When she sat in as herself in the scene she could see the fear, but as she examined the feelings she was having at that moment, she was also feeling deep anger. She realised that the fear was of what would happen if she got angry. When asked what would be the best way she could allow that anger to be expressed to her boss, she decided she should be telling him he was wrong. She visualised herself stripping down her boss's arguments before giving him a piece of her mind on his deficiencies as a manager and a human being, finally ending with a stinging rebuff on the size of his sexual organs. She saw the bully fold and start to cry.

Later she would find that the seed cause of this incident was something her father used to do. Her father had not particularly liked or wanted children and made it clear that they were not allowed to be noisy. He actually hit them until they realised that loud noises were a bad idea. When she was four, she fell down the stairs, broke her arm and howled in pain. The father, not realising, shouted at her for being noisy, cuffed her and returned to the living room. The child's mother intervened, but the father, probably ashamed, didn't apologise and pretended that it didn't happen. The child had received the impression that it was important never to express anything, even under extreme conditions, and that it was acceptable for men to bully her.

In Psychological Magic, the seed of any problem is revealed deep in the tree's roots. After nearly half an hour tracking the various branches, the person is led into a hole in the corridor and told that it leads to the roots of the complex. They go into the hole and slide down the inside of the roots. Deep into the earth they slide until they emerge in a dark cave. They are reassured that their guide is with them.

They are told that after a while some symbols will come into their mind which must be interpreted quickly by the leader. This takes some skill, particularly as a leader has to intuit what that symbol may mean for that person, but the task is made easier by the earlier journeys into the person's past. The person undergoing the technique will have to say everything they see, no matter how apparently silly.

The guide is then required to find a solution to the problem using the symbols that have been generated by the unconscious mind of the person performing the technique.

One of the more spectacular examples of this came with one high achieving woman who we will call Liz, who was depressed and burnt out. Throughout the initial parts of the Psychological Magic pathworking she had found out her problems were connected to a work ethic that came from her parents. Throughout her successful university career she regretted not getting drunk or having a sexual partner, because she was working too hard. One of her earliest memories was of being told off for playing in mud when she should have been cleaning her room.

When led to the dark room, she initially saw a little girl dressed in red, which was the 'naughty' side of her which she allowed to merge into her. Initially the guide thought that was the end of it, but Liz said:

Liz: "I see a little blonde haired girl in a dress skipping towards me. She seems perfect... as she gets closer I am feeling colder... I don't like this."

Guide: "It's OK ... who do you think the little girl is?"
Liz: "It's me ... when I said she was perfect, she is all that I was expected to be. She is so cold and I am getting more and more drained, the closer she gets."
Guide: "That is because maintaining that image is taking so much of you. That little girl has many of the qualities that you need. She enabled you to work hard and achieve: you don't want to abandon her. Lean into her heart and take what you want from her. See it as a ball of light. Place it in your own heart."
Liz: "She has turned into a little plastic doll's face. Like there is no life left in her. She has crumbled and vanished."

This particular image moved Liz very much and afterwards changed her view of life dramatically. No longer did she need to be the good little girl; she could do and be who she wanted to be. In fact, she left her husband, whom she married just because he asked her and she didn't want to offend him by saying no. She changed her stressful job, which she hadn't wanted to leave because everyone depended on her, and found a new life free from her parents' role model for herself.

Here is another example, this time from Colin, who was having relationship difficulties and ending up in sexless relationships:

Colin: The room is lighting up. I see a coffin.
Guide: Go over and look at it.
Colin: There is a dead person it. He looks like a Bishop, he has a crook in the coffin with him and is wearing a mitre. He is perfectly preserved, he looks like he is just asleep.
Guide: What does that mean to you?
Colin: He is a religious authority. But when I was religious I didn't like this sort of religion. I was a happy clappy – this is more Catholic stuff.
Guide: What do you know about Catholic priests?
Colin: Dunno, they are celibate… Oh that is it. This sex stuff is linked to religion. I thought it was better to remain celibate outside marriage. But I don't understand, I stopped being a Christian a long time ago and have had lots of relationships since.
Guide: But a dead bishop has been carried around in your unconscious since.
Colin: Maybe.
Guide: What does this scene remind you of?

Colin: It looks like those pictures of pilgrims visiting a saint or holy relic... holy relic of the past I guess.

Guide: A revered holy relic.

Colin: ... that I superstitiously hang on to?

Guide: Despite your religious beliefs moving on.[42]

Colin: OK. I respect those beliefs in others but I don't want to worship them any more. We need a reformation here.

Guide: OK. I want you to imagine that Martin Luther is with you.

Colin: (Laughs). OK

Guide: How does he think this reformation should go?

Colin: He is saying I must be the Bishop and wake up.[43]

Guide: OK. I want you to hold Luther's hand and allow yourself to merge with the Bishop.

Colin: Lie on a corpse, yuck.

Guide: It is worse than that, you are going to merge yourself with the corpse. Lie on top and allow yourself to sink into it.

Colin (after a while): OK I feel very cold, clinical and like part of me is not working. It is like I could soar spiritually, but at the same time I am missing the point of the earth. I feel set in this stone coffin... like I can't get out.

Guide: Are you still holding Luther's hand?

Colin: Yes, he has his eyes shut.

Guide: He is praying for a reformation.

Colin: I feel weird... there is energy coming into me.

Guide: When you feel you can, I want you to sit up.

Colin: This is hard... done it. Hang on, the body is still there.

Guide: Are you still wearing the clothes?

Colin: Yes but so is the corpse.

---

42 You should see this from Colin's point of view. He was not a Roman Catholic and was against the symbols and traditions of that Church. A Liberal Protestant, he regarded the Catholic Church as backward, so the symbol of a dead bishop is more likely to be a symbol of outdated superstitious religion that has been superseded by something better. A devoted Roman Catholic would see this symbol as something completely different.

43 Colin was used to pathworking and was comfortable about allowing these inner characters to suggest their own cure. This is risky, as the inner character might only suggest the obvious intellectual answer. In this case it would have been to bury the bishop, which would have been a bad psychological symbol as it would have suggested repressing the force rather than integrating it. I was the guide for this particular session, and I really had no idea how I could integrate a dead bishop and was relieved to have 'Luther's' suggestion – which seemed to be to force the association with the bishop then the separation from the image (waking up) and the destruction of it.

Guide: That's OK. Get out of the coffin. (Pause) Take off the mitre and the robes and place them in the coffin. Imagine that you are dressing in the clothes you are wearing today. What is Luther doing?
Colin: He is still praying.
Guide: The bishop's body is crumbling into dust... like you see in those old vampire movies. The robes and the Bishop's crook are burning.
Colin: Yes. There is nothing left.
Guide: A group of people has arrived. They are wearing modern clothes and look like modern worshippers. They slide the coffin lid shut. One of them tells you that "the past is gone, we do things differently now." The scene fades and you are left in darkness with Martin Luther.[44]

ThE END OF ThE COMPLEX

To maximise its effect, the person has to see the destruction of the complex and the flowering of something new from it. This is powerfully illustrated by the planting of a new spiritual seed in the darkness, while the tree splits apart at a molecular level. The new seed, based on a new affirmation, grows into a white rose, which is a symbol of a pure desire and replaces the tree as it collapses into dust.

In the above example there was an earthquake as the tree started to break up. Martin Luther handed Colin a seed. He visualised what he wanted to achieve as a scene taking place within the seed (in this case it was to be able to have a normal sexually fulfilled relationship). He planted the seed, which quickly grew into a huge white rose, filling the room with a beautiful scent. He sat in the centre of the rose, which continued to grow upwards through the carnage of the exploding tree, finally emerging into the bright sunlight. On looking around, there is not a trace of the tree left.

A GUIDE TO ThE RISKS

Although I would like to say this system is completely safe and easy, it isn't. It places a great deal of strain on the leader and the person.

People with the skill to become leaders in Psychological Magic are either skilled counsellors or have got the knack of entering people's

---

44 Colin went into a bit of a hedonistic period after this pathworking, but settled down to a fairly normal, expressive sex life.

psyches and empathising. Others have not. If you haven't, it is better that you don't try it.

The guide has be intuitive enough to see the direction that the pathworking is heading, while at the same time ready for it to go somewhere that they have not anticipated. They are in a position of complete trust, and information disclosed must never be talked about, other than in anonymous case studies. They have to be extremely well versed in symbolism and preferably a trained counsellor or psychologist. If you are good at interpreting dreams, you will probably be a good leader.

The leader should also know when they should back off and leave it to the professionals. An example of this was when I encountered someone who suddenly, much to their surprise and mine, started to reveal that they had been sexually abused. Initially they were unhappy to reveal this memory but thinking it was something else, I pressed. There is a certain amount of seeing ahead involved in being a guide. I suddenly saw the head of something dark start to emerge which had been so well buried in this person's unconscious that I realised that this would require more expertise. That particular session was bought to a halt and the person was recommended to see a traditional counsellor.

Another risk is that the leader might impose their perceptions onto the person and unconsciously guide to a conclusion. Unlike traditional counselling, the leader can suggest reasons why a problem may manifest, but the pathworker is always correct and the leader must not impose their morals, religious or political views upon them. If someone is covering up that they want to sleep around, it is not up to the guide to decide that is morally wrong and regard it as 'part of the neurosis'. If they have repressed a huge sex drive, it is valid that they be helped to find expression. The leader needs to know themselves well enough to put aside their own personal beliefs when taking part in the technique, as they are in a position of power. It was this power that was abused by Christian hypnotists who were convinced that Satanic Child Abuse was common and they implanted these suggestions in the minds of their patients.

The hardest position for a group leader involved in the technique is if the person divulges a complex that has resulted in a crime against children or something else illegal. I am lucky in that I have not encountered this yet, but my view would be that, if it bothers, close down the working and suggest that the person seek more professional help, as you are not qualified to deal with this. A councillor or psychotherapist using the technique will know exactly what to do and my advice is that an unqualified person should not try.

Neither should you try Psychological Magic on a psychiatrically ill person unless you are medically qualified. Although I know psychologists and counsellors who use this technique, this book is written mostly for lay-people who want to help friends who are finding their lives difficult because of their neurosis. It is best at tackling the causes of mild depression with its roots in some intangible past, neurotic behaviour, and minor obsessive and compulsive behaviour.

If you are ever in doubt about performing, taking part in, or completing the technique, don't do it! Allow the person to return to the garden and end it.

A person should not undergo more than one pathworking in a month – preferably there should be a three month gap between exposures to the technique. This is because you need the person to adapt to the fallout from the collapse of the complex, and not to confuse their psyche too much. There is also a considerable amount of stirring of the unconscious, which can make the person appear worse in the short term, as the mind processes the experience and builds a new world view.

Below is the script for the technique to be read to the person. Obviously there are gaps in the process for the person to describe what they see and feel. It is written to be read in the slow, even voice of someone conducting a pathworking. It is also devoid of much descriptive language, although it is packed with words to encourage descriptive thought.

ThE TEChNIQUE

Just relax and regulate your breathing. Slow and deep. As you breathe out, you will breathe out stress ... and as you breathe in, you will relax more. *(Pause)*

Now throughout this you will always hear the sound of my voice and you will be able to speak to me. Is that OK?

Just relax. You are in a beautiful garden.

You feel warm and comfortable, it is a bright summer's day.

All around you are flowers and trees, the garden is well ordered.

This is your garden, it represents your life.

All around you are pagodas, pools and summer houses that represent the different parts of your life. There is one for your work, another for your home.

All is content and pleasant. It is a warm, clear day and you feel that you might just want to relax and fall asleep in your garden.

Then you see a tree that you have not noticed before.

The sun goes behind a cloud.

While everything in your garden looks beautiful, this tree is out of place. It is dark and twisted. It seems to suck light out of the air and its roots have erupted out of the ground.

It is sucking the life out of plants around it and as you look, you can see the roots are spreading and where they travel, the plants look sick.

The roots head towards some of the pagodas and are undermining their foundations.

It is no good, you say, *this tree has to go.*

You go up to it. How can you get rid of it?

If you cut it down, with its extensive root network it will simply grow again.

You need help with this problem.

"You need to destroy this tree from within," says a voice. It is [insert name of guide]. In [his or her] hand is a staff. "However, the journey will be hard and you will have to face many difficulties. Are you ready to do that?"

You nod and the guide lights a lamp for you and [him or her] before striking the tree with the staff.

The bark of the tree parts like a curtain to reveal that it is hollow.

The guide tells you that you only have to think the word RETURN and you will come back to the garden and the technique will be safely over. You nod, [the guide] enters the tree and you follow.

You are in a hollow tunnel shaped out of living wood. The walls are heavily knotted and you can hear a subtle whispering.

(*Whisper*) Failure, loss, depression and despair.[45]

[The guide] tells you that to understand what caused the tree to grow, you must first examine its branches.

[He or she] takes you to a long corridor lined with doors.

"Behind each of these doors are moments when the problem manifested. When you look behind these doors, you will see a scene that will show the problem that contributed to building this tree. Then we will get a chance to change that scene so that it never happened. This will weaken the tree and make it easier to kill."

---

45 If the person is aware of their problem, several of the words in this sequence should reflect that.

[He or she] takes you to a door and tells you that this is the last time that the problem manifested in your life. You open the door and shine your light into the room. What do you see?

The person will describe the scene.

How do you feel?

The person will describe how they feel.

Now I want you to take the part of yourself in this. Just allow yourself to become part of the scene and allow it to replay. How do you feel now?

The person will describe how they feel.

Do you think that there is a better way to handle this?

The person says yes or no and describes a method they think will work. Assist them to reach a conclusion, however wacky it might appear.

Now I want you to play out that same scene, doing what we have just worked out. What happens?

The person will describe what happens.

That event now has happened like that, OK? The harm that it caused is now undone. Step out of that room.[46] Now I want you to go to pick a door from mid-way down the corridor. [Your guide] tells you that this one will lead you to a point where the problem manifested several years ago.

You open the door and go through the same sequence as before. When that is complete, repeat it about four or five times. Each time should lead you closer to the original incident that caused the problem, the last one (which will probably be in childhood) will be the situation that caused the problem, although it is important that you do not tell the person that.

---

46 The conversation will probably be more involved than this, and you should not feel bound to the script so long as you follow its general points.

Right! Now your guide believes you are ready to approach the seed of the tree, now you have a rough idea of how it has affected you. Are you ready?

Wait until the person says yes.

[Your guide] leads you to a hole in the wall. This is a hollow root that leads directly to the source of the problem. Slide down it and you will find yourself in a cave. There you will receive symbolic impressions. It does not matter how silly they appear, I want you to tell me what you see. OK?

Wait until the person says yes.

You jump into the hole, which turns out to be a long slide, deep, deep into the earth.

You emerge in a dark cave.

You are aware that [The Guide] is behind you, so you are safe. After a while you will start to see images. What are they?

The person describes what they see. You will have to think quickly to work out what they mean. Then you will have work out a fairly dramatic way of using those symbols to resolve the person's problem (see examples). When that is done…

The ground is beginning to shake, the tree is beginning to crumble from within. We do not have much time. [Your guide] hands you a seed. It is about the size of a large marble and is pearl coloured. Now I want you to visualise a scene which would show you being what you want to be, without this problem. I want you to see it as clearly as possible, living within the seed. OK?

Wait until the person says OK. It might be helpful if you have agreed on this image beforehand.

Plant the seed. [Your guide] hands you a watering can and you water the seed. Almost at once it shoots and quickly grows to a bush with an enormous white rose bud.

The bud opens and the room is full of its scent. This causes the old tree to start to dissolve quicker.

You sit in the rose petals, which feel like a soft bed.

The rose grows upwards, taking you with it.

The tree is dissolving.

The knots that locked up feelings of negativity are unlocking, freeing up the energy they contained.

Earth from the garden is rushing to fill in the void left by the dead tree.

Suddenly you burst into the sunlight of the garden. Blinking at the brightness, you see the last parts of the tree dissolving into dust.

You step out of the rose and watch it grow into an enormous tree with many beautiful roses.

Already the plants that surround site of the old tree are healing.

You look to see where its roots had undermined the pagodas and summer houses and instead see small white flowers.

It is as if the tree was never there. The garden is healed.

Lie down in the garden, knowing that all is well.

Relax for now.

When you open your eyes, you will be aware of this time and space.

You will remember everything.

Slowly and in your own time, open your eyes.

Afterwards

It is very important that you talk the whole thing through with the person afterwards so that some of the details can be made clear to them. They will also feel a bit disorientated, so it is best not to let them drive a car for a while. They should also have something to eat or drink.

PSYChOLOGICAL PAThWORKINGS

Besides the Psychological Magic technique, there are pathworkings designed to help people out of specific situations. I have included two here as examples because they will enable the reader to think about how to approach writing some of their own. Unlike the above method, these pathworkings are not interactive. The person is simply led through them. All of them assume that you have relaxed the person completely and have allowed them to visualise a doorway.

ADOPTED BY THE GODS

This pathworking is designed for those who have parental images that are so corrupted that the existence of their mother or father is a complete blight on their life. An example would be the daughter of a prostitute who I mentioned earlier. It is also for those who for various reasons lacked a father or mother figure in their life. Often children can bond with foster parents, but in some cases this is not possible and they lack a deep father or mother archetype to base their life upon. This can lead to confusion in relationships as they get older, or a tendency to find people who approximate to the nearest role model, which may not be appropriate.

This pathworking forms a link with the husband and wife archetypes of Isis and Osiris, whose love was so great they could conceive their child Horus even after death. Isis makes an ideal mother image, and Osiris, as the Father who provides support for the whole of Egypt, makes a good Father image. The pathworking is designed so that if someone has a poor mother image they can chose Isis and a weak father image they can choose Osiris. Before the pathworking the person should be shown pictures of the God or Goddess so that they can be familiar with its form. After completing the pathworking the person who has performed it is encouraged to say the word 'Mother', if it is a mother archetype or 'Father' if it is a father archetype, while visualising the God or Goddess. This builds up the association between the god form and the psyche.

The Pathworking

Now relax and regulate your breathing. I want you to open your inner vision and imagine that you are a seven-year-old child in ancient Egypt. You are in a small bedroom with a primitive bed in one corner. This is your room. It is part of a great temple of [Isis or Osiris]. You were brought here by the people of the village after your parents were swept away when the Nile burst its banks. You cannot remember them because you were a baby.

Today is the Festival of Orphans where the children, like you, are presented to the [God or Goddess] in the hope of a blessing.

You have put on your best robe and are waiting to be called to the temple.

You are nervous. This will mean that you will stand before the statue in front of all the priests, including the High Priest and selected people from the village.

There is a gentle knock on the door and it is opened by Khem, who has been teaching you how to write the complex hieroglyphs that make up the language of Egypt.

"They are ready for you now [insert your real name]," he says.

Without a word you follow him through the labyrinth of cool whitewashed corridors and into the bright sunlight of the temple's courtyard.

You hurry up the stairs to the temple and through the huge copper double doors.

The temple is dark after the brightness of the courtyard and the things you sense are the sweet smell of incense and the rattling of many sistrums.

As your eyes adjust, you see priests and others lining the brightly painted columns of the temple. They are looking towards the golden curtain that seals off the Holy of Holies from the rest of the temple. Only the senior priests and priestesses go in that room, for that is where the statue of [Isis or Osiris] is placed, far from the eyes of the profane. Only on special Holy Festivals is it brought from its resting place.

You are led down the aisle towards the golden curtain to where the High Priest is waiting. He is holding a wand in the shape of a lotus flower.

You are a little frightened of the High Priest because you have been told that he is the closest to the [God or Goddess] in the whole of the temple. He looks at you with kindly eyes and you relax.

The priestesses sing a hymn to [Isis or Osiris].

The High Priest turns and raises his wand towards the curtain and begins to chant the name of [Isis or Osiris]. The chant is taken up by the choir and seems to make the whole temple vibrate with a special power.

You are aware of a presence behind the curtain – a living, golden light.

The curtain parts and before you in all [his or her] glory is [Isis or Osiris].

Everyone falls to their knees.

You are drawn to meet the gaze of this being.

[Isis or Osiris] looks directly at you. But [his or her] look does not bring fear, only a deep feeling of love, love that you felt long before you were born.

"[Insert your real name]", says the [God or Goddess]. "Your parents were taken from you by fate, and as a result you are without an earthly [mother or father]. That which is your blood and body, is not the real you. You are a child of the stars, incarnating in a body of clay. Your true parents are the gods themselves – only most people forget it.

"You who are without earthly parents to distract you have the ability to realise your true parents and become the [son or daughter] of a [God or Goddess]. In the name of Amon, the hidden One, I declare in front of this assembly that [your full name] is now my [son or daughter]."

There is a stunned shock in the temple. This is a great honour, as few have had the right to declare that they were the son or daughter of a god.

[Osiris or Isis] walks over to you and embraces you.

There is a tremendous feeling of love, stability and security.

"Come with me, child of the Gods,"[He or She] says.

[He, she] takes you by the hand and leads you into the Holy of Holies.

The room is dark, lit by a single candle and the light radiating from the [God, or Goddess]. On a simple altar is a life sized statue of the [God or Goddess].

"My image is a gateway to me. Whenever you see it, it will call me. Whenever you need courage, whenever you need love, whenever you need security, guidance and support, all you need to do is look upon this image and I will be with you. For I am now your [mother or father], now and until the end of the age."

Look into the eyes of the [God or Goddess] and know that this is now your heritage and your future.

[Isis or Osiris] holds you in a deep and loving embrace. There is a joy which passes beyond time to this place and this reality. What was true in the pathworking is true now, [your name] is a true child of [Isis or Osiris]. When you open your eyes this will be so.

hEALING FOR ThE VICTIMS OF SEXUAL ABUSE

Sexual abuse in any form leaves a heavy legacy, often for a lifetime. If the abuse happened in childhood, it can mar the chance of a committed relationship. Rape often brings feelings of fear and distrust to sexual and emotional partnerships, where it is important to be open. Counselling and other therapy often enables a person to come to terms with the problem, particularly with those feelings that somehow they are responsible for the assault.

There are few outlets acceptable to the victim that enable a feeling of justice to be done. Most rapes and sexual assaults are never reported and when they are, they put the victim in an incredibly difficult position. Sometimes the attacker is another partner, under whom they live in total fear and unable to break free. In other cases it is parental sexual abuse, the truth is so horrible that it sometimes does not resurface until the attacker is dead. One of the things I have noticed about sexual abuse victims is that, once they have the bravery to face the fact that they have been attacked, there is an incredible anger – they feel that their attacker has somehow succeeded in hurting them and ruining their lives and gone unpunished.

This anger is the liberation of emotional energy from the emotional complex that has imprisoned it for years. It can last for years, leading to bitterness and a cynicism about life and relationships. Instead of healing, the person continues to be a victim, never mastering the situation. Sometimes they do have the strength to face their attacker in a court room. In my job as a reporter, I have seen many rape and sexual assault cases and can say that in a human court often nothing like justice is done. Even when the right person ends up behind bars, the victim feels that they have been through an ordeal that has doubled the sense of the unfairness of the whole thing. It is a pity, for if it all worked, then the situation could be incredibly cathartic.

This pathworking is designed to open a channel between the victim and cosmic justice. Its message is that not only will the Universe deal with any revenge that is required but it will correct any imbalance and allow the person to move on with their life.

The pathworking is incredibly intense for the person. They have to face their attacker and they have to reactivate their pain so it can be taken away by the universe. For this reason I suggest that it be performed by a nurturing group of people of the same sex. That is not to say it cannot be done by a male for a female or vice versa but there is always the risk that the person will project their anger and fear onto the nearest target like the attacker, and friendships can be lost in this way.

The pathworking is based around the concept of universal justice as exemplified by Egyptian goddess of Justice, Maat, who was considered so powerful that all life would have to come before her to be judged, including the other gods.

The Pathworking

Allow yourself to relax as much as possible. Regulate your breathing and allow these images to appear in your mind's eye.

Before you is a curtain, upon which is a picture of a set of golden scales.

The curtain parts, and standing before you is a being with a jackal head. This is Anubis.

He says: "Why do you seek the Temple of Maat?"

You reply: "I have been wronged and this wrong has created an imbalance, which is against the rule of Maat. I seek justice so that balance may be restored."

Anubis replies: "All calls for justice in the Temple of Maat are heard. Are you ready?"

If you agree, then the jackal-headed god will allow you to enter the gate. He says: "Enter thou then the halls of Justice, the place of truth, the Judgement Hall of Maat."

You find yourself in a vast Egyptian temple. It is the colour of flame.

Arranged in a semi-circle before you are figures, seated on thrones cut from red sandstone. They are dressed alike in kilts and a nemyss of black and yellow. Some are human, but others are animals. Each wears a necklace in the shape of a flying hawk and carries a flail in the left hand. These are the forty-two assessors, the force of cosmic justice that even judge the gods.

In front of them is a giant pair of scales.

Behind the scales is a beautiful woman, and on a crown upon her head is a feather, which represents truth. This is Maat; she is the force of cosmic balance, and just looking at her calms you further. This is a person to be trusted.

Maat asks you slowly and quietly to tell the story of what happened to you and, starting at the beginning, you recount everything you can remember. The court is hushed as you tell your story.

Maat comes from behind the scales.

She says: 'Every story has two sides. Therefore we must also hear the person you have accused. Be aware that in this place no harm can come to you, for there is not a god or demon who can withstand my power."

Then in a voice that commands the very atoms of life she says: "bring forth the accused."

A hawk-headed god enters. This is Horus and he has a sword in his right hand. In his left he holds a thick chain attached to four dog-faced demons. Between them, also chained and looking tiny and impotent is the accused. [She or He] looks at the scales with terror.

Maat approaches and asks him/her patiently to explain [his or her] side of the story. In the Halls of Truth it is impossible to lie. What does the person say?

Maat goes over to the accused and puts her hand deep into his chest. There is no blood, but she pulls out a ball of energy. This is the heart of the accused. Only in the Hall of Truth is this possible without the death of the person. She places the ball of light onto the scales.

You have the impression that something is being decided. The forty-two assessors are telepathically debating the merits of the case with exact precision.

They stretch out their arms, pointing their fingers towards the scales. The scales begin glowing with power.

Maat takes the Feather of Truth and places it upon the scales.

The scales sink on the side of the heart. The weight of the person's guilt is too heavy to support truth. There is a rumbling as the ground shakes slowly.

"My rule has been shaken by this unbalanced act. It is necessary to restore it and make the victim whole again," says Maat.

She turns to the guilty person. "You who have violated this fellow human and the rule of Maat are now free from my protection. Those dog-faced demons are your violent aspects, bestial and untamed. These are what you release onto others, creating harm."

Taking the Feature of Truth, she touches each of the dog-faced demons in turn.

"Therefore I have decided that each time these demons are released they will attack only you. This will happen in this lifetime and will continue to happen until you master these demons. This is the will of Maat."

Maat throws the heart to the nearest demon, who eats it hungrily.

The chains fall from the demons and the guilty person. [She or He] looks at them and flees the temple, closely followed by the demons who are biting at his or her heels.

Maat looks at you. "That is only part of the work of justice. Justice must be seen to heal the victim of the wrong that has been committed."

She leans into you and takes your heart. There is no pain, just a tingling.

She places it on the scales and puts her feather of Truth on the other side. But unlike the last time where there was judgement, she holds the scales in your favour, slowly moving them so that they are in perfect balance with her feather.

"I, who am the force of Cosmic Justice, restore your heart to perfect balance and harmony," she says.

She returns your heart to you. You feel momentarily dizzy as your heart moves to restore all the energy centres to their proper balance.

She looks at you: "Know this, Child of Earth, that you are truly healed and the rule of Maat is established in your very body. Go now with my blessing and live your life in balance and truth."

Still a little groggy, you thank Maat and leave via the door though which you entered.

FINDING ThE CENTRE

In times of stress it is important to be able to centre yourself and find that higher aspect of yourself. This will enable you to draw on the power of your own spiritual strength, giving you the courage to press ahead. This brief pathworking is designed to do that. Although it appears simple, it is extremely powerful, particularly when performed over time. Its simplicity means that it can be easily memorised and practised. Ideally it should be practised daily, as well as during times of stress.

The Pathworking

Visualise yourself inside the golden sphere at your heart. Before you is a great red rose. A beam of light comes from above your head, down your spine to connect to the rose, which slowly opens. You walk into it and there in its centre is a black cubic altar. On the altar, in a small golden cup, is a single flame. The flame is your Divine Spark, the real you that has built countless personalities through many incarnations. The flame is infinite, yet small and still. Commune with it. Feel it. Desire knowledge of it. Let it speak to you.

When you are finished, step back from the rose and see it close. Expand your consciousness to encompass the whole of your body. Feel the rose and flame in your heart.

Chapter Five

USING MYTHS

YTHS AND LEGEND contain many components that can be used in the construction of Inner Kingdoms or pathworkings. This is because they contain archetypal situations and powerful symbols which are essentially timeless. Encoded within the legends of its gods are formulae, which if unlocked by magical techniques can lead to the total regeneration of the self. One such formula – taken from the Egyptian Book of the Dead – was the cornerstone of the Golden Dawn system of magic. In its initiations, candidates were bought into the magical myth of the 'Judgment of Osiris', where their souls were judged by the 42 Assessors and awakened to the light of life. The Golden Dawn adepts in 1888 were even able to use the same legend as the skeleton for rituals that turned dead wood and metal into magical living talismans. But the 'Judgment of Osiris' is one formula derived from one small part of a single legend. There were many different myths, all with their own techniques and magical methods.

Carl Jung and Joseph Campbell both experimented extensively with myth as part of psychotherapy. Both of them were convinced of the universality of all myths to reflect the unconscious mind. I am uncertain if I wholly agree. Some cultures place subtly different emphasis on different aspects of archetypal symbols in accordance to their own world view. For example, a tribe which has lived in a single valley for hundreds of years worships a tree at the mouth of the valley. This tree is believed to be a guardian to the afterlife and spirits of ancestors are said to land on its top. Campbell would rightly identify this tree as a representative of the world tree, which is a gateway that links the underworld with heaven. However, the tribal priest would not say that. To him the tree is a place of fear because it stands on the path that leads to the outside world. The spirits that descend upon it are evil because they have not gone on to the afterlife. The tree does not reach heaven, only a half life hell.

In the Western Mystery Tradition we use many myths as part of our inner work and rituals. I know of one ritual group that bases its entire ritual working on the legend of Gareth, who starts out as a squire on his way to King Arthur's court. During the magic ritual the initiate symbolically becomes Gareth and then the pathworking is read out. The aim of this is for the initiate to take on the qualities of Gareth and learn the lessons that he does during the legend.

So powerful are these archetypes that sometimes they are known to bite the people who use them unwisely. For example, there was a Romano-British re-enactment group I know of who adopted the titles of characters from the Arthurian myth as part of their performances. This worked well for a number of years until the person playing Lancelot ran off with 'Arthur's' wife. 'Arthur' took refuge in the arms of a woman who was not involved in the group, ironically called Morgan. 'Gawain' was arrested in a bar room brawl and there was general dissatisfaction with the way 'Arthur' was running the group. More than half the group sided with 'Arthur' and the others with the person who called himself 'Mordred'. It all got nasty and the group dissolved.

So how is it possible to take the raw material of a legend and use it in a pathworking programme? Obviously the body of mythology is vast but to use as a case study this book will look at a single legend in the Egyptian Mythos – that of Horus and Set. By looking at the approach adopted here, it should be possible to adapt any myths and legends into useful pathworkings or other imaginative experiments. Let us look at the myth first.[47]

ThE LEGEND OF hORUS AND SET

Osiris was the greatest and most wise king, but his brother Set desired his kingdom. He killed him by cutting his body into many pieces and distributed them all over Egypt.

Osiris's wife and sister Isis gathered the parts of Osiris and joined them to make him whole again – all except the phallus, which had been swallowed by a fish. She built Osiris a phallus of gold, then with her magic she bought him back to life for long enough to have sex.

From that union she gave birth to their son Horus, who began a series of wars with Set for control of the two lands.

---

47 This version of the legend was painted on the temple walls at Edfu in Egypt. It was translated by Margaret Murray, *Ancient Egyptian Legends* (John Murray, London, 1913).

From the moment of his birth, Horus has been at war with Set and some say this battle has never been resolved. Horus suffered at Set's hands until he learnt the arts of war. Then Set refused him battle, always preferring to strike when Horus was not ready and unable to bring his strength to bear. But finally, after years of inconclusive war, the ruler of the gods, Ra, declared Set an outcast and rallied a massive army to fight him.

Set fled to Nubia and Ra barged his troops down the Nile to do battle. At Thest-Hoor, Ra was joined by Horus Edfu, whose name means harpooner and hero. For it is said that Horus Edfu enjoyed fighting Set more than rejoicing.

Thoth, the god of magic and wisdom, appeared to Horus and gave him the ability to change himself into a great sun disk with sunset-coloured wings. Thus Horus, as a great winged sun disk, sat on the prow of Ra's boat, his power flashed upon the waters of the Nile and he sensed Set's army as they waited in ambush.

Horus rose into the air and with a mighty burst of power pronounced a mighty curse: "Your eyes shall be blinded and ye shall not see. Your ears shall be deaf and ye shall not hear."

The followers of Set were thrown into confusion. When a man saw his neighbour he thought that he was looking at a stranger and their own language sounded foreign. Some killed each other, while the rest fled.

But the Winged Sun disk Horus was unable to find Set, who was hiding with his main army in the marshes of the north country. Horus returned and Ra gave him wine mixed with water – which is still poured as a libation to Horus Edfu.

Then the followers of Set shape-shifted themselves, becoming crocodiles and hippopotami, who can live under water and whose thick skins can turn a sharp spear. They rushed upon the barge of Ra, seeking to overturn it. But Horus was ready for them.

He had ordered magical arrows and spears to be made with magical words and spells cast over them. When the fierce beasts came out of the water, the Followers of Horus let fly with their magical arrows and charged with their spears. The magic metal pierced the hides and reached the hearts of the wicked animals, killing 650 of them.

The rest fled – those who faced the South ran the fastest for they were being chased by Horus Edfu and his followers. The followers of Set were defeated twice near Denderah, Hathor's city. This was the end of Set's armies in the South. But in the marshes of the North, Set and his followers waited. They had shape-shifted into crocodiles and lay hidden in the water.

Horus ordered his army to silence, as they searched for four days and nights for Set's followers. On the fifth day Horus found the ambush and he and his followers again routed his enemies – this time bringing back 142 prisoners to the boat of Ra.

The followers of Set made for the North. When they came to the western waters of the Mert, where an ally of Set had his house, they stopped. Horus followed but lost Set's army.

At the house of Rerhu, Ra told Horus where Set and his army were, and Horus marched his troops towards the rival army. They came to the point where the never-setting stars wheel around a certain point in the sky and on the banks of Mert the battle began.

Again the followers of Horus were victorious. Horus executed 181 of the prisoners before Ra's boat and gave their weapons to his followers. Now Set came out of his hiding place and he boasted he would destroy Horus.

The wind bore the words of his boasting to Ra, who told Thoth to "cause these high words to be cast down". Horus attacked Set and his army. In the thick of the battle Horus thought he had found Set. He bound his arms and tied his staff across him so that he could make no sound and placed his weapon at his throat. Horus dragged Set to Ra, who told him that he could do as he wished with his father's murderer. Horus struck Set in the head cutting him open to his back, he cut off the head and cut the body into many pieces.

Thus he treated Set's body as Set had treated his father's. This took place on the first month of the season when the earth appears after the flooding of the Nile. But it was not Set whom Horus had killed, but his ally. Set changed himself into a mighty snake and entered into the earth. No one saw this, but since he was fighting against the gods, they were aware of what happened.

Horus waited in the barge of Ra for six days and six nights, waiting to see if there were any followers of Set left – but they were all corpses on the water. Then Horus and his followers searched the two lands for his enemies and slew 106 in the East and 106 from the West – these they slew before Ra in his sanctuaries.

Ra gave to Horus and his followers two cities which are called the Mesen cities, for the followers of Horus are Mesenti, the metal workers. In the shrines of the Mesen, Horus is the god and his secret ceremonies are held on four days of the year.

Now the followers of Set gathered together. Horus of Edfu transformed himself into the likeness of a lion with the face of a man – his arms were of flint and on his head was the Atef crown which is the white crown of the North, with the feathers and horns, and on either side is a crowned serpent.

He routed this army, which took to the sea. Thoth calmed the waves of the ocean and the wind was lulled, but there was no enemy in sight. Horus' navy sailed around the coast of Africa until they came to Nubia, where he saw Set's followers gathered. Horus shape-shifted into a great winged disk and on either side of him came the goddesses Nekhbet and Uazet in their form of great hooded snakes with crowns upon their heads.

On Nekbet was the white crown on the South, while on Uazet was the red crown of the North. And the gods on the boat of Ra cried out, "See how he places himself between the two goddesses. Behold how he overcomes his adversaries."

After the battle, the followers of Set were routed, Ra – his boat moored at Thest-Hoor – ordered that on the main entrance to every temple in the two lands should be carved the winged sun disk with Nekhbet and Uazet flanking it. After months and years Set came forth and challenged Horus in the presence of Ra.

And Horus came forth with his followers on their boats with their glittering armour and weapons with handles of worked wood, cords and spears. Isis made golden ornaments for the prow of the boat and laid within it magic words and spells. Set took the form of a red hippopotamus and came from the South with his allies to meet Horus Edfu.

At the Elephantine the two armies met. Set stood up and spoke a great curse against Horus and Isis. He said, "Let there be a great wind and a raging tempest." At once a storm broke over the boats of Horus and his followers, the wind roared and the water was lashed into great waves. But Horus held on his way, and through the darkness of the storm and the foam of the waves gleamed his great golden prow. Horus shape-shifted into the form of a young man, eight cubits high with a harpoon.

The blade of the harpoon was four cubits, the shaft was 20 cubits and a chain of 60 cubits was welded to it. Horus held the weapon over his head as if it were a reed and he threw it at Set, who was waiting in the deep waters, waiting for people to fall from Horus' boat. The harpoon pierced Set's brain and killed him.

EXAMINING ThE MYTh

Firstly, when you look at a myth, it is important to work out what the central theme is. This may not be as obvious as it seems. Here we appear to have a standard good-against-evil, with an awful lot of fighting involved. On the face of it, this is a story of wars and battles between two gods and would have very little to do with magic.

Indeed it seems likely that the story of the wars of Horus could be a legendary recounting of the battles between two historical factions, the Followers of Horus (the Shemsu Hor) and the Followers of Set (the Smayu Net Set). The Shemsu Hor drew its members from every district in Egypt – probably only those highly placed in the military and administration. In later years the Pharaoh's retinue and supporters were called the Shemsu Hor. Their symbol was the golden standard – a hawk. Of the Followers of Set there is less known, and this is probably because, if the legends are true, the Followers of Horus must have almost wiped them out.

In the second Dynasty, a member of the Followers of Set became Pharaoh, taking the name Set-Peribsen. This led to a split in the country between the Shemsu Hor and the Smayu Net Set, which was only resolved when Peribsen's successor, Khasekhemwy, attempted to heal the division by giving both Horus and Set equal importance. However, there are elements to this legend that go beyond history. It features magical elements like shape-shifting and archetypal symbols which, if used magically, will result in transformation.

Transformation, the transmutation of base metals into gold, the fusing of the lower personality with the will of the higher, is the goal of the apprentice seeking mastery of magic. It is not surprising that the home of alchemy, Ancient Egypt, provides the techniques for transformation within its system of religious magic.

So, having uncovered the theme of transformation, we next start to pull apart the different aspects of the myth into their various components. The easiest way is to meditate on each aspect of the myth and try to find a deeper meaning to what is going on.

In the legend of the wars between Set and Horus we have to look for the many elements that show how it is a magical formula for transformation – both magically and psychologically – to remodel the self in the mould of its higher nature.

There are many different levels in which to read this legend. Psychologically, Horus represents the divine child, the true self that gradually becomes aware of its true nature. Set, then, is not only his personal shadow, but the darker aspects of his racial heritage. This is hinted at in the family tree of the gods in the legend. Set was Osiris's dark brother, who was able to destroy him. Horus therefore inherited his father's shadow – hence the Judeo-Christian concept of the sins of the fathers being visited on the sons. Initially Horus is ill-equipped to face these sins and loses battles to Set.

This is indicative of the state when the newly awakened divine consciousness continues to try to follow the patterns of society and lower habit, resulting in the stunting of spiritual growth. But then Horus learns the arts of the warrior – he learns to fight against his environment and discipline himself against those things which stand in the way of development.

But this is only the first stage. The young spiritual warrior finds himself continually at odds with the greater shadow. Sometimes he wins a small victory, but mostly the shadow of Set strikes when he is least expected, and injures Horus. It is only when the greater self – the Higher Self, which is depicted in this legend by Ra – decides that action must be taken against the Shadow, that the war really begins in earnest.

So far, the emerging self has only arranged small skirmishes with Set; now he meets up with the higher self and its legions to do serious work which will free it, and a piece of humanity, from the shadow's grip. This meeting happens at Thest, which is derived from the Egyptian concept of balance and 'half way'. The higher self moves down the levels of spirit and meets the ascending aspiring personality half way. It is a state represented by the symbol of the hexagram or Star of David, with its two interlocking triangles, one pointing up and the other down. Horus is often depicted carrying a spear, guarding the prow of Ra's boat. Ra is behind him but Horus carries out all the fighting in the legend.

This is a partial integration of the aspiring personality with the higher. It is familiar to most occultists who have reached the level known as 'knowledge and conversation with the Holy Guardian Angel'. In this, the higher personality telepathically communicates with the lower, either in the form of dreams, inspirations, or with a 'still clear' voice. In common terms, this is the voice of the conscience. Horus is given the power to transform himself into a sun disk by the god Thoth. This is an interesting stage in development. Communication between the higher self and the lower is still not clear enough for important specifics to be passed down, because the lower self still sees itself as separate from the higher.

So the higher self calls upon an aspect of itself to whom the lower self can communicate. This is the doctrine of the masters, or highly evolved beings, or gods, who are often seen assisting a personality to the light. In this case Horus's Thoth contact teaches him how to build an astral vehicle that will enable him ascend the levels and deal with the shadow at a more profound level. The winged sun disk symbol, which yields much to meditation, is a link to the divine self and brings with it some of the higher self's magical powers.

The first time Horus ascends, he sees the followers of Set waiting in ambush and pronounces a curse against them which prevents them seeing or hearing. He magically breaks down the cohesive power of the shadow by forcing each 'sin' to stand alone so that it can be destroyed. This is very successful, but can only be partial because some aspects of the shadow reside in complexes too deep for Horus to approach at this time. Although this legend is smeared with violence, death and killing, this is only a blind to appeal to the child-like mind of the lower self – after all, legends were written for the immature mass mind.

But the Ancient Egyptians had a strong belief in the afterlife and saw death – whether by war or natural causes – as a transformation from one life to another. In using psycho-magical techniques nothing is killed, it is just transformed into something more useful. After Horus's first victory the way is clear for the higher self to reward Horus with wine and water. Wine in this case is a symbol of the blood, and its dilution refers to a refinement and purification of the life force contained in the blood.

It is said that the blood of the adept is more refined than an ordinary person's. This is one of the reasons why the legends of Atlantis talk of breeding programmes, where priests and kings were not allowed to mate outside their caste, to keep bloodlines pure. This refined blood activates other physical centres, that enable the aspiring self to ascend still further. It is this gift of Ra that enables Horus to start on the next stage of his training – which is to refine and perfect the metallic substances in his body and aura so that they can be used as weapons against the shadow.

This is the work of metallic alchemy which is in its initial stages. This means the refining of the elements within the personality – rather than transmutation. Thus Horus is seen forging metal weapons and chanting magical words into their composition. Magically, this represents the magician working with the planetary forces to enable them to become clear channels through the personality. The battle at this point is with the negative aspects ascribed to planetary influence.

It has been said that you cannot change the stars that you are born under and you have to live with their positive and negative effects. Yet, by the refining of the positive aspects of the planets using planetary alchemy, Horus and his followers defeat Set's followers yet again.

There are now two battles around Denderah, the City of Hathor. Cow-headed Hathor was the ultimate mother goddess – often associated with the heavens, and was the female counterpart to Thoth. Horus at this point is dealing with the creative aspects of himself – he is discovering the Mother.

Although this version of the legend does not mention it, later versions speak of Isis actually helping Set to defeat her son. Reducing the legend to a human relationship, where a shadow is allowed to develop to the extent that it destroys one partner and carries on into another generation, the surviving partner must shoulder some of the blame for failing to help destroy the shadow. Worse, they must also accept responsibility for passing that sin on into the other generation.

This is clearly true in the extreme case of physical and sexual abuse, which is a problem that passes through generations. It takes two battles to deal with this issue and this brings to an end the war for Upper Egypt (or the unconscious). Set did not really dwell in Upper Egypt, all these battles were just clearing up the subjective results of the shadow.

Now it is time for Horus and the armies of Ra to meet the shadow in its more tangible aspects. In the war for the North of Egypt, much time is spent trying to find the enemy. There are no longer any subjective results to look for, so a problem is harder to find and tackle. Horus manages to find Set the first time by ordering his army to silence. Like the quieting of the self that is carried out in meditation, he stills himself entirely.

This is not the sort of meditation which Horus had previously practiced, which was more active. It is the deeper meditation that the Zen Buddhists have mastered, where all aspects of the self are brought to calm. Now Horus can still the unconscious so that it provides a near perfect reflection of the astral worlds above.

In doing so he encounters the first armies of the followers of Set and defeats them. This is the first time we hear of Horus taking prisoners after a battle, which is because the powers that had previously done him harm can be used in a positive way if turned to their correct purpose. This is why Horus brings them to the higher self – Ra – to be judged (to see if they should be integrated).

The followers of Set retreat further, hoping to escape to the Great Green Sea (the collective unconscious). They stop at the house of one of

Set's followers on the banks of Mert. This represents a major complex – for Mert was feminine and represented the night.

One of the Mert goddesses was Set's estranged wife – Nephthys. (She had slept with Osiris, giving birth to Anubis, perhaps suggesting a shadow aspect of Isis.) Horus once again cannot find the followers of Set, but at the house of Rertu (who was a hippopotamus goddess associated with Set) Ra tells him where to find them.

This is another instance where the higher self steps in to advise clearly when the lower self has run out of ideas. Horus, because of his victories in the South, knows the effects of a corrupted mother image. By approaching it in its higher aspects, he is able to come to terms with it enough to face it properly.

This battle takes place where 'the never setting stars wheel around a certain point in the sky'. It is a place of stillness, where Horus discovers the horrors of a corrupted mother image and sees its projections on the zodiac of his life. He has ceased to deal with the problem piecemeal and returns to the centre of his being to deal with the root cause.

In the battle he captures 'prisoners' and takes them to Ra. But this time the 'prisoners' cannot be controlled and Horus kills them. But he does take their weapons – in other words he transmutes their ability to hurt him into the more useful project of destroying the shadow.

Now Set himself comes forth. This is the great personal shadow, the Dweller on the Threshold, who is now nearing the end of his rulership. However, Set is still confident and boasts that he will destroy Horus. He is using the power of words, which framed in a particular way can bring about new images of destruction on the lower self.

But this time the higher self, in its Thoth aspect, intervenes to stop Set creating new images, and enabling the battle to be fought fairly. If left to itself, the consciousness will make more mistakes and programme the lower self with new complexes. In this case, the higher magical aspect of the self can assist by stopping these images before they start and creating new ones.

Through ritual, meditation or pathworking techniques, it is possible to neutralise the creation of new and faulty complexes. In the final battle, Set is captured by Horus. Set's arms are bound and Horus has tied his staff over his mouth so that he cannot speak. In other words, Horus has neutralised his personal shadow through will power.

By the time of this last battle with the personal Set, Horus is equipped magically to deal with his own shadow. When he appears, Horus can silence him. Horus takes his shadow to Ra, who says that

141

he can do what he likes with Set. Once this victory is accomplished, the Dweller on the Threshold in his current form is of no use for anything, so Horus kills him and hacks the body into as many pieces as Set had Osiris. Set at this point becomes an Osiris, a symbol of life and rebirth.

The legend is hinting that the shadow has begun the slow process of integration with the rest of the personality. This was enacted ritually when the flood waters of the Nile pulled back to reveal the fertile land. It is the point where the adept (to use Golden Dawn terminology) has crossed the boundaries between the outer and inner order. Now he begins to work magic for humanity rather than himself and seeks to damage Set in the wider world.

The legend reveals that Set has not been killed after all. Set is a cosmic force and cannot be killed as such. Horus has purged Set from the little bay that is his personality – but mankind has a shadow too and it is this greater Set who must be faced by the adept. In the legend, this greater Set turns himself into a snake and enters the Earth.

The higher self is aware of this, and while the lower self rejoices at his new found integration, warns him that the war is not yet over. This comes as a shock to the lower self because until this point it has been allowed to see itself as separate from the rest of humanity.

Now, if it is going to proceed personally, its destiny lies with helping humanity to deal with Set. New armies of Set begin to appear, perhaps because of self-doubt at the greatness of this task, and the pressures on the lower self now to integrate. Horus, however, in his meditative state, is able to destroy these niggles with new found power.

He searches the two lands for minor complexes that stand in the way of total integration with the higher self. This is what is indicated when it is said 'he slew the followers of Set before Ra in his sanctuaries'. Horus has now achieved unity. Ra gives him two cities, both of which are connected to metal working.

This links Horus to the arts of metal alchemy, the secrets of which he now perfects to take on the next stage of the Great Work. Ra seems almost to disappear from the legend at this point, as do most of the gods, other than Set and Thoth (who represents Horus's magical aspects). This is because Horus (lower self) is so integrated with Ra (higher self) that they cease to be separate identities. They are the hexagram – two that are one. This is the work of the grade that the Golden Dawn referred to as Adeptus Minor, although many of its adepts failed to live up to what was expected of this grade.

Dion Fortune described it as when the person becomes an Initiate (which she spelt with a capital I). We now begin to see Horus shape-shifting. The first form he uses is the image of a lion with arms of flint, a man's face wearing the Atef crown (the 'white crown' of Upper Egypt, flanked by two horns and two feathers). The lion is the alchemical symbol which stands for natural power – the raw, sex power of the lower self. By having a human head, this indicates that Horus is now able to place this power under will and is able to project it outwards. The green flint arms represent the ability to remove the fire from the natural kingdom of earth and bring it forth. This is a hint that natural power, represented by the lion, draws its force from the earth.

W.E. Butler said that this power comes directly from the planetary being and the earth's heart. The heart of this power was often depicted as being emerald green and could be the prototype for the green stone of the grail legends.

The Atef crown symbolizes the state of consciousness of the adept. The two feathers indicate that this rule of the Inner Kingdom is attained by balance – personified by the goddess Maat, whose symbol is a feather. The two horns indicate Hathor, the unconscious mind (represented in the Tarot by Key Two, the High Priestess) which has been stilled and raised upwards towards the one. The crown's twin serpents are similar to the Greek caduceus and represent the natural energies rising upwards to merge with the One.

Mastery of this force can be obtained by meditating on the crown and the form of Horus with a lion's body and the head of a young boy – but bear in mind that this is a point where the higher self is totally identified with the lower self.

The series of battles Horus is fighting at this point in the legend is still fairly close to his own self. It is the evil he sees in his own immediate environment. Set and his followers have escaped to the Great Sea, which as described earlier, represents the collective unconscious. In this turbulent mass it is much harder to find the root causes of complexes.

To remedy this problem Thoth calms the waves to enable Set's navy to be seen. This is the effect that an Initiate has on the mass mind; they are the peacemakers, to whom Jesus Christ referred in his sermon on the mount. But the effect has a function, which is not to create peace for its own sake but to reveal the deeper problems and complexes of the mass mind so that they may be corrected. The stillness fails to reveal the forces of Set, who have long since fled deep into the aspects of the lower mass mind. They are unable to immediately affect the life of the two lands, but in the long term they can repair and return.

Horus and Ra sail around Africa, searching for the armies of Set and finally locate him in Nubia (the deepest aspect of the mass mind). Horus uses a very high powered technique to destroy the armies – he shape-shifts into the winged sun disk, with the twin snake gods Nekhbet and Uazet, wearing their red and white crowns, flanking him. Previously in his form of a lion with a human face, he has used the earth power to destroy the Set beasts. Now he becomes an embodiment of that power, the Solar Logos, or intelligence, using the powers of the Land.

At the legend's end, Set's influence has all but been removed from humanity and Horus is given his rewards. But the battles are far from over, as Horus must face Set again at the end of the great cosmic cycle. In those times Set will challenge humanity's rights in the presence of the Cosmic Ra and humanity will come forth armed with the weapons of its experience – our bodies glowing with the power of spiritual alchemy. The aspects of our collective unconscious will buffet us for the last time, but we will overcome it. Set will rise up and will be transmuted by us, so that we will become the vision of the One for which we were intended.

IMAGINATIVE TECHNIQUES DERIVED FROM THE LEGEND

Having pulled apart a legend as much is possible, now it is time to work out ways that you can use the magical power of the imagination to bring it to life. The following are two magical techniques that have been developed using the 'Battles of Horus' legend.

A reader could, without too much difficulty, develop pathworkings, or rituals, using other parts of the legend. The first is a pathworking which is designed to transmute part of the personality so that it can overcome a particular complex. It should be used at the climax of any personality work into a particular problem or habit.

This is a 'lighter version' of the technique that we used in the last chapter. Unlike that one, however, it is not personalized and relies on the psychic pressure caused by the legend's symbolism to bring about change. The effect is to plant a suggestion deep into the unconscious and, on another level, to show the self a new reality.

What is unusual about this particular pathworking is that it incorporates a technique called godform working. A magician using a

144

godform seeks to unify with the power and images that the godform represents. In this case the magician so strongly identifies with Horus Edfu that he will seek to destroy the Set beast and will not succumb to it. The godform will supply powers that are above the personality at that time.

hORUS'S SPEAR

Sit comfortably in a chair with your feet flat on the ground. Shift your attention to the Yesod centre, which is at the groin area – see it as a ball of vibrating, spinning, violet light. Imagine a six inch statue of the god Horus forming at the centre of this light. See it as hawk-headed, armour clad and holding a large spear – like a harpoon.

Now imagine that high above your head is the star Sirius. Visualise a beam of light coming from that star, through the top of your head, down your spine and connecting with the statue. See the statue come alive, breathe and grow, until it is just about as tall as your nose.

Then slowly enter into the mind of the god Horus Edfu, until you feel that you are the mighty god. Look with his eyes, hear with his ears, for now you are Horus.

Visualise the following…

Before you is a pylon gate of pink sandstone, with a winged sun-disk across its top lintel. On the other side is the mystical land of Khem – Egypt – the land of the Legend.

Drawing a deep breath, you walk through the door into a sea of silver mist.

The mist clears and you are standing on the fertile Eastern banks of the Nile. It is a hot morning and there is not a cloud in the sky.

You feel that it is just the sort of day for an adventure and you and your followers are planning an expedition to find one. You are saluting the sun with your spear when you hear the drums of approaching ships – a war fleet.

Excitedly, you look down the Nile to see bank upon bank of ships navigating their way up the river. Their sails are of gold and all bear the device of the hawk-headed Sun god Ra-Hoor.

Leading the flotilla is the mighty barge of Ra and you strain your eyes to see the mighty god on his throne at the back of the boat.

The sight takes your breath away, but the image brings with it a feeling of sadness – for Ra-Hoor and you share the same symbol but he is mighty and all powerful and you are just a refugee from your uncle's attacks.

"Where are they going?" you wonder, for this is the sort of adventure that you would like to join. You rush to your followers, who are making ready your boat for your hunting trip. You bid them to hurry and together you push your boat into the water.

You initially intend to join the wings of the flotilla, but much to your surprise you see a signal from Ra-Hoor's flag ship signalling you come alongside. With some steering, you navigate your tiny boat into the shadow of the mighty flagship. Then there is another signal. Ra-Hoor wants you and your followers to come on board.

Your mind is a whirl as you run your boat alongside the ship and throw mooring ropes to draw you alongside. A ladder is lowered over the side of the flag ship and you climb. As you emerge over the side of the boat, you find your feet on rich pink and gold carpet. But your eyes are instantly drawn to the mighty golden throne that towers above the deck.

Sitting on the throne, masked in a great golden hawk's mask, is Ra-Hoor. You bow before him. You notice at his feet is a magnificent war spear that seems to glow with magical power. You rise to look at him but Ra-Hoor does not say a word. "My Lord Ra cannot speak with you at this time." There is a voice gentle as a summer wind.

You look up and see the ibis-headed god Thoth. In his hands he holds an ankh cross (which is a cross but with a loop on the upper arm). "However, he bids me to ask you to stand your guard in the prow of his boat. Is this acceptable to you?"

You eagerly nod and ask, "Who is my Lord's enemy that he shall be my enemy?" Thoth replies: "Our enemy is indeed thine – for it is the slayer of your father Osiris: your uncle Set, whom we seek to kill." Your hand instinctively tightens around your spear at the mention of your uncle's name.

"It would give me great pleasure to help Ra-Hoor in his quest – for indeed revenge for my father's death has been my goal from before I was born," you tell Thoth. You bow and take the place of honour at the prow of Ra's boat.

Hours pass with nothing happening but the sound of water rushing against the prow of the barge. But you remain alert, for you know that your uncle will only attack when you least expect it. Then your sharp eyes see it – a mile off.

A crocodile?

No, something much bigger.

A hippopotamus? Much bigger.

Then it dawns on you. It is something that has always frightened you. A nameless beast that your Uncle Set used to frighten you with when you were small.

You grip your spear and yell a warning to the fleet. The warning is shouted along the fleet and you see warriors grabbing their bows and arrows.

Yes, good, you think.

Kill the thing before it can get close and sink our boats.

At your command they send wave after wave of arrows at the creature. But the arrows seem to be turned long before they get to the beast. Invisible shields of energy smash the arrows aside before they get close.

The creature does not seem to want to move, but bars the way for the fleet.

"How do we kill something that cannot be killed?" you say to yourself out loud.

"We make a special weapon," says a voice, and you turn to see Thoth.

"What weapon can get through the many shields that creature has?" you ask.

"Something like this," says Thoth, and in his hands he holds Ra's spear. But before you can take it he says: "Each spear belongs to the man who must cast it. It becomes magically empowered by every evil that is killed. You must make your own magic spear, Horus."

"But how? I don't even know metal working skills."

Thoth says: "I, who am the teacher of all things, shall teach you."

Ra orders the fleet to moor at the side of the river and you and Thoth leave the boat. You walk along a path until you come to a wayside temple. Over the door is the winged sun-disk.

Thoth tells you to take from the temple a vessel of holy water. As you enter, you find yourself in a tiny room. At one end is a statue of your mother Isis and in her lap is a silver bowl of water.

With a courteous nod to your mother's statue, you take the water and join Thoth. Before him is a great ladle, a mighty hammer, and a cubic stone anvil.

Then together you gather wood into a pile for the fire. "Not too much, hawk fledgling," says Thoth. "For this fire needs no fuel."

"Then why have any wood at all?" you ask.

"There must be some kind of sacrifice for the divine fire to touch earth," replies Thoth.

Once the fire is ready, Thoth lifts his arms towards the Sun and calls a mighty name of power. Note what this name is. A ray of sunlight strikes the wood. But you notice that the fire does not burn, it just seems to dwell there, turning the wood white hot.

"Where are we going to get the magical metal to smelt?" you ask.

Thoth smiles and reaches into your body. It does not hurt, it just tickles. He takes his hand out and opens it and you see a ball of metal about the size of a fist. Note what type of metal that Thoth is holding.

Thoth tells you to place it into the ladle and into the heart of the divine fire. Soon the metal has melted, but the top of it is covered with a black crust. You scrape the crust from the top of the metal and throw it into the heart of the fire, where it burns to nothing.

Taking the ladle from the fire, you pour the molten metal into the water. The water steams and the metal explodes, but becomes hard before it can escape the water.

The metal is contorted into a strange shape that reminds you of one of the followers of Set; but as you wash it in the holy water, it becomes totally clean and pure. Now the metal is purified, it is time to make it into the spear point.

Thoth takes Ra's spear and pushes it into the ground to form a mould. Then you melt the ingot again in the fire. This time, the metal is clear and bright and glows with a rainbow of colours. Then Thoth teaches you a chant to sing to the metal that is within the flame. This may be a word of power, or it may be a vibration, it may even be a repetition of your mystery name or motto, but after a while the metal starts to boil with a new light. You then pour it into the hole in the ground made by Ra's spear. The metal bubbles for a minute and then darkens as it cools and hardens.

You dig the spear point from the earth and hold it to the light. You are disappointed because it is only roughly spear shaped. As if detecting your disappointment, Thoth smiles: "What, fledgling – you think that a magical spear can be made without work?" He gives you a hammer and tells you to beat the spear into shape. You hold the spear point in the sacred flame to warm it, place it upon the cubic forge and then strike it hard.

Bang! With each strike of the hammer, Thoth recites a litany of names of power – some are of gods, others you do not know, but soon the vibration of these names starts to affect you.

Bang! The names seem to be passing through you, down the hammer and being stamped on the spear point.

Every now and then you quench the point in the water and start over again. Soon the spear point is bright and as sharp as a razor. But more than that, it seems to glow with power. Taking your old spear, you remove its point and cast it into the sacred fire.

Then you place the new point on the old staff. Thoth seems to grunt with satisfaction and you think that your spear looks much better than Ra's original. The pair of you board the boat, and at Ra's command, the fleet moves towards the waiting Set fiend, with you standing at the prow of the boat, your spear at the ready.

The Set fiend seems to sense your presence and this time turns to attack. Closer and closer he comes, foam spraying outwards from his limbs.

You see teeth, dark red eyes and for a brief moment you are gripped by a fear. You realize that you are on the peripheries of the beast's shields and you are starting to feel its power.

Its head comes out of the water spraying foam, its jaws speaking of death and destruction to the fleet. You aim your spear and cast it towards the foul head with all the strength in your body. The spear sings as it leaves your hands.

The creature's shields move like tentacles to snatch the spear from the air, but the spear just passes through them. The spear hits the creature between the eyes and it lets out a mighty bellow – a thousand screams of fear, pain, tears and terror. Images come rushing to your mind – incidents from your current life, each charged with emotion and power.

Then you discover the nature of the beast you have killed and the power you have released. The beast dissolves into thin air and the world is quiet again.

There is a buzzing noise and instinctively you lift your hand in front of your face. You clasp your spear, for somehow it has returned to you. You look at the spear tip – it is clean. It is as if the beast had never been. But as you hold the spear, you realize that it has more power than before. It is glowing with the magic that the Set fiend had imprisoned in itself.

You turn to face Ra and bow. Ra raises his sceptre of power and says:

"Behold Horus Edfu. Mighty is he, slayer of the Set beast. Surely shall he inherit his father's kingdom".

You have won a small victory in a big war, but from this victory you have the key to win other battles. Before you is the pylon gate. You step through it and into this time and place.

You sit in your body and visualize the statue of Horus Edfu shrinking. See the beam of light from Sirius free itself from the statue and your body. See the statue shrink until it is a speck and the centre of Yesod stops spinning and grows dim. Be aware of your own body and personality. It is a personality that has been reformed by the victory of Horus.

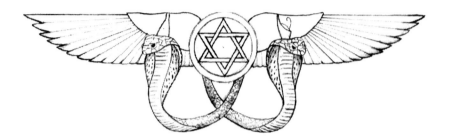

TЬE WINGED SUN DISK

The purpose of this pathworking is to ascend above emotional problems and see life as it really is. It is like a miniature version of the Inner Kingdom working that we looked at in Chapter Two. With practice, it is possible to see the people you associate with, your workmates, your family, from a hawk-like perspective.

You will see people operating within a symbolic framework which cannot be taken too literally; however, it will enable you to see where people are coming from, where they are going and how they will influence your life.

With skill at this exercise, it is possible while talking to someone to rise above the situation and see where they are coming from. It should also be possible to start seeing things that are coming up in your own life and problems that you will be expected to face.

Keep a record of your visions and when you start to notice that they are 'proving true' then start acting on them.

The process:
1. Perform the complete Middle Pillar exercise (see Chapter Six).
2. Focus on a sphere of light above your head. Equate that with infinite divine power.
3. Draw down power, like you would in a middle pillar exercise, but stop it in the mid-brain area.
4. See this light spiral into a sphere that fills your brain with power, move your consciousness so that you are sitting within this sphere.

5. In your mind's eye, place your hands over your face and see them slowly turn into wings. The wings should be the colour of sunset – turquoise, carnelian and lazuli, shot with gold.

6. Stretch out your wings, move and flap them, so that the disk of fire, in which your consciousness is placed, begins to ascend.

7. Feel your emotions and automatic mind fall away as you rise upwards.

8. What is immediately below you is your personal world – you see people, and inner world beings, that are important to you. Further away from you are distant friends, associates and contacts that are of less importance to you at the moment.

9. Watch the way these people interact. What symbols are attached to them? What is happening to them?

10. If you want to get a close up view of a person, or situation, see an Eye of Horus appear before your face and look through it.

11. Look at the body of yourself. What is happening to you? What needs to be done?

12. When you are finished, sink down into your body. Close the wings about your face. Let the light withdraw to the crown centre.

13. Perform a Cabbalistic Cross (see Chapter Six).

The winged sun disk exercise has many magical uses, ranging from long distance communication and healing to self and interpersonal discovery. My own experience in this technique has proved to me that it is very effective at neutralizing the emotional clouds that prevent you making a decision at a time of crisis.

Chapter Six

IMAGINATION AS A MYSTICAL TOOL

THROUGHOUT THIS BOOK we have looked at the use of imagination to access mental, emotional and psychological states of consciousness. However, there is another state of consciousness which so far has only been hinted at. This is because its use has been a heavily veiled secret in the various mystical and magical schools. I am talking about the use of imagination to actually link to the divine. I do not mean something like we have experienced with the Olympic Spirits, which is more like communication, but more of a mystic union with deity.

When I say veiled secret, some aspects of the various techniques have been published, usually by those who have stumbled across them as part of their mystical experiences rather than by occult training. However, specific mention of the use of imagination in attaining these mystical states is usually only made obliquely rather than using anything like specifics.

Earlier I said that the Inner Kingdoms which we access in our imaginations are real and that our imagination is not so much creating them as giving us the vision to see them. If this is true of our own physiological, emotional and mental states, it must also be true of the higher spiritual realms that are behind them. I would go further and say that it is extremely hard to experience spiritual states without the language of imagination to understand them. If you look at any documented religious experience, it is usually packed full of imagery which had meaning in the mind of the person who experienced it.

Take for example the religious experiences of the Biblical prophet Ezekiel, who experienced angels and a vision of God. Have a look the first chapter, it is packed full of imaginative symbolism.

"4: And I looked, and, behold, a whirlwind came out of the north, a great cloud, and a fire infolding itself, and a brightness was about it, and out of the midst thereof as the colour of amber, out of the midst of the fire. 5: Also out of the midst thereof came the likeness of four living creatures. And this was their appearance; they had the likeness of a man. And I saw as the colour of amber, as the appearance of fire round about within it, from the appearance of his loins even upward, and from the appearance of his loins even downward, I saw as it were the appearance of fire, and it had brightness round about. As the appearance of a rainbow that is in the cloud, so was the appearance of the brightness round about. This was the appearance of the likeness of the glory of the LORD. And when I saw it, I fell upon my face, and I heard a voice of one that spake."[48]

Here we can see fire, whirlwinds, clouds and angels, even that most evocative of symbols – the rainbow. This is material that could easily find its way into a pathworking. The Bible is packed with it. The problem is that we don't know half of what some of these symbols mean, because we are from a different time and culture which has new and different symbols.

However, it is not surprising to find techniques much like pathworking being used by mystics that use the Bible as their main source.

The founder of the Jesuits, the counter-reformation's champion, *St. Ignatius of Loyola* (1491-1556) had members of his order visualise the life of Christ. Ignatius had a month programme for the members of his Order called the Spiritual Exercises. These worked much in the way of a modern esoteric school's correspondence course. Each week you would be required to perform these pathworkings, which were designed to enable the Jesuit to key into the thinking of Loyola and to have spiritual experiences.

In the second week you would build your 'imaginary' kingdom based on a visualisation of the villages and towns where Christ lived. Then you would equate that kingdom with a good wise modern-day ruler. Then you would attempt to link that King with Christ as ruler.

In the third week you would start to visualise the life of Christ's last days through to the last supper. And finally in the fourth week you would visualise the death and resurrection.

However it is important to realise that the Spiritual Exercises would have a person watching the scene and contemplating its symbolism. The esoteric pathworking would have the same person interacting with the

---

48 King James Bible, Ezekiel 1 verses 4, 5, 27 and 28.

characters, feeling that they really were there. In my view it would have allowed for an intellectual understanding of a spiritual event, but may have stood in the way of a true spiritual awakening.

Closer to the esoteric schools is the mystic St. Teresa of Avila (1515-1582). In her book the 'The Interior Castle' the central technique was much more hands on. It is a journey through a 'diamond' castle of the soul with the goal being the centre of the building, to attain union with God.

> "You must not imagine these mansions as arranged in a row, one behind another, but fix your attention on the centre, the room or palace occupied by the King. Think of a palmito, which has many outer rinds surrounding the savoury part within, all of which must be taken away before the centre can be eaten. Just so around this central room are many more, as there also are above it."[49]

St Teresa's castle is broken down into seven rings.

First Mansion
This is where a person begins to meditate, but is still attached to the outside world. It is a period of humility and the beginning of discipline.

Second Mansion
This is when the person desired closer contact with God and actually starts to work hard at moving forward in the practice of meditation and prayer.

Third Mansion
Exemplary Life begins as the person has attained virtue and is controlled by discipline and penance and is disposed to performing acts of charity toward others. However, they still lack the full, the inspiring force of love, as love is still governed by reason. The person suffers from aridity.

Fourth Mansion
Mystical life begins as the person realises that it is not by the effort of the personality that the soul gets what it needs. The soul is seen like a fountain built near its source and the water of life flows into it, not through an aqueduct, but directly from the spring. Its love is now free from servile fear: it has broken all the bonds which previously hindered

---

49 *Interior Castle*, Chapter two (St Teresa of Avila).

its progress; it shrinks from no trials and attaches no importance to anything to do with the world.

Fifth Mansion

This is a very close contemplation of God. The faculties of the soul are "asleep". It is of short duration, but, while it lasts, the soul is completely possessed by God.

Sixth Mansion

If the fifth mansion were a betrothal, in the Sixth, Lover and Beloved see each other for long periods at a time, and as they grow in intimacy, the soul receives increasing favours, together with increasing afflictions.

Seventh Mansion

The soul has a Spiritual Marriage with God and is transformed.

However, the irritating thing about the Interior Castle is that Teresa does not give us specific images of what a person might expect to see in each room, leading some to suggest that it is simply a metaphor and she is not actually doing anything like the magical use of the imagination. However, Teresa could not help but slip into some very beautiful imagery when describing her castle. Why would someone go the lengths to describe it as a diamond or a crystal if it were simply an allegory, not meant to be seen by the inner eye? Certainly those mystical friends of mine who use Teresa's castle do visualise it as a 'physical' reality. My own experience with it was that I was taken to various rooms in each ring of the Castle by a guide and led to understand certain spiritual ideas. However, in one instance I tried to advance deeper into the castle than I was ready for. The light of the room was overwhelming and I had a sudden nosebleed which snatched me out of the meditative reverie. Oddly, years later I tried the same thing with no ill effects, perhaps because my physical frame was ready for what I experienced.

But now we have looked at the public presentations of mystical imagination, it is time to look at the more occult version.

ThE DIFFERENCE BETWEEN MAGICIANS AND MYSTICS

Before embarking on looking at the use of imagination for mystical experience, it is important to get a definition. Like the mystical writer and scholar R.A. Gilbert, it would seem that finding a definition that was neither grandiose nor limp is impossible. Quoting Evelyn Underhill, who believed that Mysticism is the art of union with Reality, Gilbert says that a Mystic:

"…is seeking to unite his whole soul, the core of his being, with the Divine."[50]

Definition is difficult, as a mystical experience is something that is often unique to each person. However many people talk about it as a union with God. Sometimes mystical experiences happen to those who are not looking for them. An agnostic friend of mine once had an overwhelming mystical experience when riding her bicycle in the New Zealand countryside. It had no spiritual effect on her life, other than to lead her to question her notion of reality more.

Similar experiences with other people might have caused a change of life patterns. The classic case of this is Paul of Tarsus on his way to persecute Christians, suddenly being blinded by a divine light which lead him ultimately to Christianity. A mystic would say that such experiences brought without any personal efforts were rare and the product of divine grace.

However, mystical experiences do not have to be dramatic blinding lights either. They often are small steps which have dramatic consequences for the soul. My move away from orthodox Christianity was one such experience. In meditation at a Christian camp, I opened my eyes and saw the camp all around me and it felt like a two dimensional image of a divine reality that had many dimensions. All around me I saw swirling shapes which suggested that the pattern of the universe was more complex and exciting than I could perceive with my religion. There must be more to God than this, I thought and resolved to find it. Yet with this awakening came an inner calm and excitement. It was the sort of feeling of the Fool embarking on a quest.

Ultimately both the mystic and the occultist are looking to achieve the same thing, either by a direct route in the case of the mystic or by the slower, less direct method of the occultist. Both occultists and mystics report the same essential experiences, a feeling of dying and being reborn, seeing light, experiencing union and a feeling of total liberation. Generally mystical experience starts with some fairly basic realisations. The first is that there is more to life than appears in physical reality. Most mystics would consider this reality God. They would say

---

50 *Elements of Mysticism*, RA Gilbert, 1991, Element Books.

that this God pervades everything but somehow remains out of reach of the ordinary consciousness and certainly is unknowable. Some identify this God with a divine aspect of themselves; others consider that God is somehow separate and that a true mystical experience is a marriage between God and themselves.

It has been said that all magicians land up as mystics in the end, but that is only after a different journey and, although there are similarities between the goals of the mystic and the occultist, their methods for getting to the same destination and what happens when they reach it are two different matters. A mystic will often sacrifice their participation in the world to attain this union at a higher level. They seek to 'be in the world but not of it'. Their path is of non-attachment, removal of the ego, never working for personal gain etc., a gradual stripping away of everything that is not God until they find the part that is. Once this is attained, there is only this unity to bask in.

As the 16th century Spanish mystic St John of the Cross (1542-1591) said, "When thy mind dwells upon anything, thou art ceasing to cast thyself upon the All."[51]

The mystic has travelled so light to reach their goal that there is nothing more that can be done other than live the remainder of their life in a state of bliss and hope that others will be helped by contact with them.

The mystic will try to divorce themselves from too much use of symbol and imagination because these will become an attachment and a distraction from their ultimate direction. As the great 15th century Catholic mystic Thomas à Kempis said, "Shut fast the door of your soul – that is to say your imagination – and keep it cautiously, as much as you can, from beholding any earthly thing, and then lift up your mind to your Lord, Jesus; open your heart faithfully to Him."[52] Whereas the occultist will use symbols and imagination like buses to carry them towards the goal.

Magicians not only participate in the world, but aim to build a ladder between the material world and the divine through their lives. This ladder of imagination enables people to journey to the throne of God and then return the same way. The process enables the personality to be purified and a vehicle for God to express itself in matter. They

---

51 John of the Cross, *Ascent of Mount Carmel*. Trans. E. Allison Peers, Book 1, Chapter 13, Paragraph 12.

52 Thomas à Kempis, *The Imitation of Christ*. Trans. Richard Whitford, modernised by Harold C. Gardiner. New York: Doubleday, 1955. (p58).

can use their knowledge to practically manifest their experience on the material plane of existence.

But this takes them only so far.

BUILDING MYSTICAL EXPERIENCES INTO PATHWORKINGS

A pathworking can be adapted to make it less psychological or magical and more spiritual. The approach has to be less narrative and more intense. Patience is required, as a mystical experience cannot always be guaranteed, must be waited upon and the person performing the pathworking has to be properly prepared.

The main focus of a mystical pathworking is a symbol of devotion. These are usually a token of faith from a religion, a symbol of a god to whom one feels attached, either by birth or by conversion. This could be a crucifix or a cross if you are a Christian, a Talmud if you are Hebrew, a Tree of Life if you are a Cabbalist, a statue or image if you are a Neo-Pagan – anything that suggests a link between you and God. In this book, which is multi-secular, I have shied away from conventional forms of worship so that the information is accessible to all. To do this I have adopted the powerful and accurate symbol of God being light or energy. This is common to practically all religions.

The next thing involves some form of worship. Now I don't mean the mindless devotion where a person prostrates themselves before something they perceive as much bigger than themselves and which needs appeasing. That approach only aims to create some kind of separation between God and the person. If you think that God is too big and powerful to enter into a personal relationship, then you will never believe that you can truly merge with that force. If we look at Teresa of Avila's description of a mystical experience as a marriage, then the first thing that needs to happen is some sort of friendship between you and your God.

A pathworking can help this process by allowing a person to meet in their mind the God or Goddess in the safe space of their imagination. A relationship can then develop as you start to see the God appearing in your life. This relationship will be like any other; there will be moments when you disagree, argue, fall out, fall in, share highs, lows, etc. There is a certain naïvety involved in this approach and indeed it is based on how a child sees God. But that is because, in the initial stages of relating to God, we are children who need a divine friend. It is not heresy to see God in this way unless you forget that this particular 'friend' is God.

Humour is very important. If you look at the truly great mystics, those that were not insane had very good senses of humour, and a mystical pathworking should allow this aspect of divinity to come through.

This phase of the relationship is often the most dangerous. It is where the ego and psychological weaknesses manifest to eclipse what would be a beautiful experience. The lower self will always try to shout down the voice of God with its own. Unfortunately, this is all too easy for it to do. We all want to think that the way we live our life is God's will and if the lower self can put words into God's mouth to justify laziness, or even atrocities, then it will. The answer to this is to be careful and also know that God is not interested in controlling you. It is unlikely that it would have given you free will if it wanted to do that. So you will never be commanded to do anything by your God. God wants to see the world through your eyes and your experiences, and approaching it with those things, good, bad or indifferent, leads it to an understanding all of its own.

Moreover, God will not step away from the boundaries set by the religion through which it chooses to manifest to you. If you are a Christian and are using pathworking to deepen your mystical relationship with Christ, you are not going to find him telling you to hate or kill. A Moslem or a Jew is not going to be told to eat pork or ignore the call to worship or to disobey the written tenets of their religion. In this way it is possible to test some of the stranger things that your 'God' may say by comparing them with what is written in the Bible, the Koran, or even the legends of the Gods themselves.

After a while, this human side of God should be allowed to fall away and more of its true nature will be revealed; it becomes less anthropomorphised and more divine. However, because the mind has been conditioned by repeated pathworking, it will connect this newer, more powerful version of God with the friend with whom a relationship was forged. As the God separates from the human images, generally the worshipper goes with them. In fact, the changes are often so gradual that the worshipper does not notice.

The pathworking is becoming something less subjective. Not only is the relationship 'real' but the lines between the personality and the God start to blur. Ultimately this would lead to a total union but even in the short term can lead to a gradual awakening of the divine self.

Mystical pathworkings must always have this end in mind. Whereas a normal pathworking might lead to a realisation about the nature of the Universe, or an understanding about the self, a mystical pathworking always ends with some kind of union. A description of this union can be found in the German mystic Meister Eckhart's 'Sermonds and Treatises':[53]

> "You should love him as he is; a non-God, a non-spirit, a non-person, a non-image; rather as he is a sheer pure limpid one, detached from all duality. And in that one we may eternally sink from nothingness to nothingness."

Somehow a pathworking must lead to this almost Zen-like state where there is nothing, but everything. One would think it impossible to do this, as words would instantly limit the vision. However, where words limit, imagination provides the rainbow bridge that connects Earth to Heaven. If you have used just enough words that can point to the mystical experience without describing it, you have the essence of a good mystical pathworking.

What follows are a series of exercises and pathworkings that provide a mystical curriculum that will lead you over a period of months through several mystical experiences, perhaps ending up with some form of real awakening.

Preparation for Mystical Experience

Before you start, you should have a visualisation exercise that declares that a more mystical exercise has begun. It also works to balance the person's aura, so that more serious work can be done.

The one most commonly used in the Western Mystery Tradition is the Cabbalistic Cross. Although this appears Christian, the symbolism is generic to most religions in the West.

THE CABBALISTIC CROSS

Much of the teaching of the thought behind the exercises below is given within the Order. However, the Cabbalistic Cross is a ritual visualisation exercise which balances energy and seals the electro-magnetic shell around the body that is known as the aura. It places you

---

53 Meister Eckhart's 'Sermonds and Treatises' Vol II Trans by M.O.C. Walshe (1979).

under the protection of Divine forces and, with regular use, strengthens the aura. It is performed before and after a working to harmonise the energy that you have received in your meditation work. Like many magicians, I would perform the Cabbalistic Cross before I do any work and afterwards to help integrate the energies from the experience into my aura.

Cabbalistic Cross

Standing upright, close your eyes and visualise a bright, white ball of light above your head. This is the highest expression of the power of God that you are capable of conceiving at this time. Visualise it until you can almost feel the warmth on the top of your head. See it beginning to spin.

Say the Hebrew word ATAH (Ah-tah), which means 'thou art'. Touch your forehead with the fingertips of your right hand and see a line of light from the white sphere travel down to where your fingers are touching your forehead.

Draw your fingers in a straight line down the centre of your body and your breast. See the light follow your fingers and carry on down towards a white sphere which is just below and encompassing your feet. As the light pours into this sphere, see it glow, brighten and spin.

Say the Hebrew word MALKUTH (Mahl-kooth) which means 'the Kingdom'.

Tap your right shoulder and see a white sphere start to spin. Say the Hebrew words VE GEBURAH (Ve-ge-boor-ah) which means 'and the Power'.

Draw another line of white across your body to your left shoulder and visualise another sphere of bright light starting to spin.

Say the Hebrew words VE GEDULAH (Ve-Ge-doo-lah) which means 'and the Glory'.

Now bring your hands together over your heart, where the lines of light meet. Hold your hands as if you were praying.

Say the Hebrew words LEH OLAM (lay-oh-lam), which means 'forever', AMEN (ah-men).

See white light expand from your heart until your entire body is enclosed in a sphere of white light.

See yourself as a cross of light, tipped with glowing spheres and your aura filled with white light.

PURIFICATION OF THE BODY AND MIND – THE MIDDLE PILLAR

The Middle Pillar is a key part of your preparation work and will have a noticeable effect on you within a few weeks. It opens energy centres, balances out the personality and awakens a realisation of the Divine within. Although much of it starts as an imagination exercise, it is far more than that and is in actual fact a form of practical magic. This is why it involves chanting a divine name to make it more powerful.

The exercise was developed into its current form by Israel Regardie from a complex Golden Dawn technique called Building the Tree of Life in the Aura. It has echoes of Eastern Tantric practice in that it involves a purification of the aura and the body by raising personal energy, or Kundalini, to meet divine energy. By linking the two energy flows, it has the effect of purifying and revitalising the aura and raising it to a higher state.

As the energy flows through the body, it ejects coarser matter and refines the body so that it can handle more mystical experiences. It also sends a powerful message to the unconscious that it is in alignment with divine forces.

The Middle Pillar differs from Eastern practice in that it does not deal directly with energy centres or chakras, but works on a level above them. This makes it safer for those who cannot practice under a trained guru because it does not allow different parts of the body to become over stimulated. Over-stimulation leads to body imbalances, illness and sometimes organ failure.

Regardie considered the exercise so important that he recommended any serious magical or mystical student to perform it twice a day at least. I agree that anyone who does this exercise as often as they can, will truly transform their life extremely quickly.

The Middle Pillar

Take a deep breath and visualise the white ball of light above your head. See it expand and begin to spin. Vibrate the divine name *Eheieh* (eh-hey-yay) – which means 'I am'. Do this six times.

Imagine the light flowing down to a white ball of light at the nape of your neck. See it expand and begin to spin. Vibrate the divine name *YHVH Elohim* (Yod-hey-vav-hey El-oh-heem) – which means 'The Lord, God'. Do this six times.

Imagine the light flowing down to a white ball of light at the heart. See it expand and begin to spin. Vibrate the divine name *YHVH Eloah Va-Daath* (Yod-hey-vav-hey El-oh-ah ve-Dah-arth) – which means 'The Lord, God of Knowledge'. Do this six times.

Imagine the light flowing down to a white ball of light at the groin. See it expand and begin to spin. Vibrate the divine name *Shaddai El-Chai* (Sha-dye El-Chai) – which means 'Almighty living God'. Do this six times.

Imagine the light flowing down to a white ball of light at the feet. See it expand and begin to spin. Vibrate the divine name *Adonai-Ha-Aretz* (ah-doe-nye-ha aretz) – which means 'The Lord of the Earth'. Do this six times.

Allow the light to begin to encircle your aura. Begin on the left side at about the same distance as your outstretched arm. Let it flow over your head to your right side, then under your feet to your left side. Continue to do this for a while.

When the light reaches the top of your head, change its direction to flow down your front to your feet, then under your feet to your back, then up your back to the top of your head. Continue to do this for a while.

Then, when the light reaches your feet, breathe out and, as you breathe in, draw the light up your spine to the sphere of life above your head. Breathe out and let this centre explode with white light, which showers through your aura, cleaning and purifying it. Allow the light to gather at your feet and repeat the process 10 times at least. Finish with a Cabbalistic Cross.

Note that when you vibrate a divine name, you take a deep breath; push the sound to the roof of the mouth while contracting the throat. When it vibrates, you will feel it deep within your throat and nose. The best place to experiment with this is in the bath, where the acoustics will help you find the right pitch. It is somewhat loud, so it is best to practise when there is no-one else at home.

EXAMPLES OF MYSTICAL PATHWORKINGS

There are as many ways to approach God mystically as there are mystics. It would be impossible for any writer to give a definitive mystical pathworking that is guaranteed to resonate with the reader. However, here are several pathworkings which have worked for me. As I have said earlier, I have attempted to keep these as free as possible from a link with any specific modern religion.

LIGHTING THE PHAROS

This pathworking adapted from a workshop run by David Goddard, which I attended in the mid 1990s. His idea was to take the person through the building of a light house or Pharos on the inner planes and then turn it over to contacts to use that light for their own purposes.[54] However, when it came to the lighting of the Pharos flame, I experienced a beautiful white light with shafts of gold. This was a true mystical experience for me and it occurred to me that if the symbol of the light house were adapted, it could be used for personal mystical experiences. This version is a hard pathworking to get right and do not be surprised if it takes several goes and you return exhausted.

Before you is a doorway with a blue curtain upon it. On the curtain, in silver, is the outline of a light house or Pharos. It looks like this:

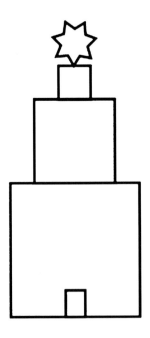

---

54 Although I still think this is an interesting idea, I would not do it in that form now nor do I quite see 'contacts' in the way I did then.

You concentrate on the doorway and the outline glows with power. The doorway becomes transparent and you step through into the silver mist of the astral.

After a while the mist clears and you find yourself standing on a headland, overlooking the sea. It is an overcast day and the sun is beginning to set.

In front of you, the land falls away – there are sharp jutting cliffs with dark rocks at the foot of them. The waves crash against the rocks in an ever rolling din.

To your right there is an ancient Pharos, standing tall against the twilight.

Its lamp is not yet lit.

You walk over to the huge double doors of the Pharos. In your hand is a key. You don't know where you got it from, but somehow you realise that this Pharos is yours and you are responsible for it.

You enter the Pharos and find, much to your surprise, that you have not walked into a functional light house but something that looks more like a temple.

All around you are intricate mosaics depicting aspects of creation, animals, people and places. When you look closer, they are all scenes from parts of your life, all moulded in semi-precious stones and crystals.

On the roof there is painted a night sky with a zodiac border. Planets have been laid out in the shape of your astrological chart. In the centre of the room is a spiral staircase.

This room represents your material world. However, the material world is not the light. You seek the light and that is on the upper levels.

You start to climb the staircase. You are aware that as you do so part of you is being left behind, your family, your job, and the life that is around you. But you have to find the light of the Pharos.

You reach the next floor. It is filled with a silver astral mist. Around the walls are seven statues of angels, each of them representing a planetary force. There is an angel of the Sun, Mercury, Mars, Venus, Jupiter, Saturn and the Moon. They look very lifelike and the energy around their hearts beats with a special kind of inner light. They are very powerful, but their light is not enough for you. You seek the main light of the Pharos.

You continue slowly up the stairway again. You are aware that you are slowly allowing your attachment to your emotional and intellectual existence to slip away as you climb each step.

It is an odd feeling as you climb past this room. You cannot think or even feel, you just are.

The next room is full of light – a rainbow of colours and energies. In the midst of these you can make out four bright lights. These are the very energies that the universe, thought and emotion are made from. They are fire, water, air and earth, but these are not just in a physical sense but in a deep and symbolic way.

But the light of these Archangels is not bright enough and somehow even the hint of matter seems hollow in comparison to the bright light that you know must be at the top of the Pharos.

You keep climbing. You are aware that there is nothing really left of you, other than infinity of thought. Not intellectual, or emotional, or controlled thought. You feel timeless and free.

You come out on top of the Pharos into absolute darkness. Cold winds whip around you. There is driving rain. Below you, the sea is whipped to a frenzy. But at the top of the Pharos there is only an empty golden bowl and no light.

But after all you have rejected, how can it be so lightless here? You feel crushed.

Lightening carves the sky. The storm is getting worse. It seems there is nothing you can do. You are cold and alone and have rejected everything that could have given you balance.

But in a moment you realise that in the midst of darkness there must be light. That the darkness is but an expression of the light you have been seeking. That even the storm is but an expression of light. Suddenly you are at home in the darkness, but still hungry for the dawn. In your heart there is a call for the light which you shout at the top of your lungs.

FIAT, FIAT, FIAT![55]

Suddenly bursting on the golden dish is a bright diamond light. The light is not white but something more. It is everything born of nothing. It is outside you and within you. It just is. It lights up the storm.

But more, it burns you.

It burns away the last of all feelings of separateness.

You are the light and it is you.

You are timeless.

Limitless.

ONE.

(There is now a very long pause)

---

55 FIAT means 'Light', and so this means "three-fold Light" and not three Italian cars triple parked in front of a popular ice cream shop.

Slowly, the feeling of separateness grows again and your find yourself looking into the diamond light. The storm is stilled.

Beside you is a golden lamp.

You take the lamp and light it from the Pharos' flame.

You walk to the staircase and into the next level, taking the lamp with you.

The Archangels glow with power as you enter, singing a beautiful devotion to the light you carry. They start to move and you are aware that they are moving in a new life pattern to the one you had before this vision of the Pharos light.

You enter the next level and again you find the statues of the angels moving to form different patterns. You feel they have been awakened strongly by the sight of your lantern. You descend further into the final level.

To your surprise, all the crystals and semi-precious stones that depict your life glow with the light of the lantern. Every picture seems centred on the light, vibrant and living. You put your lantern down and marvel at the beauty of the divine light reflected in all you do.

Then, leaving your Pharos and knowing that you will remember all that you have seen, even if you can't express it, you walk towards the doorway.

Before stepping into this time and space, you turn to see the Pharos lighting up the whole night's sky.

You step through the doorway and become aware of this time and this reality.

TRIAL BY MAAT

This pathworking has a Golden Dawn flavour and works with the symbolism used in that magical order. Its aim is to try the candidate so that they will be free from the bounds of earth and may become truly connected with their Higher Self. It uses the symbolism of the Judgement Hall of Maat, which we first saw in Chapter Four. Only here the symbols are tuned in a slightly different way for a different end.

Unlike the Pharos pathworking, this particular one aims at a purification of the soul, the turning away from the lower self and the integration of the Higher Self within the personality. This is a mystical experience, for the Higher Self is said to be a reflection of the unity that is God.

This pathworking is in two parts. This is to allow its power to filter into your life. It is not to be undertaken lightly, because it is turning the forces of cosmic justice upon you. While this is unlikely to do any long term harm, it *is* likely to force a balance in your life very quickly.

Imagine a huge doorway before you. On the lintel is a sun disk with rainbow wings. On the door is a painting of a huge set of scales. Focus your attention on the scales until they glow with power.

Say to yourself "I (state your name) proclaim myself to be a humble seeker after the Light of Wisdom and the Splendour of the Divine. I invite the beings behind the creation of the universe to test my resolve and enable me to find the Divine Light."

There is a voice from behind the door.

"Why do you seek this?"

What is your reply?

The door opens and standing before you is a being with a jackal head, wearing a nemyss of white and black stripes. He has in his left hand a caduceus and in his right holds a lantern with a red flame. He is Anubis.

He says: "All beings who wish to partake of the Divine Light must be tested. Are you willing?"

If you agree, then the jackal headed god will allow you to enter the gate. He says: "enter thou then the halls of Justice, the place of truth, the judgement halls of Maat."

You find yourself in a vast Egyptian temple. It is the colour of flame.

Arranged in a semi-circle before you are figures seated on thrones cut from red sandstone. They are dressed alike in kilts and nemyss of black and yellow. Some are human, but others are animals. Each wears a necklace in the shape of a flying hawk and carries a flail in the left hand. These are the forty-two assessors – the force of cosmic justice that even judges the gods.

In the centre of the room is a black altar and behind that are two pillars, one white and one black. In front of them is a giant pair of scales.

Between the pillars is a woman wearing a nemyss striped black and white. Her linen gown is white and she holds a mitre-headed wand – this is Maat.

Behind her on a throne is a human with a nemyss of striped while and yellow. He is wearing a white crown and is holding a white crowned sceptre. This is Osiris.

Looking to your right, you see another jackal-headed god in a black and white kilt. He has a red sword in his hand.

Maat looks at you with eyes that pierce your very soul and says: "Inheritor of a dying world, arise and enter the darkness."

Anubis turns to you and says: Unpurified and unconsecrated, you can go no further.

Two goddesses approach you. One carries a torch and the other a silver chalice. The one with the torch passes the flame through you. You feel no pain, just a feeling that some dross has been removed from you. Then the other goddess pours the water over you. You don't feel wet, simply cleaner.

Osiris says: "Inheritor of a dying world, thou hast sought admission to the mysteries of Light. But before you may enter into one of its lamps, the assessors who administer cosmic justice must test you. These tests are subtle – are you willing to face them?"

What is your reply? Remember, you are still allowed to leave.

Osiris says: "Very well. I shall give you a symbol that shall carry you through this test. Meditate on it often and uncover its meanings."

What is the symbol?

Maat comes from behind the scales.

She says: You are a being of light, incarnate within a personality, call upon your higher self in times of stress – now are you prepared to be tested?"

What is your final reply?

Maat says: "Thrice (s)he has been asked and thrice (s)he has accepted."

Anubis stands to your left hand, Maat to your right. Osiris points his wand at you and you find yourself in a triangle of force.

The assessors outstretch their arms, pointing their fingers towards the scales. The scales begin to glow with power.

Maat says to you: "You must answer the following questions truthfully to see if you are worthy of the light that you seek. All that falls short of the Glory of Truth shall be bought into balance over time. Do you understand?"

Then begins the questioning. Each assessor stands and asks a question which you must answer either yes or no. Each question is meant to be interpreted in its widest possible sense. Take your time in answering each one.

Have you committed sin?
Have you committed robbery with violence?
Have you stolen?
Have you killed?

Have you stolen food?

Have you taken things that were meant to be offerings for God?

Have you stolen the property of God for your own purpose?

Have you lied?

Have you wasted resources?

Have you cursed someone?

Have you wasted your sexuality?

Have you made people unhappy?

Have you worked to destroy your own spirit?

Have you attacked anyone?

Have you deceived?

Have you tried to take another's life work?

Have you been an eavesdropper?

Have you slandered a person?

Have you been angry without just cause?

Have you corrupted someone sexually for your own ends?

Have you tried to destroy another person's love?

Have you respected your body?

Have you terrorised someone?

Have you broken the laws of society?

Have you been an angry person?

Have you ignored the truth?

Have you blasphemed?

Have you lived a life of violence?

Have you stirred up strife?

Have you acted with undue haste?

Have you pried into another's life?

Have you spoken too much?

Have you wronged anyone or done evil?

Have you performed black magic?

Have you prevented people from finding God in their life?

Have you raised your voice?

Have you cursed God?

Have you acted with arrogance?

Have you sought to undermine religion?

Have you refused to honour the dead?

Have you stolen from the innocent or not respected the gods of your
land?

Have you persecuted those who have a different religion?

The assessors and gods return to their seats.
Maat says:

> All things of which you have spoken shall be forgiven.
> If they are allowed to be corrected on my scales.
> Unbalanced Power is the ebbing away of life.
> Unbalanced Mercy is weakness and fading away of the will.
> Unbalanced Severity is cruelty and barrenness of mind.
> Therefore my judgement shall be that you shall become balanced.

She walks over to you and leans into your heart, and takes the energy of your soul, which manifests as a pink ball of light.

She places it upon the left side of the scales and takes the red feather of truth from her head and places on the right. The scales start to dip but instead she moves them with her hands so that they reach perfect balance.

She takes your soul and places it back into your heart. "In balance, the higher self may come to thee. You are a being of light incarnate within a personality – call upon your higher self in times of stress."

Osiris says: "Inheritor of a dying world, return to this place in a month to face our judgement." Anubis returns you to the pylon gate and you return to this place and this time.

Part Two

Perform a Cabalistic Cross and Middle Pillar. Relax and get into as deep a stage of relaxation as possible. Visualise before you a gateway of pink sandstone. On its lintel is a winged sun disk and it has a curtain of red silk instead of a door. On the silk curtain is an image of a pair of golden scales.

Speak the following to the door:

"I (state your name) proclaim myself to be a humble seeker after the Light of Wisdom and the Splendour of the Divine. At the request of Maat I return to receive judgement at the Halls of Maat, for reward or punishment."

Nothing happens.
After a while you grow impatient and part the curtain yourself.
Inside the Judgement hall of Maat is empty and dark. The thrones are bare and all that you recognise are the scales of Maat, which seem unbalanced. You walk towards them.

There is a crash of thunder.

You hear a howl of some unearthly creature behind you.

You remember what happens to people who fail the Judgement of Maat – their hearts are fed to the crocodile headed god Ouammoout peSatanas. Your heart races and you fear for the first time that you may have actually failed the test of the Gods and now must face divine judgement.

There is a flash of lightning and to your left, you briefly see the outline of a beast that has the head of a crocodile and the tail of a serpent.

It is everything you fear.

You recoil into the scales. You call for Anubis, or Maat, or indeed anyone, but you are alone with this beast.

There is a flash of lightning and you again see the beast, this time walking towards you.

"Inheritor of a dying world, doomed to death and suffering, why do you tarry here?" it says.

Its form changes into a human. Who is it?

It continues: "Return to thine own realm to live and die in my clutches."

It walks towards you, its hands become claws.

You turn and run towards the east of the temple.

Each step becomes harder to take. It is as if you are running in slow motion. But Satanas is walking quickly towards you.

You can almost smell his breath.

And you are alone.

Then you remember the words of Maat.

"You are a being of light incarnate within a personality – call upon your higher self in times of stress."

You focus on your heart centre and see it as a closed rose.

"Divine spark, reveal thyself," you say.

The rose in your heart opens to a blinding white light.

From the centre of the white light comes a golden boy sitting on a lotus.

He is wearing a crown and has his index finger from his left hand touching his lips. This is Harparkrat.

Deep within yourself you realise that you and this God are one. This divine spark is born of the infinite.

Time stops.

There is just you and Harparkrat.

"I am thee and thou art me," he says. "Purified and consecrated by flame, water, judgement and life in the material world, we are partakers of the Light Divine. Let us join and be One and never forget this truth."

He merges into you.... What do you feel?

[Long pause]

You turn to face the frozen face of Satanas. You are energised by the combined power of you and your Higher Self. Time begins again.

Satanas flees.

You hear the most beautiful music.

Processing into the temple come the gods, closely followed by the initiates from countless traditions, each wearing the different robes of their orders.

They are all singing a welcome into the mysteries for a human who has met their own shadow and realised their divine nature enough to send evil fleeing.

You turn to see Osiris again on his throne.

"Creature of Earth. You have met and passed our test, although the fruits of this combat will continue for some time to come."

He hands you a golden box.

You open it.

What is the gift of the gods?

The gods and initiates of the Mysteries raise their arms in a salute of acknowledgement.

Anubis returns you to the gate.

He says: "May you find the truth you are seeking."

You say farewell, step through the gate and return to this time and this place.

ASCENDING TO ThE ThRONE OF GOD

This pathworking is one which I wrote for a reasonably experienced group. It does require abilities that will initially be beyond the beginner; however, the more you practice, the easier it will become. You will also experience an ever increasing depth with it until the experience becomes incredibly special.

It uses a similar technique to that called 'Rising on the Planes', which was developed by the Order of the Golden Dawn.

The process used is similar to the one you will undergo after you die, where you ascend through the levels of creation, casting off those elements of yourself that are transitory and not your true spiritual self.

While the pathworking flippantly describes the casting off of the different aspects of personality, this is harder than it seems and can really only be done at death! However, each time you practice this pathworking you can push away more. The extent to which you can do it will mark your success at this exercise.

Because of the way the pathworking is written, it is best to make sure you do it just before bed or not do much else afterwards. It will take a while for the various parts of yourself to catch up afterwards. This is written deliberately to enhance the experience. There are some who say that I should return the person the way they came, gradually taking on the various emotional and intellectual bodies that were shed along the way.

In actual fact these bodies will align themselves fairly quickly after the pathworking is complete. However, the aim of this pathworking is to not only give the person a profound mystical union with God, but to also give them the feeling of what it is like to be a divine being incarnate in matter. It will also give the person a break from their complexes, roving thoughts and emotions for a while – which can't be a bad thing!

Relax deeply until you cannot feel your body any more. In your mind's eye, feel yourself become lighter and ascend your consciousness until it is hovering above your body. It feels wonderfully light to be free of your body.

You feel yourself rising through the ceiling above this building and into the sky. But soon you are aware that this sky is the astral level – you are surrounded by sparkly mist. There are images in the mist and part of you wants to explore, but you feel you must press on further upwards.

After a while your upward journey is halted. It feels like a barrier. You find it hard to go on and then a quiet voice inside you says "your intellect is not needed here, let it go". You push away your intellectual understanding of what is going on, taking it off like a cloak. From now on what you see will not or cannot be intellectually understood.

See for a moment what it is like to sense things just with feeling. Not understanding them, they just are.

You feel lighter again and start to ascend further.

Ahead of you is a light, like a beautiful star. With your emotional vision you know it is that which you have been looking for. It is your missing part, your divine self.

As you get closer, you start to see that space is bending around the light, pushing it backwards so that is at right angles to reality and appears to be at the end of a tunnel. The tunnel walls are made up of swirling energy of colour like a rainbow.

You ascend toward the tunnel, seeking to enter it. The walls of the tunnel are not just energy, they are beings. They are singing the most beautiful music, you feel all the emotion and joy within the song.

However you can go no further. You are standing, beholding this vision of the light yet there is something standing in your way.

"Your emotions stand in your way, you must let them go too," says the voice again, which is somehow louder.

You shed your emotions like a cloak. All that you have ever felt is no longer with you. All that remains is a seed of your own personality, a centre of consciousness that is timeless.

Take a moment to experience what this is like with spiritual vision. The tunnel is so much more alive now and the song you hear can now be felt with every essence of your being. Symbols whirl in the rainbow-coloured vortex.

In front of you, the light is diamond, pure, not white but clear.

You move towards it, through the tunnel, toward the light. As you get closer it burns and yet attracts you at the same time. Suddenly you feel you can get no closer to the heart of the light and never leave the tunnel. Although it is beautiful, it is not as lovely as the light you see before you. You feel disheartened, it is as if there were an abyss of darkness between you and the light you seek.

Then the voice says: "There is no difference between you and the light. The I that watches is the same as the Light at end of the tunnel."

Then you realise. You must shed that concept of who you are. You are not an incarnate being, but you and the light are One.

The moment this happens you step into the timeless and limitless light. You dissolve into it like sugar into water. You become it.

Timeless.

[Long pause]

After a while you feel that you want to know something. Something unique about yourself. You imagine the Universe.

You imagine the world with a life on it.

You imagine a person in that world.

You imagine their life up to this point.

Then you shift a part of yourself into that person.

Open your eyes.
You are the rider in a chariot.
An infinite God expressing itself in a personality.
See the light around you with your divine eyes.
See your life with the new vision.
Know that this is how you truly are.

When you are ready, allow yourself to centre down. Have a drink and write down what you have experienced.

BECOMING A STAR CHILD

In the film *2001: A Space Odyssey*, a human is transformed from a mortal into a Star Child. In the Golden Dawn this 'Star Child' was called the 'Babe of the Abyss' and they made it a grade equal to Daath on the Tree of Life. Many Golden Dawn groups say that it is impossible to attain this grade while you are still alive and it can only to be managed by an advanced magician after they've died.

In some ways they were right. If you literally became the Star Child, or the Babe of the Abyss, you would be a god. But then if you take the Roman Catholic Communion literally, you are eating the blood and body of Jesus in a cannibalistic rite which does not allow a vegetarian option. Literalism is the biggest curse in mysticism and magic.

The most detailed account of someone trying to cross the Abyss was written by Aleister Crowley, who seems to have either taken the idea too literally, or written down it down in such a way that many of his students think it should be approached that way. To be fair to him, Crowley admitted the concept was difficult to explain.

"It corresponds more or less to the gap in thought between the Real, which is ideal, and the Unreal, which is actual," he wrote. But then he went and spoilt his definition by saying that "in the Abyss all things exist, indeed, at least in posse, but are without any possible meaning; for they lack the substratum of spiritual Reality. They are appearances without Law. They are thus Insane Delusions. Now the Abyss being thus, the great storehouse of Phenomena, it is the source of all impressions."

This gives you the impression that the abyss is a spiritual location and has things inside it which, according to Crowley, are not that pleasant. Crowley claimed that he crossed the abyss by taking a packed lunch into the Sahara, allowing the worst demon in his Enochian file-o-fax to possess him and rape the poet Victor Benjamin Neuburg. Somewhere along the line, something went wrong, but Crowley did not admit it.

Crossing the abyss is part of many mystical spiritual religions. It represents that state where the personality is jettisoned and the microcosmic mind merges briefly with that of the infinite macrocosmic one. This is sometimes called Cosmic Consciousness. It is not only possible to catch glimmers of this state, but it is important for any magician to do so. It is by doing this that we see how the magician ends up becoming a mystic.

It is a serious and difficult path and one which should not be lightly attempted. It does often create a psychological backlash from the personality and a feeling of sadness when dealing with the material world. At its deeper levels of experience, a more mystical soul might feel that they have achieved all that is important to them and they might reach the state and die.

But a magician, who is probably more optimistic than your average mystic when it comes to the created world, looks back upon it and returns. They stand between these two states and manage to become both at once. This dual state of conscious looks towards the higher, more abstract worlds of Binah, Chokmah and Kether and becomes a conduit for them.

Being a 'Babe of the Abyss' or a 'Star Child' is not a mystical state that can be held. Once the experience is over, the shadow play on the back of the cave wall takes over. To get back into that state, the magician must force themselves back. But the more it is practised, the easier it becomes. The Star Child grows within the magician over time and through repeated contact with the Absolute. It is able to exist in both the abstract world and the mundane.

Arthurian Legend is full of symbols of Sword Bridges which need to be crossed to get to the Holy Grail. Obviously crossing anything that thin and sharp requires balance. You cannot be too attached to the material world or that will hold you back, and you cannot hang on to the world of spirit because that will take you over completely (you will be like Galahad, who sees the Grail and then dies. To a mystic this is the perfect death, but the magician has work to do).

The issue of non-attachment to matter is a tricky one. Many mystics hate matter. Some Gnostics were convinced that the Devil must have created it to trap our souls and prevent us from seeing divine perfection. But there is a certain spiritual feeling which does lead both mystic and magician across the abyss.

This was expressed in a mantra which was given to those reaching a high grade in the Golden Dawn off-shoot, the Stella Matutina, and was an inspiration for the poet W.B. Yeats.

> Earth born and bound, our bodies close us in,
> Clogged with Red clay, and shuttered by our sin – We must arise.
> Flowers bind round and grasses catch our feet,
> Bird songs allure and blossom scent is sweet – We must arise.
> Mountains may beckon and the seas recall:
> Cloud-forms delude and rushing streams enthral – We must arise.
> Planets encircle with their spiral light,
> Stars call us upward to our faltering flight – Thus we arise.
> Sun-rays will lead us higher yet and higher,
> Moon-beam our souls scorch with their purging fire – Thus we arise
> Into the Darkness plunge, fearless of pain;
> Coldness and silence cleanse us again – Still we arise
> Open ye Gates of Light, Doors open wide;
> Gaze we within at the Glories you hide – We have Arisen.

This is a state where you feel you have done everything and realise that the material world is dissatisfying. This is not a rejection of the material world, which would be just as wrong as a rejection of the world of spirit. Both are fragments of the One Thing. If you want to be a Star Child you have get beyond fragments and ditch a lot of dualistic thinking.

What is needed is a realisation that what you are watching is a shadow play and you can take your chains off whenever you like. It happens to everyone at a certain point, but not everyone gets their chance to do something about it.

The spiritual process of 'crossing the abyss' initially means starting to observe the world totally without involvement, emotion or preconceptions. This is done whenever it is possible until it becomes second nature.

Observation without attachment takes you to a state which you will not have been in since you were a child. A child sees the world as entirely focused on them. If a person disappears from sight, there is no proof that they actually exist any longer, they 'disappear'. Perspective changes too. You will notice that all points in your vision stretch away to a vanishing point which stems entirely from you.

This might seem like it is being egotistical, but with further meditation you see that the ego is what you say you are, rather than what you really are. There is little proof that others actually exist and they might simply be shadows on the wall of the cave.

This sometimes leads to a feeling of isolation from humanity and an understanding that all around you is like a plot of a bad film which the real you is watching. In fact the biggest danger is that as you practice watching, you become more cynical and stop caring about the rest of the world. But before that leads to a rejection of the material world, you use it to provide momentum to search for the Divine One.

But the problem for the magician is that he has gone so far by using symbols. True, they might have come from the Divine, but they cannot take you into the macrocosmic divine states which formed them. Once the macrocosmic consciousness is seen, then all symbols become null and it takes a new consciousness to understand what is happening.

This half-world has all sorts of different symbolic metaphors. In traditional Cabbalah you cross over a desert, where you are tempted by the devil, and find an abyss which you must get across, usually by casting yourself into it and having faith that God will uphold you.

A literal understanding of this is probably the reason why Crowley went into the desert (although he did not throw himself off any cliffs) but in fact what happens is that each person is given an image that is unique to them. Explaining this is tricky because the temptation is to say that the experience is psychological, which it is not. It is a vision which might be interpreted as psychological after the dust has settled, and the records are looked at. But to the person who experiences it, the vision is real and impersonal. It overwhelms.

I encountered my own abyss in a minor way when I was happily married to a nice, non-magical person. I had reached a certain point in my magical life where I was simply writing and initiating people into the magical group to which I belonged, but living a normal 'muggle' life.

One winter's day I was walking with my wife down a city street when I just 'stopped'. I didn't faint, I did not fall unconscious, as far as I was concerned, my awareness stayed the same but time moved. I opened my eyes and I was lying on the ground. My shoe had come off. From my perspective the scene changed and I was in an ambulance. There was no pain, or fear. I was warm and happy. Then time moved again. Next I appeared in the hospital. As far as the doctors were concerned, I had a Grand Mal epileptic fit, but no one could actually say why or how, and I have not had one since.

My biggest fear has always been that I would lose my mind and reasoning, and that death might end up as some oblivion. But when I experienced it there was no fear. Mind created reality and placed it in a neat order. If this was switched off then time slipped. I had briefly been shown how the universe worked on a macrocosmic level.

Many people think that when they have visions there should be a cast of a thousand angels and a bearded bloke on a throne. I had not *seen* anything but what I *experienced* was macrocosmic and it brought me out of myself.

I decided it was pointless playing at magic, I had to *become* the magic and that would mean some drastic changes. It took some time for these changes to happen, and the universe I had created had to be slowly destroyed and a new one created. I failed a couple of times before I got it right, but it is safe to say that after the vision, nothing was the same. That was my first experience of the abyss and it was also direct demonstration and 'unvarnished' by symbol.

What follows is a pathworking which will give you an idea of a sequence that can be followed. It is a *training* pathworking so that you may understand the symbolism involved. It is only a starting point and not meant to be taken literally. As I have said, to truly approach the abyss you have to use that symbolism in your own way. Once you get to that state you will have to abandon symbolism to really comprehend it.

The training pathworking will have an effect, and will open the way for you to experience the abyss and start to understand the divine consciousness. I suggest that this one is read to you or you record it on tape.

The pathworking should be performed in sacred space and you should have repeated the above mantra at least ten times before you start.

STAR CHILD

Before you is a door. Upon the door is the image of a baby with stars in its eyes. Focus on that image and let the door fade until it opens into a scene of astral mist. You step through the door and the mist clears. Look at your feet. You are standing in the desert. It is not the sort of sandy desert of the Sahara. It is hard, hot stone desert, devoid of life.

You are dressed in a plain brown robe which is the colour of the earth and in your hand you hold a staff. The staff represents your steadfast will and aspiration.

You look behind you. There is the city of manifestation. It is bright, with flashing lights. In this city, from which you have come, you know people will be busy with their lives, chasing amusement, filling their lives with whatever they define as meaning. Shadows. You have played with the shadows and now even your body feels like a tomb. Now you must escape. In your hand is the lamp in which is the spark of the Indwelling Glory leading you towards something new.

You walk into the desert. Never to return the same again.

Walking in the heat. You have no water, no food, you don't feel you need these things. Dust in your mouth. Dryness. The lamp you carry feels heavy. Truth be known, you have been walking for so long that you have even forgotten what the lamp you hold looks like. Your eyes are fixed on the horizon. One foot trudges wearily after the other. What is it that you are heading toward? You have no idea.

On the horizon you see a building and you head towards it. If it gives you anything, it will give you shelter from the sun. But as you come closer you see that it is a mausoleum and there is something living there.

As you get closer you see the jackal-headed Guardian of the Necropolis, Anubis.

He carries a sword and has the job of protecting the mysteries from the profane, or unbalanced forces, that would seek to destroy them. He wears a white kilt with a lion's tail at the back and a black and white nemyss. He carries a sword with a red hilt. He has a necklace of black and white beads. His head is black, with golden eye make-up.

You take a deep breath said say:

"As I approach the Gate of the Mysteries, I meet its Guardian and pass without fear, for we are the one and the same.

I invoke thee, oh Guardian of the Sacred Mysteries
Come forth and judge my soul, oh Anubis
Protect me as I enter the holiest of holies
Speak for me before the Throne of Truth
For I am like unto thee
A manifestation of the Most High.
Take me in your arms
As the tempest rages
Uphold me as I reach toward the stars
For thou art the defender of the sacred circle
My strength and refuge."

He bows to you and takes you by the hand into the tomb. All around you on the walls are images of your life. Then you realise. This tomb is yours and Anubis is death.

You do not have much time to worry about this until you come to the sarcophagus itself. On it is a realistic depiction of your own face, dressed in the form of Osiris.

Anubis looks at you.

"It is time," he says. "Your life is over and this personality has done all it can. If you would become a Babe of the Abyss its time is over and must pass."

You nod and open the sarcophagus. It has been a full life, but hard, and you must now pass on. You hand your lamp and staff to Anubis and lie down in the sarcophagus.

It does not feel uncomfortable. It is like getting into bed after a hard day of work. You shut your eyes and the next moment time moves.

You are standing outside the coffin, looking down at the image. Anubis is there and he hands you the lamp.

What happened?

"You died," said Anubis. "The old self is no longer, the personality which held it is being absorbed into the Universal Mind as a memory. It has done its work."

You do not feel sad. In fact you do not feel anything, nor do you think. You just are there. It is an odd sensation. You do not think or feel any more. That was part of the personality. You can feel expansive, like you have just escaped from a confined space. Anubis has changed too. He still holds your lamp but your staff has become a caduceus.

The phrase "He Who is Upon the Mountain" comes into your head and you feel moved to say the following:

"O Thou Lord of the Hallowed Land,
Sky hunter of dawn
Master of the feather of truth;
I call upon thee as a son (or daughter) calls to a father.
Hear my call and indwell my Soul-Temple.
Extend thy hand through the veils of time.
O Anpu, who stands upon the Mountain,
thou who art upon the pillar of the north,
hear my call and indwell my Soul-Temple.
O Sah, who guards the heavens at night-time,
shine thy beams of Divine Light upon this supplicate.
Hear my call and indwell my Soul-Temple.
I have cleansed myself in thy sacred lake,
I have offered unto thee incense,

now indwell my Soul-Temple with Holy Fire.
The Paths to the Gate are cleared,
Anpu is within his House, he puts
his hands on the Lord of the Gods,
Magic and protection are knit about him.

O Great One, who became Sky,
You are strong, you are mighty,
You fill every place with your beauty,
The whole earth is beneath you, you possess it!
As you enfold earth and all things in your arms,
An indestructible star within you!

The Sky is cleared, the Horizon dwellers
rejoice, for Ra arises from the Double gates.

For I am the Companion of Anpu
within the secret places of the Great Hall."

Time moves but you stay still. You are no longer in the tomb but in the desert. Before you are seven flames, each a different colour of the rainbow: Violet, Indigo, Blue, Green, Yellow, Orange and Red. These are the gods of the earth, each holy and pure in their own way. Each stands over you and you feel a little of its power given to you. It strengthens you. You start to remember.

You crossed this way before as you walked to the city to live your life. But you forgot. Now you start to remember who you really are.

Time moves again.

You are standing on the edge of a cliff. It descends into darkness. In front of you the air shimmers like heat on a hot road. You look up and the shimmering extends into infinity. One step forward and you could be swept upwards or fall downwards.

You look across the abyss and you see that on the other side it is darkness. Not an empty darkness, but a darkness which contains all. You know that darkness is your real home and you want to return to it. That longing seems to seize you and you realise that all you have to do is surrender to it and you will come home. You feel a hand on your shoulder. It is Anubis.

"Your task is not to return, unless you want to, but to become something new. That is much harder."

You nod. Without thinking, you take the lamp from Anubis and cast it into the void. Instead of falling, it floats between the two cliff faces.

You focus your mind on that point of light, which stands out against the darkness. Suddenly you are floating above the abyss. You look across and you see the shadowy form of yourself standing next to Anubis. But you are also aware of the darkness at your back. You shut your eyes and try to surrender to it. It feels like a stream of blackness, of potential. You melt into it and expand into it.

You are not.

You are aware of symbols forming within you.
Ideas, new teachings, new beginnings.
They flow through you like a river.
Your eyes have become stars.
You become the universe.
Ever forming, ever changing.
Your brown robe has become a white robe of glory
And you have the stars in your hands.
Before you is the globe of the earth
You know that on that globe is the city of manifestation.
From behind you, from the divine potential, you have a new idea.
A new way that this universe will go.
You are the magician shifting the elements.

You feel yourself begin to re-assemble and then you are reborn in this time and this place and in this reality.

Chapter Seven

IMAGINATION AS A MAGICAL TOOL

"What makes magical ritual hard is the thing that most people forget. They forget to visualise the god-forms and the Inner Temple and then the whole thing degenerates into a badly scripted costume drama with only psychological value to the candidate."
Paola Farrell

IMAGINATION IS THE KEY to making ceremonial magic work. This appears to be a great secret which no one seems to talk about much. You will hear a lot of magicians talk about Will or working with their Holy Guardian Angel, but few of them will admit that the core of magic is to do with imagination. In fact there are even some who insist that imagination is not part of the equation at all, and that those who insist on using such techniques are just deluding themselves. Instead they call for ritual to be performed perfectly. An example of this is masonic ritual, which is stripped of all visualisation and imagination.

But ritual is designed to assist visualisation and make it easier to interact with the forces you are using. In ritual you allow yourself to fall into a state where the images come easily. Some modern magicians play down the need for ritual to achieve this state. If they use ritual at all, it is simple and perfunctory. There is nothing wrong with this idea, but to me it is a bit like trying to do a high jump without making the run up beforehand.

What happens in a good invocation is that an image of the god, goddess or angel appears strongly to your mind. A well written one will give you a description of the being you want to call, and capture the essence of its being.

Here is a short one to the Egyptian God Osiris which is adapted from the Book of the Dead:

Osiris

Homage to thee, O Osiris, the lord of eternity, the king of the gods, thou who hast many names, whose forms of coming into being are holy, whose attributes are hidden in the temples.

You are the substance of which we are made. You are the chief of the company of the gods, you are the beneficent Spirit among the spirits, you draw your waters from the abyss of heaven. Your heart germinates, you produce the light for divine food, the height of heaven and the starry gods obey thee, thou openest the great pylons of heaven. The stars which never set are under the seat of thy face, and the stars which never rest are thy habitations.

When you write or perform a ritual, you use words and actions that create images in your mind which stir the emotions. This is one of the reasons why rituals can take a while and are full of often long speeches. They are designed to create a particular type of imaginary image which is packed full of meaning and symbols. Once the magician has the flavour of this image they then interact with it and intensify it. Understanding this takes a bit of time, particularly if you are used to shorter and simpler systems such as Wicca, which creates its images with short repetitions or charms. The first time I carried out a long invocation, the god I was calling showed up after a paragraph of speech and it seemed redundant to keep on with the invocation.

I brought up this point to my Golden Dawn teacher, who told me that once the god had arrived then the rest of the speech should be spent interacting with that force. When it is mastered, that first stage of the invocation is a little like getting into a boat and pushing off into the river, while the second part is like paddling down a rapid. Images and feelings are supposed to come flying into the sphere of sensation so fast that it becomes real.

There is such a thing as over-egging the pudding. I have seen, and written, rituals and evocations which were too long, complex and dull to work properly. Some rituals work better for me if I did not write the words, and used ancient invocations based on things like the Egyptian Book of the Dead or the Orphic Hymns. Others however have more punch if they come from my own creative powers.

This use of imagination, where symbols come to the mind unbidden, is acceptable even to those who follow the masonic approach to magic. They say that the use of symbols and these sorts of rituals are what it is all about. When I underwent a masonic initiation, I remember clearly being swept away with the imagery of the ritual until I found myself making my oath before King Solomon. Making this point to my initiators, they told me that this was normal and one of the reasons the founders, who were all members of the Golden Dawn, had formed the Lodge in the first place.[56]

But there was another more important use of imagination which is a part of the ritual. The first is the use of what are called Inner Temples.

INNER TEMPLES

While there are those who spend a lot of time and effort on their temple furniture, the most important part of a temple was technically not in the room where the rite took place. From the Golden Dawn onwards the rite would be visualised as taking place in another, bigger, temple. Not everyone was in on this particular piece of information, as it was only the senior members who would be doing the visualisation. While some of these temples might have appeared spontaneously to the psychic visions of the senior members of the temple, very often they were consciously built.

The Order of the Golden Dawn built a general inner temple based on the Egyptian Book of the Dead. Specifically it was the Temple of the Goddess Maat, where the soul of a dead person would go to be judged after they were dead. While the ritual was carried out, the senior members were seeing the officers of the ritual being replaced by the gods.

While this temple was well documented, what was less known was that each group in the order had a different one with a different inner plane location. The chiefs of the Order built their inner plane temple and then arranged the furniture to become the Temple of Maat.

Needless to say, descriptions of these Inner Temples are thin on the ground and we only have references to them in the writings of those, such as Dion Fortune, who were taught by former chiefs of the Order. The reason for this level of secrecy is that once you know what an inner temple looks like, you can visit it, spy on rituals, and also destroy any inner workings that the group might have done. The Inner Plane technology was also developed over time, so that rules and other information were provided from one chief to another.

The person who revealed how the Inner Temples worked was Dion

---

56 This caused them all sorts of problems with the Masonic Grand Lodge, who seemed terrified of anything that vaguely sniffed of magic.

Fortune, who passed the information on to her students so that they could actively participate in the same process that had been left to the Chiefs. Her Inner Light Order would start each of their rituals by pathworking to their temple through a desert. As far as I am aware, this temple was later abandoned by the Inner Light, although it was still left open and some students found their way to it.

Once the group working was completed, the students would visualise the inner temple over the space they were in. The effect of this is quite alarming if you are not used to it. The space, whatever the size, feels much bigger. Energy, godforms and other visualisations are much easier to see. Psychologically it is possible to see this as a form of collective hypnosis, but magically it is something different. What you have done is use imagination to bring an inner plane location down to this world.

There are two sorts of Inner Plane Temples. Both of them are, to some extent, alive and very real.

The first is one which belongs to an original temple or the magical group which built it. While the group might have shut down on the physical, its Inner Plane Temple is still operating. Sometimes groups that work in the same tradition can find themselves patched into these temples. More psychic members suddenly find new inner scenery appearing within their workings. This happens when the group is in total sympathy with the original egregore. Needless to say, this is incredibly rare and can even be undesirable. Things might get heated if you patched into an inner temple of a group working during a period where humanity thought it was a good idea to lop heads off. Another problem is that the ruins of some physical temples are often visited by tourists, and New Age types who love to go and "feel the energy". If your temple is built around such a place, you often get some residue from them, even if you are working at levels that are much higher.

For this reason it is sometimes better to create your own.

Building an inner temple requires a lot of thought. While it does not have to conform to earth plane issues of gravity, it should fit into ideas of proportion. It should also fit into the overall mythos of the group or Order. Remember that an inner temple is a symbol of the root of your tradition.

A group which is connected to Ancient Egypt should make their temple using architectural features of that period; it should not have a dome installed on top of it just because it "looks pretty." You should not attempt to build an inner temple based on fantasy novels either, because that would be wired into a symbolic set which never really was. You might think that having an ice wall which looks like something from *Game of Thrones* will provide you with lots of security, but since it only existed in imagination, it can only provide imaginary protection for your group.

One of the best books to get on the construction of Inner Temples is *The Canon: An exposition of the pagan mystery perpetuated in the Cabbalah as the rule of all the arts* by William Stirling. This book explains how esoteric teaching was used to build temples, churches and cathedrals and was a major influence on the later Golden Dawn.

This sort of information is important because, unlike your castle in your Inner Kingdom, this cannot represent any one member's unconscious. The last thing you want is a group entering a person's own psychological Inner Kingdom. This is often a problem if a group leader builds an inner temple for the group on their own. When this happens, symbols which relate to their own fears and unconscious mechanisms can become features when they should not be. For example, if the leader associates a garden with a place which they escaped to when they were a child, they could place one in an inappropriate place within the temple grounds. Another one is when the leader is paranoid and builds an Inner Temple with more security than Fort Knox. This is less likely if the structure of an inner temple 'follows the rules.'

Unless you are really interested in messing with people's heads, it is not a good idea to use underworld symbolism for a group's Inner Temple. While Inner Temples with underworld themes are great places to visit, you do not want your Order's base temple to be in one. They tend to drag up the darker aspects of the group's psyche. This rules out having symbols associated with them, such as caves, lakes of fire, multi-headed dogs etc. The pseudo-magical group the Hellfire Club used a lot of this sort of symbolism in its rituals. Fortunately it was just a fantasy group which enabled rich British nobles to shag prostitutes, but the fact that its reputation has survived as "something more" is an indication of how much underworld seeped out through the group's faked rituals.

There are some exceptions to this rule. If you were working on a Mithras tradition you would meet inside a cave, but the roof would be painted like the night sky.

Each symbol within an Inner Temple should be carefully thought about before it is placed and it should all be themed carefully within your tradition. The temple should also be built within an appropriate landscape.

Building an Inner Temple is done by a group of pathworkers who are led to the site by the group leader. It pays to have researched how ancient and medieval workers would have built their sacred temples, so that you can write this sequence into the pathworking. As far as workers are concerned, it is usually better if the group asks the gods, to whom the temple is to be dedicated, to send workers to help. Say, for example, you have decided to build a temple to Thoth. You would pathwork to an appropriate place on the Nile and invoke the god to send beings to assist you, such as an army of Egyptian workers and craftspeople. Your ritual team would then begin to visualise it being built. Although it might appear that these beings are building the structure, in fact what is really happening is that they are building it from their own essence and it is just the observers' perception that sees something different.

Once it is built, it is important that you visualise that it is brightly lit. It should always be seen on a bright day, hardly ever at dawn or twilight, and rarely at night. The reason for this is that the temple has to be seen as a symbol of light and brightness. You might be a member of the Golden Dawn, but if you know the symbolism of that order, you would not want your temple to be locked in a perpetual state of morning gloom (unless you really want to live in the shadows).

One important thing which has to be thought about is security. You do not want every stray astral being wandering in. Some groups are also of high enough prominence to find themselves on the receiving end of other groups' attacks. You also do not want former members to have access once they have gone. Most magical orders have things called the Password of the Aeon, which is a watchword given to the Inner Temple guardians.

These guardians are astral shells that are built by the leader of the group in an appropriate form. Often these forms are gods or angels who are asked to protect the group. Sometimes they are elemental beings who are ordered to serve by their Elemental King, who has to be approached by the group. Usually there is more than one guardian who is spoken to but never more than three. One guardian can often be a multitude of beings who operate under a single control, such as a unit of guards. At other times it can be something like a tree which does not move at all but just radiates power to those who approach.

Some groups use some fairly exotic godforms which require advanced techniques to build. For example, there are some which use an artificial elemental. These are similar to the concept of a golem in that they are made by a magician out of the essence of group members and then bought to life using a specific ritual. Golems are as strong as the collective mind of the group, but have been known to get out of control, which is why they are only a tool for experienced magicians and orders. Even more exotic is a human guardian, who is a former member who has died but wants to remain with the temple on the Inner Planes to protect it.

It is possible to become too obsessed with Inner Plane guardians and detail their activity so specifically that their function is neutralised. For example, one chief told his group that his order was completely safe from outside attacks. I left his group, somewhat under a cloud, and he told me that getting into the Inner Temple would be impossible because I would not know the password. But his pathworking to his inner temple was badly worded and if you said the right thing to the guardian they had to let you pass.

But over the years I have seen that guardians have often acted against members who were causing trouble even before anyone was aware of what they were doing. In one group I was involved in, a person secretly joined another order "to see what it was like." This new order used symbolism in a way which was antagonistic to his old one. When he appeared at the next meeting, he complained that he could not "get into" the ritual because the temple guardian had forbidden him, even though he knew the password. A week later he left the group completely and is happy with his new order.

In another case a person who failed an initiation and was projecting his psychological anger onto others found it difficult to get into the temple. He was carefully examined by the temple guardians who let him in eventually, but his behaviour was closely watched until finally they refused to let him in at all.

It is these entities which are part of the selection process of candidates into the group. When a person applies to join, the group leader approaches the guardians and asks for the new candidate to be tested to see if they should be admitted.

The more sensitive candidate is often aware of this particular process, as it sometimes involves night-time visits. In other situations it involves dreams where a meeting with the temple guardians is arranged. Some groups facilitate the process by giving the candidate a pathworking where they meet one, or more, of the guardians and are asked searching questions.

In creating your guardians you should be careful not to use symbols which contain their own destruction within them. A guardian Medusa, who turns people to stone, might look scary, but every child who has read Greek legends knows not to look at her and can come up with good ways to defeat her. Harry Potter pointed out that a three headed dog could be sent to sleep with harp music, and you kill hydras by cutting off their heads and burning the stump. St. George godforms are jolly good at killing dragons.

Once a temple has been built, and the guardians put in place, then a ritual has to be written to connect it to the contacts of the Order. Traditionally this was just done by the chiefs; after all it was only them who knew who the contacts really were. Modern groups, who don't tend to keep their contacts secret, often allow their members to take part in the consecration. It actually helps fuse the temple into the group mind of the order.

Over time these temples build up power and start to develop a life of their own. If they are not closed down, they can continue to operate long after the group's members are dead. They act as a focus for that group's work and its astral memories. Sometimes they are shut down, but the shell remains and this forms a skeleton upon which a new group is built.

Some groups do not believe that temples should be allowed to be left up and running after the group has ceased to exist. In some cases inner temples have to be closed if they are part of an Order and the members have departed following a major conflict. I have had to close two Inner Temples in my time and the experience was not pleasant.

The first time I was told to shut down a temple which had left the Order. In that case the group had not used it and the head of the Order was worried that the connection between her contacts and that Inner Plane space might be contaminated. That structure was fairly simple and closing it involved shutting down the four elemental gates and taking the sacred flame from the temple. In another case an inner temple had been built by a group in one phase of its history, but had been forgotten by those in a new phase. The new phase had a different set of contacts which were incompatible with the older group, but because of the similarities there was a risk that the newer members might find their way into the older temple. In that situation a dead member of the older group assisted in breaking the contact's link to the temple and took the light to where the work was being continued.

Both situations were sad occasions and there was a feeling of a vacuum in each of the temples after the light departed. Afterwards I visualised the site returning to nature, before melting into astral mists.

PERSONAL TEMPLES

There is nothing to stop you building or finding your own personal inner temple. This can be used for all your personal rituals. It can obey all the rules of the group temples, only it is usually linked to your own idea of God or your contact. It is handy for those who find themselves constantly on the move. It is possible to enter your inner temple from anywhere on the planet and you can be guaranteed to get the same connections wherever you are operating. However, if you are in a group, you will find that entering its temple is a lot more powerful. Most groups expect that you will do personal workings in their temples, provided that you do not do something which you know will get people cross. Summoning demons, or necromancy, is usually frowned on and could get you thrown out by the astral bouncers of the temple.

EGREGORES

At the turn of the century the Order of the Golden Dawn booted out its autocratic founder and Scottish romantic Samuel 'MacGregor' Mathers and set up a committee to do his work. According to Aleister Crowley, Mathers responded by performing a black magic rite involving baptising some peas with the names of the committee members and shaking them about in a tin. Then he sent a young Crowley wearing a kilt and a mask to seize the group's temple equipment. Assisted by a bouncer from a local pub, Crowley managed to get into the building and change the locks, only to be ejected by the police. Mathers had better luck with his pea magic and the committee was soon at each other's throats.

These sorts of dramas are common to many esoteric groups dedicated to the development of spiritual enfoldment and fraternity in a way that they would not happen at your average drama group or sports club. But a group of occultists is a little more 'intense'.

An outsider can put a lot of this down to fancy and the fact that esoteric groups are populated by people that are either eccentric or nuts. But there are some sane people in magic groups and there might be a less obvious answer.

Psychologists have noticed that people do funny things when they are amongst groups of other people. They suddenly become easily manipulated and can do things that they would not normally do. This is the psychology of the mob, which suddenly forms in a group of people who then as a single body go off on a rampage.

This is exactly the sort of energy that an esoteric group uses to achieve the levels of faith needed to move mountains.

In esoteric terms we call this group mind an 'egregore', which is like the soul of the group, only in magical organisations it has a personality that is almost as tangible as any actual member.

This egregore is made up of the sum total of aspirations and beliefs of all group members past and present. It is powered up every time a rite is performed and the longer and more often a group meets, the more powerful it becomes, until it has the power to do lots of interesting things: some good, some bad.

On the plus side, it means that all the magic you do, whether you are with the others or not, suddenly develops a special power. It is like you are tapping into a reservoir of energy that you never had as a solo magician.

An egregore has a personality, much in the same way as a human. There are some group egregores that are slow, plodding and methodical and there are others that are light hearted and ephemeral; some are intellectual while others are touchy feely types.

A good group is aware of its egregore and does many different things to preserve and empower it. We have already noted some imagination techniques that assist groups to empower their egregore. Here is another one which has been used by many different groups for many years. In groups I have been involved with we arrange for an image of the egregore to be drawn. This usually shows an image of the gods or contacts of the group, one or two of the guardians, a symbol which sums up the group and what it aspires towards. This image acts as an icon and provides a direct doorway for group members to access the inner temple, but it also means that they have to pass through the egregore every time.

ThE ChALICE VISUALISATION

In the chalice ritual the group acknowledges the existence of the egregore and gives it a shape – that of a cup. This sends a powerful suggestion that the group is a passive vehicle from which we can draw all things needful. There is also the image of a hexagram above it that shows us that we are under the will of the Higher, that reflects into the group influencing its direction.

We do this rite at times of conflict to remind ourselves that we are actually one group working towards the same goal – whatever our individual state is at the moment. Temple members stand in a circle around the altar holding hands. The group leader says the following:

Let everyone aspire to their highest idea of God and see it as a ball of white above their head. Allow this energy to send a ray of light to their heart centre, which is the place where the soul dwells within the body. See it turn into a golden ball, like a brilliant sunrise. Feel it warm the chest. See the light descend to the groin, where it becomes a moon surrounded by violet light. This is your unconscious self.

Now become aware of your brethren around you. See a line of light connect each of these three spheres to everyone in this circle. Spirit to spirit. Sun to sun, Moon to moon. So that all are connected by silver cords to each other – like spokes in a wheel.

Look to the centre of the wheel. In the hub you see forming a silver chalice, built by the combined energy of the group.

Send your consciousness through the spokes of the wheel into the silver chalice. You are inside the chalice with all of the members of the temple. Slowly you merge. You feel thoughts and feelings which are not your own, but you are … together. One.

You look up and there you see a glowing golden hexagram, which represents the divine light manifest in humanity. You see the light of the hexagram reflecting onto the waters of the group mind. Transforming, changing, supporting, helping the group to become something new. Dedicating it to the Divine. No longer a smaller ego, demanding attention, but a group uplifting each other.

You leave a part of yourself as a sacrifice within the chalice and then return to your body. Allow the lines of connection to draw themselves back into your body.

Watch as the chalice rises, as the group rises.

It absorbs the hexagram and it turns to gold.

Then it rises further and becomes white, golden light.

The chalice disappears into the heavens.

IMAGINATION IN SIMPLE RITUAL

One of the most used rituals in the Western Mystery Tradition is the Lesser Ritual of the Pentagram, so we are going to use this as a case study for the ritual use of imagination.

The Lesser Ritual of the Pentagram was devised by the Golden Dawn as a method of creating sacred space to give students some basic protection within workings. It has been kidnapped by others who have unintelligently hammered it into their own traditions.

Before we look at the use of imagination to make this ritual come to life, it is important to clear up a few misconceptions. Firstly, the Lesser Ritual of the Pentagram [LRP] has about as much to do with elemental magic as a packet of peanuts has to do with the workings of the poetry of William Topaz McGonagall. This particular myth has come about because of a fundamental lack of understanding about the Golden Dawn and how it worked. The failure to understand the depth and power of this simple ritual has led many armchair occultists to develop 'improved' versions. While these improved versions might 'work' within their own traditions, they do not work within the context of the Golden Dawn system.

In the early Golden Dawn, the inner order with its emphasis on elemental pentagrams had not yet been developed. True, elemental pentagrams were drawn by the Hierophant in the elemental grades, but few would have been aware that this was happening. Even if they were aware, no candidate would ever see a "banishing earth pentagram".

To an innocent candidate, the pentagram in the LRP was a complete, classic 'magical sign' that was drawn in four directions by the operator. Also the mindset of the order, and the people who went through it, was you did what you were told. Only the stupid would *not* realise that the angels were Archangels, but the impact of a six-rayed star between the columns would have passed most by. As for colour, the GD was most protective of the use of colour in the outer order and it is extremely likely that the whole operation was monochromatic. It was only in the inner order, when this was developed, that colour became important. Some of this material was leaked out into the outer order. For example we find that in the later Whare Ra temple, 0=0s were given black cards with the divine name and the pentagram in colour to stare at, to add their visualisation of the ritual.

We also know that it is impossible for the LRP to be linked to any elements because it lacks a spirit pentagram as part of the rite. It would be an anathema to the GD's rule of always "invoking the highest first" before doing any working not to have included a spirit pentagram first. When elemental pentagrams are used, they have to be accompanied by a spirit pentagram. Something which is clearly lacking in the LRP.

The first reference to an LRP pentagram being used in an exorcism within the GD is in *Flying Roll XXXIV,* where Brodie Innes uses a pentagram to deal with an Earth elemental that was bringing sickness to his wife. However, on examination of the case, Innes does not perform an LRP at all and instead invokes the elemental to give it form before blasting it. Innes was also an adept at that point and well capable of using the full versions of the pentagrams.

Another case is recorded in Dion Fortune's *Psychic Self-Defence,* where she draws a pentagram between her and an astral creature and vibrates a divine name. Again nothing like the LBRP, although it shows similarities. Later in her book, she gives a watered down version of the LBRP as a tool for exorcism but strips it of a lot of its GD symbolism.

Much of the alchemical and exorcism attributions for the LRP seem to have come from Aleister Crowley. While it is possible that he got these from Bennett or Mathers, it is also likely he obtained them from his own meditation.

It is from him that we get the idea that pentagrams light you up on the astral. By the time Israel Regardie appeared on the scene, these attributions were being adopted – at least outside the existing GD.

ThE SYMBOL OF ThE PENTAGRAM

The pentagram is associated with the planet Venus, because when viewed from Earth, successive inferior conjunctions of the planet plot a nearly perfect pentagram shape around the zodiac every eight years.

Another attribution is its association with the five pointed star of Geburah. In this guise the pentagram is showing humanity's ability to control elementals because of its five-fold nature. Since most of the universe is populated by elemental or pure spiritual beings, the fact that a human is a mixture of both gives them considerable protection and power.

Within the symbol of the Pentagram is the Golden Mean, or Divine Proportion, or the Divine Section. This is a mathematical ratio expressed as the Greek letter φ (Phi) which is a number with the value of 1.6180339887, or 1.618. This 'Golden Ratio' fascinated Pythagoras and Euclid. The Pythagoreans used the pentagram as their symbol. Euclid defined the Golden Ratio: "A straight line is said to have been cut in extreme and mean ratio when, as the whole line is to the greater segment, so is the greater to the lesser." It can be used to divide a line or rectangle into two unequal parts, so that the proportion of the two new parts or portions is the same as the proportion of the larger part of the original line or rectangle.

But as far as occultists are concerned, the pentagram is a symbol of a perfected human being. It is a symbol of spirit ruling over the elemental nature.

ThE PRIMARY FUNCTION OF ThE LRP

Within the Golden Dawn there were several advantages to making a trainee magician learn the LRP. Firstly it would teach them how to vibrate names and make correct ritual gestures and visualisation. The LRP helps to integrate spiritual energy within all aspects of daily life and a balancing of the personality. The use of a regular ritual has been applied in many religions as a method of rooting the spiritual within the mundane.

However, there is more to it than that. There were magical meanings held within the ritual which linked it to the student's 0=0 initiation and to an extent the whole of the first order work. This aspect of the LRP is missed by those groups who use it, but are not part of the Golden Dawn.

One of the things that needed to be understood alongside the LRP was the Tree of Life, the traditional 'flat tree' which we see used by Israel Regardie and Dion Fortune. It is a five pillared Tree of Life, based around the middle pillar, with Binah, Geburah and Hod extended to the front right and back left pillars and Chokmah, Chesed and Netzach on the front left and back right pillars. Only the middle pillar of Malkuth, Yesod, Tiphareth and Kether stays the same.

All this information would not be known to the outer order candidate. In fact they would not even hear about the Sphere of Sensation until they reached the 5=6 grade. However this did not mean that their own sphere of sensation had not been orientated to this particular format. Mathers, in his magical instructions for a 0=0 ritual, tells the officers that they must visualise the candidate's sphere of sensation as having these pillars within them.

In the Golden Dawn, whenever you see pillars, they represent some form of gateway. In her private articles for the Society of Inner Light, Dion Fortune hinted that the two pillars in front represented the future, those behind represented the past, while the gateway formed on the right and left hand, and the Middle Pillar are the present.

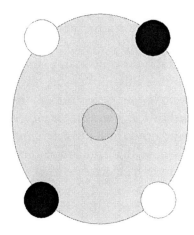

So what you are looking at when you look straight ahead is your future. Symbols that you might see in your own Sphere of Sensation are those that are gearing up to actually manifest. Those behind you are what have already gone. Symbols close to you are those which are with you now.

The Sphere of Sensation and its Relationship to the LRP

The LRP makes changes to the Sphere of Sensation so that the person gradually develops. It does so by placing powerful symbols within the sphere of sensation which become enforced over a period of time.

First you perform the Cabbalistic Cross. This draws down power from the crown to the feet. It balances and energises the sphere for more important work. It also opens the Tiphareth centre to control the operation.

Next, you draw a pentagram between the pillars of the sphere of sensation in front of you. You vibrate the name *YHVH*, which means "I am what I am" – again aspirational. In other words, you are placing the symbol of the pentagram into your own future and energising it with your own will. In this instance you are looking towards your own portal ceremony, where the completed pentagram is unveiled for the first time. The YHVH name is important because you are talking about integrating the elements under the power of spirit.

When we draw the pentagram on the right hand, we are making a statement of who we are 'now'. The divine name here is *Adonai*, which means "Lord". We are saying that we are rulers of ourselves.

199

Now the operator turns around again and is placing a pentagram over their past and saying the name associated with YHVH, *EHVH*. This means "I am what I will be." The operator is looking at their own past and saying "I am not trapped by my past, I am going to be something better." You will note that this name is in this position because the operator at that moment has his or her back to the future.

The last pentagram is placed between the pillars of the left hand. This represents the gateway to the North, which is connected to the Earth. But again, it is also the now. The left hand gateway leads to the 'now' of the outside world, the right hand gateway leads to the inner kingdom.

The divine name here is *AGLA* ("Mighty art thou, Lord of the Earth"). What is being said here is that the operator is the ruler of the Earth. Not the planet, but our own personal Earth. Notice that the person has their back to the right-handed pentagram where they are talking about being Lord of their own Inner Kingdom. Now they are claiming that what they see is a product of their own rulership.

The Archangels in the LRP

The next part of the ritual visualises the placement of the Archangels. Most people see the Archangels as wearing their elemental badges. Alternatively they are just seen in the light of the Jewish child's bedtime prayer. However, it is important to look at who these Archangels are within the GD system.

"Before me, Raphael"

'Before me' refers to the future. Raphael means "God has healed". We are asking that God will heal us and guide us. He is also the Sun angel in the Western Mystery Tradition and therefore the initiator into Tiphareth.

"Behind me is Gabriel"

This refers to the past. Gabriel is the ruler of the Moon. We are making him the guardian of our unconscious mind and preventing our past from destroying us either now or in future. His name "God is my Strength" tells us to build our life not on our past but on the foundation of God.

"To my Right Hand, Michael"

Michael means "who is as God". He gives us the image of our inner Kingdom as matching that of heaven.

"To my left hand, Uriel"

Uriel was the Angel of the Mysteries. His name means 'Fire of God' and by placing him as the Guardian of Gate of the Earth we are allowing the Earth to be our teacher. The "Fire of God" is the serpent force represented by the staff of the Kerux.

In the next part of the LRP the operator says a phrase that only makes sense when you see it in terms of the sphere of sensation with its four pillars.

"About me flame the pentagrams but within the columns shines the six rayed star."

The six rayed star refers to Tiphareth and the Middle Pillar. Until now the operator has not activated the Middle Pillar and in doing so causes the magnetic balance of the four pillars to come into harmony. Once in harmony, you are bringing the light of spirit into the heart centre of the Sphere of Sensation, using the symbol of the Hexagram. This causes the Sphere of Sensation to glow with integrated power.

IMAGINATION AND THE PENTAGRAMS

The angels, pentagrams, divine names and archangels have to be clearly visualised, usually on some form of inner landscape. This information was not given to Neophytes in any documents of the Golden Dawn but the oral teaching which was passed to me from Whare Ra confirmed that this was the case. The Whare Ra students were given, or told to draw, the pentagrams with the Hebrew letters inside to aid their visualisation and make sure that it was as clear as possible.

Colours did vary. Some were told to visualise white, others were told blue or red. The letters were either gold or of flame.

I was told that the pentagrams should be seen as containing a sphere of astral blue light. Hexagrams would be visualised above, below and in the centre of the circle. Over the years I have not seen the point of the upper and lower hexagrams for anything other than symmetry. When you are standing inside a circle it is hard to see yourself as being inside a sphere, but I have noticed that psychically the area contained by the pentagram is tinged blue.

The emphasis of all this is that the ritual should be seen as working within the imagination. The ritual gestures and words were actually less important than the visualisation. Golden Dawn papers do talk about doing the pentagram entirely in the imagination, without having to move about at all. This does take some concentration, but it also indicates how important the imagination formula within ritual was to the Golden Dawn.

In the Magical Order of the Aurora Aurea, we teach students to visualise them performing their pentagram ritual in an inner space. Normally, they are told to start out looking at their feet and seeing themselves standing on rich green grass. Others like to perform them floating in space.

A typical landscape involves a green space which looks towards some wind-swept hills. In the centre there is a plain altar and two pillars.

The magician then projects this landscape upon the room in which they are working. When they shut their eyes they visualise the landscape more clearly. And when they draw their pentagrams, angels and divine names, they see them in both realms.

This not only makes the pentagrams and godforms easier to see, they are also a lot stronger.

In time the furniture of this Inner Landscape becomes more detailed. Some place Towers of the Winds in the Quarters, or they visualise additional godforms, such as Elemental Kerubs or angels. The astral location starts to build in power which comes into action whenever the LRP is used.

At its most basic, and with these 'imaginary' images, the LRP has many different uses.

LRP TO PROTECT A WORKING

There are two different types of pentagram – invoking and banishing. In modern magic the banishing is considered the most important. For years I had known that the Golden Dawn had an invoking ritual of the pentagram, but had never actually used it.

When I was reviewing Golden Dawn material, I found that the two pentagram rituals have been consistent, but when I re-examined them I saw something I didn't expect. Firstly, the ritual described is called the *Lesser Ritual of the Pentagram*, **not** the *Lesser Banishing Ritual of the Pentagram*. Secondly, the knowledge paper hardly describes the banishing ritual at all.

"Make in the air towards the East the **invoking** PENTAGRAM as shown, bringing the point of the dagger to the centre of the pentagram."

The banishing ritual gets an aside in the last paragraph of the paper:
"For Banishing use the same Ritual, but reversing the direction of the lines of the Pentagram."

The first thing that crossed my mind was that the Lesser Banishing Ritual of the Pentagram was considered much less important than its invoking cousin and simply a footnote. This is the complete opposite of received wisdom, particularly as it is used to protect space before a working. Mathers wrote:

"This lesser ritual of the pentagram is only of use in general and unimportant invocations. Its use is permitted to the outer order that neophytes may have protection against opposing forces and might have some idea how to attract and come into communication with spiritual and invisible things."

So now we have some idea of how the Lesser Ritual of the Pentagram is supposed to be used by those in the outer order and how it is just as important to use the invoking pentagram as it is the banishing one.

The banishing is designed to protect by repelling lower astral nasties from the sphere of sensation and connecting the person to their higher self.

However, the invoking ritual is more important to this process. The invoking allows you to bring things into your life that you want and brings about your connection with spiritual forces.

The GD material implies that both the invoking and the banishing provide protection, by nature of the divine names, the angels and the pentagrams and the fact that the six rayed star is placed in your aura. When you are drawing your spiritually empowered pentagrams and calling up your angelic guardians, you are saying that you are human and manifest the elements of spirit, fire, air, water and earth. You are asserting the dominance of spirit over the elemental nature. You are binding this statement into a magic circle, powered by the divine energy of your higher self. This is most of the protection you need. This divine force spiritualises the room so that anything that does not operate on that frequency cannot get in.

All you need to do is to tune your sphere to either throwing things away or drawing things towards you.

The banishing protects you from internal and external harm *when you need it.* If you are being attacked by the denizens of hell you would use the banishing ritual to get rid of them. If you aren't, you don't. The likelihood of the forces of darkness being interested in the first magics of a 0=0 is incredibly low.

If you want to attract an angel, you would use the invoking one before your working. So if you were doing your general daily meditation, you would perform the invoking pentagram ritual because you would want to gain information. However, if you were meditating on your own shortcomings you would do a banishing, because you would want to get rid of something inside you. If you were doing a middle pillar exercise it would be an invoking pentagram because you would want to draw the powers of those divine names to you.

Besides drawing other forces to you, the Invoking Pentagram has a direct effect on the person performing it. Rather than becoming 'guardians' and 'protectors', the Angels and divine names work differently when you perform an invoking pentagram. What you are doing is drawing their energies into your sphere of sensation. Over a period of time this should have a tremendous positive effect on your spiritual life.

The rule of thumb is that you would perform a Lesser Banishing Ritual of the Pentagram if you are working in public space that you are unfamiliar with. Otherwise you would use a banishing if you were doing a ritual to get rid of something, and an invoking if you wanted to draw something to you. In the rare cases where you were doing a ritual in public space but wanted to call something to you, you would do a banishing when you arrive at the venue, but start your ritual with an invoking.

GODFORMS

It has been said that a magician uses gods in the same way that other people use buses. In other words they are used to get from one spiritual place to another. This is not to say that we don't worship gods or goddesses; some people find this an important part of their spiritual lives. However, an occultist generally sees gods and goddesses as symbolic masks for the One Thing. This enables them to be a little more clinical about what a god or goddess is, rather than getting bogged down in having to literally believe. One of the best esoteric theories I have come across about gods and goddesses is based on the holographic and morphic field theory. These are two ideas which come from the field of modern physics.

Basically the universe is made up of energy which contains the sum total of all memory. In Tarot this is seen as the water of the High Priestess. Everything which ever was, or will be, surrounds us. Ideas, and that includes the ancestors of every race of beings, are vortexes within this energy field. There is a theory that they were created outside of the universe in two dimensional space and create a three dimensional hologram. These ideas attract others to them, associations which web things together. Plato called these vortexes ideas, while Jung dubbed them Archetypes.

From these spinning ideas, other vortexes are created and some of these are called gods. Since we are actually built from this morphic field, these ideas are hardwired into us. The gods and what they stand for are an intrinsic part of our DNA. It is for this reason that most of the gods are essentially similar and the differences in their myth unimportant. Like many ideas, they are tools for the One Thing to discover itself. From our perspective, as incarnate humans, the eyes and ears of the One Thing within its creation, we have the job of building gods to perfection. They are masks built by humanity in a bid to understand how the One Thing operates in its creation. The gods are the keys for humans to understand divine forces.

Ancient humanity wondering why the grain grew, personified that action as godlike, and gave that god a name and an associated symbol. Osiris was a corn god in Ancient Egypt and his green face and symbols of death and resurrection built the complex religion that resulted in huge temples and elaborate rituals.

Gods themselves come and go. One nation's Osiris is another's Christ. None are particularly important to the scheme of things. They are tools for the mass mind to focus on important spiritual ideas.

But the magician is in an unusual place. Ultimately they have to believe nothing and everything. Each magician has an idea of what the One Thing is, and they know they can't all be right. But gods, angels, spirits provide us with the ability to understand a part of that force and use it.

The use of godforms in magic in the West has been a slowly evolving thing. Other than Egypt, where the technique of becoming a god was fairly standard, Western magic largely relied on techniques that were designed to become ecstatic. These involved long evocations and chanting of religious texts like the psalms. The magician drifted away in a mystical ecstasy until the barriers between the mind and the One Thing melted. It is a hard technique.

However the Golden Dawn bought the idea of godforms back into the mix. It is not clear where it came from, certainly it was not seen in the masonic roots of Mathers and Westcott. It is strikingly similar to the techniques used in Tantra and may be as a result of the contacts between the UK and India during the period of the British Empire. When I was taught the technique, the method which I am showing in this article was identical to Tibetan Tantra.

The Golden Dawn's system was harder. It involved the magician building a godform out of their own astral material and then asking it to be activated by the God with an invocation. This godform would then be placed over the magician who would become the godform. This method has several weak points. First, for it to be effective the magician has to totally surrender themselves to the energy that has been invoked. This is risky.

No religion, however wonderful it once was, has escaped without some form of blood on its hands. The name of the god or goddess which sets the mystic's soul ablaze has been uttered as his or her followers have raped, murdered and stolen. Also such gods and goddesses come from an era in history which was considerably bloodier than our own civilisation. Thus those who invoke such gods and goddesses do so at the risk of calling upon tainted waters.

When you place yourself in the vortex of a godform it works directly on your sphere of sensation to express itself through you. Surrendering your conscious faculties to this godform can lead to what the Golden Dawn called "obsession". This happens when a part of the person's sphere of sensation resonates too strongly to the force which is called. The godform overwhelms the personality and it leads to forms of megalomania and insanity. It is rare, and the GD's main safeguard against this problem was fairly effective. What they did was keep the knowledge and use of godforms within the inner levels of the order. Only the person in charge of the ritual, the Hierophant, would project the godforms over the officers without telling them what he was doing.

Not telling an officer you were about to throw a godform over them in a 0=0 was a fine way of making sure that they did not allow the god they were carrying to take them over. However as the number of higher grade officers, who were supposed to know about godforms, took the role of floor officers, this was no longer useful. Once you tell an officer that he is supposed to be the god Horus they will assist by visualising it themselves. To avoid the problem of obsession, Whare Ra used to sew talismans within the tails of their Egyptian headdresses. Each was cut from tin and was designed to protect the person from obsession.

All this would have been unnecessary had they used a method which came into the British magical tradition through Dion Fortune. It is not clear where she got it from and it might even be a later AO technique.

ASSUMPTION OF ThE GODFORM

Perform the Cabbalistic Cross and the Invoking Ritual of the Pentagram. Then chant the name *IAO* at least ten times. Once you feel that light everywhere, in your mind's eye allow it to form into a ball about two inches above your head.

Visualise the god as a small statue inside your groin area. Visualise it as clearly as you can. Then draw down a line of line from the ball above your head, down your spine and connect it to the statue.

As you breathe in, see more light descend and the statue get bigger. As you breathe out, see the statue start to come alive. Allow it to grow until it occupies a space up to just below your nose. *Do not allow it to get any bigger.*

Pause for a moment and then allow your mind to make contact with the godform. You will receive all sorts of feelings, and thoughts. Just make a note of these. The goal here is to feel what the godform is thinking. Open your eyes. See with the eyes of the godform. If it is too alarming for now, just shut them and feel the energy of the godform. If you feel able, you might like to try to move as the godform, seeing your room with its eyes and touch.

Hold this feeling for as long as possible. Then sit down and pull your mind from that of the god. Allow the godform to shrink until it is the size of a statue again. Pull out the white light cord and allow it to retreat until it returns to the ball of light above your head. Perform a Cabbalistic cross and allow all the images to fade.

The effect of the above method is to keep the magician in total control of the godform. True, it still has a direct magical effect but it sends a powerful message to the unconscious. It is saying "the god is part of me" and not "I am the god." It is a lot harder to identify with something too strongly if you can shrink it or make it bigger at will.

The use of godform techniques improves the focus of your magic and the ability to make something happen. Nick Farrell might not be able to make something happen, but in a partnership with a godform anything can happen. This is particularly true if you are tapped into the mask of God which is supposed to bring about what you wish. If you are doing a ritual to improve your writing and you use the godform of Thoth you are tuning into the very essence of writing, or the divine idea.

Instead of the negative association of dealing with energies and vortexes, the magician finds their sphere of sensation charged with the energy they need to bring about their will.

ThINGS YOU CAN DO WITh A GODFORM IN RITUAL

Channelling

People who have assumed a godform can pick up a sense of the right thing to say in connection to that being. In the years I have worked with them, I find the literal information which comes from channelling godforms needs to be taken with a heart-stopping-sized pinch of salt. This is mostly because, unlike mediumship where the person has less control over the godform, the personality is alive, loud and kicking when it comes to channelling. The unconscious mind, which is usually suppressed, is given a medium in which it is allowed to speak. If it feels it is being taken seriously it will overwhelm any energy being given off by the godform and speak its mind.

Dance

The idea of dancing the godform comes from shamanism. It is a way of mixing the divine energies with your own and allowing them to manifest in this world. It is true when you are mediating animal godforms, which do not speak but teach by the way they move.

Dancing was an important part of Ancient Egyptian worship. Archaeologists have found depictions of female figures from the pre-dynastic period, perhaps of goddesses or priestesses, dancing with their arms raised above their heads. The act of dancing was an important ingredient of ritual and celebration in Ancient Egypt.

One example were the Muu-Dancers. These wore kilts and reed crowns and danced in a goose step at funeral processions. It seems they might have been a remnant of shamans whose job it was to follow the dead person to the Otherworld.

Godform assumption works better if the magician practices it and works with the godform before the ritual starts. Let us use a ritual where the magician is dealing with the dead a month or so in the future. The magician knows that he will be using the godform of Anubis and his function in the ritual will be to conduct the soul of an earthbound dead person on to an appropriate post mortem state.

During the first week or two of your godform work you should study all you can about the god Anubis. This can be found on the internet and though many books, but your goal is not to become an expert on Egyptology, it is to think "how does this god work?" In this case all knowledge of the past is available to Anubis, the Opener of the Ways, and he can share it with you if you work with him.

All your unconscious problems, fears and phobias can be cured by interacting with him. Although he has the face of an animal, he is a mask for the One Thing which is behind all.

Then produce or acquire a drawing of the god, to frame and hang on the wall.

Once it is on your wall you should always pause to think about the god. Start to talk to it. Your interactions don't have to be formal – a casual chat will do. Don't cover the image or hide it, let it see all your life. When you feel that the image has become a part of your life, and a bit more real when you look at it (it might even talk back!) then you are ready for the next stage.

Each day you perform a lesser invoking ritual of the pentagram in front of the picture. Then say the following invocation at the picture.

Place a candle, white or gold, before the drawing.

Say the following:

"Grow O light, come forth O light;
Rise O light, ascend O light."

Light candle.

"O darkness, remove thy self from before me!
O light, bring the light into me!
O these four winds that are without, bring in light to me!
O thou in whose hand is the moment that belongs to these hours, bring in the light to me!
Anpu the Lord of the Hallowed Land, bring in the light to me!
For thou shalt give protection to me here today."

Pause and contemplate the picture and then say:

> O Thou Lord of the Hallowed Land,
> sky hunter of dawn
> Master of the feather of truth;
> I call upon thee as a son (or daughter) calls to a father.
> Hear my call and indwell my Soul-Temple,
> extend thy hand through the veils of time.
> O Anpu, who stands upon the Mountain,
> thou who are upon the pillar of the north,
> hear my call and indwell my Soul-Temple.
> O Sah, who guards the heavens at night-time,
> shine thy beams of Divine Light upon this supplicate.
> Hear my call and indwell my Soul-Temple.
> I have cleansed myself in thy sacred lake,
> I have offered unto thee incense,
> now indwell my Soul-Temple with Holy Fire.
> The Paths to the Gate are cleared,
> Anpu is within his House, he puts
> his hands on the Lord of the Gods,
> Magic and protection are knit about him.
> O Great One who became Sky,
> You are strong, you are mighty,
> You fill every place with your beauty,
> The whole earth is beneath you, you possess it!
> As you enfold earth and all things in your arms,
> An indestructible star within you!
> The Sky is cleared, the Horizon dwellers
> rejoice, for Ra arises from the Double gates.
> For I am the Companion of Anpu
> within the secret places of the Great Hall.

Now you should see the drawing become alive and as real as you can. Don't see the lines or other things, you should imagine it in 3D and glorious technicolour. However, see a line of silver light coming from its heart and upwards into the sun.

Then say to the image:

> O Divine Magician, guide me through the celestial halls,
> part the Veil of the hidden world and clear my vision.

Initiate your humble servant into thy Secret Mysteries,
cast thou the Holy Circle of Starry Light.
O Royal Child, may I see thee through the veils of time,
May I enfold thee in my Ka and rejoice in thy Divine embrace.
The Ancient Ceremonies are performed,
the chants echo across the temporal halls.
May my Temple be rebuilt, the faith renewed.
May we become One, twin beams of light entwined,
the Soul-Temple glows as a Golden Dawn,
the Ancient Twilight glows across Space and Time.
May we be an Indestructible Star, a Power of Heaven.
May you indwell my Soul-Temple.
And make me complete.
Ankh, Bah, Mert

Perform a Cabbalistic Cross. Leave the candle burning.

After you have done this for a time, change the practice so that, as you contemplate the picture, you see the small figure of Anubis step out of it and advance towards you. See him move into the middle of the Yesod centre in the groin.

Look up to heaven and see a ball of white light above your head. This is the Crown of Kether, the highest form of God. Say:

"In the name of the One Thing let the spark of Divinity descend!"

Vibrate the word *Eheheh* and as you do see the white ball begin to spin and a line of white light slowly come downwards in a line down your spine until it connects with the Yesod centre and from there into the form of Anubis. Still vibrating, see the statue grow bigger until the top of its head reaches up to your nose. Don't allow it to get any bigger.

This time, speak the following as if you were the god (you might be surprised at the voice you get when you speak it).

I am the Divine Magician who guides you through the celestial halls,
I part the Veil of the hidden world and clear your vision.
I initiate you into my Secret Mysteries,
I cast for you the Holy Circle of Starry Light.
I enfold thee in my Ka and rejoice in your embrace.

The Ancient Ceremonies are performed,
the chants echo across the temporal halls.
Your Temple is rebuilt, your faith renewed.
We are One, You and Me
twin beams of light entwined,
the Soul-Temple glows as a Golden Dawn,
the Ancient Twilight glows across Space and Time.
We are an Indestructible Star, You and Me
a Power of Heaven.
I indwell in your Soul-Temple.
And make you complete.

Allow yourself to make mind to mind contact with the god, feel its ancient memories cross your mind and feel your consciousness expand. Do not try to hold this for too long. When you have had all you can take, step back from the god form and feel it below your nose. Allow it to shrink as before. But this time allow it to remain in your sphere of sensation as a small statue. Then do the sign of silence and a Cabbalistic cross.

During the ritual you would assume the godform and use it to speak your lines. This creates an unusual effect. If it is done properly then it will not feel as if it is your voice saying the lines. More psychic people will see that your face has begun to change to become more jackal-like.

Chapter Eight

OBJECTIVE PATHWORKING

OVER TIME some types of pathworking connect into the wider sphere of sensation of the Universe. This is a great moment in terms of any pathworker because it means that they are literally outside themselves and able to understand something greater. It does not happen all at once. A pathworking normally goes along its comfortable subjective way; all the symbols make sense in terms of the person's unconscious. And the next thing something odd happens. Symbols become less familiar, and more from the unconscious of humanity.

The first thing that gets difficult to understand is the concept of colour. Different cultures have colours mean different things. In the west, red is associated with passion, war and Mars, whereas in China it is considered to be good luck. What happens when a pathworking becomes objective is that the colour attributions no longer have that meaning.

Shapes of inner world beings also lose their cultural map. Angelics, which might appear to your mind as being at least human shaped, suddenly take on forms of geometric shapes, or other forms of structured energy, or even flashes of intelligent light. Landscapes often melt and are replaced by energy patterns. What is happening is that you are starting to see things as they really are, rather than as the shadows on the wall.

You also do not always 'see' things, you just pick them up with other senses. Part of you will 'know' what you are seeing, but the rest of you will be confused. This is because your mind has no terms of reference for what it sees. When it sees something that it thinks is familiar it will show it to you as a symbol. This sometimes creates Dali-like landscapes with objects which should not be there, such as the odd melting watch.

My first experience of this was when a conventional pathworking suddenly 'burst out of itself'. One moment I was watching a sacred flame in a temple and the next second it became a white gold light which was suddenly more real than anything I had seen before. I felt it and knew that it was alive.

Other times you suddenly become aware that you are seeing something outside your normal world from such an abstract or chaotic point of view that it has nothing to do with your knowledge of life. This is the inspiration behind a lot of apocalypse symbolism. A good vision like this can keep your intellect busy for years trying to piece it together.

Schools of magic trained people using pathworkings so that they became used to understanding these states when they happened. The features of many of the pathworkings in this book, for example, have ingredients which could allow contact with beings from objective reality. These components include gaps in the pathworking to allow an Inner Plane being to say something to you, or the opening of a door to a reality which is not described. True, 99 per cent of the time those voices are going to be shouted down by the Lower Self, but they still train you so that in moments when an Inner Plane being really does want to talk to you it has a space in the pathworking where you are at least open for a spontaneous piece of information to be received.

But it is more than information that is being looked for. It is possible to be in a position to actively serve while in this state. Sometimes Angelics or other inner plane beings can use a hand in dealing with some problems.

This might seem a little odd, given that angels are supposed to be all powerful, but one thing that humans understand better than angels is other humans.

For example, you find yourself looking at what appears to be an energy vortex trying to untangle 'a ball of string' of energy. Communicating with it, you discover that this is the mess that a certain idea has created in the Middle East, where confusion is the order of the day. You, being a human, know what sorts of messes humans can create when they communicate. Working with the angel, you will be better at unpicking the string and allowing communication to flow again. It might take several sessions, but there have been situations where occultists have done just that, only to find later that this was time when some new peace deal was brokered.

Below is an unpublished Whare Ra paper which was written by its then Chief Mrs Felkin. It is has close similarities to a paper written by Dion Fortune and is related to what I call the Inner Temple method. Fortune said that she acquired the Inner Temple method from the

AO Chief Maiya Tranchell-Hayes, where it was a Second Order AO procedure.

The idea of using the astral counterparts of important landmarks was very important to Dion Fortune's work. She used the astral aspects of Glastonbury Tor, but she had the additional advantage of living there. I have been lucky to have a similar site in Rome where the astral reality and the physical overlap.

As this paper points out, these are powerful sites to work for humanity rather than individuals. Rituals which take place at these levels can help humanity.

To seek out these places, even using this paper as a guide, is a lot of work. Even then they are 'protected' by their own guardians. If you do find your way into one, it pays to be very polite. If you find entrance is easy then you are in the wrong place.

The TEMPLES OF The EARTh

Whare Ra knowledge paper

There are certain areas on the earth's surface which are surcharged with ritual force. These we call 'Temples', for on them, or most of them, men have erected buildings set aside for Spiritual Teaching.

It seems probable that in the first place such areas were marked by some natural phenomenon, such as flames or hot springs in some cases. At all events they have formed sanctuaries for the wild creatures in time of stress

Having once been recognised and dedicated by man, they continue to be used by whatever form of religion prevails at any given time. As for instance the site of St. Paul and Westminster Abbey, which are known to have been Temples of the Sun and Moon in pre-Christian days. There are at least 12 such sites and there may be many more. It seems likely that our own Temple at Whare Ra is such a spot.

These areas have, from time immemorial, been associated with the Astrological Signs and Planets. We know of one on the bank of the Euphrates, which is dedicated to the Sun. One on the Ruenzori Mountains (between Lakes Albert and Victoria), which is associated with the Moon. One in Central Europe, which is linked with Venus. And another in North Italy linked with Mercury.

There are some others in China and elsewhere.

Mesopotamia (Sun) Northern Persia (Mars) North Asia (Saturn)

Mountains between China and Tibet (Jupiter).

To contact any of these, it is necessary to be quite clear which you desire to visit, and how you would reach it if you were travelling there by ordinary methods.

In these days we can go almost anywhere by air, therefore you can imagine yourself entering an aeroplane .

First protect yourself by the Ritual of the Pentagram.

Then enter your plane and behave exactly as though you were going on an actual physical journey. Follow mentally the route you have already plotted out. Descend at a convenient distance from the selected site and then endeavour to see with the interior eyes, what is before you.

It may be added that all these sites are distinguished by the presence of mountains, water (either river, lake or springs), pure invigorating air and abundant light.

So far Whare Ra has lacked the near presence of water. The Order should aim at boring, for there is at least one underground stream and there may be two.

One of the easiest Temples to reach is the Sun Temple on the Euphrates. It is simple to follow the course of the river until you are on top of a hill in a loop of the river. After a short distance a canal cuts it off from the surrounding ground and it is therefore approached by crossing a bridge either North or South of the building and climbing steps. On the South side steps begin on the far side of the stream and thus form a bridge in themselves.

On the Northern side the bridge crosses the stream first and the steps are broken into three sets of twelve, seven and three, each marked by a square landing and supports. The lowest of these is a pair of obelisks, the second two palms, the third two lion headed sphinxes.

The southern approach is unbroken and has a hundred steps with a balustrade on each side. At the top on either side there are great doors opening down the middle and giving entrance to a large square portico: on the inner side of which hang heavy embroidered curtains.

The aspirant must be ready with all his Order Signs, Grips and Passwords. If he is a Mason he had better be ready with these also.

Remember that you must always enter such a place with the saluting sign and the sign of Silence. Stand still and await further guidance and instruction; use your eyes and intelligence, make a careful note of whatever you see or hear so that you can write out a short, clear account when you return.

Remember that these Temples are not simply astral, you should receive spiritual vibrations from them and the Teaching should not be merely personal.

These places are cosmic and are concerned with world affairs, not petty personal contacts. Most of them seem to use some form of ceremonial and you may be called upon to take part in this, but if so it is for definite reason and purpose.

OThER WORLDS

The Golden Dawn and those who followed held the view that there were other realms of reality which could be visited by those who were suitably trained. As we saw in the last section, suitably trained means to have stepped out of the subjective world so that you no longer see the flickers upon the walls, but what is really there.

There were two methods that were used and they had some colourful language, which meant that many people missed the point of what they were doing.

Firstly there was *deskrying* (or sometimes just skrying) *in the spirit*. This was a subjective pathworking where someone skryed or "looked at" a particular plan of existence. This is similar to a passive pathworking. You would go to a particular location that you had not seen before and allow the symbols related to that place to build up a form of reality, populated with creatures which could tell you about themselves or the plane of existence you were visiting. This is the astral equivalent of bucket shop tourism. A tourist really has no idea what it is like to live in that particular place, and while a local might tell them all about it, point to the important features, they still have not experienced that country. You might visit the right place, take the right pictures, talk to the natives, but you would be left with all your preconceptions. But that does not invalidate those impressions. Skrying in the spirit does allow a person to experience those planes of existence without getting so badly kicked by them. It allows a person to explore before a serious visit.

The next level was *astral projection*. These days astral projection is a populist subject, but I am not convinced that many of those who practice it are having 'objective' experiences. From the Golden Dawn point of view, the distance between Travelling in Spirit Vision and deskrying it was small. When you deskried, you were seeing the image, and when you astrally projected you were trying to make the vision as real as possible. You could look at your feet and see yourself there, rather than looking at a scene through a crystal ball.

As Moina Mathers wrote in her *Flying Roll 36:*

"For example, in the room in which I am now, I see reflected in a mirror a portion of the garden. I obtain an impression of all within my range of sight, but not nearly so powerful a one as when I step out into the garden to the spot in question, and examine all the objects therein, feel the atmosphere, touch the ground, smell the flowers, etc."

The rules for skrying or astral projection, according to Moina, were complex by today's standards. You would have to work in an especially prepared magical room with an altar in the centre, on which were placed representatives of the four elements and the Cross and Triangle, incense burning, lamp lighted, water in the cup, bread and salt.

The magician would wear a white robe and the insignia of the order, they would have their magical sword and lotus wand beside them. They would sit at the side of the altar facing the Quarter of the Element, Planet or Sign with which they are working.

The room would be purified and consecrated with Fire and Water and the Lesser Ritual of the Pentagram. Then the symbol would be focused upon while the appropriate names of God would be invoked over them. The magician would then vibrate the divine names connected with the symbol before allowing a brain picture of some scene or landscape to appear in their mind's eye.

However 'skrying in spirit' or astral projection are by nature subjective and touristy and play a poor second to the last one, which was 'Rising on the Planes' and this was much harder to do.

As one of the founders of the Golden Dawn, Samuel Mathers, pointed out, it required you to believe yourself in the place. This is no small matter. You cannot have faith that you are seeing reality, you have to know that it is as real as the house you are living in. It also has to be seen just as clearly.

In *Flying Roll 11*, which was an advanced paper for Golden Dawn adepts, Mathers said Rising on the Planes was a spiritual process which aimed for spiritual conceptions, and higher aims, by concentration and contemplation of the Divine.

His technique was to formulate a Tree of Life passing from you to the spiritual realms above and beyond you.

You would picture yourself as standing on Earth and then use divine names and aspirations to "strive upward by the Path of Tau toward

Yesod, neglecting the crossing rays which attract you as you pass up. Look upwards to the Divine Light shining down from Kether upon you. From Yesod leads up the Path of Temperance, Samekh, the arrow cleaving upward leads the way to Tiphareth, the Great central Sun of Sacred Power." He then calls on the student to "invoke the Great Angel HUA, and conceive of themselves as standing fastened to the Cross of Suffering, carefully vibrating the Holy Names allied to your position, and so may the mental Vision attain unto Higher Planes."

Like most of the Golden Dawn Flying Rolls, it contains some significant teaching to allow objective pathworking, which cannot be seen if you take the instructions literally.

Rising on the Planes does not just apply to Cabbalistic techniques, although it works rather like what Mathers is describing.

What you have to do is soak yourself in the images of the place you want to go to. In Cabbalistic vision you would chant the Holy Names until you began to disconnect yourself from your body. First you would be in your sphere of sensation, but Mathers is suggesting that to go further you have to sacrifice part of yourself. He uses the symbol of the Cross of Suffering, which is what an adept has to be crucified upon before they can reach higher states. While this is a Golden Dawn symbol, and has Christian connotations, what it represents is something that is universal. To really visit these states you have to surrender your personality with all its baggage and visit these places truly in spirit.

Say for example we wanted to visit the plane of fire, to really understand the nature of that level. We would surround ourselves with fire symbols, read poems inspired by fire, looking up everything we could find about radiant energy. Then we would relax and chant a name of a divine aspect of fire until we entered an altered state. We would see a fire symbol on a door before us. We would step through it and subjectively enter into the plane. But that would not be enough. We would have to leave behind all logical thought, emotion and preconception. We would have to truly be.

ATTEMPTING TO REMOVE THE SUBJECTIVE FROM CONVENTIONAL PATHWORKINGS

Sacrificing personality really is aspirational. Few people can drop their personality as easily as Elijah's mantle. So the Golden Dawn came up with a system of symbols which were designed to make their adepts' pathworkings as objective as possible. Mathers worked out that pathworkings have special errors which cause them to be subjective. The first was memory. When we look at a scene, it reminds us of something we have seen before. So what our mind does is fill in the gaps with memory. For example, we find ourselves standing on a high place. Something reminds us of a high place we have visited before, and the next thing we know our imagination has created that scene from memory. A scene would also be changed by our emotional state before the pathworking. If we are feeling down, the scene will become muted, if we can even reach the correct level at all.

The Golden Dawn answer to that was to use the symbols of the Hebrew alphabet to magically tune the scene so that it was less subjective. This might work for other groups and orders, but it has to be remembered that the Golden Dawn spend a lot of time meditating on the meaning of Hebrew letters and this gave them a magic all of their own. I am showing the Golden Dawn method here, but it might be that you will have to come up with your own symbols, something you accept will have the same effect.

For memory problems you would formulate the Hebrew letter Tau ת in white. Tau was the symbol of Saturn, so it represents reality and stability. Visualising this letter would then cause the scene to correct itself to what is really there. You could also call upon the god Saturn, or vibrate the divine name *JHVH Elohim* and ask for the scene to be shown as it really is.

If you suspect that what you are seeing is a wish fulfilment, you would visualise the Hebrew letter Kaph כ, invoke the God Jupiter or vibrate the divine name *El.*

If the deception is that of a being which is lying – intellectual untruth – you would visualise the Hebrew letter Beth ב, appeal to the God Mercury and vibrate the divine name *Elohim Tsaboath.*

If you have problems focusing, which causes the scene to constantly change, use the Hebrew letter Gimel ג, invoke the Goddess Luna, and the divine name *Shaddai el Chai.*

If you find that your scene turns into an inappropriate erotic fantasy then use the Hebrew letter Daleth ד, call upon the Goddess Venus or vibrate the divine name *JHVH Elohim.*

Use the Hebrew letter Peh פ, invoke Mars and *Elohim Gibor*, to coerce a sense of anger and violence. Use the Hebrew letter Resh ר and invoke Sol to coerce a sense of haughtiness and vanity.

Mathers adds:

"Never attempt any of these Divine processes when at all influenced by Passion or Anger or Fear – leave off if desire of sleep approach, never force a mind disinclined. Balance the Mem and the Shin of your nature and mind, so as to leave Aleph like a gentle flame rising softly between them."

All this might appear cryptic, but if you have an angel appearing before you and telling you that you are supposed to be a Messiah for a new religion which requires everyone to think your poetry is perfect, but they must show their individuality by signing all their letters with numbers instead of names, then you would visualise the letter Resh appearing between you and the 'angel', and then, just to make sure, you would also add the letter Beth. If the angel still insists that you are a prophet of the most high and you can become one with the infinite by crucifying a toad, then it probably is meant to be.

The other thing that the Golden Dawn insisted that a student should do is 'test' the vision by using the signs of their grade. The first thing you do when you encounter an Inner Plane being is do either the sign of the element that you are in (if you are doing an elemental working) or the sign of the highest grade you hold. If the being does not reply with the sign, then they are supposed to be ignored or banished.

This tradition has dropped by the wayside over recent years, because many modern magicians think it is silly. After all, an angel is not going to be a member of your magical group, whatever flavour it is, and so is not going to know any grade signs or secret handshakes. However, this is your subjective head talking – the grade sign is not literal. You are sending out a statement that you are on one wavelength and the astral being has to adjust to that energy so that you can communicate. If they can't do this, then nothing they tell you will be any use anyway. It will probably just be static, which your unconscious will spin into a nice story. It is also useful because it means you do not waste time talking to beings that can't answer you. During some of my early Enochian work, I once spent half an hour trying to talk to a life-form which looked a bit like a cactus, which did nothing other than peel itself like a banana. Since it was unable to give any grade signs, I gave up and found a being which could. It told me that the cactus thing was one of the types of plant on that realm, so not only could it not take me to its leader, it was not going to perform any grade signs either.

The grade sign thing does make for some unusual stories when you are in a more objective vision. Once I was led to a being which resembled something like a giant purple photocopier which somehow managed to give me the right grade signs by projecting the image of a human doing the signs for me.

PATHWORKING INTO PYRAMIDS

The Golden Dawn had an interesting technique which unlocked the primal ideas behind what became modern day symbols, while at the same time integrating them into the magician's sphere of sensation.

These were called pyramid workings and they are less popular now because they are a little tricky.

To understand how they worked, you have to realise that the Golden Dawn layered all its symbolism together so that one thing could lead to another. For example, the Hebrew letter Heh also meant the Emperor Tarot key, the element of fire, astrological sign Aries and the Earth symbol of Puer. It was possible to lay this information out in the form of a pyramid.

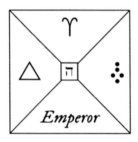

This was particularly important when it came to the use of an Enochian chess board, or elemental tablet, where each square was packed full of meaning. The arrangement and attributions of these pyramid squares are outside the scope of this book, but I recommend Tabatha Cicero's book *Concourse of the Forces* which shows the detail that the Golden Dawn took this.

To complicate matters further, each of the pyramids could be capped by either a godform or a sphinx. The sphinx was a composite symbol of each of the elements.

After studying the pyramid, the adept would visualise themselves sitting in the centre of it, with the symbols making up the four walls and the godform or sphinx above them. They would then visualise themselves rising up and merging with the sphinx before entering into a landscape which represented the combined energy of the four, which was supposed to be an archetypal manifestation of the letter.

But to make matters more complex you could use it to understand the powers of an angel or a spirit by visiting the all the letters in its name over several workings.

Say for example you wanted to understand the powers and energy of the spirit of Saturn, Zazel. This was spelt in Hebrew זאזל (Zain, Zain, Aleph and Lamed). You could take the magic square of Saturn:

4	9	2
3	5	7
8	1	6

Then 'enhance' the square using Golden Dawn information, and make them into Pyramid squares. In this case I have made the Pyramids topped with Saturn because we are trying to learn about an aspect of a Saturnian spirit.

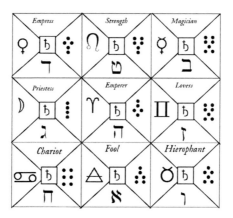

Saturn Square

From this we can see that the square is centred on the Tarot card The Emperor, so we know that Saturn energy sets things in order. Paul Case would say that the top lines were the initiating energies, the second line were the catalysts and the third line were the results.

More interesting stuff comes when we start to use the planetary square to create a sigil of a spirit or angel. Here we have created the sigil of Zazel by connecting all the letters of the name onto the square. (The Lamed is missing but is converted to Gimel to be found by using the Al Bekr chart below).

300	30	3	100	10	1	200	20	2
	Binah			Kether			Chokmah	
שׁ	ל	ג	ק	י	א	ר	כ	ב
500	50	5	600	60	6	400	40	4
	Geburah			Tiphareth			Chesed	
ך	נ	ה	ם	ס	ו	ת	מ	ד
800	80	8	900	90	9	700	70	7
	Hod			Yesod			Netzach	
ף	פ	ח	ץ	צ	ט	ן	ע	ז

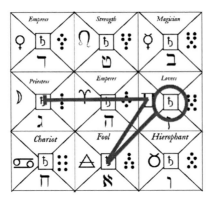

Saturn Square

What we can learn from this is that Zazel is heavily committed towards communication and Gemini, which is something we would not expect from a Spirit of Saturn. Indeed, with the Fool we would think that the spirit is pure air. The only thing that seems to root him to anything would be having his feet in the waters of Luna and the High Priestess.

But this is just intellectual information: what we want to do is to visit the plane of existence for each of those squares and ask every being we see there about the nature of Zazel. Once we have finished, and as above experienced, all the letters that are attributed to his name, we could place his sigil on a piece of paper and invoke the divine name of Saturn. Then we could visualise the sigil on a door and step through into the inner landscapes and attempt to meet the Spirit itself.

If you find the Spirit then you can negotiate its agreement to appear at a ritual to charge a talisman, for example. All the inner work you have carried out beforehand will have saturated your sphere of sensation so that it responds to the spirit better.

What follows is a description of a Pyramid working by the Golden Dawn adept Dr Edmund William Berridge into a square on the Enochian Tablet of Air. The idea was to find out about the Egyptian god Kabexnuf, who ruled the square that was being visited.

"Having enclosed myself within a pyramid, vibrating the Names, I followed the ray and found myself in a hot, very dry atmosphere; I therefore invoked the God Kabexnuf, on whose appearance I used all the tests I knew, whereby he was strengthened. At my request he then made manifest the Sphinx of his power, who became visible to me.

He was resting upon a black cube. Having once more used the Signs and applied the tests, I asked for information respecting the Square, when my repeated invocations brought before me the Angel, a powerful, virile figure of exquisite proportion and strength. He then showed me the action in the Macrocosm, which appeared to be the solidifying of Nebulae into Worlds by mutual attraction of the particles. Then, on this planet, we rested in the mouth of a volcano in active eruption, so much so that we were surrounded by flying lava. It was intensely hot, and almost mechanically I formulated in myself the idea of wrapping myself in an Apas, but a stern voice said: 'You must not, if you want to learn you must bear the discomfort.' Embedded in the sides of the volcano were crystallised jets and drops of fire which, I was told, was living gold.

I asked for another scene and was taken on to a higher plane where there was a luxuriant forest of tropical plants of gorgeous scarlet and orange, waving to and fro in an imperceptible breeze. The earth in which they grew was of a rich black colour, but there poured on them such fierce rays from the Sun that I looked to see them wither, but was told that they were on a higher plane than our flowers, and defied the scorching rays by virtue of their own internal heat which sustained their life. This Square being akin to our tropics, we went there, and saw a beautiful scene smiling in the heat of the Sun; suddenly a hot wind arose, bearing with it stones and dust with which it devastated the whole landscape. Here I was shown many tigers, and for flowers tiger lilies and Japanese red lilies in abundance. The type of human being I was shown was such a man as Chopin, playing madly on a piano in a large empty room. The elemental is a bird like creature which hops rapidly over the ground; its influence on human nature gives the desire for violent sensation."

225

Chapter Nine

GATES TO THE INNER KINGDOMS

THROUGHOUT THIS BOOK I have referred to the use of gates as methods of entering your Inner Kingdom or the astral plane. So far their use has been confined to a fairly controlled experiment with a particular gate important to the flavour of the pathworking, described at the beginning and end of each journey. However in this chapter we will look at the different types of gate where you are uncertain of the territory that lies behind it.

The Western Mystery Tradition uses many different types of gates with the aim of experiencing different aspects of reality. Each gate has a symbol upon it and what lies beyond them always relates to an understanding of it.

Generally these gates are used to access emotional or spiritual principles. Such principles might be abstract ideas like love or power, which are experienced within a symbolic landscape. Someone entering a Gate of Mars, for example, could find themselves visiting the scene of a battle or a blacksmith's forge. These principles have definite locations, flora and fauna and creatures.

It is tempting to think of these as dream worlds. However, as we saw earlier, such landscapes have both a subjective and objective reality. Remember these are built on the principle of Plato's world of ideas. What happens in these worlds may have an impact on the reality below or reflect it in symbolic form.

Visiting such worlds through gates shows you firstly what you think of the principle and secondly how it really is. Some of these symbols are extremely abstract, others are fairly obvious; however, all need to be picked apart after the pathworking is completed.

These gates are like the film *Stargate*, in that the person making the journey has no real idea where they are going to end up, or what they will see on the other side. A person passes through them with an open mind after reflecting upon the symbol and gazes upon these landscapes as if they were a tourist visiting a place for the first time. No one describes what they see, they are just entering into it and describing it for themselves. This is clairvoyant vision and does not need a person to be particularly 'psychic' to achieve it.

However, this free-form clairvoyance makes such journeys more dangerous than guided meditations because the beings on the other side of these gates often have little understanding or interest in humanity. This does not necessarily mean they are 'aliens' in the *X-Files* or *Close Encounters of the Third Kind* sense. Normally they are creatures which are associated with the particular force or the spiritual building blocks of the universe, or elementals, and see them as of little consequence.

In dealing with such creatures it is important to remember that, if they notice you at all, they are unlikely to want to do your bidding or give you much time. Some entities lack the ability to communicate at all. I remember one memorable working where I spent ages struggling to communicate with something that looked like a walking cactus, only to be told later that they had the same function as sheep on that level.

Sometimes it is possible to call upon a being to help you understand this level. These guides will prove extremely helpful if they show up and can be trusted. In a gate working you cannot guarantee anything!

Generally you would ask for help in the name of the god which applies to that level. These are given later. If the guide shows up then they must promise to help and protect you *in the name of the god or goddess of that level.* For example, here is an example of a journey to the elemental plane of Earth using the triangle of earth as a gate, which is described later.

After stepping through the gate, I found myself in a red cave, lit by glow worms, there are three stalactites but there is nothing else around. I call for a guide in the name Adonai Ha Aretz. Nothing happens. I try again. This time I notice a dwarf-like creature leaning on a shovel. I ask him what he is but he appears disinterested. He takes the shovel and hits it against the wall and there is a loud resounding ring against the cave walls.

I ask him if he will help me in the name Adonai Ha Aretz. He turns and looks at me with fear. "That name is not for the likes of me, for it burns like molten fire in my blood."

I sit and wait and still nothing happens. I resolve to chant the name Adonai Ha Aretz until something happens. After a while I have attracted an audience of the dwarves, none of whom are interested in communication.

Then one of the stalactites says to me "Who is it that calls the Name of the Lord of Earth?" I give my name and ask him if he will be my guide in the name Adonai Ha Aretz. He says he will do so to the best of his ability. "However, you will be aware that I am unable to move from this spot!"

I ask him various questions about the dwarves (who are gnomes). He tells me that he is a being that is slowly grown from the top of cave roof to the floor of the cave. After a while he would grow to reach the cave roof again. Then he would be a pillar for the cave and help support the roof.

The dwarves are earth elementals who are responsible for placing jewels in the earth. Without these jewels the earth would grow sick and die, said the Stalactite. There was a pause as I wondered out loud how I could use this information. The Stalactite said I should see this scene as if it were an allegory.

In other words, the earth (matter) is made up of congealed living energy which flows down from heaven. It grows in power until it has evolved to the point where it touches heaven. Once it has achieved that, matter will become a support for the rest of creation. It is an extremely slow process, but it means that even stones and rocks are evolving (using the widest possible definition of the word).

TECHNIQUE FOR ENTERING A GATE

This technique is taken from a Golden Dawn paper entitled *Attaining to Spirit Vision.*

1. Allow for an hour or longer of absolute freedom from interruption. Then enter the meditation room in silence and contemplation.
2. Relax.
3. Stand and perform the Cabbalistic Cross. (The GD would also have you say a prayer to the God associated with the gate you are entering.)
4. Place before you the symbol that you will want to see on the elemental gate. Gaze at it until you see into it.
5. You should then deeply sink into the abstract idea of the card. Consider all its symbolism (particularly if it is a Tarot card).

6. Shut your eyes and visualise the symbol on a door way in front of you.
7. Step through the doorway.

"The vision may begin by the concentration passing into a state of reverie; or with a distinct sense of change, something allied in sensation to a faint, with a feeling urging you to resist, but if you are highly inspired, fear not, do not resist, let yourself go; and then the vision will pass over you."

Upon completion of the pathworking it is important to return through the same gate. When you are approaching the gate from the inner plane side, the symbol will be there in clear detail on the door but will be reversed.

It is important to leave the way you came in for several reasons. Firstly it helps the process of integration to spend some time journeying back. It allows the various aspects of the self to focus itself back on the physical body. More importantly, it unconsciously trains you to return to your body after your work is finished. This is not to say that in a pathworking there is a possibility that you will become lost and never return. However, it is possible that you will start to make the same journeys in your sleep or as part of an astral journey where conscious control is harder. If you are unconsciously trained by habit, it will be easier to come back!

However, if for some reason it is too difficult to do this (you might have wandered a long way from the gate) you can call the gate to you by asking for it to appear in the name of the god (or goddess) of the level and visualising it appearing before you in detail but *reversed*.

Now we will look at some of the gates used in the Western Mystery tradition. I will give a brief explanation for each, describe where they take you, the Cabbalistic name of power associated with them, and the pagan god or goddess which can be used if you are not using the Cabbalistic system.

It is important to remember that, although some of these gates may appear to mean the same thing, they will all lead to different places and different experiences. Sometimes you will enter the same gate and end up in a different place (this will be because your mindset has changed).

TATTVIC GATES

Tattvas were one of the few techniques from the East that entered the Western Magical Tradition at the end of the 19ᵗʰ century. Brought over by the Theosophists, one book in particular, *Nature's Finer Forces* by Rama Prasad, was a great influence on the magicians of the Golden Dawn. They were a series of symbols which represented the four elements that make up creation: earth, fire, water, air and a fifth: spirit.

| *Prithivi* | *Vayu* | *Tejas* | *Apas* | *Akasha* |

The idea of the Tattvas was that there were unseen tides in the universe that were influenced by the elements. The tides, or Tattvas, flow in an unseen medium known as Prana or 'etheric matter'; surrounding the Sun and in which move the earth and other planets.

The Element of Akasha (Spirit) is strongest at sunrise, then slowly changes to Vayu (Air). This in its turn becomes Tejas (fire) and then turns to Apas (water), finally merging into Prithivi (Earth) and the cycle begins again.

According to one Golden Dawn magician, John Brodie Innes, the first Tattva Vayu can induce restlessness, while Tejas produces anger, Apas promotes receptivity and contentment, and Prithivi produces indifference.

"You get mental activity from Vayu and mental fire and genius, invention from Tejas. You get receptivity and plastic turn of mind from Apas. You get firm and steadfast mentality and an admirably sane and founding upon a rock from Prithivi. And so you may trace the mental condition of every human being and you may know precisely what tattvas have operated to produce that particular mind." As each tide moves on the earth they influence people and objects. If two people were feeling angry at each other, the appearance of the Tejas current at that time might move them to violence.

However people have tattvic tides of their own that are influenced by these forces and sometimes counteract them.

These tattvic symbols may be combined, i.e. the red triangle of Tejas may be placed in the centre of the yellow square of Prithivi to give subtle elemental combinations that show, for example, the fire in the heart of the earth.

The Tattvas are placed on a piece of black card in their appropriate colours. They are to be stared at for a few moments. Then they are visualised as being placed on a doorway.

The divine names for each of these Tattvas are *Eheieh* for Spirit, *El* for Water, *Elohim Gibor* for Fire, *Shaddai El Chai* for Air and *Adonai Malek* for Earth.

ELEMENTAL GATES

These are a simpler version of the Tattvas. These symbols, again painted on a piece of black card, give a more general overview of the elemental nature of the universe. There are five cards: fire, water, air, earth and spirit. These can be combined in much the same way as Tattvas by placing two cards in your hand and visualising them both on the doorway you formulate in your mind's eye.

The God names for the elemental symbols are *Eheieh* for Spirit, *El* for Water, *Elohim Gibor* for Fire, *Shaddai El Chai* for Air and *Adonai Malek* for Earth.

Spirit   *Fire*   *Water*   *Air*   *Earth*

HEBREW LETTERS

There is a Cabbalistic tradition that God created the Universe using the Hebrew letters. It follows that using them as gates will unlock a considerable amount of information about how the universe works.

Each Hebrew letter has a number and a meaning and this can reveal much about the sort of life one might encounter beyond the gate. For example, the letter Aleph is attributed to the number one and means 'Ox'; therefore one might expect to see an ox at some point in the pathworking.

In the Western Mystery tradition each path on the Tree of Life has a Hebrew letter allocated to it. Since these paths show the mixing of energies between the Sephiroth on the tree it gives an idea of the sort of energy one is likely to encounter. For example, the letter Tau connects Malkuth with Yesod. This would mean a connection between the earth energies of Malkuth and the lunar energies of Yesod.

Not only does a journey give an understanding of each Hebrew letter, it also gives a deeper understanding of the names of power that are made up by those letters. If you have visited the three letters

LETTER	POWER	VALUE	FINAL	NAME	MEANING
א	A	1		Aleph	Ox
ב	B	2		Beth	House
ג	G,Gh	3		Gimel	Camel
ד	D, Dh	4		Daleth	Door
ה	H	5		Heh	Window
ו	O,U,V	6		Vav	Pin, Hook
ז	Z	7		Zayin	Sword, Armour
ח	Ch	8		Cheth	Fence, enclosure
ט	T	9		Teth	Serpent
י	I,Y	10		Yod	hand
כ	K, Kh	20	500 ך	Kaph	Palm of hand, fist
ל	L	30		Lamed	Ox, goad
מ	M	40	600 ם	Mem	Water
נ	N	50	700 ן	Nun	Fish
ס	S	60		Samekh	Prop
ע	Aa	70		Ayin	Eye
פ	P, Ph	80	800 ף	Peh	Mouth
צ	Tz	90	900 ץ	Tzaddi	Fishhook
ק	Q	100		Qoph	back of the head
ר	R	200		Resh	Head
ש	S,Sh	300		Shin	Tooth
ת	T, Th	400		Tau	Cross

that make up the name of power Yod, Heh, Vav, Heh יהוה you will unconsciously link up with those experiences each time you vibrate it during a ritual.

The letters themselves are names of power and high level angelic forces. Therefore when doing a pathworking and you need to call upon a name of power, you should use the name of the letter.

They should be written in black on white card.

PLANETARY AND ZODIACAL SYMBOLS

Although planetary and zodiacal symbols have become commonplace in modern astrology, their use as elemental gateways has rarely been looked at. In fact each symbol provides direct access to that planetary or zodiacal state of consciousness, and using them as gates can greatly enhance your knowledge of their meaning.

This proves extremely valuable for astrologers seeking to deepen their knowledge of these planetary energies for chart interpretation. It also enables a deeper understanding of the various planetary and zodiacal influences in your own chart.

Another use is that of planetary magic. It is extremely useful for a magician or Wiccan to know in advance what the energy they are trying to use in a ritual feels like before invoking it. If you are doing a working that uses the planetary energy of Mars, for example, you will know that you have pulled through enough energy when the room feels like the Martian pathworking that you had performed before the rite. You will also have a clearer idea of how that energy works on you.

Remember that the effect of a pathworking is to often bore holes through the consciousness and allow better access to that energy. Working with the planetary and zodiacal forces will intensify and enable those forces to be expressed on the material levels much better.

Unlike the elemental gates, planetary and zodiacal symbols are best painted on a round disk the size of a dinner plate using a technique called 'flashing colours'. The disk should be painted in the appropriate planetary colour with the planetary symbol painted in a complimentary colour. This optical illusion gives the impression that the symbol is vibrating.

Planetary Colours

Planet	Background	Gate Symbol	Symbol Colour
Saturn	Black	♄	White
Jupiter	Blue	♃	Orange
Mars	Scarlet	♂	Green
Venus	Emerald	♀	Scarlet
Sun	Gold	☉	Purple
Moon	Violet	☽	Yellow

Zodiacal Colours

Zodiacal Sign	Background	Gate Symbol	Approximate Flashing Colour of Symbol
Leo	Deep purple	♌	Yellow
Aries	Red	♈	Green
Sagittarius	Yellow	♐	Purple
Taurus	Deep indigo	♉	Yellow
Capricorn	Black	♑	White
Virgo	Grey	♍	White or black
Aquarius	Sky blue	♒	Orange
Gemini	Pale mauve	♊	Yellow
Libra	Blue	♎	Orange
Scorpio	Brown	♏	Blue green
Pisces	Buff	♓	Blue green
Cancer	Maroon	♋	Blue green

The effect of using flashing colours as elemental gates is tremendous. This is partly because the adepts of the Golden Dawn placed these symbols in their flashing colours on devices called flashing tablets that attracted blind planetary forces for use in talisman making, ritual or alchemy. Using them as planetary or zodiacal gates means that the practitioner is exposed to the planetary energy before they enter the gate. This means that they would experience the energy at a much deeper level because their inner vision is properly attuned.

TAROT

Tarot cards are the perfect magical gates to interior realities. The more esoteric hermetic packs include the *Builders of the Adytum*, Chic and Tabatha Cicero's *Golden Dawn*, the Aleister Crowley *Thoth* pack and the *Golden Dawn Temple Deck* which are designed with this purpose in mind.

Not only do they contain symbols of inner realities that effectively stir the mind, they also feature Hebrew letters, colours, planetary, elemental and Cabbalistic attributions that could take a lifetime of study.

Builders of the Adytum was fond of saying that if you were washed up on a desert island with nothing but a tarot deck, you would unlock the secrets of all esoteric wisdom. There is some truth to this and if you used the tarot cards as gates you really would know a considerable amount by experience.

The Major Arcana of the tarot deck is closely linked, by modern occultists, to the paths on the Tree of Life, and the Minor Arcana with the spheres (the aces represent Kether, the twos Chokmah, the threes Binah etc.)

This means that they can be used to unlock the secrets of Christian Cabbalah, with each tarot card leading you to a mystical experience of that path. Dolores Ashcroft-Nowicki wrote a modern occult classic called *The Shining Paths* which gives pathworkings up the Tree of Life using tarot cards.

On a more mundane level using the cards as gates considerably enhances your ability to understand their meanings in divination. Once you have visited them all, turning over a card is like opening a photo album to a place that you have visited. When you apply what the querent is asking in relation to that experience you will be able to give them a much deeper answer.

One of the Builders of the Adytum's magical techniques suggests that you become the central character in the Tarot key. This gives you a deeper sense of the energy of the card and the characters within it.

ℶ   **THE MAGICIAN**   ☿

MAGICAL AND ALCHEMICAL DRAWINGS

For a long time mystical and magical information was portrayed in symbolic form in drawings. These were particularly common in alchemy, where the process of transmutation was shown in obtuse symbolic language and pictures. Many of the keys to this language have been lost to modern minds. However, by using these drawings as gates we can unlock these mysteries. When using alchemical drawings it is important to realise that the illustrators were not simply showing chemical reactions, but rather a spiritual process that led to a total transmutation. The work represented in these drawings and their equally obscure writings could be enacted in a test tube but also in the mind. Such drawings show in symbolic form a snapshot of a spiritual state. If this drawing is placed on an elemental gate it is possible to visit that state and experience what it is showing you.

I should point out that alchemical drawings should be experienced, in order for them to have the best effect. However don't start using them unless you are serious and ready to face the consequences of the change they will bring. Alchemy is advanced work and potentially dangerous.

Drawings of an alchemical process can be found in *The Book of the Lambspring* (translation by Adam McLean) or *Splendour Solis*.

IMAGES OF THE GODS

This is especially effective for Neo-Pagans who want to have a deep contact with their particular deity. All that needs to be visualised on the doorway is an image of the god or goddess that you feel most closely reflects your understanding of it. Sometimes it might be an image of a statue or a painting, at other times it might be a symbol of the god or goddess.

Chapter Ten

LIFE IS BUT A DREAM

I N ALL THE imagination experiments you have carried out so far you have been aware that there is an essential 'you' that has been participating in the exercise. It did not matter if you were approaching the throne of heaven or the deepest aspects of your darker side, there was always a 'you' that was the observer.

Once the pathworking is over and you are awake within your physical body, the 'you' is still there observing. It may have better tools to perceive the world around it, such as the five senses, than it might have in any pathworking, but it is still the same observer. This begs the question, is this material world any different from any of the other worlds that we may have visited?

Essentially there is little difference, other than the fact that for some reason the spirit of humanity seems particularly attached to the material level. It has a material body which is designed to live in this world and makes it appear more real, but it also binds us to its rules. These rules are expounded to us by modern science, which has been very good at telling us how the material world works. While we dwell in our bodies we have to maintain them with food and exercise. Shelter is needed to protect our body from the extremes of climate; we need a partner to procreate to make sure its genetic material survives into a next generation.

This material world contains so many elements similar to our dream or imaginative worlds and when we start to see this world as just one of many that we live in then it is possible to interpret life as if it were a dream.

Think of some event in your life and then describe it as if you were telling a friend about a weird dream you had. Here is a fictitious example:

"I am in work and I am bored. The work is below what I am qualified to do and I am always trying to make it seem more important than it is. There is a problem with my boss. He always seems to be finding fault with everything I do and it makes me feel very depressed. He is also a sexist pig who has made passes at girls in the office and makes life difficult for those who don't play ball."

The crucial symbol here is the person's boss. The boss could be symbol of an autocratic father figure who constantly belittled her when she was small. The fact that he also sexually harasses women in the workplace could be an indication that her father perceived women as sex objects. There are elements of sexual blackmail which be a reflection of the way this woman unconsciously sees what she has to do to please men.

The other symbol is the work, which is a symbol of self-achievement and progression. In this woman's case it indicates she lacks the confidence to face the world with all her abilities. Instead she tries to make do with second best. The fact that she is bored, depressed and unhappy indicates that she is holding on to the status quo even though she knows it is hurting her.

So putting the two symbols together, we are left with an interpretation which might look like this:

"This woman has had an autocratic father who constantly belittled her. This has damaged her self-confidence to the point that she is scared to be her true self. Her success, which should be working on her own direction in life, is instead being directed into appeasing her father."

The 'dream' would be suggesting that changing her work would be the best thing for her as it would take her from the clutches of the bad father figure. The work should be something that she is qualified for and finds fulfilling.

Here is another example, which is a little more commonplace in Britain.

"I went to work today and the train broke down due to leaves getting on the railway track. The train driver apologised for "any inconvenience that the delay might have caused" but no one believed him. I was angry because it is bloody typical of the inefficiency of Britain's public transport system."

Here is an event, which might happen every day, in which case it could be a symbol that life's journey is frustratingly slow as your life's direction is being thwarted by small things beyond your control. Sceptics might say that not *everyone* on that train could be suffering from that same problem. While it would be tempting to point out that *anyone* who has to commute between Nottingham and London on the train has this problem, it is certainly true that this is a symbol that affects everyone differently. For each commuter the delayed train is a symbol for something different depending on their own emotional reaction.

The key word in the above description was that the person felt angry. Another person might have felt bemused about how a big train could be stopped by something as silly as leaves on the line. Another might have found it a joke!

The man was 'angry' and was using words that were similar to a parent who is scolding a child. This is further emphasised by the comment about the apology not being accepted. In effect the man wants to be angry about something, to tell someone off because his life is not progressing the way he would like. This is someone who blames things outside himself for the situations he is facing.

Another commuter who found it bemusing that such a big train could be stopped by something so small could see the incident as symbolic of the tiny obstacles that seem to be getting in his way even when life seems to be going so well.

The commuter who finds it funny is not the sort that worries much if his life's path is blocked. He sees obstacles as a temporary and amusing diversion.

So in every incident in your life it is important to see how you feel and then interpret the symbol accordingly.

The more unusual some aspect of your life is then the more important it is as a symbol of the way your life is going. The above example is not unusual in most people's lives and therefore cannot be taken too far, but if the train was delayed because a lion had escaped from a theme park and was lying on the track it would be a much more important symbol.

WhEN ThE DREAM BECOMES A NIGhTMARE

Major life crises, such as death, divorce, job upheavals, are packed with the most important symbolism which if correctly interpreted can often prevent suffering in the same way again.

The nightmare situations in our life are mostly of our own making; we pick the wrong partner, or job, or lifestyle. We usually have symbolic warnings that something bad is going to happen, which we blissfully ignore and then our world collapses. If we see these crises as we would any other inner kingdom, with the key players as symbols, then we start to understand the nature of the world we have created around us. Our lives become fairy stories in which we experience and learn.

For example, Jemima is a victim of a man who wants to control every aspect of her life right down to the clothes she wears. A talented artist, she finds her skills put on hold as the duties of looking after her boyfriend become the key focus. She never leaves the house because her boyfriend is always suspicious of her movements. When he is away on business he rings her every two hours to make sure she is still at home.

This is similar to the story of Cinderella, where the beautiful heroine is forced to cook and clean for her ugly sisters despite her ability to catch a handsome prince later in the story.

Into Jemima's situation a person comes and shows her that there is an alternative life for her. Not quite a fairy godmother; the person explains that she is in this situation because she does not want to realise her full potential out of fear that success will bring responsibilities far more important than getting a meal onto her boyfriend's table.

She enthuses about the possibilities of a new life and determines to escape, and if she had left to start her new life at this point then the fairy story would be over. But like the Cinderella story there is an evil wizard involved.

Jemima decides to flee the boyfriend, but being insecure and still too frightened to risk starting out life on her own, she looks for another man to build her 'new life' upon. She finds someone who seems to fit the bill, but he is actually a carbon copy of her boyfriend – only worse. He is married and is stringing her along with empty promises of a 'new life' with him where he will protect her from all life's worries. Since he does not really want to care for her, he advises her to live with her boyfriend, even though he makes her unhappy, and sneak a few moments of pleasure with him when she can.

Now Cinderella is under the spell of an evil magician, and still trapped by the wicked stepsisters in her hellish existence.

The Universe never gives up in trying to move a person closer to their true destiny and so enter the fairy godmother figure again… this time in the guise of a twist of fate. The boyfriend finds love letters from Jemima to her married lover and understandably makes a scene and throws her out. She looks to the evil magician to protect her, but since he is married he turns his back on her for anything more than casual sex.

Jemima is now alone and facing her worst nightmare. I made the remark that her life was remarkably like a fairy story. "But where is the handsome prince?" she cried.

The handsome prince was something within her. It was her personal strength, self-control and the ability to make decisions for herself. These qualities frightened her because they brought responsibility, and her need for them was still great and she looked for them in her partners to balance herself out. Her fear meant that when she chose her men with those character traits she only chose those with the unbalanced aspects of them.

"But I never picked these men," she said. "They picked me!"

This comment, which is really common in cases where people pick controlling or violent partners, assumes that the 'victim' was coerced, or 'under some spell', when they entered into the relationship. It has been my view that people enter relationships to fulfil some psychological need, either good or bad. In Jemima's case it was to look for the missing part of herself, which she did not want to spend the time acquiring the discipline, or self-reliance, to find.

By working with the men in her life as symbols of her own self, Jemima could try to find the qualities she needs to develop.

But what of the other nightmares we develop in our lives? A particular bugbear is illness, which seems to spontaneously appear, often in a very nasty way.

The psychologist Wilhelm Reich (1897-1957) worked with cancer patients in the 1940s and became convinced that a particular type of person was more susceptible to it. These were people who gave up, refused to fight the problems in their lives and were content to be victims. Those who were more aggressive about life were less likely to have cancer or, if they did, were better at fighting it off. Reich's observations were noted by the authors of *Getting Well Again*, Carl Simonton and Stephanie Matthews-Simonton, who in 1978 concluded that people predisposed to cancer often had a poor self-image, had a tendency towards self-pity and to hold in resentment.

While this is clearly a factor in the development of cancer, there are others as well, and it is simplistic to say that because someone has cancer they do not affirm life or want to give up on it. I know of two cases where the opposite was true. In the case of Karen, cancer was hardly a sign of her giving up. She had been fiercely independent all her life. To her, cancer was going to be a hurdle that she was not only going to overcome but was to be a proof of the powers of her own mind. She refused treatment and held workshops for fellow sufferers to use their minds to fight it off. She died of a fairly trivial cancer that would have responded to medical treatment. When her friends looked at her life they concluded that she had never really had the courage to look beyond herself or to others, life was always "her way or the highway". As a result, when cancer appeared, she saw it as a method of showing herself a leader among people. The cancer was a symbol of how she really needed to be dependent on people sometimes. If she had trusted the medical system a little, her fight against cancer would have been successful.

There was no evidence of self-pity in the mind of Kimberly either. Initially a computer programmer, she stopped work in the middle of her soul-sucking marriage and became obese. Then she suddenly woke up to her own potential, lost weight, and dumped the useless husband to take a job in computing in another part of the country. After a moment's breathing space in what was turning out to be a life-affirming existence she was also diagnosed with a rare form of blood cancer. While Kimberly was in hospital wondering what the symbol of cancer was all about her work fired her for being off sick so much. Then she worked out that she had not really wanted that career and really wanted to do something with writing. She changed her career, and took a course in journalism and at time of writing was responding well to treatment and was on her way to being a sub-editor. To her, cancer was simply a way of getting to realise that the path she was on was leading her to the same mistakes she had made in the past.

Terminal illness is sometimes the only way that a soul can leave incarnation when their time is up. With all their life's work achieved, their body has to die of something.

Cancer, or any illness, is a symbol, and its nature is up to the individual to interpret. While for some it might be the all-encompassing final nail in the coffin that ends their miserable and repressed lives, for others it can be a call to arms. Many who do fight off cancer say that they tend to live for each second, and this could be the symbolic result they need to understand. Whatever illness you might face, it is important to see what it represents to you with clear understanding. If approached with the same care and testing that is used for an inner kingdom being then it can reveal much.

You will notice that unlike many New Age writers I do not say that illness is all in the mind and that you can overcome it entirely by using mental techniques or dealing with psychological blockages. By the time an illness has manifested on the material level from the level of the mind it is often too late to stop its effects and no amount of mind control will work better than a course of antibiotics. The body is a creature of the material world and as such responds quicker and more effectively to physical things like chemicals and operations.

Magical Imagination techniques will dispense with the need for the illness to manifest as you will start to see its appearance in the imagination and can deal with it long before it affects you physically. But it is silly to refuse medication for asthma simply because you know it is caused by an emotional need for affection. If you can't breathe properly, take your inhaler and as you start to understand your emotional needs you will have to take it less.

Also I would be a little careful about focusing on health too much. By all means see health, particularly symbolic mysterious illnesses, as something to be looked at, but be careful about allowing health to become an obsession. When physical health becomes too much of an issue it creates a self-feeding complex within your Inner Kingdom. Legendary magician Aleister Crowley noted that the Christian Scientists who allowed health to be a key part of their belief structure were some of the sickest people. The same can be said for many New Age groups where health is a major theme.

A healing group dominated a study circle I once belonged to. The healers were well meaning and loved to discuss the various holistic cures they had tried on themselves and friends. But after a while I started to notice that every week they seemed to have developed a new complaint and a corresponding cure for it. Every week there were the vegetarian healers (at one point drinking their own urine), coughing and spluttering through the meeting while the meat-eating disbelievers were the epitome of health. Focusing on their illnesses to cure them had created the circumstances where they always needed to be cured and their illnesses were not symbols of their inner state of consciousness but rather proof of their ability to create sickness as well as health.

So what of the so-called 'random unlucky event', the mugging, the plane crash, the tragedy of the pedestrian mown down by a car?

It is possible for a particularly paranoid or nervous person to generate random events within their outer world. People who are frightened by muggers or burglars are sometimes likely to frighten themselves so badly by the experience that they will suffer from repeat offences.

Most of these random events can be understood by interpreting them as symbols. If you are the victim, write it down and interpret it as a dream. Like a dream you will be surprised at little details that have no meaning except as symbols of something else.

When processing a street mugging, Jason commented on how the thing that struck him as odd was he never saw his attacker. He was struck from behind and did not remember losing consciousness, yet he found himself in confusion on the ground with his wallet apparently spirited away as if by an invisible force.

"The first thing I thought of was that I must have tripped, yet my coat was ripped off my shoulders. Then came the realisation of what happened followed by a profound sense of loss," Jason said afterwards.

I asked him what that loss was like and he said suddenly that it reminded him of when his lucky blanket was taken away from him by his father, who thought he was too old for such things. His father had simply thrown it out while he was at primary school. Jason thought it odd that he should remember that event which had taken place some thirty years before.

If the mugging was of symbolic importance then Jason had all the pieces to work out what this event was trying to tell him. He was an obsessive saver and his wife had complained that although the money was in the bank he never spent it on anything. He never invested it, or even bought a house, because he was worried that something would go wrong and he would lose his security.

After a while he realised that for him the robber was a symbol that anything material could be taken away and that security needed to be based on things that were less tangible.

The death of a friend or family member also has an incredible symbolic meaning for you. While it does not mean that something in your life actually caused it, but rather the event has happened at a time when it can have the most meaning for you. People learn a lot about themselves when faced with the enormity of death close to them. Often their response is to question their own mortality and decide to find more meaning in their lives.

Sometimes the deaths of strangers become symbolic for a whole nation. The death in a car crash of Princess Diana evoked an emotional response in many people. But what I found interesting at the time was that many people who rushed to place flowers or attended the funeral procession in London were not actually mourning the death of a well-heeled woman who had led a rather privileged life. Many used her death as a symbol to remember members of their families or friends who had died in similar circumstances. She was a symbol of their own loss that they could re-examine and process.

BEING A SYMBOL

If other people and circumstances are symbolic to you, it is fairly obvious that you can be a symbol to other people. To your family you might be the Black Sheep or the Wonder Child in whom all their dreams are realised. At work you might be the Heartless Boss or Moaning Employee or Hard Worker who Lacks Recognition. You might find yourself being someone's father or mother figure and get a lot of surprising flak as a result.

This causes problems if the symbol does not suit you; if your boss sees you as the same symbol of wayward daughter and is always telling you off even though you work hard, if people think you are Stupid rather than Ditzy, or Sex Pest instead of Sexual Novice.

It is possible to change the symbol that people see you by. Politicians, press officers and other masters of spin work very hard to achieve this all the time. They seek only to associate themselves with situations in which they appear in a positive light. To a greater or lesser degree they succeed until they become a symbol for something else. Generally it is easier to become a negative symbol than it is to be a positive one. Bill Clinton will always be remembered as Serial Adulterer and Richard Nixon as Liar, no matter what merits their respective presidencies might have had. John F. Kennedy will always evoke positive symbols because of his tragic death, and his indiscretions were always kept from public view.

The power of people as symbols, particularly public figures, can never be underestimated. I found this out to my shock when I first met members of the Royal Family. I am not a royalist and see them as a harmless constitutional anachronism and even harboured a dislike for the Queen Mother for the way she seemed to be so nasty to members of her family who crossed her. The British press had carved them into particular Royal stereotypes – the Queen was a symbol of untouchable Sovereignty, the Queen Mother was everyone's Grandmother, Prince Charles was the eccentric and Princess Diana was glamour personified. It was with some surprise that I discovered how much these symbols had even on journalists like myself, who might have written our news stories using these royal symbols while at the same time not believing a word of it ourselves. Imagine my surprise when covering the opening of a military barracks in Windsor that I found myself, along with the crowd, let out the collective sigh that a person reserves for seeing a beloved grandmother when the Queen 'Mum' got out of her car. For the same reason Princess Diana was far more attractive in real life than in any picture anyone took of her.

Margaret Thatcher, who managed to cultivate herself as a symbol of iron authority, hanging on to power despite extreme unpopularity in some quarters, made a huge mistake late in her rule when the British public saw her trying to usurp the trappings of royalty – for example starting to speak like Queen Victoria with such memorable quotes as "We are now a Grandmother". In placing herself as a symbol of Royal Usurper, her cowed cabinet found the courage to stand up to her to defend the True Queen symbol. Any hope she might ever be asked to lead the Conservative Party again were finally dashed when she cried as she left number 10 after being sacked – her Iron Authority image upon which her power depended was shattered.

Most people do not have to deal with the collective belief patterns of an entire nation, but the same principles apply. If you want to appear in everyone's eyes as a symbol of efficiency, you must adopt all the trappings that make you appear efficient – the slick suit, the personal organiser and the tidy desk. It does not matter that the drawers are stuffed full of rubbish, the desktop must be extremely organised.

Con-artists are always the most convincing if they manage to incorporate the symbols of what they are trying to impersonate. At the time of writing, a moderately successful con-trick where an email is sent to a person asking for their account details turned into a spectacularly successful one when the team directed potential victims to a website which looked like a leading South African Bank. The web page was covered with symbols of authority and stability that were unfortunately not real. Victims were prepared to overlook the bizarre requests for cash because they thought they were dealing with a legitimate bank.

This leads to an important point. Attempting to associate oneself with a certain symbol will only work so far, unless there is a genuine change behind it. This is because as people start to associate you with the symbol you wish to create they will expect you to be like it all the time. When you fail to respond the way they think you should, you will fail to represent that for them. This is true of any politician who has attempted to cover their failings with spin doctoring. After a while people start to realise that the avid reformers they thought they voted for are just playing with their minds.

If you decide that you are going to represent a particular symbol, you should work with it to allow it to slowly reform your behaviour patterns. You can act this out in your Inner Kingdom so that the subtleties of the symbol get played out in your mind first. Then act out the new you in a fairly safe environment so that you see how it interacts with others.

The internet is an excellent way of forming a halfway house between your Inner Kingdom and the outside world. In an internet chat room you can be anything you want to be without anyone questioning you, and many people do. For example while recovering from a lack of self-confidence caused by his marriage break-up, David did not have the courage to ask anyone out for a date. Aware that he had to create a new image for himself, he created a character called Wizard who was a supremely confident flirt. In the half-world of the internet he found he could be this person. Even though at times David felt that Wizard was too much, many found the character attractive. Soon David had to play the role of Wizard at an off-line party and much to his surprise he found it easy – he also found it easy to get dates. Later he was able to integrate the aspects of the Wizard character so it reflected more of who he wanted to be.

There are some who feel that tinkering with your personality in this way is wrong. They believe that a person should feel confident to be himself or herself and not attempt to be someone they are not. I do not believe that the True Self, which is trying to be reflected through the personality, is at all negative and when people want to be themselves it is that Higher Self they want to be, not a little bag of neurosis. One of my clients, Joan, said she was shy, and for six months she attempted to be self-assertive and yet she hated it. "I am shy and I cannot be someone else," she said. Later she described the feeling of being shy as negative and I asked her if she felt her higher self was a negative being. "No," she said. "My Higher Self always appears as very powerful."

"So, not particularly shy then?"

"No."

So when Joan said she was shy and could not be someone else, she did not mean her true self. She was living in her personality and believing it was her real self, rather than the somewhat broken vehicle of her Higher Self. When she realised that her Higher Self was not shy, she started to work more seriously on building her self-confidence.

INNER AND OUTER KINGDOMS

Earlier I mentioned the case of a woman who was starting to see her life as a pattern similar to a fairy story. The archetypal nature of fairy stories was first looked at by Carl Jung and is very popular with students of Joseph Campbell. Although I prefer using the Inner Kingdom as a good method of looking at archetypes affecting our lives, if we start to see ourselves and others as symbols in the material world it is inevitable that they will form into patterns which start to look like legends or fairy stories.

It is common in esoteric groups for the leaders to find themselves adopting a mythic status to their role. One common myth they tend to adopt is that of a Priest or Priestess of Atlantis. Often they, or their students, will say they had a previous life in that mythic history. But while Atlantis is seen as a place of magical power, it is also an allegory for magical arrogance – of power misused to gain authority over others. Is it any wonder that after a while such people start to become supremely arrogant and insensitive to their students? It creates what has been dubbed High Priestess Syndrome (HPS) or its male equivalent Atlantean High Priest Syndrome (AHPS), among the British occult community.

Another common problem is Merlin syndrome where a person's life starts to mirror the myth of that ancient sage. They tend to be loners, who appear in others' lives and provide sage wisdom before moving on. Their one weakness is a belief that they will find a person of the opposite sex who they can share their life and their magic with. What ends up happening is the 'Merlin' becomes so infatuated that he believes that the partner, who is often much younger and or less experienced, is capable of more than they are ready for. They sometimes burn out but they always end up leaving a very battered Merlin alone and miserable.

This was certainly the case with the legendary occultist Dion Fortune, who pushed her husband Dr Penry Evans deeper into occultism faster than she should have done. While observers thought Evans would have made a formidable magician if developed at a normal speed, Fortune thought he was ready for the 'Greater Mysteries' far sooner than he really was. In the end, after lots of arguments, Fortune's marriage ended and Evans lost interest in occultism.

Aleister Crowley cheerfully courted the myth of the Black Magician. If the press of the time is to believed, Crowley was the 'Wickedest Man on Earth', who practiced black magic. Anyone reading Crowley's biographies or his autobiography may think that such titles somehow validated him and gave more magical credence to the man than he deserved, one whose life was emotionally crippled by an extreme Christian upbringing. Throughout his life Crowley seemed to want to shock, simply to get attention, and by today's standards his 'shocking antics' are somewhat mundane. Yet living the myth of a black magician led him to the inevitable Faustian end – alone, drug dependent and forgotten. If Crowley had adopted another myth for his life, it might have been different, but history will always record him as a black magician – whatever the cleverness of his magical system or poetry.

I often wonder if John F. Kennedy's life might have been different if he had not taken the Arthurian myth. With his administration labelled 'Camelot' and his battles with the "might is right" military and FBI of the day, he fits snugly within T.H. White's *Once and Future King* version of the Arthurian myth, right up to the tragic end of his reign. Theoretically he should have been sunk by an illegitimate son being discovered, but being bumped off by someone who wanted control of the country fits nicely too.

Adolf Hitler, a man for whom myth was of paramount importance, saw himself in the role of Siegfried in Wagner's *Ring* opera, saving the world from the 'evil Jewish dwarves'. He forgot that the end of that opera has Siegfried and his girlfriend dying in flames as everything around them burns, and a new order is born without the gods or a master race.

The message of these lives is to choose your myths carefully or know when would be a good time to change them. All myths of greatness start with the hero doing well, but generally there is a seed which is overlooked that eventually leads to destruction. Arthur, Roland, Merlin, Theseus, Helen of Troy, Cassandra and Ophelia meet bad ends. All had the option of changing their fates and if you are going to live these myths then it is important that you learn from them. Be wise like Arthur, but stand up to evil within your kingdom; be brave like Roland, but not suicidal; find your treasure like Theseus but don't marry ill-fortune (Medea) to get it.

It is important to remember that your sex has nothing to do with the myth you are leading. I know several females who are living out the myth of Heracles and two 'Merlins', likewise one of my male friends is living his life as if he were Helen of Troy!

AND ThEY LIVED hAPPILY EVER AFTER...

By seeing material world as a myth and by looking directly at our internal myths in pathworkings and meditation, we are in a powerful position to forge our lives into the shape we want. We can stand like the archetypal Magus as a link between heaven and earth. With symbols as our magic wands, we no longer have to have our universe shaped by the neurotic programming of our childhood or early teens. We can find within ourselves our own counsel and guides, free from the weakness of our teachers, friends and family. Without fear we can build an Inner Kingdom of peace and then see it manifest in our environment. Everything we do or see around us becomes a reflection of our inner state and can be seen as God teaching us how to be more than human.

The key to 'living happily ever after', or at least to individual fulfilment, is that divine gift of imagination. Life is a dream, so make sure it is a good one.

INDEX

Lightning Source UK Ltd.
Milton Keynes UK
UKOW04f0751160115

244533UK00001B/302/P